TRAVELING

WITH

SPIRITS

VALERIE MINER

LIVINGSTON PRESS
THE UNIVERSITY OF WEST ALABAMA

Hardcover binding by: Heckman Bindery
Typesetting and page layout: Joe Taylor
Proofreading: Gonil Gveiro, Joe Taylor, Jovel Queirolo
Cover art, design, and layout: David Schorr

The quote on page 77 comes from Thomas Merton's
The Seven Storey Mountain, Mariner Books.

first edition

6 5 4 3 2 1

TRAVELING

WITH

SPIRITS

This book is dedicated to Marcia Dillon with gratitude

The Guest House

This being human is a guest house. Every morning a new arrival....

Welcome and entertain them all! Even if
they're a crowd of sorrows, who violently
sweep your house empty of its furniture,
still treat each guest honorably.
He may be clearing you out for
some new delight....

Be grateful for whoever comes, because
each has been sent
as a guide from beyond.

By Jelaluddin Rumi,
Translated by Coleman Barks with John Moyne, *The Essential Rumi*
San Francisco: HarperSanFrancisco, 1995

ONE

January, 2001, New Delhi

Crowds of savvy people weave confidently through the thick, smoky atmosphere of Indira Gandhi International Airport. Monica is as startled as a body can be at 11:30 p.m., after 19 hours of travel. Desperate for air and space after the marathon flight in her small, stuffy seat, she's overwhelmed by the viscous, jostling environment of the vast terminal. Muslim men in succinct knitted caps bustle past Sikhs in the urgent baggage room turmoil. Women hurry, too, looking astonishingly fresh in vivid saris and salwar kameezes: pulsing blue, alarming chartreuse, beaming yellow. In contrast, the few Westerners appear pretty ragged—the denim backpackers and the suited executives—with tousled hair and grey faces.

Momentarily dazed, Monica leans on a wall. Everyone else in this enormous cold, damp, room has grabbed a trolley or staked out a position at the baggage carousel. Ashok Nair, the cordial professor who flew in the aisle seat next to her, snatches his battered brown leather suitcase and strides toward the exit. He doesn't bother to wave good-bye. Ridiculous to feel abandoned. Of course he's not her guardian angel. And he has invited her to lunch this week.

Magically, her three blue bags arrive together. She readies herself to heave them from the carousel, then grasping the first one, strains at its weight.

"Ma'am, these are belonging to you as well?" inquires a sturdy Sikh man in his fifties.

Panic rises—at the sight of this tall, strong man gripping her luggage—and falls at the sound of his kind, courteous tone.

"Yes, Sir, thank you," she manages as he removes the second bag. She tugs off the third.

"You are most welcome." His voice lowers. "If I may offer some advice?"

His skin has been pocked by some childhood infection. "Please do."

"Pre-paid taxi. Go to the booth outside this customs area. Accept no other transportation."

"Thank you." She smiles as they both load bags on the trolley. "Thank you very much."

Powder blue bags. She didn't want her luggage confused with a stranger's. How many weeks will the color last in India? She tries not to think how long she will last.

"Pre-paid taxi. Pre-paid taxi." She repeats the phrase silently, steering the wobbly trolley. "Pre-paid taxi," Father Koreth has emailed her. "Pre-paid taxi," Professor Nair advised over their miniature dinners on the flight. "Pre-paid taxi," she repeats over and over to calm herself through customs. Of course she has nothing to declare. (Nothing except: she's thrilled, terrified, dazed to be here, to be so far from home.) Father Koreth and others have explained that Indian immigration is watchful of doctors working for Catholic missions. "They regard us as religious proselytizers, if you can imagine!" he wrote. "One must arrive with a single entry visa and strictly obey regulations." So far she's been very obedient. Still, she's nervous as hell and can smell the sweat rising from beneath her tired deodorant.

"Nothing to Declare" lines are nerve-wracking. She tries to forget that last trip to Ireland where she splurged on Waterford crystal bowls and Belleek vases for Mom. Definitely over the customs limit then. Perhaps she's over all kinds of limits here. The limits of her flexibility, courage, forbearance.

"Pre-paid taxi," the mantra steadies her as indifferent customs agents flip through her documents.

Outside. Finally. The night is surprisingly cool. No, not night, early morning now. She peers through the thick soup of fog and smog for Taxi 1451. All around people are pushing and shouting.

"Hilton?" asks one young man.

"Intercontinental?" A hipper guy.

"Good price anywhere Madame goes." A third driver seduces.

"No, thank you," she answers each one. Her voice jars with broad American syllables.

At last. Number 1451 license plate. Gripping the trolley with one hand, she waves frantically to the driver with the other.

A legless man slides his wheeled platform close to her shoes. "*Namaste ji,*" he calls upward.

Too ashamed to be surprised by her recklessness, she steps away from the beggar, directly into the chaos of honking and darting cars. Taxi 1451 screeches to a halt.

The cabbie stuffs her bags in the small trunk.

Monica summons the address of Mission House from her muddled brain.

He looks puzzled.

Maybe it's her accent. She has to get used to having an accent. Slowly, she repeats the address.

A blank stare.

"Near the Bengali Market." The synapses are reconnecting.

He nods vaguely.

As they withdraw from the airport melee, she breathes a huge sigh of relief. *Pre-paid taxi. Pre-paid taxi.* The chant rattles through her sleepy head.

Bumpy road.

Utter darkness.

"Headlights?" she asks.

"Not necessary."

"Please switch on your headlights." Her friendly, but firm, physician's tone.

"Wearing down battery. Safe driving. Don't worry," the driver states with finality.

Monica is in his taxi, in a strange city, half a world away from home.

Her exasperated, anxious moan morphs into a cough. She replaces *Pre-paid taxi* with *Jesus guide us.* Same number of syllables, same soothing rhythm, and a more useful chant at the moment.

Eyes adjusting to the night, she sees, or thinks she sees, an elephant lumbering along the road. The city air is heavy with smoke and an odd, pleasantly sour smell. Parked near a brightly-lit intersection in a turquoise truck, vibrantly painted with flowers, a god she can't identify and large, red stenciled letters. "My India is Great."

"You are a priestess?"

The driver's sudden curiosity startles her. "Pardon?" She leans forward to catch his words.

"Madame is a holy woman, a priestess? A nun?"

"No," she grins, "no." She imagines what her sister would say about her. Wicked Witch of the West, more likely.

"No?"

Monica answers his lilting question with her strangely thickened Minnesota accent, "I am a doctor."

"Ah," he readjusts the plastic statue on his dashboard.

Krishna, she's fairly certain. An avatar of Vishnu and one of the most popular Hindu deities. Brain continuing to return. Positive sign.

"We have our own religions in India," he objects quietly.

"Oh, yes."

She wants to tell him she's studied Indian spiritual traditions. Wants to ask, do you know that Catholicism is one of those practices? That six million of your citizens are Catholic? St. Thomas brought Christ's teaching here centuries before they reached Ireland. Rather, she says, "Indeed, you have a wealth of religious paths."

"We also have excellent Indian medicine," he asserts more vigorously now. "Madame has heard of Ayurvedic health care?"

"Certainly." She's irritated by the pointless tension between them. "I received Ayurvedic massages at home."

"Home?" His musical voice lightens. "Where would your good home be?"

"Minneapolis." Monica glances out the window, spotting three more elephants being led on a rope. Quite docile. This isn't the Serengeti; she reminds herself not to gape.

"The Minnesota Twins!" he proclaims.

She laughs.

"Do you know Torii Hunter?"

She racks her brain for players' names, strangely compelled to please.

The taxi slows in front of a large block of flats.

"104 Wills Road," he announces.

"Yes, yes," she shakes her head and rummages through her purse. *Pre-paid taxi*, the words float through her drowsy brain.

He holds open the door.

Surely he'll help her with the heavy luggage. Surely.

Surely there's so much about this country Monica has yet to imagine.

TWO

January, 2001, New Delhi

"Coming. Coming."

A flashlight slices through the cold dark.

"Welcome, Ma'am, rather," the stout middle-aged man corrects himself, "Welcome Dr. Murphy." He shivers slightly in sandals and a rumpled beige uniform.

Clearly she's wakened the poor guy.

"Mr. Alexander?" Monica suddenly recalls his name from Father's letter.

"Yes, yes. Welcome. Welcome. Come in before you will be freezing to death."

He hoists the heaviest two suitcases on his shoulders before she can protest, leaving her the manageable roller bag and briefcase.

He's right about the cold. Frigid night air pierces her airplane numbness. "Sorry, sorry. The lift is broken. But only three flights."

"Yes, of course." She can't get more tired.

Astonishingly nimble, Mr. Alexander scurries up the zigzag stairs and she scrambles after him. He sets the luggage down and opens a door to her "suite."

As he flips the switch, an overhead bulb glows dimly. Once he turns on the table lamp, these large, tiled rooms appear dingier. "In here is the bath. You ignite the inverter for hot water."

She's grateful for the sit-down toilet. Looking forward to a bath in that tub. Hot water, the very thought revives.

"And here…" He's disappeared.

Monica trails him into a tiny kitchen.

"Bottled water. Please dispense water from the cistern. Do not drink from the tap," he cautions, rubbing his stomach vigorously in explanation.

She's about to laugh. Monica won't explain she specializes in gastro-intestinal infections. That she took a special international health course this fall to brush up on tropical diarrheal diseases, shigellosis and choler-typhoid fever. She remembers the cabbie, tells herself that this is Mr. Alexander's country. "Yes," she nods. "Thank you."

"The cooker—please watch how you start it."

Monica blinks. She expected meals with colleagues during orientation week here in Delhi. Is this another American presumption? Do they want her to shop and cook for herself? She knows a few words. *Sabzi mandi,* is "vegetable market." She can ask for *sag, aloo, gobi.*

He twists knobs, points to burners. "Cooker is for making toast and tea. Here are the provisions. Meals are served in the refectory."

She grins.

"Ma'am, they wouldn't bring you all the way to India to cook!"

Exhausted, she glances at the gloomy bedroom.

"A long journey. You must be tired," he says kindly.

Perhaps everyone at Mission House is suffused with charity. Monica hopes to recover hers by morning. Only one side of Mr. Alexander's shirt is tucked in his trousers. His left sandal strap is torn.

"Yes, thank you. We'll both feel better after a good night's sleep."

"*Namaste, ji,*" he bows over tented palms.

She dodges a memory of the legless man. "Yes, good night and God bless, Mr. Alexander."

The place is damp, so she plugs in a space heater which looks—and smells—as if it predates independence.

Brushing her teeth with bottled water, Monica sees a strange woman in the mottled mirror: stringy red hair and blotchy freckles. What did Mr. Alexander make of his crumpled, honorable guest?

Clammy, ugh, the towel is so damp. India is twenty degrees closer to the equator, but she feels colder tonight than in Minnesota, cold in her bones. Sister Margaret did write about the lack of central heating. Who needs heating in the Indian plains, she thought. She hears her mother's complaints about the deadly dank of Dublin.

Monica imagines Mom walking with her back to the cavernous bedroom within range of the heater's small province of comfort. "I would have been with you in the last days, if Jeanne had called," she wants to say.

Enough, and off to bed with you, Mom insists.

She races into a nightgown and crawls beneath the damp sheets. Tomorrow will be better. Tomorrow. Later today. Who knows what time it is? This is only the beginning of the journey. Let go. Let God.

The knocking is tentative. Light taps. She could ignore the noise, roll over and return to sleep, to that strange dream about her neighbor stealing the tree. Maybe he'll return it. She's always loved the Japanese maple.

Another light rap on the door.

Worn out, but pathologically polite, Monica sits up. "Coming."

2:30 on her watch. Does this mean 2:30 a.m. here? 2:30 p.m. in Minneapolis? Daylight outside. How long has she slept?

"Coming," she calls louder, slipping on a robe. The chill rises from her toes straight up her legs, gripping her stomach with something like panic.

Outside the door, she finds a small, dark-skinned woman in a crisp black and white habit.

"Good afternoon," she extends a delicate hand. "I am Sister Margaret. We've been corresponding for so long, I feel as if I know you, Doctor. I'm happy to be among the first to welcome you to Mission House."

Afternoon? How has she slept so long in this strange, new place? And who is this woman impersonating Sister Margaret, whom she's always imagined to be the twin of her first grade teacher, with big bosom, ruddy face and ageing blue eyes?

Sister Margaret laughs. A friendly, pleasing trill.

Monica joins in.

"Pardon my attire, Sister. You can see I haven't caught up with the time."

"Indeed," the young nun grins. "You must acclimate yourself. Do sleep more if you like. But some of our newcomers like to be alerted to the time."

It's 2 p.m., Monica realizes. Delhi is 11 ½ hours ahead of Minneapolis.

"I wondered if you'd care to take an early evening tea with me at Nathu's?"

"Nathu's?" Almost awake now, Moica sees a nun in her late twenties, not much younger than herself, just fresher, familiar with the surroundings.

"A local café." Sister Margaret studies her guest. "In the Bengali Market."

Bengali Market. Prepaid taxi. It's all coming back.

"Yes, thanks. I'd enjoy that."

Sister Margaret shakes her head from side to side, an Indian gesture for agreement, Monica remembers.

Overcome with remorse, she splutters, "Oh, dear, friends were phoning."

"Yes, Professor Nair said he will ring again tomorrow. And Dr. Nelson, from your Embassy clinic, has left her mobile number."

Monica takes a long breath of relief, anticipation. How astonishing that Tina Nelson is working in Delhi. She didn't think she'd have a friend here until Beata visited. And now she has two, well one-and-a-half, with Ashok Nair.

"Sorry to be a bother."

"Hardly a bother." The young nun waves her fine-boned fingers.

Why does she seem young? Innocence? No purity perhaps. Sister Margaret exudes a kind of serenity. Monica understands she, herself is the innocent here.

"Shall we meet in the foyer about 6 p.m.?"

"I look forward to it."

"A light lunch awaits you in the refectory, whenever you fancy it."

"Thank you, Sister."

Craving a latte, Monica pokes around the kitchen for tea bags. While the water boils, she opens her suitcases, digs out woolens.

The first bureau drawer is discouraging. The second even riper in mildew. Maybe she'll leave the bags packed and withdraw things day by day. She'll only be at Mission House a week before traveling up to Moorty Hospital.

*****

Walking downstairs to the lobby, Monica notices the windows on each landing have been removed. (Broken? Shot out? Never installed?) No wonder the place is freezing. She shivers in her black wool sweater and skirt, then sees the nun.

Sister Margaret rises from a bench by the chapel, smiling. "The refectory is this way."

Outside in the early evening dark, crowds rush along the raised sidewalks. The sidewalk is a good nine inches higher than the street, how many sprains, how many broken ankles per week?

Noises begin to penetrate. Honking. Grinding. Whistling. Screech-

Traveling with Spirits

ing. The combustive dissonance of buses, scooters, auto rickshaws, trucks, cars.

Drivers weave in and out of lanes. "Use horn!" a popular bumper sticker.

Gently, Sister Margaret takes her elbow. "You must watch yourself on the crumbling pavement."

Pavement, not sidewalk. Are all the pavements like this? Last night's dreams return in fragments: cars without headlights; people without heads; the stolen tree.

Wait, she wants to say, India already? I need more transition than a taxi ride and one night's sleep.

Then turn from the busy main road and walk on several blocks to the Bengali Market where she sees Krishna convenience store, two stationery shops, two green grocers, several flower stands, a bookstore advertizing photocopies.

On one corner is the Bengali House of Sweets. On the other is Nathu's, which also specializes in cakes and other confections.

"How do you choose between them?"

The nun raises a wry eyebrow. "We visit one this month. The other next month. We don't eat out very often."

The meal will be an occasion for each of us in different ways, thinks Monica.

As they enter Nathu's, a burly man nods. "This way," he guides them around the tables crowded cacophonous families and whispering young couples, then gestures to a booth at the back.

"English menu?" A waiter barks.

"*Kripaya*," Monica nods.

"*Please*. On your first day. That's excellent," beams Sister Margaret.

"A minimal achievement." Monica cocks her head.

He tosses two menus on the small table.

English, sure, but what are these? *Uthapam. Dosa*. "I've eaten a lot of Indian food at home but never encountered these words."

"Time to try them, then," encourages Sister Margaret. "You'll need to know what to ask Cook to prepare for you at Moorty Hospital."

Cook. She blanches at the thought of servants.

"Let's sample a variety." Sister waves to the waiter. "Biju, please bring us one tomato onion *uthapam*, one plain *dosa*, some *sambhar* and *raita*."

He turns.

"Oh, yes, one bottled water and one regular water, please."

Monica thinks wistfully about the Kingfisher beer she always ordered with Indian meals at home.

Three men arguing. Children crying. Two couples in animated conversation. The place smells of oil and sugar and who knows what all these spices are. Monica is here, finally, after months and months of planning. After years of childhood fantasizing. How can she convey the momentousness of this simple meal?

Sister Margaret is saying something.

Monica tunes out the clatter.

Sister regards her steadily. "Dr. Murphy, we are grateful to have you join our modest mission."

"Please call me Monica." She squeezes the nun's hand, then remembers Indians don't touch each other as often as Americans do.

Sister shakes her head.

"*I* am grateful to be here." Monica draws a breath of satisfaction. It's been a year of making the decision, backing away from it, then finally embracing this long journey of body and spirit. She didn't anticipate nine months of forms and inoculations and more forms. She wonders, idly now, where all her documents are stored. Where does a country with a billion citizens put an extra file?

Their meal arrives promptly. The *uthapams* are large, pungent pastries—a cross between pizza and latke. The *dosas* resemble crisp pancakes folded burrito style around fragrant, savory mush. How long will she continue to compare each meal to American dishes?

Sister precisely divides the meal, serving half of each to Monica.

"Your family, they are in America a long time?"

"Oh, no," she exclaims. Simple questions: this is how to get to know people. Monica tells herself to be less self-absorbed, to inquire about Sister Margaret's life. "My parents came from Kildare, in Ireland."

"Ireland is a Catholic country," Sister Margaret observes, then crunches into the *dosa*.

"Most of it." She sips mineral water and studies Sister Margaret's technique of eating with the fingers of one hand.

"You know, we Indians were Catholic before the Irish. Before the Spanish."

Monica resorts to knife and fork. She'll have to practice hard to become as dexterous as Sister Margaret. She chews slowly, relishing the subtle spices. Next time, she'll just order the uthapam.

"Yes, St. Thomas," she finally answers. "I know the stories about him, converting people on the Malabar Coast, traveling all the way to Madras."

Sister shakes her head approvingly.

"We Catholics in India are six million. You have come to a very old Catholic country."

THREE

An entire morning of paperwork. Perhaps bureaucracy is the real religion of India. Monica stretches her jet-lagged shoulders, then dresses to meet Ashok Nair for lunch.

"No, not Nathu's," he rebuffed her suggestion, mildly appalled, very professorial. "I'm inviting you for a proper meal. Please be my guest at the India International Center."

"I'm not sure how to get there."

"Simply catch an auto rickshaw," he spoke with more of a lilt than he did on the plane. "Everyone knows the IIC, near the Lodi Gardens."

"Yes, the great Mughal Park," Monica noted, eager to show she wasn't ignorant. She simply had a lot to learn.

"That's it. Shall we meet in the dining room at 12:30?"

She weighs his brusqueness as she approaches the auto rickshaw. Maybe he feels trapped by an invitation offered after two glasses of airplane wine. His asperity is at such odds with the graciousness of Sister Margaret and Mr. Alexander. Perhaps he learned abruptness in grad school at NYU. He'd fit right in with her Minneapolis colleagues. Thinking about those tensions, now 12,000 miles away, knots her stomach.

*****

Winter sun spills through generous windows of the handsome dining room.

Behind her, a voice.

"Dr. Murphy. How nice to see you looking rested after that beastly journey."

She turns to a slim, strikingly attractive man in a navy sports coat, white shirt and black slacks. "Likewise," she smiles.

The waiter directs them to a window table. Outside, people stroll through Lodi Gardens in the thin blue winter light.

Now she's glad she chose the new green wool dress. These jade beads were Eric's last Christmas gift.

"India!" Eric burst out. "Who do you think you are? Mother Teresa?

You could die in India."

She wanted to tell him she was already dying in Minneapolis, from grief over Mom's death, anguish at the way Jeanne handled it, rage at her clinic colleagues. But he'd patiently listened to her troubles for months. He was waiting for a recovery, unaware she was being eaten alive. Soon there would be no Monica Murphy.

She returns to Ashok. "You look refreshed, yourself."

The prematurely graying hair is an intriguing touch of vulnerability. His assured voice conveys dignity. And those brown eyes reflect fierce, determined intelligence.

After they are seated at his favorite table, he gestures to the garden.

"It's a lovely place." She feels suddenly girlish.

"Hmm, I suspect if you stayed in Delhi, you would come here often." He waves to the waiter.

"That depends on whether the food is as tasty as Nathu's."

Not a crease of a smile.

The waiter brings two English menus.

Ashok holds up his right hand. "I noticed you forwent meat on the plane. May I recommend their vegetarian *thali*? It's one of the best in Delhi."

Ignoring her craving for another savory *uthapam*, she says, "How can I resist?"

"Fine," Ashok orders the *thali*, then instructs the waiter. "A bottle of mineral water." He turns to her, "And what? Scotch? Wine?"

"A Kingfisher?"

"Two Kingfishers, please."

The waiter nods to Ashok, smiles politely at the lady.

Her companion stares out the window.

She babbles, shy and unnerved by the silence. "Delhi is such a fascinating city. A cultural amalgamation. It's so Indian, yet so much more Western than I anticipated."

"Yes," he sighs in amusement, annoyance. "Once you recover from gawking at tree trimmers on swaying elephants, once you get used to cows delaying traffic on Kasturba Gandhi Marg, you start noticing the Reebok and Nike logos, the mock fast food outlets."

"Mock?"

"*Fast* is not an Indian mode. Do you know that in Bombay, it is required to have 47 certificates before one can complete a building?"

"I've had a few encounters, myself, with your civil service."

"Somehow neither 'civil' nor 'service' seems an appropriate word for red tape dispensers in any country. You should try being an alien in your land."

She nods.

"On a serious note, I'm glad your entry was scrutinized. You cannot expect us to leave doors open to any wandering foreigner."

He's aiming for irony, not rancor, surely. Monica knows she's feeling too sensitive today, from physical and cultural jet lag.

Beer and water appear. She sips each gratefully. In some ways, Ashok reminds her of Eric. Maybe academics break into lecture the way tenors break into song.

Ashok gazes out the window once again, looking pensive, or perhaps worried.

Why did he invite her if he's so averse to foreigners? And why did she accept during her first chaotic week in this daunting country? Do the mission staff consider her absence rude? Indeed Father Koreth expressed surprise at her "appointment."

"Cheers," he raises his glass.

"Cheers."

"Apologies for the lecture," he shrugs. "Once you've lived abroad for an extended period, it's hard to accept all the 'contradictions' of contemporary India. Do you know we have a middle class of over 200 million people?

She recalls yesterday—the Mercedes Benzes and cell phones. She glances at the bejeweled, elegantly attired women at two adjacent tables.

"Yet a tiny minority pays income tax."

She waits.

"Fifty percent of our kids under five are malnourished. Forty percent of Delhi is illiterate."

"You're helping to change that," she insists.

"How?" He studies her face. "By educating children of the elite who will go to graduate school or jobs in England, Canada and America?" His jaw stiffens.

"Well, you went to the U.S. for grad school and you returned." She fiddles with the jade. Bad habit. Once during a tense phone call with Jeanne, she broke the strand. Hours later, she was still searching for pale green balls under the couch and chairs.

"More fool me." Again, he browses the garden.

Maybe his distraction is solace in the garden rather than boredom with her. He's clearly shy, too.

"I'm just perpetuating divisions here, suffering an anemic wage as a result."

"No." She's slipping into deep water. "You're smart. Committed. That counts for a lot."

"So are you, no?"

He seems to be looking through the bones in her face.

"Do you know what you're doing for, or *to*, India?"

"What do you mean?" Sweat trickles inside her dress and she hopes he can't smell the fear, confusion.

"For Madame."

They're locked in a stare.

"Your lunch," her companion cocks his handsome head.

"Thank you!" She's dazed by the array of vivid, pungent vegetables.

"Any questions?" Ashok asks.

She takes advantage of his new lightness. "What are these white cubes?"

"Curd cheese. Many Delhi-ites will tell you it's like cottage cheese. But I've met cottage cheese in your country and the resemblance eludes me."

She takes a bite, rolls her eyes with pleasure.

He laughs.

"What kind of philosophy do you teach, Professor Nair?"

" 'Ashok,' please. Didn't we exchange first names when were were packed into that airborne sardine tin for so many hours?"

"You've been addressing me as 'Doctor Murphy,' " she hesitates, "so…"

"An old habit," he declares. "Monica it is, then. Monica and Ashok."

He peers out the blasted window again. Then answers her question. "Ethics for the first years. When I believed in, or was interested in, moral judgment. Lately I've moved to philosophy of science."

"You don't think you're still a bit of a moralist?" Instantly, she regrets the forwardness.

"Because of my questions on the plane?"

She closes her eyes, chary of reviving that stressful exchange.

"Well, tell me, Monica, aren't there clinics in poor areas of the States? Why come to India? More interestingly, why not as a Fulbrighter or as a *Médecin Sans Frontières*? Why come with a Catholic Mission?"

"People are people." She leans forward, noticing the small scar beneath his lower lip. "Because I was born American does that mean I have no connection to, no responsibility for, people who happen to be Indian?"

"Don't be naïve, friend," he draws his right hand into a fist.

"Don't be so cynical."

"Even if you're right about there being some 'world community,' as the journalists say, what about the Catholic piece? India is a Hindu country, a Muslim country, a Buddhist country."

Monica hears Sister Margaret's proud declaration and shuts her eyes. "I'm sorry if you are offended by my work." She's not going to cry.

"Offended. Hurt. The American preoccupation with social comfort is truly astonishing. What matter if I'm *offended*? We are two adults having a serious difference. That doesn't mean I'm devastated by your words. It doesn't mean we can't be friends." He blots a bead of sweat from his left temple.

"Friends," Monica repeats softly. "I'd like to be friends." She glances outside as a bright green bird flies into view. "Such a beautiful creature. Look!"

"That?" He restrains his astonishment. "That bird? It's a rather ordinary parrot. Oh, my friend, I see this India of ours is going to dazzle you." He's laughing.

It's a kind laugh, she believes. A friendly laugh.

FOUR

January, 2001, New Delhi

A warm, late afternoon. Grateful for rising temps, Monica lounges in a vintage rattan chair and footstool, on the tiny bedroom veranda. Buzzards and finches call from above as she reads more documents about "her" hospital.

This morning's orientation session, their third, was particularly helpful. She learned much more about the facilities and lack thereof at mission hospitals. Once she arrives in Moorty and confirms the shortage, she'll write to Alonso for the supplies he's promised. But she won't make any presumptions before talking to the staff there. If she's learned anything from Louise's hubris at Lake Clinic, it's how consensus should trump individual ego.

Parrots sail back and forth. Ashok can keep his laconic indifferences: these radiant birds flickering through Delhi smog inspire her to believe she, too, can flourish in this dense atmosphere.

Now she has the answers for Ashok. She's been obsessing for days. About how Catholic hospitals treat people of all faiths. She longs for people who share common beliefs. How much richer her life has been since returning to the Church. She wants to say spirituality might be a dimension missing from his rational philosophy. She wakes up each morning thinking of retorts.

He's right about one thing: the bureaucratic hurdles persist.

The Americans want her to get more shots. (Well, this will give her an excuse to see Tina at the Embassy Clinic sooner.) The Indians require more forms. A clerk at the American Express Bank holds her hostage for two hours while she ensures each signature on each page matches precisely.

*****

Arriving at the U.S. Embassy in a yellow and black auto rickshaw, she feels her heart sinking at the endless queue of people snaking around the block. Men leaning on canes. Women hoisting toddlers on their hips. Older boys in t-shirts and jeans joking with each other. She heads to the back of a long, long line.

Someone calls to her. "Ma'am?"

An American voice.

She turns to a tall, erect African American soldier, marine, some military person.

"Ma'am, what are you looking for?"

The pickles. Kosher dills. No, he won't appreciate her humor.

"The infirmary," she summons a professional tone. "I need an inoculation."

"Follow me, please, Ma'am."

Is she being arrested. Because she helped block the Federal Building in Minneapolis during Desert Storm? Her penchant for paranoia swells in this land of perpetual surprises.

Again, her cool, doctor's voice: "May I ask why?"

"Because this is the line for visas to the U.S., Ma'am and, from the sound of your Minnesota accent, I'd guess you're not fishing for a visa."

She laughs. "How can you tell I'm from Minnesota?"

"I'm from Duluth, myself."

Duluth, she blocks memories of Mom's last months with Jeanne. "Minneapolis here. Do you really think we have a regional accent?"

"You betcha!"

She can't wait to tell Beata about this guy. A witty Minnesotan in Delhi.

As she follows the young man into the imposing modern embassy-fortress, no one looks up to protest her jumping the queue. She imagines Ashok deconstructing her privileges here. She's conscious of entitlement. This is her embassy. She pays taxes for it. Even if she often protests U.S. policies, she is an American. "America": a label. In India a particular brand of foreigner.

Rows and rows of hard chairs are filled with people who have finally made it to the front of the queue. One reward at a time from the land of gilded thoroughfares.

Because of her citizenship, she doesn't have to stand for hours, then sit for more hours. She can walk straight into the clinic. Inalienable rights. Not a comfortable thought. Still, more comfortable than the queue.

She registers, fastens her ID badge, and takes an elevator down to a brightly lit clinic used by the Embassy staff and their families. Waiting on an over-stuffed couch, she flips through the latest copy of *Time*, distracted by thoughts about her perforated arm: hepatitis A, hepatitis B. cholera, flu, Japanese encephalitis, polio, tetanus, and now rabies shots because of the wild dogs and mountain monkeys. Monkeys?

"Monica!"

She swivels to the familiar voice, beams at her tall, blond friend, elegant as ever even in baggy white doctor's jacket and pants. "Tina!"

Embracing her old friend, Tina whispers, "You don't look a day older than you did in med school."

Monica grins. "It's only been eight years. You look great too. More worldly, somehow."

They both notice the turned heads.

Tina fingers a blond curl behind her ear. "Come, come back to the exam room. I have the serum ready." Then in a softer voice, "We can talk there."

She feels her body relax as it hasn't in two weeks. Ashok would assign this ease to being with "her people" now. No, she'd argue, everyone unwinds with old friends.

"Business first, OK? Then you can chill out and chat a bit. These preventive rabies shots don't hurt like the others. Simple jab. Maybe some swelling this week."

Monica rolls up her sleeve. She hates the sensation of needle piercing flesh, any flesh. She was happy the Lake Clinic lab techs handled the blood tests and shots. She knows she'll get used to giving shots and drawing blood in Moorty. Of course she will.

Her tall, fit roommate looks all grown up now. Friend of her youth. Monica always wondered if they'd make it through med school. Yet here they are: practicing physicians living in India. Eight years along.

"I was flabbergasted when Edward told me you were in Delhi." Her face is all delight at seeing Tina. "Thanks, again, for getting me the appointment here."

"Pretty neat that we wound up in the same town again."

Tina always had flair. She knew how to dress, where to eat. She discovered the best jazz places. Monica never imagined jazz in Minneapolis until Tina. But India?

"I did write a couple of letters, to your parents' address in New York. Maybe you never got them?"

"Done!" Tina discards the needle. "Hey, sorry, I'm a terrible correspondent."

"So why India? Why Delhi?"

Ashok's inquisition.

Tina blinks her pale blue eyes. "I had to pay off those mega med school loans. And foreign service seemed like an adventure. It is. The country is fascinating. I've made close Indian friends, so I'll stay a while. What's more interesting is you being here, Ms. Big Time Fellowship. You didn't rack up student debts. What's the scoop?"

"Maybe it's about a different kind of debt."

"Yeah," Tina pauses, probably summoning tact. "Edward said something about an evangelical mission?"

Monica covers her eyes, shakes her head wearily. "No, absolutely not. Just a basic Catholic hospital in Moorty. Nothing evangelical."

"I couldn't really feature you with Holy Rollers. Remember those parties in school?"

A knock on the door. "Your next patient, Dr. Nelson."

Monica stands.

Tina leans on the examining table. "So listen, how long are you in Delhi?"

"Another week, at least," she sighs. "Until I scale the mountain of rules and regulations."

"Hey, no one ever reaches that summit. But I know you'll excel at running through the paces," she laughs.

Again Monica is filled with nostalgia for their youthful days and nights, mostly nights, when everything seemed possible.

"Come to dinner, Monica. Maybe we can have an expedition. Have you seen the Jama Masjid? The Red Fort? Fab India?"

"Fab India?"

"Oh, girl, you've been spending too much time around the nuns and priests. I see I need to take sober Monica in hand."

*****

Tina waves as Monica descends to the lobby of Mission House.

"Well, this pad is *très* convenient," she says. "Close to Connaught Circle, the Janpath, Kasturba Gandhi Marg."

"And the Bengali Market."

Tina is mildly surprised. "With such local savvy, you'll become a Delhi Wallah in no time. Why not stay here? They're looking for a replacement at the clinic."

The head concierge, Mr. Asnani, tries to look invisible as he eavesdrops. Monica understands his curiosity. Tina is a stunning woman.

"I told you," she whispers, "I need a break from American medicos." She takes a breath. Yet another friend worried she's gone over the brink. "From blitzkrieg appointments, impossible triage options…"

"You're looking for a serene pace in this rural Indian clinic?"

"My colleagues will be different. I won't be battling American insurance companies."

"But…"

"Listen. I've made the commitment for six months. I hope to stay longer, if I'm useful. Besides, I've invited you to Moorty."

"Right," Tina swallows. "My bucolic weekend in the hill country."

Monica nods, firmly closing the argument.

Tina brightens. "Let's hit the road or we'll be late to 'Beating the Retreat.' "

As their wobbly auto rickshaw threads through frantic traffic, Monica raises her voice over the street noise. "Now, explain this again? We're celebrating what?"

"The British military withdrawal. A yearly commemoration." She's shouting above the blaring horns and screeching tires. Two bicyclists almost collide and curse a truck driver. "Fabulous pageantry. You'll adore it. Bands from all the services."

Monica suspends disbelief. She and Tina used to march in protest rallies together—"U.S. Out of Panama…Americans Divesting from Apartheid…" Now they're off to listen to military bands? Perhaps Embassy life has changed her.

"Sir," Tina calls to the turbaned driver, "to the left; to the left."

"*Achah*," he says, then, without looking over his shoulder, slips two lanes to the left.

Use horn, Monica thinks. *Use horn.* Even though St. Christopher was de-sainted years ago, she carries the medal Beata gave her at the airport.

"Glad you remembered not to bring a purse. They're sticky about high security. No water bottles, binoculars, cameras. Just money and keys in your pocket and your ID."

The driver pulls over to ask a soldier for directions.

The whole area is swarming with uniforms.

He drives until they're stopped by a policeman.

"This makes no sense," Tina argues with the officer, half in English, half in Hindi. "See all those cars ahead of us?"

The officer shrugs incomprehension.

"OK. OK," grumbles Tina. "We'll hoof it from here." She hands the relieved driver twenty rupees.

*****

Enveloped in a crowd of rich Indians, poor Indians, scattered foreigners, Monica savors her anonymity in this huge city. She feels even freer here than in New York. Certainly Moorty is a small place and she'll be visible as a clinic doctor. But, she won't be known, not in the same way she was in Minnesota. Will she still feel like the same person: sister of angry Jeanne; daughter of Saint Marie and vagabond Tim: erstwhile girlfriend of Eric, whom she misses although she's glad they broke up. If she hasn't left it all behind, at least it's in the background. She has yet to discover who she will be in Moorty.

As Monica and Tina approach the staging area on the Rajpath, she notices a line of five or six mounted camels standing at attention on a rise to the west in the muggy winter light.

"They'll hold that posture for an hour," notes Tina.

VIP cars deliver government officials to their central seats.

Mounted soldiers escort the very VIPs arriving in better cars.

Once the big guys are settled, music commences.

Marching bands.

"Aren't those English tunes?"

Tina laughs. "For some, Britain remains the Apex of Western Civilization."

They sit next to an excited little boy and his watchful father.

The band uniforms are a marvelous fusion of green, orange, red.

Bagpipes? Monica wonders. *And those must be Indian tartans. Definitely not Scottish.*

An extended family settles in front of them, get up, move to better seats.

Another family. More shifting. Bobbing up and down.

Monica and Tina watch, like proper school marms, each clucking under her breath.

Finally, a Sikh man implores the popping audience members to settle down. Their view is clear for five minutes before the next wave of people arrive, stirring and fussing.

Then a hush cuts through the chaos.

The lone trumpet moans. The tune is echoed by the bands. A carillon chimes. Also answered by the bands.

Call and response. Moving in its familiarity and poignant strangeness.

The ceremony ends as the camel riders head farther west, into the horizon.

As the sun sets, electric stars outline the stately buildings.

They eat at one of the big hotels halfway between their homes, the Hotel Barrington.

An astonishing buffet offers *aloo gobi, sag paneer, uthapams,* baked chicken, mashed potatoes, string beans with almonds, *nan, parathas, rotis.* Their fellow customers are well-dressed Westerners or Indians in fine attire. Monica recalls the family they passed on the street ten minutes before, all of them seated on the sidewalk as the woman stirred a pot heated over a hibachi.

"This bounteous display; it's like the opening of the O'Henry story."

"You never get used to it," sighs Tina, "the disparity between rich and poor here. You learn to live with the contradictions."

Monica sips her Kingfisher pensively.

"So what do you think of the ceremony?"

"Like a history book. Are there other events like that?"

Tina winks. "Tons. Bureaucracy and ceremony are first cousins."

Tina is still her teacher and guide—from Minneapolis jazz to Indian culture. Monica may have found academia easier, but Tina was always better at living life.

"Haven't you seen the bumper stickers? 'Our India is Great.' They outdo American chauvinism by miles of bunting. And thousands of years."

"No."

"Wait, old friend, just wait."

Waiting has never been her strong suit. It is especially hard now that she has so much to look forward to—a new country, new colleagues and a reunion with this long lost friend.

She starts to weep.

"Honey, what's *up*?"

"Everything, Tina." She sniffs back the tears. "Everything, absolutely everything is up."

Tina reaches over and squeezes her friend's shoulder.

Excited, grateful, terrified, Monica wishes she would never let go.

FIVE

January, 2001, New Delhi

From her third floor room, she hears drilling from down the street. Riveting on nearby pavement. Horns from two blocks away. Dozens of voices.

Delhi is exhausting. She's fit, young, optimistic. Yet it takes such effort to accomplish a few errands, to battle through to evening. She'll set out after daily mass with a mundane list—posting letters, buying milk, finding Beata a birthday card, photocopying a document, procuring government forms, searching once again for an ATM that will accept her very common bank card. By the murky dark of late afternoon, she'll only accomplish half the tasks.

Monica lies down to rest from paperwork, a "wee nap," as Mom would say.

Disasters loom. Yesterday the printer blew up because she forgot to use the transformer, and she abandoned the electric kettle to the point of mini-conflagration. She's learned to say to herself, "I'm having an Indian day."

She should open her eyes and get back to the paperwork, but sometimes fatigue overwhelms her straight after lunch.

Rapping on the door.

Around the Christmas table: Mom, Jeanne, Ashok and Tina. Everyone is arguing as they eat roast beef and aloo gobi.

Louder knocking.

She blinks into the afternoon. Stands up, a little wobbly. "Coming." After splashing her face with cold water, she repeats, "Coming," and answers the door.

Sister Margaret's face radiates joy.

She's been visited by the Holy Spirit? Wake up, Monica. Focus.

"Please excuse the disturbance."

"Not at all, Sister. Will you have a cup of tea?"

"No, thank you very much. I have duties. I couldn't wait to relay the news."

She stares at the serious nun whom she's come to admire in many ways. She guesses the news and suddenly her body roils with conflicting emotions. "My documents are approved."

"Yes, Dr. Murphy. Yes. And we are all so happy you can finally begin your journey after so long in our humble station."

"Hardly," she balks. "Everyone has been so hospitable. I've learned so much and I'm profoundly grateful." She wants to add, *Just as I'm beginning to understand Delhi a little, to make friends, to feel semi-comfortable. Maybe Tina is right. Maybe I should stay here. They say the Missions are rarely staffed by Western doctors.* Instead, she says, "When do I leave?"

"Alas, Doctor, there will be one more week's delay. But the Moorty staff are thrilled about your imminent arrival. They are in grave need of your skills."

One week's reprieve. She can keep the dates with Tina and Ashok. She has time to buy the rest of the books and personal items she now knows she can't get in Moorty.

Her mind wanders. Fifteen degrees here this afternoon. And the temperatures in Moorty will be much lower. Thinking in Celsius makes her colder. Of course, she'll be glad for Moorty's climate in the summer when Delhi bakes at 40-45 degrees.

"We'll offer a special prayer of gratitude at Mass tomorrow morning," Sister beams.

"Yes, Sister. Thank you."

*****

"So you're actually going through with it?" Tina is annoyed, resigned, stunned.

A farewell lunch at the Imperial Hotel: Tina's treat. "A proper Indian meal." A feast.

"Of course," she keeps the tone light. "This is very tasty. What is it?"

"Vegetable *jalfreze*. Looks easy, but believe me, these dishes aren't simple. I took a cooking course last year, but I still can't blend the spices properly."

"Mmmm." Enjoying Indian food is one of her own less tricky accomplishments.

"So you're leaving me just when I've found you after eight years."

Monica rolls her eyes. "Visit me in Moorty." Overwhelmed by loneliness, she hopes Tina will come. She'll be a stranger in a place as distant from Delhi as Delhi is from Minneapolis. Not quite. Still, very different. She'll have busy days and empty nights. Sometimes Monica wonders if

Eric is right about this trip being a penance. For being American. For succeeding beyond her parents' imaginations. For losing Mom. And Jeanne.

"Moorty isn't, well, the most cosmopolitan hill station, sweetie. It's picturesque, but nowhere. Which, indeed, is why they need you. We'll plan reunions in Delhi. My spare bed is always available. Come down whenever you like."

"Thanks."

Tina folds her rich cloth napkin. "Are you ready for adventure?"

"Oh, right, the market." She really should return to Mission House and pull together all those bloody papers. Still, this will be her last sight of Tina for a while.

A wide street, busy with all manner of vehicles zipping past tall, colonial storefronts. Sidewalks crowded with tables of face cloths, men's underwear, Wellington boots, double boilers, girls' frocks in pastel colors. Tina's right again. She's never seen anything like Chandni Chowk.

Her old friend is on a serious jewelry quest. She's saved a sapphire from Sri Lanka to be set by the superior craftsmen in India.

Sapphire. Monica loves the way Indians pronounce the word—*safire*—emphasizing the stone's blaze. She's been dazzled by these multi-colored gems since her fifth grade project on the British Royal Jewels. The blue sapphire, she knows, is quite rare. Proletarian, artless little Monica writing about the Kings of England found herself seduced by gleaming stones and the distant lands where they were mined.

"First let's cruise the silk stalls." Tina yanks her hand.

Heat. Crowds. Monica feels faint. Perhaps she ate too fast.

Shoppers swarm the small stalls of the indoor market. Loquacious men sit, chatting to each other, their backs to yardages of vividly colored and subtly patterned silk. Women lean forward, fingering the fabrics knowledgeably, then consult each other in whispers, their bracelets jangling.

"One day we'll buy you a sari," promises Tina. "Green. I think you'll look super in lime green."

"Where did you say your jeweler is?"

"I'm serious, Monica. Indian women love saris. They know their attire is more elegant. They will expect you to dress appropriately."

"You wear a perfectly average doc's coat and slacks." She shakes her head, smiling.

Someone pushes from behind.

Monica turns to face a frazzled mother, three children in tow. Stepping aside, she lets them pass. The beguiling boy turns and grins widely.

"I work at the U.S. Embassy with Americans mostly, not at a hill station treating local people." Tina directs her back to the street.

Monica's head throbs from the racket of clattering carts and incomprehensible voices. The still Delhi air—which everyone says will lift any day now—presses against her eyelids. "Where did you say the jeweler is?"

"Over here, see the sign, 'Capital Jewellers.' "

"Do they mean 'capitol' as in Delhi? Or 'capital' as in 'foremost?'"

"Hon," Tina sniffs, "there are lots of things worth puzzling about in India. Spelling isn't one. Just be happy when you see English signs. Until you learn Hindi."

She's made minimal progress with Hindi despite her resolutions. Maybe Moorty will accelerate the pace.

Tina stops at a darkened shop and presses the buzzer.

That picture book on Raj jewels aroused a lifelong curiosity about Indian history. Monica recalls her eighth grade teacher being surprised that she wanted to do a geography report on Bombay. Amazing how those school projects provoked an abiding affection for India. Maybe that's why she and Ritu became fast friends in med school.

Finally, someone comes to the glass door of Capital Jewelers: a bald man peers drowsily as he parts purple velvet drapes.

"Hi Ayan, it's me," Tina laughs. "Wake up from your mid-day snooze."

"Oh, many apologies, Dr. Nelson." He opens the door. "I was forgetting your appointment."

"Good to see you! Ayan Dutta, please meet Monica Murphy, another doctor from America."

"*Namaste*," they say in unison.

He calls to the back of the shop, "Tea for the ladies, please, Sukemar."

Monica watches artisan and customer dicker heatedly and cheerfully about the design, the thickness of gold around the *sa-fire*, the appropriate chain.

"Yes," says Tina pensively. "The right width, but can you make it *flatter*?"

Feeling voyeuristic at the unexpectedly intense exchange, Monica glances into the dusty showcase containing glittering earrings and bracelets and necklaces. She wanders over to study the rubies, diamonds and emeralds. Suddenly, she's completely dislocated. It's one thing to read pretty books, but to confront so many real gems is, well, unnerving. Take me back to the costume jewelry counter at Target, she thinks.

Tina is standing now, smiling happily with Ayan Dutta.

"Come," Tina says playfully. "We'll take a small excursion."

Before Monica can protest, she's atop a bicycle rickshaw, her driver speeding ahead of Tina's.

Giggling, Tina manages to instruct, "Hold on to the sides. Keep your feet on the floor board. Don't lean forward too much."

"Right, thanks." She's laughing too, despite her terror.

"The Red Fort," Tina directs her driver.

*****

The Mission House staff practice silence at breakfast. Monica sips tea, recalling Father Koreth's sermon. Christ's suffering is a model, a reminder that we serve God on this earth so we may glorify him in heaven.

She's distracted by the letter from Beata she noticed in her box after Mass. She's torn between her appetite for the *idili* and *sambhar* and her longing for home. Discipline: as a child she was never as good at physical restraint as Jeanne. Is that pious restraint what drove her sister to alcohol? Clearly the alcohol intensified her righteous dismissal of Monica's revived Catholicism.

She glances at her companions—the nuns and Father Koreth all absorbed in meditative reflection. For a week now, she's been the only lay person at Mission House. All the other docs and nurses have departed for postings.

Contemplate the journey ahead, she tells herself. Instead, she wondering about Beata's new boyfriends, about whether she's seen Eric and how he is. Discipline, she's never had enough. Not for the first time, she worries she's a fraud at this religious community business.

A big bell rings. The harsh metal sound carrying profound relief. Saying farewell to the others, she leaves the table.

Monica settles on the veranda wearing her new parrot green shawl. Tina's Bon Voyage gift. The sari is next, her friend promised.

Morning is almost warm. Birds call. Across the street two elephants lumber along the pavement, half-adorned in satin and tinsel for a Hindu wedding.

Wonderful that Beata prefers old-fashioned correspondence to email. You can be so much more reflective on the page than on the internet.

My Dear Monica,

Great to hear about your arrival. I wish I could join you on those fascinating streets, at those delicious meals. A much more inviting scenario than Minnesota life at the moment: tentatively picking my way over ice to the car, driving through the unplowed streets (seven inches of snow last night!) to work. Your life is adventurous and worthwhile. OK, some days my job is useful, but on others I feel I'm just doing admin work.

Monica loosens the shawl. Beata always underestimates her own contributions.

It's another lavender morning in Minnesota: that brief blush of pastel against the white sky, land, flakes. I headed straight for the Coffee Shack which was heated with laughter and conversations of a dozen people who awoke earlier than I.

Espresso. Monica still often wakes up yearning for a half-hour chat with Beata at the Coffee Shack before work. They had such good conversations there—about jobs and men and Mom's illness and Jeanne's kidnapping Mom to Duluth and Mom's death and returning to the Church and breaking up with Eric. And preparing for India.

Clumsily, I dropped my change on the muddy floor and Alfred, the wiry blond youth who beams friendly greetings each morning, handed me a warm, wet rag for my hands. I felt genuinely happy for the first time today because I remembered the compensations of winter: people taking your coat, asking about your health, telling you to watch the ice. Damn, I'm getting carried away with Mundane Minnesota. By the time this is forwarded from Mission House, you'll be settling into your clinic. What are the patients like? And your colleagues?

Monica laughs at the questions, which she's still asking herself. Beata will be surprised that she's still in Delhi, not contributing anything except shit to an already stressed sewage system.

I saw Eric at the Coop. In the herbal remedy section. Apparently he's had bronchitis for weeks. More like a broken heart. He asked after you, of course.

Her throat catches. No, both she and Eric agreed it was over months ago. What she misses is ephemeral: a sense of belonging with someone: holding hands at the movies. Really! She surveys her library of Indian history and literature. She glances out the window at another pair of elephants swaying down the street. And the parakeets!

You must be wondering about James, the new guy I met at the Y. I've seen him twice. He's smart and funny. I just don't know if I want to date a banker. Yes, I do use a bank. And James is politically savvy, campaigning against redlining. He tutors prisoners. You know all too well it's hard for a black woman to find a black man in the Cities. He's a decent guy, but will I fit into his scene? Of course, I can hear you saying, "How do you know until you've tried?" Your voice comes in loud and clear.

I miss you. I wish we weren't so many time zones apart. Do you have a cell phone yet? Can you do email there? Write again soon about your health and spirits.

God's blessings.

Much love,

Beata

She blinks back tears. Natural to miss a best friend. She also misses the bitter beauty of Minnesota winter. She misses the optimism and excitement she brought on this journey weeks ago. Monica simply never imagined the difficulty of getting settled. Where did she find the hubris for this trip? Where will she find the grace to survive it?

****

She waits for Ashok on a paisley padded bench in the spare, cold lobby, admiring the clean blue of these walls, the simple crucifix, the small statue of Our Lady. She's never been a rococo Catholic.

Mr. Asnani connects a caller to Father Koreth and looks up from the reception desk. "Good evening, Doctor. You are going out?"

"Yes, Mr. Asnani. I am meeting a friend."

He returns to his newspaper.

She admires the sari-like length of her long dress, pleased with her choice.

"And you are going to the Catholic jamboree?"

"No, I'm attending a concert at the India Habitat Centre."

He scrutinizes her. Those tiny oval glasses and the grey hair make him look like a skeptical scientist searching for empirical evidence.

"The India Habitat Centre?"

"Yes, have you been there?"

"You are meeting the Professor again?"

"That's right, Mr. Asnani." Does he disapprove? Does he think she's a nun? "Professor Nair," she says evenly.

A buzzer rasps and Mr. Asnani slowly rises to open the large door for Ashok.

He looks particularly natty tonight in his brown Nehru jacket and black shawl.

Mr. Asnani clears his throat. "Enjoy the concert, Dr. Murphy. You will remember that we lock the doors at 10 p.m. After that, you shall have to summon the night concierge."

"Yes, thank you, Mr. Asnani. And good evening."

Descending the broad stone steps together into the boisterous Delhi evening, she grins and notices that Ashok has barely contained his laughter.

"What's with that fellow? Is he your long-lost father?"

She shrugs. Catching her breath, she wonders if in her jet lag she's told Ashok about Dad skipping out to Wyoming. Of course not. Just an uncanny joke.

"Does he think I'm abducting you to a rave?"

She hoots. "The man likes everything in place," she explains. "Apparently my place tonight is The Catholic Jamboree."

"I trust I'm not keeping you from it?" Ashok takes her arm as they cross the wide street.

She likes the light feel of his hand, blushes, quickly concealing her embarrassment with chatter. "I have a feeling there will always be Catholic Jamborees in my life. Not sure how often I'll get invited to the India Habitat Centre."

Ashok's face softens. "Depends how well you behave."

Blaring horns. Men in brilliantly colored and sequined outfits play instruments loudly as they prance down the street, followed by two festooned pachyderms and a handsome man on a white horse.

"You have attended a Hindu wedding?"

"Oh yes. I mean no. This must be the groom, arriving for the rituals?"

"Yes, the Bengali Market is a prime location for this nuptial season."

She's suspected this from the booming music that beats long into the early morning. Are these elegantly garbed giants the plebian elephants she watched clearing the branches yesterday?

"I should have invited you to my cousin's wedding last week," Ashok scolds himself. "Well, when you return to Delhi for a leave, we'll find a wedding."

Her heart skips the presumption of, what, well, something, between them. Best to ignore that. And isn't it amusing that Tina and Ashok are already planning her imaginary furloughs.

At the taxi stand, she steps back under an acacia tree while Ashok haggles with the drivers about the fare. Delhi wallahs enjoy bargaining. Moorty people too?

He holds the door as she climbs into one of the ubiquitous white Ambassador cabs. She hasn't ridden in one since the pre-paid taxi. How many years ago? The Mission House staff use auto rickshaws. She hopes Ashok isn't spending a fortune.

"Will you tell me a little about the concert?"

"You've heard of raga: different Indian instruments playing traditional melodic shapes and rhythms?"

More statement than question, she notices.

"A couple of times." Before coming, she spent months watching Indian films, reading novels and poetry, attending music and dance. Still, she's culturally illiterate.

"This is idiosyncratic stuff. Indian and Western instruments. You'll hear. I don't want to spoil it."

They pull up to a lavish performance hall. Monica realizes she hasn't been terrified once during the ride, not even when the taxi came to a screeching halt two inches from a brawny lorry. She's getting acclimated. Or losing her mind.

She holds out several bills.

Ashok chivalrously waves them away.

The contemporary hall is filled with light and the happy bustling of excited patrons in flowing fabrics. The crowd is mixed. Young couples on dates. Large family groups. Old women in pairs. Everyone chatting, shifting seats. Surely they'll stay put during the performance. Maybe not; she recalls the commotion at Beating the Retreat.

Ashok nods his head with pleasure at the program. "This guy," he points to the unpronounceabley named saxophonist, "is terrific."

Opening her program, Monica is flooded with exhilaration and uneasiness. When she closes her eyes, she's on a ship docking in Bombay, arriving the way people did fifty years before. Tonight she feels as if she's finally landing in India. All vestiges of jet lag have disappeared. If she had traveled by sea the transition would have been more natural, the arrival more convincing.

During the first set a flutist plays with a violinist, who holds his instrument upside down, the bow pointing to the floor. Their music is dynamic, startling, and she's sorry when it ends. As the stage is prepared for the second act, a family of four in the first row makes ready to leave.

"Is this intermission?"

"Oh, no." Ashok is puzzled, then instructive. "No one stays for a whole concert. Intervals are frequent and unpredictable. We'll have to leave after a few sets if we're going to get a proper dinner."

Newcomers side-shuffle in, claiming the still warm seats.

The saxophonist is superb. Astonishing to hear him riffing with three tabla players. Half-an-hour of spirited improvisation. The drummers are so deft, yet she wonders about the stress on their thumb joints.

Waves and waves of applause.

A tall man presents the saxophonist with a white shawl.

"Now?" Ashok inquires. "May we leave now? Or shall we forgo dinner?"

"Thanks, I'm happy to eat. As long as leaving in the middle is customary."

"Customary." He grins. "So many customs in India: almost everything is customary."

They walk through the dark, warm evening, past several attractive restaurants.

Hungrily, she asks, "Where are we going?"

He leads her over uneven pavement down a small side street, humming parts of the saxophonist's last piece. "A surprise."

She hadn't pictured Ashok as a music lover. What a curious man. Acerbic. Considerate. Gentle. Irascible. Sometimes he acts annoyed by her presence. Sometimes suspicious. During the past week, he's been quite welcoming.

The brightly lit, small café is called The Malabar Coast. A thin, elderly man greets Ashok warmly and escorts them to a corner booth.

Already part of her dream is realized: a quiet refuge from Delhi's crazy pulse. She imagines Moorty's mountain tranquility.

The owner serves two Kingfishers, compliments of the house.

"The father of a student?"

"Brother-in-law of my cousin in Cochin."

Remembering Tina's jeweler, she considers how many people in this huge country seem capriciously linked to so many others.

He regards her expectantly. Something new in his eyes tonight: a kind of fond, teasing familiarity.

"I thought you grew up in Delhi." Her stomach rumbles at the aromas of garlic and butter and heady spices.

"I did. But I belong to Kerala. My father moved to Delhi for a government post."

"Your family is from Cochin?"

"Nearby," he allows, returning to the peacock-shaped menu.

Then he must know about the large Catholic and Jewish communities there. All this time he's been baiting her about Indian history. OK, maybe she's enjoyed the sparring. Dad used to say lively opponents sharpened your wits. Mom shook her head, despairing over a quarrelling world.

"Well, what would you like?" He pushes his glasses higher on his nose.

Quickly, she peruses the menu. "Uthapams!"

He smiles indulgently. "Since you enjoyed the rubbish at Nathu's, I thought you should taste some authentic South Indian cuisine."

Clearly he belongs to Kerala.

Before the first bite, from the delicious smell and vivid presentation, she knows he's right about the food. He specializes in being right. This cooking is far more subtle.

"Mmmm," is all she manages.

Still, she'll always love Nathu's for the atmosphere, for Sister Margaret's hospitality. Because she ate her first dinner in India there.

"You leave on Tuesday." He clenches his jaw, readjusts his glasses.

"Yes, the flight is about an hour." She concentrates on facts, rather than on emotions. "Then I take a car to Moorty." She sounds excited, doesn't she?

"That road is labyrinthine. A three hour ride at least." A dour voice.

"You've been to Moorty?"

"On a family holiday. I don't recall much. Moorty was much cooler than Delhi. One of the minor Raj hill stations, you know."

"I've heard."

"You have a postal address?"

"Somewhere in my purse." She digs around the black Sportsac anxiously.

He hands her a business card. "You must have cards made. Indians love to exchange cards. Of course one throws half of them away."

She scribbles the address, surprised by the trembling of her hand.

"I have a conference in Calcutta on Monday," he takes a long breath. "Otherwise I would escort you to the airport."

Airport. The chaos of that first crowded, smoky night engulfs her. Maybe the domestic terminal is easier. Ridiculous to worry. How sweet of him to think about it.

"You'll be fine," he reassures both of them.

"Thanks."

"Email me once you get settled. Or drop a note."

She nods. Is he speaking out of friendship or something else? Does she want to know? Her life seems too full right now for…for what?

"But not a post card. They don't often survive in the mail. Use an envelope."

"Yes, Professor," she smiles.

Ashok frowns.

"Stay in touch." He squeezes her hand.

As his fingers reluctantly release hers, she imagines herself in a hot air balloon ascending daringly, fretfully, expectantly.

SIX

February, 2001, New Delhi and Moorty

Mr. Asnani carries her luggage out to the white blockish taxi.

Gripping her briefcase and a small bag, she surveys the cool blue vestibule one last time, already nostalgic for her home of three weeks.

Mr. Alexander was probably enjoying a well-deserved sleep after his encounter last night with three young thugs in the chapel.

"R.S.S.," Mr. Asnani explained, cryptically. "Right wing Hindus. Much anti-Christian violence."

Father Koreth admonished him not to jump to conclusions.

Regardless, she'll worry about her friends here.

Last year she read so many articles about the Rashtriya Swayamsevak Sangh. About how they had collaborated with the British against Gandhi because of the Mahatma's ecumenism. How they assassinated Gandhi one ordinary winter day. Somehow the R.S.S. seemed like history then, nothing she'd encounter herself.

Silently Sister Margaret and Monica follow the concierge to the curb.

Mr. Asnani steeples his palms. "*Namascar*, Dr. Murphy. God bless you."

She can barely hear him over the horns and sirens and shifting lorry gears. The unseasonable heat wave makes everyone anxious and louder.

"Thank you for all your kindnesses, Mr. Asnani," she speaks at the top of her voice. "God bless you."

Sister Margaret is tearing up. "Dr. Murphy, I wish you the best. I will pray for you."

"Thank you, Sister. Thank you for everything."

She bursts into loud sobs and tugs a white handkerchief from her pocket.

"Sister, don't cry. We'll see one another again." How can she bear that heavy black habit in this heat? She probably roasts all spring and summer.

"Yes," Sister sniffs into her plain cotton square. "It is wrong to get attached. You see we don't normally have extended visits at Mission House from our foreign friends."

She touches Sister's thin shoulder. All too aware how long she's stayed, Monica is startled by the nun's attachment and by her own tender regard for these people, especially Sister Margaret.

The nun is weeping inconsolably now.

The taxi driver finishes loading bags. He stands within earshot, hands on his hips.

Monica has a thought. "Do you ever get a furlough?"

"Yes, we do." A ragged, almost inaudible voice.

"Perhaps you could come to Moorty for a few days of your leave. You'd be doing Mission House a service by getting more acquainted with the posting. Then we can continue our games of Scrabble and our sampling of Indian teas."

Clearly pleased, yet embarrassed to dwell on the invitation, she tells Monica for the twelfth time, "Remember Mr. Menon, a good Catholic, will be waiting at the airport with his limousine to drive you to Moorty. Don't go with anyone else. Taxi drivers can be persuasive. Mr. Menon will stand with a sign bearing your name. He speaks English fluently and has worked with the Mission for many years."

"A pre-paid taxi?"

"Pardon, Doctor?"

"Silly joke, Sister. Thank you for arranging the transportation. I'm confident everything will proceed smoothly."

"Yes," she says shakily.

Hesitantly, Monica draws Sister into a hug.

Mr. Asnani looks away.

Sister embraces Monica tightly.

The driver guns his engine.

Monica steps into the car and is suddenly jolted into traffic. She waves.

Mr. Asnani raises a hand in salute.

Sister Margaret flutters her hankie, smiling through the tears.

Ignoring the cabbie's daredevil driving, Monica considers yesterday's rush: saying good-bye to Ashok and Tina, having a farewell interview with Father Koreth, a parting tea with Sister Margaret. She was taken aback by their touching gifts. Ashok presented a small enamel Ganesh on a silver chain. Tina bought her favorite chocolate from the Embassy commissary. Sister Margaret gave her a medal depicting Sister Alphonsa, a beatified

Kerala nun. Even Father Koreth offered a sandalwood rosary. She had no time to reciprocate, but resolved that on her first trip back to Delhi she'd bring everyone mementoes.

What a morning! The farewell mass was mercifully brief. She was moved by the crusty priest's ardent prayers for her safety and success and *happiness*. At communion, he bestowed a traveler's blessing. Perhaps she overstated Koreth's severity in her letters to Beata. Still, she looks forward to meeting Father Freitas, Director and Chaplain at Moorty. People say he's youngish, pliable and energetic. Sister Margaret explained that most mission stations have fewer non-Indian doctors, but Moorty has faced unprecedented shortages. At any rate, Father Freitas is a skillful administrator, powerful spiritual director and an abiding presence.

****

The small airport is more crowded than she expected.

"Dr. Murray," a tall, wiry man in a dun-colored suit clutches the sign.

She looks around to confirm that she's the most likely suspect, then walks forward. "Mr. Menon?"

"Ah, Doctor Murray, welcome." He smiles broadly and bows.

"Murphy," she says pleasantly.

"Quite so. Welcome. We shall collect your luggage, then transport the bags to my cousin's car."

Fast talker. New accent. His cousin's car?

An hour later, they pull into a tiny auto repair shop on the city outskirts.

"One moment, Doctor, one moment," Mr. Menon implores, slipping out before she can reply.

Monica recalls Sister telling her the trip was in God's hands. She summons Beata's last letter. She hopes her friend gives James more time.

A firm rap on the passenger window.

"He is ready for you, Doctor." Mr. Menon opens the door with a flourish. "Who? Ready for what?"

"My cousin is a first-rate driver. Poor English, but a first-rate driver, never an accident on these devious hills, you know, my cousin Emmanuel will take you to Moorty in one fine piece!"

OK, time for a little American assertiveness. "Sister Margaret informed me that you were the driver, Mr. Menon. She has a special confidence in you."

"Other tasks, Doctor, other tasks. You will be most satisfied with my honorable cousin."

She takes a deep breath. "Where is your cousin?"

Mr. Menon points to a beige van with a cockeyed bumper. "Waiting, Doctor. This very minute waiting to escort you safely to your new home."

She wished he'd stop repeating the word 'safely.'

Forestalling further protest, Mr. Menon briskly launches her bags into the back of the dilapidated vehicle. He secures the rear door with a rope.

Emmanuel stands by the driver's door. Eighteen at most: a tall, handsome man with a repaired cleft palate. "*Namaste, ji.*"

"*Namaste,*" she tries for a kindly voice for her kidnapper.

"Emmanuel was cured at Moorty Hospital," Mr. Menon speaks rapidly. "Our family is eternally grateful for this sterling care."

She nods, overpowered by tension from the flight, the hectic race through town and the confusion.

"Actually, he does know a few English phrases," Mr. Menon's words zip past. "But you won't be chatting much. Such a beautiful ride. Be assured Emmanuel has made this trip many, many times. He knows the way with perfection."

She steps into the van, discouraged by the hard seat, wishing she'd brought a pillow for her spine now that she's been turfed out of Mr. Menon's limousine. Monica knows how spoiled she is. During the last month, she's seen vans crammed with dozens of people. She and Emmanuel have the whole vehicle to themselves.

She pivots, waving good-bye, but Mr. Menon is already speeding his comfortable car in the direction of the airport. She fumbles in her pocket for Ashok's Ganesh and Sister's medal, rubbing each of them for luck and blessing and simple comfort. She reaches into her other pocket for Beata's St. Christopher.

Slowly the van rattles to a start. Coughs. Then enters the road. She closes her eyes and sighs. Already they'll be two hours late. She sees from the map that Emmanuel must drive way back to the airport to catch the road to Moorty.

Flexibility. Patience. Acceptance: all virtues she needs to develop. India will offer boundless practice.

Emmanuel inserts a cassette of Bollywood music as they reach a narrow highway which snakes up the mountainside.

The thoroughfare barely permits two lanes of traffic. It's congested with coaches and elephants and cars and auto rickshaws and clattering vans the same vintage as Emmanuel's. She folds her map, watches the road ahead.

Up, up.

Up, up, up they travel. Around and around the ever greening hills, all the while breathing black exhaust fumes from lorries and buses. Would Emmanuel mind closing he window, she wonders, then notices all the other drivers have theirs rolled down.

Trucks are painted with radiantly colored flowers and images— sometimes of Krishna or Ganesh; sometimes Christ; sometimes a scene from a driver's hometown.

Bumpers and mud flaps are meticulously lettered in English and Hindi: "Happy Journey." "Have a Good Day," and the ubiquitous "Use horn." What a macabre camaraderie among the death-defying travelers. Ashok says almost 2,000 people were killed by cars on Delhi streets last year. How many more perish on these hazardous regional roads? One contribution to preventive medicine would be a set of traffic rules. She hears Ashok's laughing at her Western rationality.

Her bags rattle and roll in the back. She's packed the fragile items diligently, so they probably survived Mr. Menon's energetic tossing. A long crack on the van's side window has been mended with masking tape. The mustard yellow vinyl bench is wearing away her tail bone. Get a grip. Real pilgrims suffered hardship, not just discomfort.

The scenery is stunning. Small, terraced farms score the hillsides. Occasional peaks of white promise the snow to come. Stately green trees border the road. Occasionally, she glimpses mountains. *The* mountains. The Himalayas.

Suddenly, Emmanuel wrenches off the thoroughfare.

"Rest. Tea. Toilet." He grins at her in the rear view mirror.

Someone did an excellent job on the cleft palate. They say Kevin Walsh, Moorty's senior doctor, is a fine surgeon.

Toilet. That will relieve half her discomfort.

He drives a kilometer down a dirt road to a small cottage.

"Mother," he explains haltingly.

Standing in the doorway is an ancient woman with brilliant eyes.

Warts crowd furrowed cheeks. Over her turquoise sarong is a white sweater secured with a safety pin.

Emmanuel opens the van door.

She steps down as gracefully as she can after that bumper car journey, unsure just how her bones and joints have been rearranged.

Beaming at her son, the woman approaches. "*Namaste, ji,*" she greets Monica.

"*Namaste!*" Monica folds her hands.

The small parlor is decorated with magazine advertisements featuring European children. Very prominent are a large refrigerator, a small TV and a VCR. But where's the bathroom? She digs in her purse for the Hindi phrase book.

The old woman touches her elbow, directing Monica to an outhouse.

She washes her hands at a faucet next to the pristine privy before returning to Emmanuel and his mother.

What trouble they've taken. The table is covered with a lilac wool blanket. Set before the cup and plate is a small tray of English digestive cookies.

Emmanuel's mother appears with a steaming cup of chai.

It dawns on Monica that she'll be having tea alone. She gestures for Emmanuel and his mother to join her.

Emmanuel nods toward the kitchen.

"*Dhanyvad.*" They probably have a lot to talk about, she rationalizes.

The chai is syrupy with rich evaporated milk and heaps of sugar. How generous to share these expensive provisions with a stranger. Ugh, the cloying sweetness. She sips a little at a time, gulping the last bit.

Dusk, as they return to the highway. Traffic looks worse. An unfazed Emmanuel inches ahead. Up and around. Higher and higher they climb. When they aren't idling at a complete standstill. "*That road is fairly labyrinthine.*" Ashok is right again.

Father Freitas, Dr. Walsh and the others at Mission Hospital expected her at 6 p.m. They planned a special welcome service before dinner. Well, people up here must be used to delays. She sips water sparingly as she doubts there will be more rest stops.

Rising in the dark foothills, the headlights shine on patches of snow and ice. She prays for safety and tries to anticipate the dazzling views she'll see tomorrow morning.

"I hope you have found the weekend...provocative," Father Daniel said after that fateful retreat in Minnesota. Provocative enough to propel her to these winding foothills. He's back in Chennai now. She'll write to him tomorrow.

The trees have changed shape and color. Even in the dimness, she can see this is an evergreen land.

Emmanuel's lights catch a billboard: "Slow Drive. Long Life." Then another: "Always Avoid Accidents." She closes her eyes and imagines she's in India. Emmanuel's scratchy music has become almost soothing. She recalls the films she watched with Beata this year: the dazzling saris, swirling dupattas, dancing hands.

*****

"Welcome home!" A stranger's voice. Friendly. Crisp. Another new accent.

She awakes, bewildered. How long has she napped?

Ah, she's here. This is Moorty.

A slim woman with large green eyes and red hair—a shade lighter than Monica's—stands next to the van smiling. "Welcome, Dr. Murphy."

She blinks, rolls down the window. "Sorry to be late." Calm down, this isn't the Mad Hatter's Tea Party. "We were delayed, as you must have gathered."

The night air is cold. Winter in the mountains. Everyone is wearing a heavy coat. Monica buttons her parka snugly.

She's supposed to disembark. This is it, the end of the journey, the beginning.

"Yes." The woman is nodding, sliding open the door. "I'm Brigid Walsh, Dr. Walsh's wife and a nurse here at Moorty." She helps Monica to the snowy ground.

"Monica Murphy," she clasps Brigid's warm hand. Her eyes adjust to this disappointingly dark world, gradually making out shapes and people. If only they had arrived in daylight.

An Indian in a clerical collar steps forward. "A very, very warm welcome, Doctor. I am Father Freitas."

"I've heard so much about you," she bows. "Delighted."

Emmanuel is driving away.

"Where?" she begins.

"Don't worry," says Father Freitas. "He's just delivering luggage to your rooms."

"I didn't get a chance to thank him."

"So American, the thanking," chuckles the bespectacled fair-skinned priest.

"Emmanuel will join us for supper," Brigid explains.

"Oh, no, you shouldn't have delayed your supper. I'm terribly sorry."

"Too many apologies!" Father raises his eyebrows. "We'll find a cure for that."

A tall form approaches.

The ghost of Hamlet's father. Weird association. She feels a chill. Of course, she's standing in the snow. Moorty is 6,000 feet above sea level. In the Himalayan foothills. Yes, she's here. Tugging the green shawl tighter, she manages a direct, alert gaze.

"Dr. Murphy?" His voice is an Irish rumble. (She now places Brigid's accent. Brain returning.) "Welcome. I'm Kevin Walsh, senior doctor at Moorty Mission."

"Thank…"

"I see you believe in fashionably late arrivals," he says archly.

She hopes this is a joke.

Father Freitas stares at his shiny black shoes and shakes his head slightly. The priest is a foot shorter than Kevin Walsh and a quiet, compelling presence.

After a brief supper at the refectory, Father Freitas accompanies her to their quarters, a three story yellow house renovated into flats.

"May I assist you with the unpacking?" He cocks his head.

"No, thanks Father. I may go straight to bed and put my life in order tomorrow morning."

"An ambitious woman. To accomplish such a task in one morning!"

She laughs.

"Welcome, again, and good night, Dr. Murphy."

She wants to hug this genial spirit. Instead, she smiles. "Good night, Father."

He climbs downstairs to the flat he shares with Dr. Sanchez, who is out of town.

Her bedroom and living room are spacious, with windows facing north and east.

Imagining her new life on the middle floor between the Walshes and her other two colleagues, she is surprised by the comfort. The flowery curtains on the north and east windows. She'd expected a single room, something more monastic than this cozy flat. Here's a couch, a large desk, two bureaus, a single bed. Across the hall, she discovers a toilet, shower and tiny kitchen.

Bed! She sprawls on the hard narrow mattress. She needs sleep. She's traveled to yet another new world.

Her mind races about tomorrow's orientation. About the cases they've scheduled for her. She has to be alert. She must sleep.

Restless from rocking in that wretched van, she bounces up. Up, up and around. And around. "Always Avoid Accidents."

Just a whiff of mildew in the closet. She begins unpacking. So many slacks and blouses, a ridiculously profuse wardrobe. She needs more hangers. How embarrassing.

On the ancient mahogany bureau, Monica spots a small shortwave radio. Shortwave: how far can it reach? How far back? How far forward? Taking a long breath, she presses the power button.

SEVEN

February, 2001, Moorty

Shivering, Monica clutches her collar snugly as she walks from the ward to the refectory. Sharp winds send moist air straight to her lungs. Brigid Walsh cheerfully advises they'll all be grateful for altitude in May when the plains are baking. Right now, Monica is grateful for her sturdy Minnesota boots crunching on the fresh, white snow.

Nearly the end of her first week. Thank God for the grace that got her through six frenzied days. Sister Margaret was right about needing an extra doc at this small hospital where the demands are endless.

Monica pauses as mountains come into view. Oh, how Moorty's atmosphere is more conducive to healing than Lake Clinic. If she needs more than twenty minutes with a patient, she takes it. No insurance forms. No unctuous visits from drug company reps. She jots notes on lined paper, writing at a pace that permits her to listen to patients. No invasive, dysfunctional pseudo-efficient system here. By mid-day, she always feels exhausted, but not constricted by anger and frustration at time wasted on bureaucratic ritual. A year ago, she couldn't have imagined being so useful, feeling so excited.

Clapping to keep warm, she continues toward lunch, determined not to be fashionably late. She hopes Dr. Walsh lightens up; she's developing a definite aversion.

Yesterday's dark was misted with stars. Cold and crisp: perfect February night. How does the moon shine on these Himalayan foothills? Will it look like the one at home? The one in Delhi last month?

Monica remains stimulated by the morning's chat with head nurse Sister Catherine about preventive medicine, about initiating simple programs. At home, she never left the clinic thinking. Worrying, maybe. She'd hop in the car, switch her brain to NPR. Reality was elsewhere—Somalia, Iraq, Peru—not her 10 hours of doctoring.

The sudden wind catches her by surprise. Perhaps this is a two-shawl day. Father Freitas enjoys teasing her about feeling cold. Yes, she explains, Minnesota's climate is harsher. But in Moorty, it's impossible to warm up indoors. What would she do without all the sweaters and shawls left behind by the two Kerala doctors who returned south this year? What will she leave behind, and when? She has no idea if Mission House, or the visa office, will let her stay if Indian doctors become available here. Of course she's always known this, but now that she's feeling at home, the tentativeness feels more real.

Monkeys screech from behind. Noises are different from the Delhi racket, yet just as loud. People arriving at dawn, chatting, chatting. Road construction outside the clinic. Frightening shrieks from orange and brown rhesus monkeys. Scarier are the plump black scorpions she saw snuggled in the doorjamb of her bedroom the first morning. Nothing lethal up here, Sister Catherine joked, except the automobile drivers. Then she mentioned her aunt who died of snake bite or scorpion sting in Bihar last summer. "We are lucky not to live in Bihar."

Monica accepts the new experiences one by one, offering up her confusion and fear. Praying for courage, patience, ingenuity, transcendence, whatever's available. She'd hoped to move nearer to God, strengthening her newly recovered faith up here in the foothills. She thought the closeness would come from actual grace, useful actions. She didn't anticipate needing divine reassurance about scorpions, monkeys and snakes.

Pausing now, she savors the fragrance of the stately deodar cedars. Nothing like this scent in Minnesota, simultaneously sharp and sweet. Gazing down toward the streets of Moorty, she anticipates where she can spend her half day there next week. Father Freitas says there's a new internet shop offering email connections.

The patients are friendly and grateful. Also tolerant of, sometimes pleasurably amused by, her fragmented Hindi. The reserved but cordial Sister Catherine is a gem. Almost as radiant as Father Freitas.

Just a few more feet to lunch. She wonders about Dr. Walsh's conventional self-importance and Mrs. Dr. Walsh's subservience. Did he drive away the Kerala doctors with his arrogance? And when will the mysterious Dr. Sanchez appear?

The aroma of chilies and coriander drifts from the small kitchen. As she pulls open the creaking wooden door, she spots a letter from Beata on the white rattan foyer table. No, don't get distracted. Focus on collegial lunch and talking about the out-patient clinic. The letter will be tonight's reward.

They're all gathered at the table—Sister Catherine, Father Freitas, the Walshes.

Quickening her pace, she slips into a chair next to Father.

"Ah, finally, Dr. Murphy," Kevin appraises her.

How does Brigid cope with his superciliousness? And the others? Maybe she can talk with Father Freitas. A complicated relationship: can Father be friend, boss as well as confessor?

"Good afternoon, everyone," she stifles an apology. A minute or two late at most.

"I believe it's Mrs. Walsh's turn to lead us in grace," Kevin instructs.

All bow their heads.

Monica concentrates on Brigid's sweet-sharp Irish intonation.

"Bless us, oh Lord, and these Thy gifts, which we are about to receive. Amen."

Cook appears with a steaming, fragrant platter.

Father Freitas leans over. "Cook heard that you enjoy vegetable *jalfreze*, so he has been working all morning on our feast. We owe you our gratitude."

"Lovely," she bows to the small man in the plaid shirt and lunghi. "Thank you ..." she wants to say, *Matthew*, but people call him *Cook*. A respectful term like *Sister, Father, Doctor*? Maybe she'll get the nerve to say *Matthew* in a few weeks. "Thank you, Cook."

As the platter approaches, Monica notices how many vegetables in her special dish are carrots. She doesn't remember carrots in *jalfreze*. She didn't expect carrots in India at all. They seem such an American vegetable. She loves the sweet crunchiness of raw carrots, the way they sate hunger in the late afternoon. She hates, has always hated since childhood, cooked carrots. A miserable, soggy contrast to the refreshing raw vegetable. It's puerile; still she also loathes cooked turnips, rutabagas, parsnips. Perhaps it's a family gene, passed down from generations thinned out on roots wrestled from Irish soil. At home, she pushes aside the carrots, but her childish loathing is trivial in impoverished India. She gulps water after each dose.

"Thirsty, Dr. Murphy?" Kevin Walsh teases. "*Jalfreze* usually is a spicy dish."

Monica gazes at the crucifix hanging on the yellow wall behind him. "The lunch is delicious," she speaks loudly for surely Matthew is listening behind the kitchen door.

"Perhaps Monica is simply getting accustomed to our altitude," Father Freitas intervenes. "When I first arrived, I drank gallons of water."

She nods, pleased to find only two carrots left.

"Dr. Sanchez returned late this morning," Sister Catherine reports.

Monica has noticed the canny nun deftly shifting topics several times this week. They've all developed strategies for coping with Dr. Walsh.

"Why is he not at lunch?" Brigid asks anxiously. "Is he unwell?"

"No, no illness," reassures Father Freitas. " 'Rattled,' so he said. Exhausted from the journey. He'll join us for supper."

Kevin Walsh clears his throat and begins a report about fundraising for the new hospital wing. "I'm contemplating another U.S. 'money safari,' that is if I can be spared, that is if Dr. Murphy can acclimate soon enough, that is—"

"Dr. Murphy is up to speed already," Father Freitas declares.

"Oh, she is indispensable," Sister Catherine agrees.

"No one is indispensable;" Kevin Walsh retorts, "we are each God's servant."

Moorty Chapel is a plain, wooden structure located in front of the refectory, sheltered by a stand of deodars. Monica appreciates the modest furnishings: an altar, twelve pews, no vestibule. In February, the church is chillier than most buildings. Shivering, she yanks the heavy wooden door, which, unlike all the other mission doors, isn't weather warped. The low whoosh of the opening is almost reverent. As her eyes adjust to the dim light, filtering through simple stained glass windows, she realizes she's not alone.

A tall man in the second pew.

Shaking his black curly hair, he looks upward, then rests his head on the forward bench. Dr. Sanchez.

Sliding silently into the last pew, she gazes at the tabernacle. Making a visit to the Blessed Sacrament, as Sister Henrietta urged her fourth graders to do every week. She's always felt closer to God sitting alone in a pew. Since returning to the Church, she's discovered Catholic traditions of meditation, not unlike Buddhist practices.

Dr. Sanchez doesn't seem very serene up there, rocking back and forth, sighing heavily. He begins thumping his fist on the bench.

*****

The compact white clinic has a reception area, two examination rooms, a pharmacy desk and an equipment pantry. She hears the low chatter of patients and checks her watch. No, she's not late. Sister Catherine explained people arrive hours early.

She meets the young charge nurse, Sister Melba, and nods at the people waiting on folding chairs. A pregnant woman; an old man with an arm oddly bandaged; an adolescent boy and his striking mother. The pair hold her attention—the kid's anxiety; the mother's calm, almost an ennui. Ten or twelve other patients in back rows.

Panic rises. At Lake Clinic, she entered a side door after lunch. Patients were escorted to her, already weighed and measured and partially screened. Here she's conscious of people waiting, endless lines of them.

"Just a moment, Sister Melba, and I'll be ready for the first patient." She retreats to the tiny exam room, washes her hands, reminds herself she can only see one person at a time and says a quick prayer for guidance. All the afflictions of India are not her responsibility. She'll do better if she concentrates on the person before her than if she frets about those on folding chairs.

Sister Eleanor stations herself in the corner to help with translation. Monica likes the young nun, but looks forward to the time when she knows enough Hindi to see patients alone.

The sun gradually drops lower and lower in the trees. It's several hours before she can see the boy and his mother.

The mother greets her in English, "Good afternoon, Doctor."

He follows shyly, "Good afternoon, *Doctorji.*"

"I am Sudha Badami, a teacher at Walkerton School. This is Vikram, one of our finest students."

The boy drops his gaze.

"Thank you, Sister Eleanor," Monica smiles. "We won't need translation for this patient. Would you like to take a break?"

The nun regards her warily.

"Really, Sister, we'll be fine. Why not have a cup of tea and stretch your legs?"

Sister Eleanor smiles hesitantly and withdraws.

"You speak no Hindi?" observes the teacher.

"*Thora Sa.* I am learning." Monica is embarrassed by the teacher's challenge. "How can I help Vikram?"

"Something is occurring in his eyes." She tilts her pretty dark face, concerned.

Monica notices that Sudha Badami is her age, mid-thirties—a poised woman wearing an elegant green silk sari. Saris make Indian women look older, more grown up. In comparison, Monica feels bleakly utilitarian in her brown skirt and black sweater.

"Vikram, do you speak much English?"

He glances uncertainly at his teacher.

"He speaks more than he lets on. But if I may be permitted to translate, you both might be more comfortable."

Edgy lady. Focus on the patient.

"How long have your eyes been red?" Monica asks.

"He has suffered four days only."

Monica examines the boy's shy eyes. "Vikram, you have conjunctivitis. Do you know what that is?"

"No, *Doctorji*."

"There's an infection in the membrane over your eyeballs and inside the lids."

Sudha Badami translates.

Vikram's face grows solemn.

"We can treat this relatively easily if you take the medicine as directed."

She notices a flicker of reprieve in Vikram's rich brown irises. She loves how examining eyes reveals patient's deeper feelings.

Sudha Badami sits back in relief.

She hands him a scrip. "You can show this to Sister Melba in reception and she will direct you to the pharmacy desk."

Sudha Badami watches.

"And Vikram, please keep your hands away from your eyes. Conjunctivitis spreads easily and before long your entire class will be ill."

"Yes," the teacher complains. "We have much eye disease here. It's the wind."

"It's hygiene," Monica says automatically. Too brusque; she needs a tea break.

"Families do their best. Sometimes wells function. Sometimes not," her voice simmers. "Indians wash more than any other people on earth. Here the dust, the dust..."

"Indeed," Monica's voice softens. "I don't mean to impugn. Still, there are certain precautions, even in this challenging climate..."

Sudha Badami studies her. "I believe you are the perfect person to present a lecture about hygiene for my afternoon students. Do you ever get away from the hospital?"

She pictures her half day, exploring Moorty and visiting the internet shop. However, she came here to serve. Wasn't she discussing preventive programs this very morning? The invitation is a blessing.

"I might come on Tuesday." She leans against the wall, yielding to exhaustion.

The teacher stares. "The cross hanging from your pretty silver chain, does that mark you as a member of the clergy?"

She shakes her head. "I am a doctor."

"But the cross. Do you preach?"

Is she baiting her? Is she confused? "Many Catholics wear crosses."

"So when you come to the school, you will not speak about religion?"

How annoying can she get? First the woman challenges her Hindi, then usurps her half day leave, then accuses her of indoctrination. Monica waits for an apology.

The teacher seems to be expecting an answer.

Vikram sits tight and still.

Too tired and busy for games, she speaks deliberately. "If I were to come to your school, I would speak as a physician on the requested topic. I believe you were interested in hygiene as preventive medicine."

Vikram shifts to the corner chair, his eyes alert. If he doesn't understand every word, he's catching the tone.

The woman lowers her eyebrows, looking satisfied. "Tuesday it is. I will organize the room for 2 p.m. if that is acceptable."

"Perfectly," Monica suppresses her irritation. "What age are the students?"

"Between fourteen and eighteen. Why do you ask?"

"They have had HIV/AIDS education?"

"We do what we can. Be my guest, Doctor. As you know, the virus is spreading fiercely in this country."

She makes notes.

"Vikram will come to escort you."

"Yes," Vikram smiles for the first time. An attractive boy. "Tuesday, *Doctorji.*"

Her heart lifts. One patient at a time. Vikram, not Sudha Badami, is the patient.

*****

At five o'clock Monica peeks into the waiting room, distressed to discover six long-suffering people. She's shattered, wants to sleep for twenty-four hours. Her stamina will build as she get used to the altitude, the language. Monica invites Sister Melba into the exam room.

"No, Doctor. No critical cases. All can return tomorrow."

"Thank you," Monica sighs.

She exits through a newly discovered back door and heads for the residence.

They're serving cocktails in the refectory to welcome back Dr. Sanchez from Manda. She should attend. No, she needs time to herself.

Still some natural light, she notices, making tea. Kevin Walsh has warned not to be profligate with electricity. The emergency generator is for hospital use. She collapses in the window chair, a blanket wrapped around her weary legs. Monica inhales steam from the hot tea as she opens Beata's letter.

Dear Monica,

Great to get your letter from Delhi. What bureaucracy! And your visa is still insecure? I'm sending this to Moorty, assuming you have to be there now. Glad to know your health is fine. And nice to hear about running into Tina after all those years. More details on Ashok, please.

She hasn't heard from either since arriving in Moorty. Chances are, of course, that both Tina and Ashok have sent emails. Her heart sinks, remembering it will be another week-and-a-half before she can visit Moorty's internet palace.

I miss our talks. In fact, I'm looking into long distance plans that allow you to call India without losing your old age pension. I want to know about your patients, the other doctors? Is there a real spiritual community there?

She muses about her own early quixotic hopes of landing with kindred souls sharing faith and work. Still, what can she judge after one week? Father Freitas and Sister Catherine are devout, humble, insightful. And she hasn't met Dr. Sanchez. Glancing at the clock, she sees there's time to finish Beata's letter. She's not going to be late for two meals in one week.

We're in that part of winter when I wonder why I moved back from Seattle after grad school. It's not the cold; it's the ice. Also, I hate the milky skies. Usually the saving graces of our winter are blue skies and glistening *snow. But we've had skim milk overcast for a week and no fresh snow. The back garden has lost its creamy texture—dead grass gets exposed and the lawn is beginning to resemble those glazed sugar cookies. Do you get much snowfall in Moorty?*

She grins at Beata's excellent manners; following her own news with questions.

You must be wondering about James.

Well, yes, dear.

Last night we went to that funny restaurant: Sushi Tango in Calhoun Square. He surprised me with his expertise about sushi and sashimi, which he picked up when he was a soldier in Japan. A hard posting for a black man, but he made several close Japanese friends and he's devoted to the cuisine. The evening was full of stories. He asked about me, too. The one disappointment is that he attends Westminster Presbyterian. At least he's a man of faith. We have plans to see each other on the weekend.

Yes! Beata was beginning to give up finding a good man in Minnesota. Here's a woman who deserves happiness, after all she's done for others. Finishing the tea, Monica realizes she's not at all jealous. She must truly be recovering from Eric.

The gong echoes. She stretches, folds the blanket, grabs a blue sweater to wear under her shawls. The walk back to the residence after dinner will be freezing. Hurrying, she notices excitement about meeting the elusive Dr. Sanchez. She trusts he found some peace in the chapel.

Father Freitas walks into the refectory at the same time. "How was your afternoon, doctor?"

"I met an interesting woman, a teacher. Perhaps you know her—Sudha Badami?"

"Yes," he smiles. "A good person. She often brings students here. She's made an unusual vocational choice for a Bombayite with such fine training—did she tell you she has a degree from St. Andrews?—to opt for village education. She's very dedicated. A missionary in her own way."

"But definitely not a Christian."

"Ohhhh, most certainly not." He holds out a chair at the dinner table for her. "At first she was leery of us. Worried we were peddling doctrine with our medical care."

"She quizzed you about this?" Monica recalls the woman's imposing manner.

"Quizzes are her specialty," he chortles. "We had a coffee in town—

now you must let me introduce you to the Kerala Coffee House on your half day next week."

The Walshes enter, chatting intently. Rather, he talks rapidly to his nodding wife.

"Ms. Badami has invited me to speak on hygiene to her class Tuesday afternoon."

"But of course." Father rocks in his chair. "She got to you quickly! It took her two months to persuade me to speak about Goan history. She does all she can to introduce those children to diverse voices."

She's intrigued. "So you two sparred about religion?"

"It was more temperate than sparring, a lively discussion. She questioned why the Church has established our own clinic. Why we needed a priest here. After all, what practical use am I, aside from administrative work, any sensible non-Christian might inquire."

"She asked that?"

"Not directly," he lowers his voice. "I did explain that I served those who asked."

"I guess you didn't reveal the local congregation has trebled since you arrived."

"Now where would you get such a notion?" He frowns, then checks to see who's assembled for diner.

Dr. Sanchez is still missing.

"Sister Margaret in Delhi told me. She's one of your greatest fans."

"God bless Sister Margaret, but she shouldn't be telling tales like… ah, here he is, Dr. Sanchez!" He whispers as the dark-haired man approaches. "A fine person, but excitable. Very tired. The last journey was arduous."

Kevin Walsh announces, "I believe everyone has arrived. Shall we sit at table?"

Sit at table: where does he get his arcane idioms? Do the others find him pretentious?

Monica takes a deep breath, striving to be more charitable. Perhaps Dr. Walsh is attempting Indian English.

"Before we begin," Father Freitas raises his melodious Goan voice, "I believe Dr. Sanchez and Dr. Murphy have not met."

They smile shyly to one another.

"Monica Murphy," she extends her hand.

"Raul Sanchez," he grins, tenting his palms in response.

Sanchez is taller than she imagined in church. Very fit, with an olive complexion and arresting gray-green eyes.

She tents her palms as well. Part greeting; part prayer. A much more sanitary salutation, especially at mealtime.

Sister Catherine offers grace.

Cook enters, bearing platters of curry and *biryani*.

Kevin Walsh declares. "Dr. Sanchez was telling us over drinks—so sorry you couldn't join us, Dr. Murphy, you must have had an abnormally difficult day. He was telling us about being detained by *dacoits* on the way to the station."

Sanchez stares blankly out the window into the early winter dark.

"I'm not familiar with the word *dacoit*." Monica says.

"It comes from the Hindi, *daikait*," Kevin Walsh intones, "meaning 'bandit.' "

"Bandits prosper on the remote back roads," Brigid Walsh explains. "Detaining, sometimes attacking, travelers for their gear, for what little money they carry."

"Praise heaven you are safe," says Sister Catherine.

"Sí," he murmurs. "Heaven and Sanjay the driver. But it's all over now, so…"

Monica strains to hear him. He's stopped mid-sentence. Sister Margaret alerted her to his odd speaking habits. She's alluded to several family members among "the Disappeared" in Buenos Aires. "A good man," Sister Margaret had said, "but not the easiest companion."

"The thing we should be discussing is the need for a real satellite clinic in Manda," asserts Raul Sanchez. "It would serve people from nearby villages. These once-a-month forays are bandages, not very effective ones."

Walsh leans forward. "We've discussed all that. Once we're sorted out here, we might expand, but first—"

Raul interrupts, "First you want to create the perfect hospital with state-of-the-art equipment. Meanwhile, people need basic medications for malaria, dysentery, cholera. We could do important preventive work with a little money."

Yes, Monica thinks. Maybe Raul and I and a couple of *dacoits* could hijack the clinic from Commander Walsh. Although Father is the Director, Walsh wields a puzzling clout.

"And who will raise that money, Dr. Sanchez?" Walsh reddens.

"It's not just a question of new money," he leans on the table, glaring at Walsh, "but also of allocating what the board gives us. I'm sure that if we wrote to them—"

"Unless I'm mistaken, I was hired as senior doctor."

"In Spanish, *senior*, and *despot* are different words." Sanchez's hands shake so much, he sets down the fork.

"Dr. Sanchez, Dr. Walsh, please," Father Freitas begins.

"Sorry, Father," Sanchez stands, rasping his chair back over the wooden floor. "Apologies to all. I'm too shattered to be decent company."

"Listen, Dr. Sanchez, there's no call to walk off in a huff," Walsh rises.

"Yes, Doctor," implores Sister Catherine, *nurse* Catherine, also rising. "You need to eat after that difficult journey."

Raul Sanchez signals them to be seated. "Really, the best nourishment for me right now will be bed."

The rest of the meal passes in virtual silence (*No, Beata, not yet a spiritual community.*)

Monica is relieved that Cook, so undone by Sanchez's abrupt departure, forgets to serve one of his alarmingly sweet desserts. Everyone one seems happy to leave the tense room as quickly as possible.

Strolling to the residence, she pauses to drink in the cold mountain air. She's almost cleaned out her lungs after that month in sooty Delhi. Stars gleam in the moonless sky. She recalls that final night in the Boundary Waters with Eric; this same Milky Way shone down. She's glad that thinking of Eric these days brings more fondness than sadness. She hears something from the road. A woman walks alone, carrying a shopping bag. Wind catches her *dupattas* and the long, silky scarf trails her like a private cloud.

Monica approaches the residence as quietly as she can in heavy boots, so as not to disturb Dr. Sanchez. From the flat on the bottom floor, she sees lights blazing in his room.

EIGHT

March, 2001, Moorty

Crisp, clear mountain afternoon. Infused with optimism, Monica sets out for Walkerton School. Wearing a heavy woolen skirt, two sweaters and a shawl, she's prepared for the hour's walk. The invigorating air should sharpen her mind. She's glad she phoned Sudha Badami and suggested that Vikram simply meet her at the campus entrance. He needs rest, not a long hike.

"Indian life isn't conducive to rest," Sudha responded, but finally acquiesced.

Four coolies pass her, plodding at a steady, almost easy pace under tanks of propane, stacks of lumber, bureaus, boxes of glass and bags of family groceries. They climb higher into the hills from the lower town markets. "Coolies," it's hard to believe they use that term here.

"Porters," Monica said to Sister Catherine, who looked through her.

"We'd never survive without those fine coolies," the nun explained, "since our road is closed to cars. Finally we Indians are doing something about air pollution before we lose sight of one another completely. Why, coolies transport all our food and supplies from the outside world."

It's a pleasant journey, past houses and stands of deodar cedars and paths meandering into the hills. In a cotton bag, she carries sandals, an umbrella. She'll change shoes near the school. How do people walk these uneven roads in sandals?

Ahead, she sees three women chatting at a road construction site. One balances a heavy bowl on her head. All wear saris and carry wood. She pauses to watch as two men heat tar by placing it on top of metal barrels then setting a fire under each barrel. Once again she feels she's landed in the 19th century.

"*Namaste.*"

She turns to find a man dressed in a grey suit hurrying toward town.

"*Namaste,*" she nods back.

Everyone travels by foot in this part of Moorty. Further down the mountain, where driving is permitted, cars, trucks and coaches negotiate a cart road. She's getting used to long distances—sixty to ninety minute walks are routine. A sensible, low-tech solution to limiting fumes. Smog in the Himalayan Foothills, she never would have dreamed. Yet on some days, you can't see the peaks through the grey haze. She takes a deep breath, inhales a mixture of piquant deodar and road tar.

Last night, snuggled under the heavy comforter Sister Melba gave her, she felt both relieved and distressed, recalling tense exchanges between Sanchez and Walsh. Relieved that she wasn't the only one who aggravated "the chief." Distressed that his imperious behavior would apparently be a constant. Did Father defer to Walsh because of his surgical skills? His fundraising abilities? Sanchez seems at the end of his tether. Monica looks forward to a private conversation with him. The remote village outreach intrigues her. Smiling, she realizes that she hasn't thought about Dr. Jill at Lake Clinic in weeks.

Some houses face the street. Other residences are marked by gates and long driveways. Father Freitas says two government ministers own holiday property here. Well-hidden. She notices a modest wooden structure built into the hillside. Several pink apartment blocks stolidly claim land at a turn in the road. Now there are long stretches with no sight of habitation. Remembering the monkeys, she pulls out Sister Catherine's umbrella.

Monica loves the langurs, perched with quiet dignity everywhere. So elegant in their black and white coats. Such a contrast with the matted orange rhesus monkeys. "Rascals," Father Freitas calls them. Sister Melba has been bitten three times. Thank God and Tina for those pre-rabies inoculations.

Two large bull rhesus monkeys sit on a long, white retaining wall. She swings her umbrella vigorously and quickens her pace.

"Don't carry sweets or bread or anything they might want to snatch from your bag," Father advised intently.

"Say the rosary as you walk," suggested Sister Melba.

Belatedly, she's beginning to see the benefit of Vikram's company.

The monkeys don't seem to notice her military gait and baton. Maybe she'll be used to them by next year. Next year. She'll have to struggle with the visa people to last that long. Some missionaries fail. Missionary, she hates the inference of proselytizing, the shadows of Crusades, whiffs of Western imperialism. Surely her work is none of that. She's simply here to help. An aid worker. With the Lord's blessing, she'll be useful to people.

Finally, yes, after just about an hour, she spots a small brick building down a sharp slope on the right. She slips behind a tree to change shoes and brush her hair. She's spent more of her walk daydreaming than sharpening her mind. But she does feel rejuvenated, a little excited.

Approaching the school, her heart sinks at the broken windows. Why did Sudha Badami move from the Bombay bourgeoisie to this dilapidated institution? As Father Freitas asked, is the teacher less of a missionary than the doctor?

"*Namaste, ji,*" Vikram calls from the rusting gate. He looks smart in a freshly pressed green and white school uniform.

"Permit me to show you the way," he grins.

She notices his left eye is recovering quickly, but the right still flares a bit.

"Did you have a pleasant walk?"

"Yes, thank you, Vikram." She'll omit her death-defying sprint past the wicked monkeys. "What beautiful English you speak."

He lowers his head and falls silent.

Perhaps he's exhausted his vocabulary. Has he been practicing for days? No, he's shy. She thinks about the cocky, disarming hip-hop kids she tutored at home and wonders what Lavandas and La Rue would make of their polite, modest peers in Moorty.

He heads down rickety stairs, past a courtyard of sad trees and shrubs, into a windowless corridor. Suddenly, she's hit by the nauseating lavatory odor. Discreetly, she raises a tissue to her nose, imagining mem-sahibs with perfumed hankies.

In a small office, two women busily record in large maroon ledgers. They glance up, smile politely. From the stairwell, three teenage girls peer and titter.

Vikram shoots them a disapproving glance.

At last they reach the door at the end of the hallway. Vikram knocks.

Sudha Badami appears, lustrous in a purple silk sari. "*Namaste*, Dr. Murphy. Welcome to our school." Glass bangles jingle as she extends her arm into the room.

Thirty young people in matching green and white outfits rise to their feet.

"Dr. Murphy, may I introduce the advanced English language students."

"*Namaste*, students." Advanced English. Of course. So much for far-reaching preventive education. She needs to work much harder on her Hindi.

"Good afternoon, Dr. Murphy," they sing. "Moorfy, Muffy, Maffie," so many musical renditions of her name.

"Thank you," she turns to the teacher, then back to them. "It's an honor to be invited."

She begins with questions, although Father Freitas warned that Indian students aren't used to speaking in class. She asks about their ages, their goals.

"Fourteen."

"Fifteen."

"Teacher."

"Bollywood director."

Girls in the back row burst into giggles.

"Scientist. Epidemiologist."

Taking her cue, she voice strains slightly. "Who has heard of HIV? AIDS?"

Most raise their hands.

"How is it contracted?"

Here they clam up.

Sudha Badami stands, arms across her chest. "Remember now, we discussed this topic at assembly."

Vikram bravely raises his hand.

Monica nods encouragingly.

"By sexual transgression, Ma'am."

His teacher inhales sharply. Girls in the back giggle. Several boys roll their eyes.

"I think you mean, 'sexual transmission,' yes?" Monica asks evenly.

His face frozen with confused embarrassment, he whispers. "Yes, Doctor."

Laughter from much of the room.

Sudha Badami quashes their amusement with a stern glance.

For the next ten minutes, students listen courteously to her plain-spoken lecture.

"Let's open to questions now," she prompts. "Don't be shy. All questions are acceptable." She sits beside Sudha Badami to lessen the formality.

"Good afternoon, Doctor." A young man stands. "I am Raj Agarwal."

The erect, thin boy is poised, confident, an expert at projection.

"Good afternoon, Mr. Agarwal."

The snickering resumes, briefly.

"I am wondering what preventive tools you dispense at the hospital."

At Lake Clinic she gave condoms to anyone who asked and many who didn't. She campaigned for free needle exchange. But here at Moorty Hospital, they offer Catholic remedies of prevention and prayer.

"We advise abstinence before marriage."

A pretty girl in the front row fiddles with her embroidered handkerchief.

Raj places a hand on his slim hip. "Is this responsible practice?"

Monica sits straighter, impressed by his vocabulary, surprised by the directness. "Abstinence is the most effective deterrent to HIV/AIDS." Of course they'd ask about her deepest conflict.

Another young man raises his hand. "Ramesh Kumar, Ma'am."

"Yes, Mr. Kumar."

"Do you advocate abstinence for medical or, uh, moral reasons, Doctor?"

She represents the hospital. Her personal views are beside the point. "Moorty is a Catholic facility. Thus you might say the injunction is both medical and moral." Does this sound as spurious to them as it does to her?

She remembers asking Father Daniel these questions at the first Minnesota retreat. His nuanced replies revealed his own conflict. Yet he confidently described many contributions made by the missions in other spheres. And she was persuaded his project was, on balance, valuable.

Sudha Badami leans forward, rubbing her hands.

Monica feels a breeze through the broken window pane. The room, she notices now, is quite cold.

"Don't the girls have any questions?" The teacher urges with mock sternness. "Are we going to let Dr. Murphy leave thinking that girls are mute in my classroom?"

Bodies shift, squirm behind desks that are clearly grades too small.

A nervous Maya Sen asks about the differences between HIV and AIDS.

Poised Sita Umrigar asks about antiretroviral medication.

"A very educated group," she smiles. "You must attend an excellent school."

Raj maintains his scowl, but Ramesh and the others are grinning.

Vikram raises his hand. "May I ask a non-medical question, Ma'am?"

"Certainly," she says with relief.

"What do you think of our India?"

She exhales. "You live in a stunning country, particularly here in Moorty. And I am impressed with the rich diversity of your people."

"Ma'am," he can't contain his pride. "India is the world's largest democracy."

She nods soberly.

Silence. A small bird glides through the back window, then sails out again.

"Is there something, perhaps, you want to ask about my own country?"

Vikram stands, a little apprehensively. "Why are Americans so lacking in spiritual life?"

Drawing in a quick breath, she says, "Many Americans do lead secular lives. But numerous religions are practiced—including Islam and Buddhism and Hinduism. I believe we have the highest attendance at religious services of any Western country."

"But," he persists earnestly, "Wouldn't…"

She knows he really wants to understand.

"Wouldn't you say that the general culture is more material than spiritual?"

"On the whole, yes. Abundance. When you have wealth, you want more."

"And lack of family life?" queries the girl who asked about drugs. "Why do people live so far from their parents? Indians live our whole lives within the family."

Sudha Badami clears her throat. "What have we discussed about sweeping generalizations?"

"Most Indians, most Americans, I believe, Ma'am."

She shuts out Jeanne and Mom for the moment. And Dad. They're not asking about her life. "Many Americans have close families. Many others travel widely and this sadly takes them from their homes. I won't say Americans are anti-family. We just have different ways of maintaining ties. My friend Beata attends a family reunion every year that draws people from ten states."

A girl at the back raises a hand.

Monica strains for patience, energy. Indians are so candid—cabbies, airline seat mates, students—she's starting to see what people mean about Americans being too polite.

"Richa Tuwari, Doctor. Would you tell us about Minnesota? About the big lake there? And your snow?"

She'll remember Richa in her prayers tonight. "I wish I could take you all to Lake Superior on a shimmering July evening when…"

The class adjourns with applause and a communal, "*Namaste*, Doctor."

Suddenly she's surrounded by students with scraps of paper and little books. "Your autograph, Ma'am, if you please."

She regards the long line of eager students, who just moments ago were debate opponents. They look like kids again.

"Really, Dr. Murphy," the teacher intervenes, "you shouldn't have to put up with this."

Several students moan.

"I'm delighted. But with such a long line, I'll need to keep each salutation brief. And in exchange, you must promise not to forget me."

Most of them nod solemnly.

"And promise to use the hospital if you have need."

More nods. A couple of bashful smiles.

Raj stands at the end of the queue, moving from foot to foot, gripping an autograph book with a green cover.

At his turn, he gives Monica a big grin.

"Thanks for being so engaged, Raj."

He blinks shyly, a teenager again.

As Monica finishes, the teacher lightly taps her elbow. "May I offer you some tea?"

"That would be grand." Monica suddenly feels drained.

Sudha Badami takes her through a new wing of the school, the floor moldings are still wet with fresh blue paint. The small teachers' lounge holds a faded burgundy brocade couch and two matching yellow armchairs.

A grey-haired man stares out the window, twirling a tea bag in his purple mug.

"Dr. Murphy, may I introduce Sambit Sharma, our esteemed biology teacher."

His smile divulges two missing teeth. "*Namaste*, Doctor. I see my honorable colleague is continuing to pursue multi-cultural outreach."

Sudha Badami laughs. "Oh, Sambit likes to tease. He's traveled widely and received his degrees in Toronto. Everyone at school is excited when a foreigner visits."

Foreigner, she'll get used to the word. She recalls those long forms in the Minneapolis post office for registered aliens. She prefers *foreigner* to *alien*.

"I'd love to stay and chat, Doctor, but I have examinations to mark. Thank you for visiting our humble institution."

"Thanks for welcoming me."

Sudha hands her a mug of steaming tea. "Milk or sugar?"

"No, thanks, I prefer it plain."

"Please, sit."

"Thanks, I am a little tired."

"Sorry about the 'grilling'—do you say 'grilling?'—that they gave you."

"That's one description," she laughs. "Your students are proud of India!" She sinks back into the old couch. How good to talk with someone outside the hospital. She hasn't had a "civilian" conversation since Ashok and Tina in Delhi.

"Indians are proud people." Sudha regards her visitor directly.

"I'm beginning to appreciate that." She luxuriates in the sweet Darjeeling aroma.

"Still, I apologize for Raj, that he baited you that way. He's an intense lad."

"With reasonable questions. Just ones difficult to answer."

"Did I detect some personal conflict?" As she leans forward, her earrings gleam.

"Catholics have varied views on sexual mores, on contraception." She sits straighter. "I work at a church-connected hospital."

"Yes." She leaves the tension suspended between them.

Sipping her tea, Monica reckons she doesn't know Sudha Badami well enough for this conversation. Sister Margaret warned her to watch for those right wing R.S.S. agents. Clearly this woman isn't Hindutva. She'd have no truck with Rashtriya Swayamsevak Sangh activists censoring history texts, erasing the historical presence of Muslims and

Buddhists and Christians. The woman is a cosmopolitan. She'll write to Beata about this class today. And talk with Father Freitas.

She changes the topic. "Your students are very fluent in English."

"Unfortunately, they must know your language to succeed. We have over fifteen major languages in India. Then there are the tribal tongues and so forth. Many consider Hindi the national language; however students opt for English in the larger world."

She waits, annoyed at having English dubbed "her" language. She's tempted to recite Mom's patriotic rant about the English destruction of Gaeltalk in Ireland.

"I know what you're thinking," the teacher gazes at her ironically. "Why do I open my classroom to the larger world? They need to know about it, about you." She seems genuinely ill at ease for the first time in their acquaintance. "But I wish them to see their home in context, not to leave it."

"Yes," she gropes for the right words. "You left Bombay to come here to teach in a land where few know Marathi."

"Ah, you have been conferring with the charming Father Freitas."

Monica is glad she finds Father charming. "He mentioned his visit here."

"There you have the model Indian. He was raised speaking Konkani. Yet he also knows Hindi, Portuguese, English. He addressed our students in Hindi."

"I wish I could have done that."

"You could learn."

"I have tapes and a book." She sounds pathetic. "I haven't touched them for weeks. It's hard to find discipline and focus after a long day at the hospital."

"I could teach you." Sudha regards her directly.

"Oh, I couldn't impose on your schedule."

"A very American response. So concerned with time." She's smiling faintly. Afternoon sun pours through the windows. "What do you think a single woman does in the evenings here? I can only mark so many essays before my mind begins to atrophy. Besides, I live near your clinic. You're not the first person from the hospital I've taught."

Her heart sinks. She's been hoping this was a hand of friendship. Now she understands it's a practical campaign to train the staff and hospital to communicate with patients, part of Sudha's "missionary" work.

"Who else?"

"Brigid Walsh came for several lessons."

"Brigid?" And then without thinking, "How did she get away from her husband?"

Sudha laughs. "Indeed, he was the difficulty. When he discovered, lessons ended."

Monica is also laughing now and this feels so good.

They grow silent. It's a more comfortable silence than before.

Recovering formality, the teacher proposes, "Let me walk you to the gate."

"Thanks," she nods, a little deflated by the sudden farewell.

By the time they reach the road, Monica has summoned enough courage. "I'd like to accept your tutoring offer. But I need to repay you somehow."

She grins faintly. "Recompense is not necessary. Besides, I think we'll find the experience mutually edifying. We might even have another laugh or two."

Monica waves, wondering when Sudha Badami will answer the question about why she left Bombay. "Another laugh will be good." She smiles and continues smiling well past the gate and the long retaining wall.

Halfway home, she realizes she's forgotten to be on guard against the monkeys.

NINE

May, 2001, Moorty

She strolls briskly to keep up with Sudha, who's especially fleet when wearing a salwar kameez rather than a sari. Shopping trips with her friend always begin far down the mountain, at the *sabzi mandi*, where Monica gets to practice Hindi. *Aloo, gobi, bindi* (okra was inedible until she tasted Sudha's *bindi*), *lahsan* (lots of garlic, the international secret), *matar, palak* (so many ways to cook spinach), *tamatar* (now that had to be bowdlerized English) and an array of fruits: *Khubani, aam, tarbuz.*

When shopping on warm spring mornings like today, Monica misses her little kitchen in Uptown. Grateful as she is for Cook's attention and talents, she sometimes craves a grand salad. Of course that would lead to grand diarrhea. After two years here, Tina still doesn't eat salads.

Monica has her favorite stalls in the *sabzi mandi*. The man who sells nonfat *dahi* and *dudh* always greets her with a grin. Milk and yogurt are among the few things she takes back to her flat since Cook prepares the meals. On Saturday nights now, she and Sudha cook together after the Hindi lesson.

Today her bag is heavy with vegetables, because it's her turn to be teacher. Imagine, Sudha wanting to learn how to make pasta primavera. Tina and Monica lived on pasta during med school. Such a simple dish, especially with Moorty's abundance of spring veggies. She's pleased to repay Sudha's culinary instruction in kind, if not in gourmet nuance.

They climb the hill to the next level of shops in the Lower Bazaar. It's great to have a whole day off each week now that she's acclimated to Moorty Hospital. Even when she's doing chores in town, every exchange is a small adventure. At the general store, Sudha buys paper towels, cooking utensils, the odd bit of crockery. Crockery. Comestibles. She loves these Victorian-sounding words. There are fewer shoppers on this level of town. More men.

Every week, the general store holds new surprises. In mid-April, she was excited to find her favorite American cereal, albeit outrageously priced. Now, it's a welcome indulgence with her skimmed *dudh*. Today she buys plum nectar and a bag of cashews. *Kaju*, she says under her breath.

The merchant regards her cautiously. His eyes brighten as Sudha addresses him.

Monica knows enough Hindi to eavesdrop.

"Of course, Ma'am, we'll be able to carry your groceries up the mountain with the broom and cereal and such. No, no charge. How long has Ma'am been shopping here? How long educating our children? We are flattered by your custom."

"Sri Chawla, you are too kind."

The parking lot at Lunds in Uptown was filled with winter filthy cars. Customers trudged warily on the Minnesota ice, leading the way as young men and women in green uniforms pushed shopping carts toward capacious trunks of Subarus and Volvos and Hondas. How much more anonymous that life seems now. How long ago and far away.

Before striking farther uphill to the Mall, they graze stalls of Lower Bazaar for pens, paper, bars of soap. Not too much because after the Mall, where Monica will buy newspapers and a candy bar in a fancy shop, they'll have a steep climb to their neighborhood. Once past Mr. Chawla's store, they're accountable for haulage.

She's happy Sudha lives so near. Her small apartment block, 500 yards away, makes walking back at night easy. Thus she gets minimum flack about this "dubious practice" from Paterfamilias Walsh. She must develop a less confrontational attitude toward him. Has he simply replaced Louise as adversary in her psychological landscape?

No trip to town is complete without a stop at the Kerala Coffee House. They have a special table in the relatively smoke-free back room with a view of Lower Bazaar.

"Whew. This town does keep a person fit," Sudha sighs as she releases her packages. "But then, being American, you're probably used to attending the gym daily and torturing yourself on those monstrous machines."

Monica laughs, thinking about her gawkiness in aerobics class, then feels a pang of homesickness for the low impact course, the locker room chats with Beata. "You're right, this is a great workout. I've lost a couple of pounds since coming to Moorty."

"A pound or two, it makes a difference?"

"A pound or two leads to nine or ten. Then your clothes don't fit."

"Ah, yet further evidence of the superiority of our saris."

"Ha! You know full well those dainty sari blouses don't fit if you gain weight. You're very careful. I've seen you order *roti* rather than *naan* at dinner."

"I like *rotis*," Sudha raises her hand for the waiter.

Oh, good, Monica thinks, it's Rabi today. She enjoys the old man's smile. He always makes sure the coffee is steaming hot.

"Would you like to split an *uthapam*—or would that lead to those nine extra pounds?"

"One *uthapam* and, as always, one *dosa*. I'm starving."

"Why are you so fond of *uthapams*?"

"They were part of my first meal in India. In the Bengali Market."

"Don't tell me—at that dreadful Bengali House of Sweets!"

"No, not at all, across the street at Nathu's."

"Nathu's! Worse yet. That's not real South Indian food."

"So Ashok declared, but my first meal was delicious."

"Ashok, you haven't talked about him this week. Is he still planning to visit?"

Monica shrugs. "I guess so. If he finishes his article on time."

"Academics! I wouldn't have featured you falling in love with an academic."

"Who said anything about love? He's just a friend. An acquaintance."

"A friend who emails every few days. A friend who phones once a week."

"He's very brotherly. He looks out for the Minnesota Yankee in his land."

"Brotherly!" Sudha flicks her eyebrows theatrically.

Rabi appears with the scalding coffee and fragrant snacks.

Grateful for the interruption, Monica tries to sweep her mind of Ashok. He's an attractive, provocative, attentive man. And she does think about him. Too often. How much of that is simple loneliness in a new country? She's not interested in romance. She's here to serve, to grow in spirit. You can't love someone you've only known ninety days. Is she really counting the days?

"Actually, I've told you more than enough about Ashok, my mother, Lake Clinic. We haven't got past chapter one of Sudha's dramatic biography. When happened when you turned down that Colaba man? How did you tell him? How did your parents react?"

With the scrupulosity of a practiced teacher, Sudha divides the *uthapam* and *dosa*.

Monica taps her fingers on the table.

Sudha's head drops back dreamily. "Manil understood I wasn't going to be the docile wife who would raise four children and greet him with a martini when he returned from the office. After two dinners with our families, we knew. All of us did."

"How did you get out of it?"

"My family is middle class. They don't live in the dark ages."

"Of course not," Monica says quietly. How can she develop a friendship with this complicated, intelligent woman if she doesn't know more about her life?

Sudha chews thoughtfully.

In the far corner, chess players smoke furiously, concentrating on their board. A small audience leans over, rapt. By the front door, an ancient man sips from his cup, nodding intently, as if revisiting his youth on a coffee plantation. Why do so many South Indians migrate to the wintry cold climate of Moorty?

"Father, who's always supported my ambitions, was easy. Mama made trouble. She was looking forward to my returning from St. Andrews to settle down as a flourishing Bandra or Colaba housewife."

Monica nibbles the delicious *dosa*. "That must've been a hard conversation."

Sudha throws up her hands. "It was. It was. But Mama had successfully married off her other daughter and so she was philosophical. Except…" She pauses, laughs softly.

"What?" Monica studies her friend's face.

"She called me a 'Modern Woman!' "

"There are worse epithets." Like the names Jeanne called her after Mom's death.

"So, eventually, everyone was accepting. Papa urged me to go for a Ph.D. at Bombay University. He said I could live with them and commute to the Bandra campus. Within days, Mama had big plans for her professor daughter. A J.N.U. Professorship."

Monica finishes her coffee and wants another, but she's afraid to interrupt Sudha's self-disclosure. "What happened?"

"That was never for me. I'm not an intellectual. Don't have the patience with theory. I wanted to do something with my life. It was hard to leave St. Andrews. I loved Scotland. There was a boy there…well, anyway, I decided if I were going to return to India, I needed to contribute to this country. I always liked kids. I know what a difference one teacher made in my life. The choice was easy in some ways."

"In some ways?"

Rabi offers fresh black coffee.

"Obviously I couldn't stay in Bombay. Not only was I rejecting marriage, I was rebuffing their career dreams. And for what? To become a maiden school marm. Forever an auntie, they thought. So I imagined places where I might live. Our family traveled to Moorty once. And during my first year at St. Andrews, I often thought of Moorty: the hills, the trees. Somehow Moorty reminds me of Scotland. It's not rational, but I came here because I wanted to be in India and I wanted to be in Scotland and I wanted to be near my parents but not too near."

"Sounds like the perfect decision."

"Hardly perfect. I guess I'm useful, but…"

Monica glances down at Lower Bazaar, more crowded now during lunch hour. This sight feels happily familiar. Whole hours pass these days without a thought of "being in India." Sometimes she has to remind herself that she is 8,000 miles from Minneapolis and 6,000 feet closer to the stars. She waits for Sudha. "But what?"

"Sometimes people are suspicious of a single woman. Especially a single woman from Sin City, Bombay."

"I see."

Sudha chuckles. "Outsiders—Maharashtra and Minneapolis. No wonder we are such good friends."

Such good friends. Monica blushes. A significant statement from the reticent Sudha. Embarrassed and touched, she suggests, "Shall we good friends finish our errands before the day evaporates?"

Sudha's voice is quizzical, amused. "*Andiamo, Cara* Sudha?" My Italian friend would say when she wanted to leave the St. Andrews library. "*Andiamo, Cara* Monica."

*****

Vikram's visit is brief. He's progressing well—both his eyes and his English. She suspects this last appointment had more to do with language practice. A sweet kid.

From the waiting room, she hears an Irish voice. An echo of home. But not.

"Good morning, Mrs. Rao. It will be a day or two before Dr. Walsh is free. He has an early surgery this morning. Quite busy, you know. Quite busy."

"Not to worry, Mrs. Walsh," says Sudha's colleague from the mathematics department. "I am consulting with Dr. Murphy now. Very fine doctor. Excellent care."

Although Monica's assignments are eye diseases and intestinal curses, a number of pregnant women have begun to request her. And one or two younger men. This has happened gradually, almost imperceptibly.

"Is that so?"

Monica concentrates on Vikram. Brigid's response isn't her business. It makes sense that some women are more comfortable with her.

Then, without warning, the outside door crashes open.

Monica looks out: an explosion of noise as moaning patients are rushed in on stretchers.

"Jeep toppled over the mountain," Sister Catherine announces, calling everyone into service.

Vikram bows good-bye, looking terrified.

Facial wounds on three men. Four broken legs.

Shivering and shock.

Who knows how much internal bleeding?

They work efficiently together, doctors and nurses. Eventually the injured patients are shifted to beds. Good prognoses all around.

The examination rooms are suddenly empty.

The clinic is eerily quiet.

Monica wonders if she said good-bye to Vikram.

Her two pneumonia patients in the ward need attention. She considers skipping lunch. But yesterday she did that and regretted it all afternoon.

She forces herself to walk to the refectory.

The midday sun arches over the noble deodar cedars. Trees of the gods. Monica thinks of Eric taking her to the stunning Redwood forests in Mendocino. She inhales the clean, crisp scent. Sister Melba's flower garden is so vibrant; it's hard to believe these are the same frozen hospital grounds as four months ago. Two orange monkeys chase each other around a well. Monica walks faster.

As she climbs the refectory steps, she hears Sanchez laughing with Walsh. Odd, but good sign. The two men rarely greet each other, despite Father's attempts to mediate.

"Dr. Murphy?" Brigid calls from the veranda.

"Good afternoon. How are you?"

"Just fine. Fine, indeed."

Monica clasps the door knob.

Brigid places a freckled hand over Monica's.

"May we have a word before lunch?"

She doesn't want to be tardy. If Kevin Walsh faults her again, that's his problem.

"Sure, is everything OK?"

"With me, yes, thanks." Brigid twists her neck as if to unknot a muscle.

"But?"

"You're still new here, so let me offer a little advice." Her cheeks are flushed.

Like Jeanne's face after several martinis.

"I always welcome helpful advice." Keep an upbeat attitude, girl.

"I spoke with Mrs. Rao this morning," Brigid lowers her voice. "I've noted that she and several of Dr. Walsh's other patients have begun to consult with you."

Monica counts to ten. Listens to birds arguing on a nearby branch. Her tone is polite, formal. "I believe our procedure is to see patients as we are available and to attend to their requests for consultations when we can."

"Officially, yes." Brigid straightens her back.

"I always try to follow procedures, to avoid personality conflicts."

"As a recent arrival, perhaps you're missing some nuances here, Dr. Murphy."

"Oh," she breathes deeply, trying to summon the pleasure of Brigid's accent.

"Kevin, Dr. Walsh, is the senior doctor. With many years of medical background." She's gripping the iron railing. "And considerable experience here. If we want what's best for our patients, we sometimes have to relinquish our egos."

"You have a point." How sad to see her defending her husband's turf. Monica says a quick prayer for patience and resolves to consult Father

Freitas.

"I knew you would understand. I've come to admire your quick intelligence."

Monica's heart sinks. In the last months at Lake Clinic, she became a master of deflection. It's one thing to avoid argument and another to surrender integrity. She's certainly not going to turn away patients.

As Walsh leads them in grace, she realizes once again that if she's going to have any charitable thoughts about her colleagues, she must get to know them better. Cook serves aromatic *chana biryani* and everyone digs in.

"So, Dr. Walsh," she begins nervously, "you were asking about American Medical schools the other day. Did you train in Ireland or Britain?"

Brigid's expression is wary.

God, there aren't any safe topics with him?

"Ireland, of course," he says, then takes a long sip of purified water.

"Oh, at Trinity?"

Brigid shakes her head in dismay.

"No, Dr. Murphy, as you may have noticed, I am a Roman Catholic."

"Sorry, I forgot about the Church's ban on Catholics attending Trinity."

"I studied at University College, Dublin. A fine institution. You'll be interested to know we admitted more women at the time than Trinity."

"Yes, one of my professors went to UCD," she recovers quickly. Thank God for Dr. Smythe and those Friday nights at Stub and Herb's when he joined the younger docs for a drink and offered an hour of his seamless storytelling. "Did you do your clinical work at St. Vincent's or at the Martyr?"

"You do know something about Irish education!"

"A wee bit," she aims for her mother's charm.

"Right, a Kildare family. I forget. You seem so American."

She blinks.

"Some people mistake Trinity as the better institution, but truth be told, it was more like a privileged boy's club. I dare say we had broader experience. I have UCD to thank for more than a good education. Brigid and I met there."

Brigid nods, lips parted in a diffident smile.

Praise God for Mom's social graces ("Just ask them about themselves, dear. Everyone has a story.") Monica feels a small reprieve from recent tensions.

Raul clears his throat.

They turn to him.

"Before we resume work this afternoon," he sits forward. "I want to report that I'm returning to Manda for three days."

Walsh chews his *naan* with absorption.

Raul continues hastily, "I know we have a difference of opinion, but people are suffering there. They have no one. Now with our excellent new colleague, we have three doctors, four nurses… I'll just be gone a few days, one of which is my day off."

"I'm afraid we can't permit this," blurts Walsh.

Cook presents a tray of tea and biscuits. Then, apparently noticing the tension, exits without clearing the lunch plates.

"I've already made promises." His accent grows stronger at moments of conflict. "I've hired the car."

"With whose funds?"

"A patron from home has sent modest support."

"One of those Peronist bankers?"

"Dr. Walsh!" Father Freitas is scandalized.

"Really, that's uncalled for," Monica proclaims. Everyone knows Raul lost his family among "the disappeared."

Raul flings down his napkin. "Let's leave it there. I'm a peaceful man. But I have my limits."

Walsh watches in astonishment as the younger doctor stalks out.

Silence hangs heavily over the table.

TEN

While the tea steeps, Monica begins her morning study. She likes this private ritual an hour before Mass each day. This week, she's re-reading her worn copy of *The Seven Storey Mountain*. How important Thomas Merton was during the first months after Father Daniel's retreat. Perhaps Merton is vital to her because he's also a returnee to Christianity and was about her age when he wrote the memoir confessing his doubts, exploring his renewed faith.

Sipping the Darjeeling blend Sudha gave her, she re-enters Merton's fascinating consciousness. "*Aseitas*—the English equivalent is a transliteration: aseity—simply means the power of a being to exist absolutely in virtue of itself, not as caused by itself, but as requiring no cause, no other justification for its existence except that its very nature is to exist. There can be only be one such Being: that is God. And to say that God exists *a se,* of and by reason of Himself, is merely to say that God is Being Itself. *Ego sum qui sum.* And this means that God must enjoy complete independence not only as regards everything outside, but also as regards everything within Himself."

Light begins to lift through the wings of the *deodars*. She finds herself weeping, longing for the community of spirit Merton discovered at his Trappist Monastery. Of course working at Moorty Hospital is not the same as participating in a contemplative order. Still, she'd hoped for kindred colleagues. She hadn't anticipated Raul's disaffection or Walsh's harshness or Brigid's wifeliness.

Pouring more tea, she savors the cup's heat on her cold hands. Enjoy the small, unexpected comforts. Turn over the troubles. Remember that God exists in virtue itself.

*****

Tina's email is breezy as usual:

Glad you're used to the altitude. You must come to Delhi before it gets too hot. Work is OK. We had two windbag senators last week. Diarrhea. From their moans, you'd have thought it was cholera. Otherwise, same old, same old. Miss you. xo, Tina.

As Monica stretches for her water bottle, she marvels once more at reconnecting with Tina.

Monica prefers this internet shop to the coffee houses at home where people plug their laptops into ubiquitous wall sockets. The Coffee Shack was becoming a site of virtual socializing. Sometimes she and Beata couldn't snag a table. Here in Moorty, you queue to book a computer. Everyone is engaged in his or her own project. Students surfing the net for universities in Europe, North America and Australia. People catching up with personal correspondence. A widow and her son, befuddled by immigration forms. Backpackers from France and Germany checking on their next flights or trains.

One of these blonde Rasta-haired travelers calls loudly over to Monica. "How do you best say to the travel agent, 'We desire to have the next most possible flight?' "

She shrugs, concentrates on her screen. These kids bug her. Maybe it's the privilege of their sloppiness exposed before neatly kempt Indians. Maybe she's jealous of their freedom. When she was nineteen, she was selling hosiery 40 hours a week at Dayton's and attending university full-time. Maybe it's the cozy way they appropriate Rastafarian coiffures, which look ridiculous on fair-skinned people.

"Come, Madame, help us out." The French accent is stronger now.

"Why ask me?" She's still pissed off at Kevin Walsh. Great, Monica, imitate the blustering fool. What was she reading about virtue yesterday?

"Because English is your language."

By this time, everyone has turned to observe the exchange. Of course at least half the Indians here speak perfect English, but that's not the point. English is her native tongue. She can help the young travelers. After all, they are trying to leave Moorty.

"You're close. Just say, 'We need the next flight to X.' Shorter is better, I think."

"*Merci, Madame.*"

"*Pas de quoi,*" she grins.

Monica catches the fleeting smiles from other customers as they return to their email.

Tina's probably right. She needs a break.

Monica presses "Check Mail" again. And there—a reward for her grudging charity?—is a message from Ashok.

Dear Esteemed Dr. Murphy,

Oh, he's in one of those moods.

It is with profound humility that I report my paper was accepted in Madison.

"Wonderful," she says aloud.

Several heads turn.

Thus, with great regret, I must postpone the visit to idyllic Moorty, capital of pleasure and beauty in the handsome foothills of our country.

Our country? What happened to her threat as a cultural imperialist?

Seriously, Monica, I'm thrilled at this opportunity. But also dashed at the thought of missing you. Fancy a short journey to your beloved Midwest? Madison, they say, is close to Minneapolis. Maybe it's a long shot, but could the Mission send you on a fundraising trip? I'm not being sarcastic, well, not completely. No harm in asking.

But what was he asking? How well do they know each other? Of course she can't go. Unnerved by the invitation, she's also pleased.

How's work? That boy, Vikram, did he recover? And your Hindi lessons? How are you doing?

She gulps from her water bottle and checks the time. Running late, she fashions a quick, light-hearted reply, filling him in on her news, reluctantly declining the opportunity of a Wisconsin spring, wishing him luck on the paper.

Happy trip. Travel safely. Don't eat too many cheese curds. Ciao, Monica.

She hands Radha 600 rupees. "Thanks."

"Thank you, Doctor. See you again next week?"

"Yes, Radha, I'll be here."

Under her breath, the young woman says, "At 2 p.m.? I can reserve for you."

"Why thanks, that would be a big help. You can count on me."

"Yes, Raj told me so."

"Raj?"

"Raj Agarwal, my little brother. You spoke to his class a while ago. He was impressed."

"Raj!" She recalls the boy's challenge about condoms. You never know who is listening or what they hear. "Thanks again, Radha. See you next week."

As she walks along the mall, she is infused with buoyancy. Good to get a rest from the hospital. But it's more than that. She's beginning to feel less of a stranger. Not that she belongs in India. She doubts she'll ever feel like that. Almost every day, she's reminded of her difference. Today the Rasta fille calls her on her English. Yesterday, a well-meaning patient said, "Yes, Dr. Murphy, you foreign doctors are so precise." But if she's a foreigner, she's no longer a stranger—not to her colleagues or Sudha or the tomato vendor in the *sabzi mandi* or to Ashok.

She stops at the All Purpose Stationers to find a card for Jeanne's birthday. If her sister refuses to communicate, that's her business. Monica will send a birthday card.

The shopkeeper bows. "Good afternoon, Doctor."

"*Namaste*, Mr. Patna."

Jeanne would loathe these flower cards with Victorian messages. No appreciation for kitsch. She opts for a blank card with a photo of the Himalayas. She can write a personal birthday wish. Monica picks up a card for Dad, too. He hasn't answered her first letter from India, probably still angry that she ignored his injunction during the last phone call in the States. *You could do so much here. It's crazy to go to that dangerous country.* She wanted to say she'd wished he hadn't lit out for his own "dangerous country" when she was a kid, but she'd worked hard at reaching their current détente.

"Excellent choice," Mr. Patna states. "Discreet, understated. Friends will like."

Clearly this isn't the sort of intimate card one gave to family. But hers is no longer an intimate family.

The news vendor has sold out of *Herald Tribunes*.

"So sorry, Ma'am. Would Ma'am like me to reserve one for next week?"

Has she met this small, bald man in the spotless lunghi and purple korta? Clearly he's noticed her.

"Thank you sir; that would be very kind."

"My pleasure."

Further along, she stops at a bench for a long view of the mountains. Not just any mountains. The Himalayas. The world's highest mountains, she learned during her K2 project in high school. In today's relatively clean air, she can make out the tallest peak. Back in Minnesota, she rarely thought about mountains. She loved the flat plains, the way you could see forever, the big sky. Lately, she's been yearning to go higher, maybe along the fabled Hindusthan Road, the ancient silk route. You can travel by car at least 15,000 feet. As far as the Kunzum Pass.

Sighing, she shifts her bags and heads uphill toward "home." Just past the Anglican church, the route grows narrower, darker, under an arcade of pines. Three small boys are laughing on the road side. She walks toward them.

A bright orange monkey swings from an electrical wire to the high branch of a stately deodar. Suddenly, she's pointing and laughing with the boys.

ELEVEN

July, 2001, Moorty

Loud, continuous rain. Not music exactly, or company, but an agreeable presence, insulating the exam cubicle from waiting room conversations. Everyone says the monsoons are almost over. Another few days. End of the week, for sure, according to Sister Eleanor.

Veena doesn't seem to notice the incessant dripping outside the windows as she chats happily about the imminent birth of her third child.

Monica's mind wanders. The Walshes are due back from their fundraising tour on Sunday as the monsoons end. Dr. Walsh is always in the right place at the right moment.

"Sita," Veena suggests. "I like other names, too, of course—Maya and Gita."

"Lovely." Refreshing that Veena wants a girl, feels she's earned her daughter after bearing two healthy sons.

"Rajul is pretty. And Richa."

"All fine names."

Monica knows she's being mean-spirited about the Walshes. Summer is a good time to fundraise in the U.S. The fact that sunny June in New York coincides with soggy June here is incidental. They're ambitious for the Mission.

Banging. Loud banging. Wind blowing the door again.

She hands Veena a sheet with nutritional tips and they begin to review them.

Raised voices.

Unfamiliar men.

Veena twitches in the chair, her pretty face drawn.

"Not to worry," Monica smiles reassuringly. "The front door hinge is broken. I'm sure things will quiet down by Friday when the monsoon has passed."

Veena bites her lip, mischievous, smiling eyes on Monica.

"What's up?"

"So you know the monsoon will end on Friday? Do you have a time in mind? Morning or afternoon? It would be convenient to plan ahead."

She breaks into a wide grin. "Doctor, who told you a tale about knowing when the monsoon ends?"

"One of the nurses." She's embarrassed by her eager credulity. She hasn't credited Sister Eleanor with such a sense of humor.

Another bang.

A table crashes to the floor.

Veena blinks rapidly. "I thought this might happen." She scans the exam room. Clearly the window is too small for escape.

"Wha…what might happen?" Monica's voice is actually quavering.

"R.S.S. They just attacked a private school forty kilometers north of here."

She recalls Mr. Alexander booting thugs from the Delhi chapel. Thinks back to Kevin Walsh reciting his first encounter with the right wing Hindu Nationalists. Moorty Mission's David facing the xenophobic Goliath. He said they might return. Stupid to assume they'd come when he was here. Is she starting to rely on the Patriarch?

She's scared, but her first concern is Veena. "Come this way. Take the side door and you won't be noticed."

Veena holds her belly tenderly. "You are sure?"

She hears Raul arguing now, at the far end of the waiting room. She wants to follow Veena home.

"Go," Monica whispers urgently, grabs her hand, "that way, quickly."

She watches Veena make her way down the hill. Summoning courage, she opens the door and finds an almost vacant waiting room. The other patients have fled, too.

Three young men, arms akimbo, shout at Raul and Sister Eleanor.

Monica breathes a prayer for guidance. "God give me strength." She's startled by a longing for Ashok.

Sister looks younger than usual as she concentrates on translating Doctor Sanchez' accented English into Hindi for the visitors.

"We treat anyone who comes to the clinic," barks Raul.

"Then why display a vast cross from your roof?" asks the youngest man, with curly hair and rimless glasses.

"India is a democracy," Raul lowers his voice, "with many religions."

"This is a Hindu nation."

"Gandhiji and Nehruji insured that India protected rights of all citizens—Buddhist, Zoroastrian, Muslim, Christian and others—to follow their creeds."

"It's one thing to practice quietly. And quite another to sell religion with food or education or medical care," grumbles the oldest of the young men.

Once again, she hears Ashok's comments on the plane and the censure of the airport cabbie. Surely Raul has heard all this before. Surely he will maintain his cool.

Sister Eleanor's eyes fill with tears.

Raul's calm voice and agility impress Monica. "Oh, that's the problem," he says, "a misunderstanding. Please sit down."

They stand their ground.

"We ask no questions about faith and do not proselytize. We sell nothing. Services are free. A few patients make donations. "

"Rupees from poor Indians go straight into your gilded Vatican," the quietest man finally speaks. In fluent English.

Gilded Vatican. Either he's had foreign university training or he is mimicking the embellished prose of *The Hindustan Times.*

"All patient funds supplement medical expenses or food for the wards."

Suddenly Raul notices Monica. He makes the slightest gesture of his eyes leftward, cueing her to return to the exam cubicle.

He could be right. The sight of a woman doctor might provoke these young zealots. Admittedly, she'd be safer in the cubicle. No, she will stand by, will witness.

The intense men take no notice of her.

"We object to you preaching strange dogma to our people."

Sister has trouble translating this and says something *sotto voce* to Doctor Sanchez.

"Quite right." He rolls his broad shoulders. "Sister Eleanor asked me to remind you that she is an Indian, who comes from many generations of Christians in Kerala."

"A Communist State in the deep south," sneers the curly-haired fellow.

"Besides," Raul strains for dispassion, "we don't preach to our patients, except to insist that they take their medicine as directed and return for check-ups."

The quiet man sways from one foot to the other. He whispers to his friends.

They nod soberly.

Finally, he speaks. "Consider this as a reconnaissance trip. A first contact. We will keep you under close watch. We will return with reports from your 'patients.' "

They file out quietly, the decorous departure a contrast to their clattering arrival. If Raul has his way, they will return one day for check-ups.

She peers out the window to the white Ambassador sedan splashing through large puddles and down the hill.

Turning, she catches Sister Eleanor crossing herself.

Raul murmurs, "Jesus!" under his breath, righting the overturned table.

"Thank God!" Monica squeezes sister's cold hand. "Well done."

Monica pats Raul's shoulder. "You, my friend, were magnificent."

He shakes his head. "Brutes," he spits. "I've seen it all before."

As Sister sits, a healthy color returns to her face.

"I thought I'd get some reprieve from Argentina here," he growls. "These people are the same the world over. Different bodies, different language, same bullies."

Monica studies a tremor in his left cheek.

Raul continues. "Still, it's about domination. An international virus."

Making a show of inspecting the empty waiting room, she cajoles, "Since we have no patients and are likely to be overloaded this afternoon, let's break for lunch."

"Either a flood of patients or a drought," Raul rolls his eyes, "once the word gets out."

*****

Sister Catherine greets them anxiously. "I knew, after last month's firebombing of the church in Chennai. I knew we'd be targeted."

Raul shakes his head. "Chennai is a long way from here," he says irritably. "These men are from the north. I can tell by their accents."

"Locals?" Sister Catherine declares and inquires simultaneously.

"No one I recognized," Sister Eleanor whispers. "But, yes, they were Punjabi."

"A Tamil wing of the R.S.S. claimed responsibility for Chennai," Monica nods.

"Ten parishioners killed," Sister Catherine cries, "and one priest."

"God keep their souls." The younger nun bows her head.

"The point," Raul leans heavily on a chair, "is that these goons harass all over the bloody country. With tacit approval of the National BJP and state leaders."

Father Freitas rushes in the refectory door. "Is everyone OK? I heard on my way from giving the Last Rites to Bina Singh. Her neighbor was at the clinic, a young woman named Veena. She said there were guns and knives."

"No," Raul laughs edgily. "No dynamite either." The chair wobbles under his grip.

Monica wonders if it—or he—will crack under the stress.

"No hand grenades," he snaps. "Nothing cinematic. Just big talk from the inflated chests of small-minded men."

"But what can we do?" Sister Eleanor entreats. "They're coming back."

"We can pray," Sister Catherine clasps her hands together.

"We can indeed," declares Monica, "and we can continue our work."

Raul eyes her gratefully, finally sitting down.

"With God's help." Father moves toward Raul, grasping his friend's arm. "Dr. Murphy is right. People in Moorty know us. We will carry on."

*****

Monica lies across her bed listening to the night rain. Is she imagining the deluge is ebbing? How can she describe this morning to Beata without terrifying her? She felt so frightened today, although oddly invisible. Raul was effective, an authoritative voice devoid of Walsh's sanctimony. Imagine even momentarily missing Walsh! If Dr. Blowhead had been here, it would have grown ugly. At best, they'd be stuffed in Emmanuel's van now, winding down the mountain to the airport.

It was good of Father Freitas to say Mass after dinner. Being together in their beautiful little chapel helped. Praying helped.

Bang. Bang. Loud, piercing sounds. Her heart races.

Bang. Bang. Ring.

The telephone. What's wrong with her.

Two rings. For her.

Phone, she scolds herself. Before answering, she listens to the natural patter of rain to steady her nerves.

"Monica, are you all right?" Sudha's voice is loud, anxious.

"Just fine. A little shaken, but nothing happened, except...words."

"Hmmm."

Sensing Sudha's exasperation, she adds. "OK, the threats are frightening. But one is grateful there were no assaults."

"Indeed," Sudha sounds relieved, "this one is grateful you're safe."

Tears well up. Finally.

Sudha listens to her weep. "Good. Normal. Even saints cry. Didn't Jesus cry at Gethsemane?"

Taken aback, she remembers that Sudha's Scottish boyfriend took her to some services. And Sudha is a quick study. Monica is touched that this friend, who has her own critique of the Mission, is comforting her with Christian scripture. She cries harder, releasing the tension she couldn't betray earlier.

"Yes, cry, get it out. I would have rung sooner, but I was visiting Neela."

"How did you hear? Who told you?"

"Monica, news like this travels like lightning. Everyone is agitated. The town is behind you. I saw Raj in the street and he was shouting, 'Moorty has no room for these hooligans.'"

"Raj Agarwal?"

"People can disagree with you without wanting to destroy you."

Her tears dry up. "Neela, how is Neela?"

"Recovering. The baby is well. I offered more moral support than anything."

"That seems to be your vocation today."

"Do you need anything? Do you want me to come over?"

"It's raining." Of course, selfishly, she wants to see Sudha.

"It's been raining for a month. Indians are waterproof. It's in the genes. How about it? I haven't even put away my umbrella."

"No, Sudha, you need to rest after your journey. School starts early tomorrow. We'll have our usual long talk on Saturday. I'm much better for hearing your voice."

"You are sure?"

"Just fine. Good night now. Thanks for phoning."

Monica stands and stretches, peering out the window into the darkness. Darkness is harder than the rain. It's true that the days are a little longer than when she arrived in February. But night falls by 7:15. In July. On summer evenings, she and Beata used to go to dinner, then walk around Lake Calhoun until 10 o'clock. Friends, that's what she needs. Monica refills her tea cup and sits down with Beata's letter.

My dear Monica,

Wonderful to hear about your progress with Hindi. I bet your patients appreciate it. Your new friend Sudha sounds nice. I'm glad you have a break from the almighty Walshes. I hope they don't canvas in the Twin Cities.

Kevin Walsh won't go further than Chicago.

We've been lucky this year—just a few thunderstorms. My roses are gorgeous. Thanks again for those silvery pink ones. I think of you whenever I gaze at the garden.

James and I had a fab time in Redwing last weekend. Yeah, I can hear you say, Finally making some progress. *You'd like him. He loves jazz as much as I do. He doesn't tease me too much about the infamous shoe collection (I have gotten better, really.).*

James is a poetry reader. He's great in bed. Funny and kind. Did I say great in bed?

So what's the catch? OK, I know this shouldn't bother me. James is divorced. No children or any ties. Amicable. I wish he'd told me earlier.

Wouldn't that have scared you off, old pal?

OK, it would have troubled me a lot. He said he wanted to wait until I knew him before telling me. What's the deal? At least half of adult Americans are divorced. Of course I'm not being rational. I didn't want a virgin. Maybe I'm unrealistic because I've been alone so long.

That's a point.

So he's given me some "space" to think. Gone to visit his parents in Cleveland for a week. He's a very attentive son. Oh, Monica, I wish you were here and we could really talk. That's selfish. You're doing such important work in India.

Odd that Beata thinks of her being in India rather than in Moorty.

Let's see, what gossip. Heard the inimitable Dr. Jill twice on the radio. Diet and exercise are this month's themes. Oh, she doesn't' say anything bad. It's just so obvious. You've probably long forgotten your irritating colleague.

I'm still thinking about that trip to India in the late summer. James keeps mentioning a time share in Captiva. But he knows India is my priority.

Come soon, friend. R.S.S. bullies. Visa officials. Warring colleagues. She can't control any of it. She can pray. Sometimes all she can manage is praying for the willingness to pray.

TWELVE

July and August, 2001, Moorty

Monica and Raul linger over tea after Friday night dinner. Everything is more relaxed minus the Walshes. It's nice to spend time alone with him. Father Freitas is off on an evening call. The nuns always leave table promptly. Cook will bang around in the kitchen for another hour, washing up and preparing for breakfast.

"Minneapolis is very cold?"

"In winter, yes. Often below zero for most of January."

"Below zero *Fahrenheit*?"

"You betcha!" she grins. "January must be a different story in Buenos Aires."

He closes his eyes. "Early summer. The roses and the tourists."

"Tourists flock to St. Paul in February for the ice sculpture show."

"No!" Laughter softens his long face.

So good to see him relaxed. His large eyes are often shaded in anger or worry. Tonight the brown irises are clear. Newly washed hair drops in curls over his forehead. Does he go to the barber in the Lower Bazaar, the one who props a mirror against a tree? The intimacy of this question shifts her into bashful silence.

"It gets cold in Mendoza. Where we lived when I was small."

"I've heard of Mendoza. It must have been a lovely childhood in the Andes foothills."

"Until my father was kidnapped, *sí*."

"I am so very sorry. Father Freitas told me some of the story."

"That story," he shakes his head fatalistically, "happened long ago and far away."

"How did the rest of your family survive?" she persists gently.

"Mama moved us to Buenos Aires, to Palermo, near her family. It wasn't bad. She found office work. And on Sundays we walked the city, Mama and I, to watch the street dancers in La Boca; to browse the market in San Telmo."

"But how did you get to medical school? Wasn't it expensive?"

"When my grandfather left Italy, his siblings left too and went to

New York. A better choice in some ways. At least financially. Mama's cousin was a doctor in Texas, and he helped me get into medical school there."

"Your mother must be very proud."

"She was a wonderful woman, who died too young of a broken heart. And afterwards I had no reason to stay in that godforsaken country. I couldn't remain in Texas. India seemed the 'logical' choice," he says.

They sip tepid tea in silence. Raul taps his foot against the wooden table leg. He seems to expect her to say—or ask—something.

"Your father, you have no idea where they took him?"

"Back to Mendoza, I always imagine."

"Oh?"

"They tossed them from planes, you know. I can just picture the bastards flying back to Papa's beloved mountains and then 'releasing' him there."

"Oh, Raul, no," she automatically puts her hand over his. It's warm and she feels blood ruggling through the tangled veins.

"I must not torture you with my grisly imagination," he lowers his voice.

"You're the one who is tortured." Where is she going with this? Walking onto Lake Calhoun before the ice has frozen over. "And talking about your grief, well, that's what friends are for."

"Friends," he regards her dolefully. "I'm not a person with many friends." He gulps the last of his tea and stands. "I wasn't, as you say, socialized properly. I didn't learn the ways of normal, happy children."

Monica holds her tongue. Her own girlhood pain is nothing compared to his loss. Still, she's a little piqued that he assumes her passage has been simple.

"Thank you for the conversation." He turns. "I wish you pleasant dreams."

"Good night. Sleep well," she whispers.

He nods, waves on the way to the door.

Understanding that he prefers to walk to the residence alone, she lingers at the table. What a story. What a life.

*****

Her phone rings at one the morning. Who would call at this time? Has Jeanne had another car wreck?

"Hello, Monica?"

"Hello," she hesitates. "Ashok."

"Yes, oh, my god, did I wake you? I'm so sorry. I'm calling from Madison and I didn't really think through the time properly. Oh, no."

"It's fine," she laughs, amused by her apologetic, absent-minded friend. "I was just getting up. How is the conference?"

"Grand. My paper went over well. But I was thinking of you," he pauses.

She waits.

"Well, this is the weekend I was planning to visit you in Moorty."

"Yes," she says vaguely.

"So I was thinking about you," he stammers. "Because this was, well, going to be our weekend."

Our weekend is all she can hear.

"Monica, are you OK? Have you fallen back to sleep?"

This feels like a dream. Our weekend. She's fully awake now and thoroughly tongue-tied. He's calling from the States. Her heart races.

"So," he continues gamely, "I decided to call you from your country. I don't know, it was a silly notion."

"No, a lovely idea," she finds her voice. "Very thoughtful. Tell me about the conference, about your panel."

He describes the meeting, his observations about Madison, the weather.

"Ah, yes, July in the Upper Midwest, a soggy time."

"You forgive me for running off like this?"

"Of course." She tried not to think of Dad. This was just a weekend.

"I'd like to come in November, if that works for you."

"Yes. It will be snowing."

"I'll bring warm clothes, Doctor, so I don't catch a chill," he laughs.

"Tell me how things are at the hospital? With your friend Sudha?"

As Monica talks, she savors this simple conversation with, well, a good friend. She hopes he's more than that. And she imagines how Sudha will tease her.

*****

Sudha has promised a fête. The *mela* is crammed into a huge tent. It's almost possible to forget this site was an empty lot between the Tasty Bite Café and the derelict liquor outlet last week. Today Sudha and Monica are surrounded by a cheerful yellow canvas. Stalls display brilliant tie-dyed scarves from Rajasthan; pink and white pearls from Bangalore; *khadi* from the Punjab; appliqué from Orissa; *ikat* from Andra Pradesh.

"This is the ideal place to buy presents for my trip to Delhi." She thinks about those lovely farewell tokens. "So many gorgeous fabrics."

"You are from England?" the woman in the purple sari asks as she wraps Monica's silk scarf in brown paper.

"No," she's slightly taken aback. Sometimes she forgets how much she stands out. "I am from the U.S."

"Welcome to our country."

"Thank you."

Sudha draws her to a stall of Kashmiri shawls. "I told you the *mela* would be fantastic." She's glowing. "This shawl would suit you nicely in that Tundra of yours."

"Trying to get rid of me again?" Monica teases.

"Or for your friend Beata? You're always saying how she hates cold winds."

"Did I tell you Beata is coming at Christmas now?"

"Yes, she went off to California with that boyfriend for a summer holiday. Imagine choosing California over India."

"Florida," Monica smiles. "Indeed, what possessed her to follow her heart? The guy does seem perfect for her."

"*Perfect.* Dangerous word."

She's grinning, pleased that Sudha and Beata almost know each other, often ask after one another. She can't wait until December when they all have supper together.

"Look, look at these dolls from Haryana," calls Sudha threading her way through the bargainers to the other side of the aisle.

"Cute. I like the one carrying wood on her head."

"A worker doll." Sudha lifts the wooden doll in the air. "I can see how you would be drawn to a worker doll. But for Meenakshi, I think I will choose the one holding a baby. My niece is a traditional child." Sudha's arms are filled with gifts and she's still eagerly looking around.

"Sometimes, my friend, you're like a child yourself. We need to rest. Have lunch. A carbohydrate pick-up."

"You think I'll grow faint under the weight of all this fun?"

"*I* am growing faint. Under the weight of hours. It's 2 p.m.; I ate breakfast at dawn."

"OK. OK. I'll repress my consumerist weakness for the sake of your stomach."

Taking several of Sudha's packages, Monica shakes her head. "You could use a porter."

"Thanks." Sudha turns left and cries, "Oh, we must!"

Monica sees nothing but a bindi stall and, next to that, an old woman at a card table.

"Our fortunes," Sudha exclaims. "I haven't heard my fortune told since I was twelve."

"I can tell your fortune." Monica shakes her head. "Tomorrow over dinner you'll complain about having spent too much. Come, let's get something to eat."

"No, really, we must do this."

"You can't be serious."

"Maybe my student was right. Maybe you Americans are not a spiritual people."

She's tempted to laugh, then realizes she knows nothing about Sudha's history with fortune tellers. And what harm can it do?

"OK, but you owe me one."

"Sorry?"

"An American saying."

The old woman purrs softly to herself. Her pale skin is almost the color of her ivory sari. She doesn't seem to register their presence.

Sudha greets her, "*Namaste*."

She peers through clouded eyes, offers "*Namaste*," and motions for them to sit.

Monica perches on the edge of a rough wooden bench.

Sudha settles her packages on the dirt floor, then joins Monica on the bench. She leans forward fixedly.

Loud, raucous music intrudes from the carnival, just outside the tent. Monica finds herself oddly drawn to the rollercoaster, remembering flying high over the State Fair with Jeanne, holding her once impetuous sister in her seat as the red metal car swayed wildly from side to side. Jeanne shivered while the other kids squealed in delight.

"Do you have a question for me?" the old woman inquires feebly.

"Yes," Sudha's face lights up. "Will a professor come to visit my friend?"

"Oh, no, no," Monica cringes.

"Your hand," the woman urges.

She extends her left palm. What if Sister Catherine or Father Freitas wanders through the *mela* now?

"You must relax," the psychic instructs.

She inhales slowly. The woman doesn't examine her palm. Rather she holds her wrist and resumes humming. Of course, how could a nearly blind person read palms?

The woman's voice is hoarse, low. "I see a man from Delhi, running for a train."

Sudha elbows Monica on her right arm.

"Yes, he is catching it. Heading to the mountains. And…" She raises her venerable head, sighing and staring past her into the middle distance.

"And?" Sudha implores.

"No, that's it." She purses her lips. "That's all I see."

"Thanks." Relieved, Monica slips a coin into the chipped blue bowl.

"And now your friend?"

Sudha speaks up quickly. "Will we find a benefactor to fix the windows at the school?" She presents the woman with her right wrist.

Once again the psychic shuts her eyes and hums. Then halts. A frown crosses her forehead. "Would you repeat the question? Slowly? I must hear your voice again."

Puzzled, Sudha repeats her query about the windows.

The old woman hums, squeezing Sudha's wrist tighter, her weird noises resonating louder. She releases the wrist saying, "Unexpected benefactors will appear."

Sudha grins, and drops ten rupees in the bowl. "Thank you." She turns to go.

"Before you leave," the fortune teller sing-songs, seeming to recover her sight so thoroughly she can see through them. "You are friends?"

"Yes," Sudha says.

Monica wants to escape, to ride the roller coaster, to eat lunch, to take a nap.

"Come, then—one hand in each other's."

Sudha sits again, eagerly extending her wrist.

Monica complies stiffly.

The woman grips their wrists for a long time, so long, Monica thinks her arm will go to sleep.

"Please close your eyes, both of you."

Really! Monica fidgets on the bench. As a child she learned clairvoyants were like ministers and rabbis, people to be avoided lest she contravene the First Commandment about false religions. Still, this is a simple game to humor Sudha.

"Please quiet your minds."

The woman begins to hum again.

A vibration travels up Monica's arm from the shoulder. This is just too silly.

More purring.

"I see," she manages breathily. "One of you will rest in a high place." Gradually, she releases their wrists.

"What high place?" demands Sudha. "What do you mean, rest?"

The woman shakes her head. "That is all."

Sudha puts ten more rupees in the bowl.

"But which one of us?" Sudha demands.

"I have nothing more."

Sudha reaches for the money, but the woman deftly slips the coins into a purse.

"*Al Vidah!*" their fortune teller calls after them.

*****

The waiter brings a bottle of mineral water and two glasses.

"You were right," Sudha says crossly. "Silly superstition. A waste of money."

"Maybe she was predicting one of us will go to Heaven," Monica jokes.

"OK," she says. "Clearly it's you. I don't believe in the place. You're going to Heaven. Advance congratulations."

"I could have told you that." Monica smiles. "On a more serious note, you do have the wrong impression about Ashok and me. We're just friends. We share an interest in each other's country."

"Of course."

"Really. Sometimes I think he'll return to the U.S. He loved grad school there."

"That's not the only American thing he loves."

"Sudha, you're incorrigible."

"Since she's obviously right about you going to Heaven, I guess I can count on my benefactor and on the chance to meet Ashok and evaluate this relationship for myself. You heard her. He'll catch that train."

Monica sips her water, examining the menu.

THIRTEEN

January, 1995, Minnesota

Monica tucks herself at a corner table, looking out the restaurant window at buses trundling down snowy Hennepin Avenue and studying the white flakes landing in the dark night on vehicles, on heavy coated people hidden in caps, gloves and boots. The way these street lamps momentarily light up the flakes makes her nostalgic for a childhood which, if it wasn't blissful, was relatively safe and comfortable.

*****

Dad used to drive these buses. Maybe she expects a bus door to yawn open at the restaurant stop. To see his mop of blond hair, finely featured face, blue eyes igniting.

"Step on little lady," Tim Murphy would say. "Do your parents know you're traveling alone on a bus?"

She'd perch on a forward bench, kitty-corner to her father as he adroitly steered the huge vehicle in and out of lanes, rolling past Lagoon and Lake and 31st Streets, turning a careful left at the cemetery and then a quick right on Dupont. When a regular passenger boarded, he'd introduce his "beautiful daughter," bragging about her school grades.

She loved the winter smell of wet wool, the parade of colorful coats and jackets.

He was host to all those traveling spirits. She assisted in the hospitality. Tim Murphy's bright and beautiful older daughter.

Suddenly, after years of contented Saturday afternoons—their special time together with the guests—different adventures beckoned: homework, shopping and girl gossip. When she caught the bus—once a month at most—he seemed happy to see her. Yet, he was growing distracted, too.

Then one day the gallant chauffeur disappeared. Vanished.

Leaving Mom.

Abandoning Jeanne and Monica, too. Journeyed out to the Lady Rancher in Wyoming. An exotic, improbable, excruciating ending.

*****

Tonight, the buses barrel by without halting. Years ago, they shifted the stop one street south. The busy Bijou Café is reflected back to her in the front window—tables of people chatting, eating, laughing, sipping wine. As the tiny candles flicker, faces move in and out of focus. Black-clad waiters balance impossibly heavy trays. The server, Martin, delivers a generous glass of sauvignon blanc. Beata is always a few minutes late.

*****

Late, that's what Monica and Jeanne imagined when Dad didn't show up for dinner that Friday night. Mom told them he had a union meeting. The next morning, they found her sobbing. Shaking, she handed over the farewell note. Farewell, as if he'd been a visitor all their lives. Passenger rather than driver.

As years passed, Marie Murphy rued that Wyoming vacation. She'd had a premonition, had campaigned for Colorado. But no, Tim Murphy heard about this Dude Ranch in the Big Horn Mountains. Jeanne and Monica could ride horses and milk cows. Really, his wife said, you just have a big fantasy about the West. Monica doubted either of them fantasized Dorothea, the handsome brunette with the smoky voice. Who would have predicted Tim Murphy would run away from home at age 47?

*****

A long sip of wine and she feels the welt of Mom's grief in her throat. Monica's parents never claimed, or even imagined, the perfect marriage. They bickered about house expenses, church attendance. But the young immigrants had fun too; genuinely seemed to respect each other.

Mom had married for eternity, had followed Dad in his daft plans for a better existence on this side of the ocean. Sure, they made more money here, from his driving and her typing, but was that a fair exchange for leaving their brothers and sisters back in Ireland? Monica knew Dad was happy to escape his parents. Mom's parents, both sets of siblings, the parish, Kildare, the whole bloody country. Then after years creating a new life with Mom, Jeanne and herself in frigid Minnesota, Dad simply rode into the sunset.

Monica thinks now how for years neither Jeanne nor she could forgive the bastard. She still wonders why she sent him a card last Christmas. (Well, he's the only father she'll ever have.) Since then, each of their three short phone calls has been less strained than the previous one. It's not time to tell Mom or Jeanne about the tentative rapprochement, not yet.

Monica senses Beata's arrival before seeing her. Weather in the café has shifted. The other diners stare, catch their breaths, fantasize about this tall, willowy black woman in the stylish fake leopard coat. Movie star? International diplomat? Dancer? She'd guessed dancer when they met years ago at the Y.

"Catch you in a trance, again?" Beata laughs throatily, bends down for a half-hug.

"Brief winter meditation." Monica hugs her back, inhaling the Rive Gauche and the frost smell of her hair. "So good to see you. It's been a week. How are you?"

"Cold," Beata shivers as she slips off the leopard and zips her cardigan.

"Cold?" she teases. "It's been above zero for seven days. Weren't you born in Minneapolis?"

"Not my choice." Beata scans the wine list, beckons the waiter.

Immediately enamored, Martin grins.

"A glass of Sangiovese please."

They clink goblets.

"Here's to an early spring!" Beata sighs.

"Come on, winter is the ultimate season here. Water crystals dangling gracefully from roofs. Tree shadows on snowy lawns. The luscious quiet of night when snow absorbs voices and traffic noises."

"OK for you, Ms. Poetic Minnesota, but my people and my genes came from Louisiana. I've always pestered Dad about choosing the U of M for law school. We're Louisiana folk! And before that, we hailed from an even warmer country. Somewhere."

"I know you love the sweaty heat of August while I long for the crisp dry cold of February. It's a wonder we ever became friends."

Martin serves Beata's vegetarian tower. Even her food is elegant. Much classier looking than Monica's roast pork and potatoes.

She reminds herself not to eat too fast. She does that when she's tired and tonight she's exhausted from clinic frenzy and the weird animosity between Louise and Alonso.

Voices swell around them in the crowded bistro. She concentrates on the scents of garlic, butter, wine, basil. She's glad she nabbed this corner table so far from the smokers in the bar.

"How are things at the Center?"

"Just fine, I guess." Beata taps her fork pensively against the flowered ceramic plate. "It was one of those fundraiser days when you felt more like the chatelaine of a country estate than the director of a top treatment facility. Of course that means interrupting in the counseling schedule, the administrative calendar. Who do they think does the work while we're all sipping tea together?"

"I bet it's galling to perform for some of these donors."

"Lord, yes. Still, private facilities depend on these rich philanthropists who live in Never-Never Land."

Monica thinks back to her own tedious hours with insurance forms. "Money, if we didn't need money, we could concentrate on the work."

"So how's Lake Clinic?"

"You read my mind."

"Hardly." Beata sips the Sangiovese. "Sometimes your face takes on that distinctive 'yet another day at the clinic' expression; a cross between rage and anguish."

"One of those Dr. Jill days. She's doing a 'hot' radio series this week."

"I caught that during breakfast, some new diet for pregnant women?"

"Who knows?" Monica is abashed by her searing hostility for the prima donna wonder doc who graduated first in her Northwestern Med School class to a national column in *Women's Way* to become the Twin Cities celebrity medico. She misses two thirds of clinic meetings and when she does appear, makes suggestions that have already been tried. Louise insists she brings "visibility and cachet" to the clinic. Monica waits for the malpractice suit from neglected patients. Unaccountably, they love her too. Perhaps people like the secondhand glamour. Still, it can't do much for their strep throats.

Across the room, an abstract painting with large purple lines catches her attention. There's something cold, ghoulish, about its blobby texture, intense color. Monica likes almost everything at the Bijou except the thunderously bad art.

"Girl, you could use some detachment from that woman."

"I imagine you're not advising the kind of detachment that ends in homicide."

"Nooo," Beata takes a bite of her towering vegetables. "St. Olaf's is sponsoring a serenity retreat up at Lutsen next month."

"Thought we had a détente. I don't make snarky comments about your prodigious designer shoe collection and you don't hassle me about returning to the Church."

"Listen: Lutsen is absolutely your kind of place. Rustic cabins overlooking frozen Lake Superior. Perfect for the winter poet."

"I could ice fish while you listened to the padre ramble?" Monica eats the last of her delicious, proletarian pork. "Bizarre that we survived Catholic schools with such opposite reactions. Maybe your nuns were less dogmatic."

"Maybe." Beata grows quiet.

"Well, compared to my education in blue collar Saint Paul, your Minneapolis classes sounds like Manhattan."

Beata examines her newly manicured nails. The deep red matches her lipstick.

"Sorry about the retreat." Monica's heart sinks. "I know St. Olaf's is important to you. Retreats just aren't my thing. Truce?"

"Truce." Beata takes her hand. "Another glass of wine to celebrate Friday?"

What would she have done without Beata's friendship during these stressful years? As Jeanne distanced herself, Beata assuaged the pain and loneliness. She loves her younger sister. But now she's vanished, like Dad.

"Earth to Monica. Are you there?"

Monica glances at the dessert menus and the two fresh glasses of wine. "I was just thinking, 'Freedom is what Saturdays are all about.' "

"Pardon?"

"You said that at the Y when we were getting to know one another."

"You were pretty tightly wound then. Not that I'd call you loosey goosey now."

"Med school does that to a person."

"Family does that to a person." Beata drums her nails on the glass table.

"Not that you're a stranger to obsession, 'Ms. Dedicated to the Cause.' "

She rolls her eyes, pushes aside the menu. "You want dessert?"

"You're off topic. Aren't we both a little fanatical about work?"

Beata's face is filled with distress, even repugnance.

"What are you staring at?"

"That purple canvas," Beata laughs dryly. "Do they specialize in bad art here?"

Monica grimaces, "Not the most relaxing image. But you're still off topic."

"I have lots of interests—Jazz, shopping. The Church. And yes, like you, I take work seriously. That's one reason we became friends."

"We've been through a lot together since those early days at the Y."

"Political campaigns, good movies, bad movies. And a few men," Beata nods.

"You have to take credit for the last two jokers."

"*Moi?*" Beata raises her eyebrows, sips the Sangiovese.

"Absolutely. You dragged me to that lawyers' party."

"Dragged?"

"Alright, I was curious. Craig was pretty dreamy at first glance. I was as smitten as you were with Al."

"Remember that weekend in Chicago?"

Monica sees that only three groups of people remain in the quieting café. She loves these long, leisurely dinners with Beata. Sometimes she thinks that everything would be solved if they were lesbians and they could forget about men.

"That trip was fun," smiles Monica. "At least I enjoyed being with you and Al. Craig spent half of Saturday on the phone to his office. He was married to that job." The memory makes her crave another glass of wine. She's walking home tonight. But she has to be alert for the morning clinic. Besides, Jeanne's drinking is getting out of hand and she doesn't want to follow.

"Some might say the same about us."

"Speaking of which, mind if I ask for the bill? I'm on Saturday shift."

"You've worked a lot of Saturdays this winter. You overdoing it?"

"Not really. People get sick in winter."

"Let's hope you're not one of them."

"Thanks." This is the kind of friendship she craves with her sister. Concern. Laughter. Jeanne is so cold, complaining, resentful. Their mother tells her not to worry, that her little sister has always been the sensitive one.

"I'm fine. I did more sit-ups than you in Body Pump class."

"Never crossed my mind to check."

"Right."

They latch arms, walking to the parking lot.

"Damn!" Beata exclaims. "I didn't notice how much it snowed during dinner."

"There, there. Winter princess comes to your rescue."

Brushing away the soft snow, they work fast to ward off the cold.

"Let me give you a lift."

"It's only a few blocks and I need the air."

Beata hugs her. "You're a stubborn one."

"Take care!"

"You do the same, Doctor. Think about taking a break. You could skip the chapel part of the retreat and just wander around the snowy woodland and join us for delicious meals."

FOURTEEN

March, 1997, Minnesota

Monica slips through the dim lobby, sets the steaming latte on her desk and closes her door, careful not to disturb any other early birds.

They all share exam space. Still, this room is her home base. Attached to the ceiling is a blue and red mobile from the Farmer's Market which is particularly popular with women getting pap smears. Men rarely comment on it.

Sipping the latte, she opens the laptop, determined to catch up on the wretched computer system. As clinic director, Louise has persuaded everyone to standardize records. Her interview charts are labyrinthine. In another life, Louise designed torture instruments. Enough, she's got to clean up her attitude toward "teammates" as Louise likes to call them. The woman is a hard worker; everyone has quirks.

She squints at multi-colored tables. God, she misses the intimacy of taking notes as patients talk. Conversation. Making eye contact. Asking intuitive questions. With this computer, she's more of an admissions clerk than a physician, always waiting for the next item on the chart. OK, Louise is right in some ways. What if a patient has a crisis when she's out of town? Who could read her shorthand? She'll get this down. But not this morning because the clinic opens in twenty minutes.

Startled by Brewster's radio, she finishes her coffee and closes the program. Their charming and ever-patient receptionist always begins mornings—before he thinks anyone has arrived—with NPR news.

She opens another program to confirm her schedule: a pretty average day. Three routine check-ups. One flexible sigmoidoscopy. Mrs. Polanski is worried about her memory again. Two people with flu symptoms, a follow-up on Roger's broken arm, an anti-depressant consult, ear infection, skin cancer assessment. A crowded list—she hates how Louise limits consultations to twenty minutes—but still manageable.

Brewster turns off the radio. She hears him clicking on all the lights; his crepe rubber soles squeak on the clean floor.

She opens her door for air.

"Monica!" He looks embarrassed. "Did my radio disturb you? I thought…"

"No, it's reassuring that someone pays attention to world news. I was getting a head start on that new computer program."

He laughs knowingly. "Stunning how much work labor saving devices take."

Her first patient is giggling. Monica remembers Clare was referred by three other lesbian patients. She likes a diverse roster. Wishes it were more ethnically mixed.

"Why so merry?" she smiles.

"Your assistant Gao was refreshing my health history on the computer." She bursts into hysterics. "I guess you have to start from scratch with the new PC system?"

"Yes," she answers neutrally.

"So she asked if I were sexually active."

Monica sees it coming.

"Then she asked, 'with a man or a woman or both?' "

She nods, waiting.

"I said I've been in a monogamous lesbian relationship for twenty years. Then she asked, 'Do you use contraception?' "

Monica blushes at the system's rigidity.

"I couldn't help laughing. 'What kind of question is that?' I teased. Gao shrugged and broke into a small smile."

"Gao has no other option. Our director requires her to ask all the prescribed questions."

Clare laughs again. "It's OK, really. But I can't wait to tell Anita."

*****

Monica hates running late. "Sorry to keep you, Mrs. Polanski."

"Oh, Doctor, I thought they weren't going to let me see you. That nice Chinese lady asked so many questions. I explained I had a doctor. But that didn't matter."

"Gao is my assistant, Mrs. Polanski. She meets with each person first."

"Isn't that nice. I've always liked the Chinese: such industrious people. Polite."

No point in explaining "Gao" means "song" in Hmong; this would take them even further afield.

"How are you doing today? Gao notes that you still need a refill on the hypertension meds and that you have some questions about your memory."

Mrs. Polanski's list of concerns grows longer than either of them anticipate.

The patient's real problems often get mentioned in passing. Clinical Practice 101. She unbuttons her lab coat, realizing this hot turtleneck is a mistake.

Knocking at the door.

"Excuse me." A red-faced Gao delivers the note. From Louise.

Monica doesn't need to unfold the green paper. She's already gone over Mrs. P's allotted time. As a Medicaid patient, Mrs. Polanski isn't high on Louise's triage list.

"Thank you, Gao. Please tell Louise I got the message."

She slips it into her pocket to share with Alonso. Tonight they'll do a "mental health session" over coffee. She's lucky to have a colleague she can be candid with.

"Mrs. Polanski, please ask Brewster for an appointment in early April." Normally, she'd wait for more questions. But she should get to this clinic meeting.

*****

Outside the conference room, she pauses for two deep breaths. Detach, Beata advises. Beata schedules transcendence into her weekly routine. On Tuesdays and Fridays, she eats lunch solo, reading her meditation books.

Louise pointedly consults her watch as Monica enters. Then she continues with the meeting. "We've got to streamline the rota more."

Alonso raises a furry eyebrow to Monica, patting the adjacent chair.

"Yes," Jill is agreeing. "It's like the Peter Principle. The more minutes you have, the more time you waste. These radio spots teach me succinctness, minute by minute economy. If we spent less time, patients might take more responsibility for their own health."

"But," Monica leans forward, "isn't coming to the clinic responsible?" She bites her lip, knowing she should have sat out the first couple of exchanges. She concentrates on her sandwich. The mustard tastes vinegary.

Louise's gaze is frosty. "I believe our teammate is talking about self-sufficiency and not running to mama with each scraped knee."

"Don't you think that's a little patronizing?" inquires Amber.

Monica watches her closely, glad for the comradeship, but concerned about her job security. The nurse practitioner usually keeps to herself at these debates.

Gabe leans forward, fiddling with a tuft of grey in his beard. "We mustn't jump to a decision. We should consider the options prayerfully."

Monica looks at the wall behind Louise where a chart of the human body reveals organs, bones, muscles in garish colors. They are all competent diagnosticians. What do they understand about healing?

"Colleagues," Louise clears her throat. Monica is a little envious of this tall, handsome woman with straight silver hair. Louise's nose crooks at a dramatic angle, yet it's another of her pretty baubles. From the side, her face is magnetic because of the sculpted cheek bones and the pastel blue eyes.

"We have just ten minutes left to..." Louise begins.

She wields fragility and toughness. Monica knows she's as bright as Louise, but lacking strategic instincts. Beata and Alonso have adamantly confirmed that deficit.

"...come to a consensus on patient schedules."

"It's hard to cut off people when they're anxiously talking," Gabe sighs. "Especially older people."

"Your empathy is admirable." Louise's jaw juts almost imperceptibly. "But we're a team here."

"That's right," Jill says sincerely.

Monica wonders.

"We share overhead costs," Louise adds. "Remember the common good."

Brewster raps on the door. "Sorry doc. Patient time."

Seething all the way to the hospital, she warily concentrates on navigating her car through the new blanket of snow. As someone committed to preventive medicine, she should really avoid running over pedestrians. But, good god, the gall of Louise. The coy coolness of Jill. The ineptitude of Gabe. No, Monica, focus on the road.

Entering the enormous brick hospital, she shakes off her irritability. Realistic optimism is the foundation of successful bedside manner. Plus there's reason to be cheerful about Robert. A fit, twenty-six year-old man is strong enough to overcome pneumonia, especially with a new course of anti-retrovirals. She stops at the restroom to brush her hair and splash cold water on her face. "Leave the forces of doomed efficiency behind," she whispers to the mirror. "Let Gabe take care of them in his prayers."

Refreshed, she hurries down the hall to her recovering patient. AIDS is a lottery. Chance and genes foil all predictions.

Robert lies, pale and drawn, staring at the ceiling.

"Hey, you," she cajoles, "I thought you'd be shooting baskets when I arrived."

"Not yet." His voice is thick, soupy.

"The new meds haven't helped yet?" She tries to remain upbeat.

"Which new meds?"

She inspects the chart. "What's this?"

Robert, like most of her HIV/AIDS patients, closely monitors medication. "Insurance company nixed them."

"What? We'll see about that!" she explodes, then calms down for Robert's sake. "I'll be back."

"I'm not going anywhere soon. I hope."

Ben, one of her favorite nurses, is on the phone.

Settle down, she tells herself. Whatever happened, it's not the nurse's fault.

The short black man finishes his call, immediately turning. "Robert?"

"Yes. What happened with the new course of meds I prescribed?"

"Insurance company," he shrugs irritably.

"Why wasn't I called?"

"The resident said she phoned you. I know you were on her list. But we had two cardiac arrests…" He shakes his head. "This really sucks, you know."

"I'll phone the health plan, myself. Can you get the number?"

"Rightie here, Joan of Arc. Best of luck."

She waits five minutes in the "physicians' queue," listening to the Goldberg Variations. Damn. She can't tie up the nurses' line. She needs to get back to Robert, then visit three more people at the hospital before returning to the clinic.

"I'll call from home, Ben. Usually, I get through around midnight."

"Go Doctor!" Ben grins. "Don't wear yourself out."

Lake Clinic is hopping: a typical late winter afternoon. After four patients, Monica forces herself into a time-out, carrying a half cup of coffee to the staff bathroom. Often five minutes are enough. She lets herself get too angry. Maybe she does need Beata's serenity retreat, if only it came without droning priests.

The young man is literally wringing his hands.

"Sometimes SSRI's stop working," She checks his chart. "Five years on Zoloft?"

"No, Dr. Jill prescribed it last spring."

"Really, oh, well, sometimes these computer records are unreliable."

"I met Dr. Jill last April, after hearing an awesome radio program about depression."

"Tell me how long the prescription worked for you?"

He fights tears. "I feel like such a wimp. I drag myself to work and just sit there. I'm going to lose my job. I've already lost my mind."

"Don't blame yourself," she says fiercely. "Depression often has complicated physiological components too. Your therapist's note says you've been in counseling two years. So you've covered the bases."

He tugs a tissue from the box beside her laptop and blows his nose.

"For how long was the Zoloft effective?" she tries again.

"I'd say it lasted maybe a month."

"A month? Why didn't you check back with Dr. Jill?"

"She's been busy. They couldn't squeeze me in. I call every few weeks. Finally I gave up and told that nice guy Brewster that I'd talk to anyone."

"I see. Let's discuss alternatives, non-serotonins like Wellbutrin and Atavan."

"Do they have side effects?"

"All pharmaceuticals have side effects. I was just about to discuss them."

"First, Doctor, what do you think of flower essences? My herbalist wants to try sage."

"I've studied alternative medicines, but flower essences aren't in my repertoire."

Brewster appears at the door in his down parka and woolen cap. "Just wanted to say I'll lock the front door on my way out."

"Sorry, Doctor, I'm keeping you. I can come back when Dr. Jill has an opening."

"As you like," she says, "or you could stay to see if we find another anti-depressant."

"If you're sure I'm not keeping you."

"This is my job. Now, let's consider those possible side effects."

*****

What happened to her weekend? She steps on the gas, determined not to be late for dinner with Jeanne and Mom. Otherwise, Jeanne will snap that she's too busy for her humble family. "Humble family," she actually used that phrase last time. Wild traffic on 94 East! The sunny day has impelled thousands to head for the Wisconsin hills.

She zips off at Snelling, suffused with nostalgia. Summit Avenue—when she was a kid, she dreamed of living in one of the mansions on Summit. She'd marry a doctor and raise a girl and a boy. The poodle would be named Clarence. Most nights, she fell asleep decorating the imaginary house—overstuffed sea green sofa and chairs in the parlor. A grand piano. The shiny oak table graced with fresh flowers. Carnations—how she loved those flowers before the funerals started.

Summit Avenue fantasies evaporated with Dad's disappearance. Realism was her mode now. They had watched TV westerns together. "Wouldn't you love to gallop a wild horse across the mountains?" he'd ask. They studied the constellations on clear nights. "Nothing better, good buddy," he once told her, "than to die under the stars."

Jeanne, on the other hand, had always been Dad's "baby doll." When he left, his pretty doll began to eat and eat. These days, drink appeals more than food.

Easier to let go of being a buddy than being a baby doll. Monica dates her tenacity to those days. Sometimes she thanks him for a healthy dose of pragmatism.

Oakhill Road is five minutes and a world away from Summit Avenue: small wooden houses and carefully kept yards. The exteriors haven't changed much, but Mom's new neighbors are Hmong or Somali. "Fascinating!" she tells Jeanne and Monica.

Guardedly, she climbs the slippery steps, resolving to salt them before she leaves.

Jeanne opens the door. She's checking her watch.

"Busy at work, Doctor?"

She pecks Jeanne's flushed cheek. "Sorry, I ran into unexpected traffic."

"Yeah, I saw lots of cars on the two-hour drive from Duluth." She nibbles an olive from her martini.

Monica sighs. Her beautiful little sister is ten pounds heavier this month.

Jeanne notices Monica's worried look. "Don't get on my case. It's Sunday. Some people go to church. I have a little drink."

"What about church?" Mom appears, wiping her hands on a new flowered apron.

They each smile sheepishly.

"Has one of my daughters finally returned to Mass?"

Monica wraps her arms around this loving woman with curly blonde hair and a wide smile. She looks 10 years older than her 73 years, and Monica feels her fragility as they hug. She senses years of struggle, loneliness and hard work.

Gently withdrawing from the steadfast embrace, she winks. "Every Sunday…"

They speak in unison. "Every Sunday you light a candle for our safe return."

"Two candles," she says firmly.

The sisters smile at one another.

Mom shrugs, returns to the kitchen. "Come help me serve the food."

The table is laden with mashed potatoes, turnips, glazed carrots, roast lamb, mint jelly, like the bounteous Sunday dinners of their youth.

Monica and Jeanne wait for grace, hands folded in their laps.

"Bless us, oh Lord, for these Thy gifts which we are about to receive," Mom prays. "Thank you for bringing our wee family together on Your day. Amen."

They fill their plates, eating silently, perhaps hungrily. Monica, for one, is grateful for the distraction of the food.

Mom turns to her, "Now what happened to that tiny baby—two months premature, I think—you mentioned last time?"

"I'm happy to report—for Mary Anne's sake and for Mom's—that Little Andrea has gone home from the hospital."

"I've been praying for them," she nods in relief. "What about the old lady with the broken hip?'"

Her sister's eyes glaze over. Jeanne has fixed a fresh martini while they were bringing out the food.

"Mending nicely. Thanks for asking, Mom." Shifting the focus, she says, "So Jeanne, tell us what about the bank. How are things at work?"

"Nothing as thrilling as resuscitating preemies or venerable elders."

Monica stares at her plate.

Mom, looking deflated, passes the potatoes.

Monica tries again. "Weren't you revamping your computer system? Our new one at the clinic is driving me wild."

"Technology was never your strong suit."

"Jeanne," Mom reproaches gently. "Monica is asking about your work, your life."

"Unlike Alberta Schweitzer here, my life is not my work." She forks a piece of the succulent pink lamb.

Monica sips water, missing the wine she used to bring to Sunday dinner until she got tired of watching Jeanne consume three quarters of the bottle.

Mom tries again. "Do tell us what's new with you, Jeanne Elizabeth."

"Nothing much. I got promoted to assistant manager three weeks ago."

"Congrats!" Monica cries before she realizes her enthusiasm is bound to annoy.

"It does entail an extra hour of work each day. Remarkable stuff. I get to review the tellers' accounts. Fascinating. And I'm in charge of Travelers Cheques. Imagine the thrill."

Mom tilts her head. "Don't devalue yourself, dear. It's a good job you have. A responsible one. I was never promoted to any kind of management post."

Jeanne cradles her glass pensively.

Monica has urged her to finish college, saddened how this bright woman has isolated herself—moving to Duluth, eating and drinking too much, mocking herself constantly.

Monica recalls her last phone call with Dad: *I don't expect you to understand, honey, or to forgive. But one day on the bus, I realized I wasn't going anywhere, just around and around. I had to get out—out of Ireland first. Then out of marriage. I'm too free a spirit. Leaving was selfish. But I had to.* Jeanne, it seems, has found her own ways of leaving.

"I was remembering that time we all went down to Minneapolis," Mom begins.

Monica is always astonished by her talent for deflection. She loves how her mother says "down to Minneapolis" as if she were describing a trip to Mexico.

"We went down to one of those lakes off Hennepin."

"Lake of the Isles, Mom." Monica grins because Mom often talks about this special Sunday when "the whole family was together as family should be."

"That's right! And your father surprised us all by doing pirouettes on the ice."

Jeanne adds, "And we stopped for cocoa and oatmeal cookies."

There's no sarcasm in her sister's voice.

"Oh, my," Mom races on. "When we got home it was all you two could do to drink tomato soup for dinner. I think we watched *Bonanza*."

"We always had to watch *Bonanza* on Sunday nights until…" Jeanne trails off, draining her glass.

Until Dad followed the Cartwrights out west, she was probably going to say.

"It's strange," Mom tries again, "how sad I felt each time one of those actors died."

"Me, too," Monica nods. "Pa and Hoss and Little Joe."

"It was a stupid *TV program*!" Jeanne explodes. "For Christsake, what's wrong with you two? Jesus!"

"Jeanne Elizabeth! Using such language in this house. And on a Sunday!"

"Mom, sheez." Jeanne ducks into the living room for a refill.

Monica whispers. "She's not planning to drive back tonight in this condition?"

Mom shrugs. "That was the plan when she arrived."

"But Mom, she's a danger."

"I'm her mother. Don't you think I know?" She reddens, then lowers her voice further. "I've already hidden the car keys. We went through this last month, when you were in New York. After an hour, she gave up searching. Called in sick the following morning. And sick the lass was."

"It's been this bad before?" Monica is aghast.

Mom crosses herself.

"What are we going to do?"

"I pray on my knees every night," her voice is breaking.

Beata has suggested an intervention with an alcohol counselor, but

Mom would never discuss family problems in public.

"Her new position must bring a lot of stress. Your sister isn't as self-reliant as you. She's a sensitive one, alright."

Monica refrains from cataloguing her own sensitivities.

"Discussing the problem child?" Jeanne enters, raising her glass gaily.

FIFTEEN

February-March, 1998, Minnesota

Monica inches along the slick, shoveled sidewalk. Beata strides ahead, scoping out the neighborhood.

"Why, again, did you decide to look for a house in February?" She pulls the knit hat over her ears. "It's even more incomprehensible that you're looking in St. Paul."

Beata drops back. "St. Paul is pretty. It has a small town feel. Lots of churches. And well-kept neighborhoods."

"Precisely!" Monica declares, surveying the modest wooden houses with closed-in front porches. Picnic tables and garden chairs sag under six inches of snow. Swing sets stand brittle in the wintry landscape. She takes Beata's arm, unnerved by her own urgency. "Listen, friend, I grew up here. You don't know how provincial and stifling Irish Catholic neighborhoods can be."

Beata laughs, little white puffs of breath dissipating into the frigid afternoon. "Honey, we share a lot of things, but not the same nightmares." Then she grows subdued. "I need change. St. Paul is quieter. I work in our neighborhood all day. I'll see you at the Coffee Shack."

"Our *old* neighborhood, when you move. Past tense."

"Relax, Monica. I'm not dying, just moving to a new place."

"Won't you be lonely over here?" She knows she's overreacting. On a good traffic day, Beata will be 15 minutes away.

"St. Paul is more diverse now. Besides, I don't have your antipathy to churches."

"OK, it's your life. Your choice. And I promise I'll cross the Mississippi to see you if you cross the river to see me." She recalls the relief and freedom of finding her Uptown apartment. Minneapolis always seemed more urbane, sophisticated, indifferent and therefore safe, compared to the sociable streets of St. Paul. As a proud passenger on her father's bus, she often wondered about the differences between Minneapolis's metropolitan avenues and St. Paul streets. Why were the towns called "Twin Cities?"

A cheery realtor in a turquoise pants suit opens the door. "Welcome in from the cold."

Hot cider. Corny. She slips off her wet boots.

"Cider!" exclaims Beata. "What a lovely idea."

Trailing her friend through kitchens with their avocado appliances and compact bedrooms papered in 1960s flowers and forests, she recalls family dinners she precipitously escaped for homework or a meeting of the Foreign Activities Club.

Beata sips cider contentedly in the funky kitchen.

Monica thinks about her friend growing up, daughter of a lawyer and a teacher, in a big modern apartment overlooking Lake Harriet. Maybe what sparks their friendship is the differences. Maybe they're nostalgic for each other's childhoods on opposite river banks.

*****

She glances through the café window at the drifting snow.

"We deserved that lunch!" Beata warms her hands on a cup of mint tea.

"It's been an, um, invigorating day."

"What a true friend, following me through the shadows of your youth!"

She shrugs, savoring the chocolately dregs of espresso.

"Only two more today, I promise," she says contritely. "We're both exhausted."

"I'm not as tired as you. I'm not carrying the weight of a mortgage and renovations."

"You can't live in a rented place forever."

"Of course not. I just sense, I don't know, that something will change permanently in my life when I buy a house."

"Something with Eric?"

Monica purses her lips. "Maybe." She's ready to head back to real estate land.

Beata's dark eyes brighten. "Has Monica been keeping *quelque chose* from her loyal friend who tells her everything?"

"No, no," she squirms in the hard chair. "Hell, something has to happen one way or another. Remember that kid's game, 'Statues?' "

Beata is artfully applying deep mauve lipstick. Monica envies her friend's innate femininity. Lipstick always smears on her teeth and she hates the taste.

"I remember."

"Eric says one thing that throws me into a frozen position. Two days later I come up with a perfectly neutral idea and he freezes. Clearly we're both scared. What's not apparent is whether we're wise to be skittish or whether we're both guy-shy because of our parents' divorces."

Beata nods, deflated. "Same with Arthur. But I'm not waiting on him. I could go grey in rental housing. Working for a non-profit, I have to grab good interest rates."

"Let's get moving before the percentage rises!"

Beata snatches the bill. "My treat, with thanks for your good company."

Immediately, Monica fancies the large brick apartment house converted into condo flats. The entry door has a beveled glass image of two dancing peacocks. The wide stairway is covered in warm blue carpet.

Fact sheets are piled on the marble foyer table.

"No cheery invitation to cider, like the last three places," Monica notes approvingly.

"Crank!" Beata pulls a face. "If you don't like cider, why do you drink it?"

"I don't know."

"This is a palace!" Beata beams at the large rooms.

"Like one of those old New York apartments on the Upper West Side. I remember visiting Tina, my med school roommate, and her parents on Riverside Drive."

"Check out the fireplace! Can't you see me reading here on a cold night?"

"The look of love is in your eyes."

"Let's just sit here a second." Beata pats a cushion on the overstuffed sofa.

Green. Sea green from her girlhood dream. She grins at Beata.

"Yes, I could be peaceful here," Beata sighs. "Remember what I was trying to describe about the sensation at the retreat house? It was this very feeling of being *embraced* by a room."

Monica is happy for her friend. But there's something about the place, the clouded mirror over the mantle, that plunges her into a sudden funk about Mom.

"I'm fine," Mom shakes her head, "it's a little harder to get around, dear, is all. I'd think you'd anticipate that, being a doctor."

"Sure, a touch of arthritis is no cause for panic. Still, you need more help." She leans back in the old kitchen chair inhaling the familiar fragrance of coffee and vanilla. The room has barely changed in thirty-eight years. They repainted the cabinets in the late eighties. And the picture of the Sacred Heart has faded into pink. But she can still see eight-year-old Monica watching Mom measuring and stirring and pouring and making magical sweets with that big oven.

"Mom, did I like hot apple cider as a kid?"

"What makes you think about that?"

"Oh, I had some with Beata recently."

"Strange."

"What?"

"Well, Daddy used to fix hot cider every Halloween. After he left, why I remember you went off your cider. One Saturday I'd gone to a lot of trouble and mess with cinnamon cloves and you complained about the sugar. Bad for your teeth, you said. I thought, Yes, she's going to be a doctor. Funny, never did think you'd be a dentist wearing all that mining gear on your head and excavating in people's mouths."

Monica smiles thinly. Whenever Mom does mention Dad, she always makes a prompt detour. But she hasn't riffed on dental archaeology before.

Mom concentrates on the cookie batter. "Don't fuss over me. I have lots of company. Mrs. Casey drops by once a week. And Mrs. Farah's daughter—you know, the smart one who is following your example and applying to medical school—she still helps with the garbage, the recycling. I'm so lucky to have two lovely daughters." She bends down to the oven for the cookie tray, which has been warming. "Oh, Oh. Ow!"

"What's the matter?" Monica jolts from the kitchen chair.

"Stupid, stupid to forget the potholder." Mom reaches into the freezer. "A little burn."

"Here, let me help." She presses two ice cubes on her mother's thumb.

"I taught you this," she clucks. "An early medical lesson." Her face drains.

"Dear Dr. Mom, I owe you many debts. Now, please take a seat."

She crumbles into the chair. "Don't worry so."

"Hey, what's this?" She lifts her mother's left hand. "All these little scars."

"Now Mickey, you know I'm clumsy."

Clumsy? The nimble woman who typed liked a demon and sewed the straightest hems?

"What about this large greenish purple bruise on your arm? When did you fall?"

"Does it matter? Such little things. Now, do something useful. Just drop a spoonful of batter every few inches and then slip it into the stove. *With the potholder*. I have to have something for St. John's Bazaar."

*****

Monica has been staring at the novel for half-an-hour without turning a page. She switches the lamp to a higher beam and takes in her own pretty, petite living room. All she needs, really.

She misses Beata already. Worries that she'll grow distant in her handsome condo. She's already phoned her twice tonight. She can't be gardening in mid-March, in the dark. Maybe there's a lively condo party with her new neighbors.

She closes the book and switches on PBS, hoping for something illuminating to take her mind off Mom. Yes, she does fuss. And it's important for older people—let's face it, old at 74—to have independence. She does have attentive friends.

Damn pledge night.

She makes a cup of chamomile tea and tries to finish the latest *Guardian Weekly*. She craves international news. Tonight on every page of the paper, she sees as photo of Mom, the poor woman crumpled next to the stove, in her bedroom, grasping for the phone.

She's in the middle of dialing Jeanne before she really thinks about it.

A telephone rings one hundred miles north. It rings. And rings.

Where can Jeanne be? She doesn't know anything about her sister's life in Duluth. Why does she assume Jeanne will be home at 9 o'clock on a Friday night?

"Yes," the voice is oddly defiant.

"Jeanne?" she asks tentatively.

"Yes, this is her."

"Well, this is her sister," she aims for a lighthearted tone.

"Funny." Her voice is recognizable now. She sounds as if she's concentrating hard. "What's up, sister?"

Thunder-and-lightning. Dad's revised nickname for Jeanne in the fourth grade. "Baby Doll" had morphed into a tempest rolling in, flooding the room and extinguishing anybody's good mood.

"You there?" Jeanne barks again.

"Sorry to wake you, I didn't—"

"Wake? I'm just watching a cruddy movie on TV."

Monica identifies the tone: alcoholic, mid-evening. Maybe Beata is right about an intervention. Meanwhile, she should simply call back tomorrow morning. Late tomorrow morning.

"Mom's not doing so well," she hears her desperation to connect with Jeanne.

"Finally," Jeanne says.

"What do you mean?"

"I've been waiting for you to wake up. Obviously she needs help big time. You're the older sister. The doc. I knew you'd notice sooner or later."

Ignore the provocation. Is it too late to suggest talking tomorrow?

"Well?"

She sips the tea, begins again. "Do you think we could talk about it sometime?"

"What are we doing now?" Jeanne takes a long gulp.

She draws a breath. "Maybe this isn't a good moment for you. I can call back."

"Mickey, all moments are pretty much the same for me. I don't have a hectic medical schedule and a fancy social life and trips to Ghana or wherever. I go to work. I come home, fix dinner, turn on the tube. Maybe this isn't a convenient time for you? Maybe you just got beeped for emergency heart surgery or something?"

She's never before felt this degree of anger from Jeanne. She wants to say, *I don't have a fancy social life. I'm often lonely. I'd like to be closer to my sister. I lost Dad, too.* But she can't say this just as she can't say good-bye without alienating Jeanne further. How has this happened—her resentment and coldness?

"We want to handle this delicately, of course. We're both concerned for Mom's feelings. And our own feelings. Some siblings wind up estranged, or worse." How did she get on this track? Jeanne hates discussing emotions.

"I don't pack guns, Mickey. It's pretty straightforward. Mom can't live alone anymore. She can come live with me. I'm a grown up. I have a whole house."

Mom moving two hours north is crazy. She'd miss her friends. Her parish. Monica would miss her.

"Besides I've already invited her."

"You have?" Monica feels the panic and anger rising. "When? Just this weekend, she said—"

"We discussed it the last time I was down. Once I persuaded her to return my keys."

"You drove home that night?" This is out of her mouth before she thinks about it.

"Don't start."

Everything's moving too fast. Monica takes a long breath. "What did she say?"

"She said no," Jeanne scoffs, "because it would hurt your feelings."

SIXTEEN

April, 1998, Minnesota

Walking to Lucia's Café, Monica marvels at the crocuses in the yards on Humboldt Avenue. And the Scylla! Beata says these little blue flowers are also called Siberian Squill. Siberia in Minnesota. No, not hard to imagine. Yesterday she saw a cherry tree flowering on Hennepin. Two weeks ago, sidewalks were treacherously icy; last Monday the temps hit ninety. Now the mid-April weather is more reasonable, about sixty degrees. A truly bipolar climate. Jekyll and Hyde—these Twin Cities.

She steers her mind back to Eric—away from Sunday's family dinner. Tonight she can't do a thing about family. If she wants this sweet man, she has to focus. She's been distant for weeks. He's smart, kind, attentive. Beata is scoping out brides' maids' outfits. Discussing their honeymoon. Whoa, Monica tells her. Not ready. Not yet.

The lawns near 31st Street are dappled with tulips and daffodils. The gingko she loves is almost in full bud. The scent of lilies floats from a nearby yard.

She's wearing an olive green silk blouse for their first anniversary, not that they call it that. Still, when Eric made the date, he asked if she remembered what they were doing last April 17th. No sentimentality, they agreed. They appreciate each other's aversion to sappiness. Of course they share a lot more: political commitments, interests in experimental theatre and new music. Great sex.

He sits at a table by the window, jotting something. Eric values time, uses it well, understands her own work pressures. Sometimes she worries he's sold his soul to the Macalester History Department, but he could say that about her doctoring. Once he laughed, "We're mutually useful auguries." She likes a guy who uses the word *augury*.

From this distance, she registers a man who is handsome, unselfconsciously so—dark, serious eyes, clear olive skin—fit, but not bulked up. The balding doesn't bother her. He keeps his thin hair clipped and hilariously disparages colleagues with "academic comb-overs."

As if sensing her gaze, he glances up.

Yup, there's the dazzling smile. Her heart catches.

She waves, startled as he tucks a small package into his briefcase. Oh, no. She has nothing to give him. Unfair. No sentimentality, they agreed.

Garlic. Tomato. A trace of cigarette smoke from the distant bar. Fresh bread. She loves the aromas of her neighborhood bistro. Jeanne would call Lucia's pricey, pretentious. She needs to leave her sister in Duluth this weekend.

He busses her on both cheeks. She air kisses him back. Cosmo Minneapolitans.

"Nice blouse," he notices. "You look terrific in green."

They scan the wine menu together.

"Is red OK, despite the sudden summer?"

"Amazing weather," he laughs. "I'm not removing the snow tires yet. Remember that storm last May?"

He's cautious. The San Diego boyhood showing.

"Hardly a storm," she parries. "Two inches. Snow melted overnight."

"I love how you savor this town—in all its seasons."

She's blushing. Love? Their favorite table. The suspiciously small *cadeau* in his briefcase. She warns herself not to drink too fast.

"So what were you writing as I walked up?"

"Just notes for my meeting with the Dean next week. He's got a cock-eyed idea about consolidating departments. Absolutely clueless about intellectual integrity."

"Isn't he an academic, too? Don't you have to be a professor to be a dean?"

Eric lowers his voice. "The guy's from Marquette. A psychologist. I guess he barely qualifies as an academic."

She inhales sharply. Always an edge when he talks about Catholic schools. As much as she agrees with him about Church provincialism and imperialism, she's strangely uneasy around the anti-Catholic jokes. "A psychologist. What's wrong with that? Beata is a psychologist."

"Dear Beata is a clinical psychologist. She helps people. And makes no pretence about social science."

"At the moment," she stretches for a lighter note, "with all the fund-raising, Beata doesn't make any claims about being a therapist."

"Another thing about the dean. He wants us to go donor hunting, to help 'grow' the college."

"Reminds me of Captain Louise." She takes a gulp of the rich Pinot Noir.

"Do tell." He butters a slice of multigrain bread.

"No, I promised myself not to gripe about work tonight. Too irritating."

"If you shared the problem it could become less irritating. That's what people who are, um, dating, do, talk to each other."

She sighs, eats bread to absorb the half glass of wine. "We had a meeting on Wednesday, a 'team consult.' Louise got on my case about doing Free Clinic work."

"What business is that of hers?" he demands.

"Good question. I only volunteer one night every two weeks."

"Something I love about you is that you're such an old-fashioned good person."

She shrugs, "Anyway, Louise says it's a conflict of interest, that I can't be part of two practices at once."

"The Free Clinic isn't a practice! She doesn't have a leg to stand on." He reaches for her hand, which has been nervously shredding the label from the wine bottle. "Monica, you have the craziest people in your life. They don't deserve you. Speaking of that, what's happening with your barmy sister?"

How quickly she loses her resolve of silence. "Mom is moving in with her."

"She's going to Duluth?"

"There are some great things about Duluth."

"But living with your alcoholic sister isn't one of them."

"No." She feels the tears brimming.

He hands her a white handkerchief. It smells of Tide and Clorox. Eric is the only person she knows who carries handkerchiefs.

"Why? Why would she leave her lovely neighbors? She's lived in that house twenty-five years."

"Thirty-eight."

The waiter serves their salads.

"So why?"

"It's sad, mad. Mom dragooned me into the kitchen, whispering that this would be good for Jeanne. She wants to help my sister 'take better care of herself.' "

"Jesus Christ."

"Mom has always sacrificed for others."

"How did we become relatively normal people, coming from these nutty families?" Eric's face is long and sad. "Maybe that's what drew us together."

She takes a breath, looks around. The room is packed now. *What drew us together. What I love about you.* OK, she's shy of his affection. Beata says she has "abandonment issues" around men because of Dad. Of course, Beata is once more going over the top.

"Who says we're normal?" Monica grins. "Listen, I need a break from family. Tell me more about the Dean. Do your colleagues agree with you?"

Watercress salads. Shrimp and artichoke pastas. Eric is still venting. It's worrying to see him so wired.

"The administration starts to see you as a teaching and service machine."

Odd how they usually order the same dish. A year ago, she would have switched her choice, then sat through the meal covetously watching him eat her entrée.

"I'm committed to teaching. That's why I chose Mac over large schools. I studied at a small college; I know what a professor can give." He brightens.

Eric has the sweetness of her father, but not a trace of the vagabond. Sometimes she is stunned by his steadiness. Sometimes, just a little stifled.

"I also know that in order to continue giving, I need intellectual nourishment. And their administrative trivia eats up my research time."

He's like a patient facing surgery, naturally absorbed in the precise details of pain, the options for relief.

"That means the dean has to give you more time to research."

He nods vigorously, finishing the pasta.

If Eric is a little long-winded, she has to remember that she asks the questions. She often deflects his queries about her work and family. Why?

"While we're waiting for coffee, I have a little something for you."

Little. She's seen the gift—tiny—and is now fully aware of how much she does not want it. She can hardly breathe for intimacy. With Mom attached to one lung and Jeanne to the other, she cannot add another person.

"Hey," she cries, "unfair. We agreed not to be sentimental tonight."

"Just a small thing," he protests, hurt.

"Let's wait until next Saturday, when I can bring something for you?"

"Come on. You don't have to reciprocate. It's an expression of my feelings—"

"That's just what I don't want!" Has she said this? Can he hear the panic?

A ray of comprehension crosses his pupils. He laughs nervously. "Honestly, I think you'll like this." He presents the small silver box tied with a cherry bow.

Cruel not to open it. She takes a long breath, unknotting the ribbon. Slowly, she lifts the shiny lid.

"Oh," she gasps.

"Do you like it?" He leans forward with that inimitable smile.

"I've always wanted one of these. As kids, we used to call them fairy worlds. But I've never seen one this tiny. Ah, it's Minneapolis, right?" She tips the snow globe and watches white flakes float down the Mississippi River.

"I knew you'd like it," he laughs, relieved.

Blushing, she's startled by a disappointment welling in her chest. Damn her fears and resistance. She does love this guy; why can't she just open up. "Yes, Eric, thank you. I like this very much. I love it."

SEVENTEEN

November, 2001, Moorty

Cold. Grey. Wet. Glorious snow-slicked mountains. She hurries from the clinic to the refectory over a steep, icy path. Prying the heavy door open against late November winds, she spots a large brown package on the table. Beata's handwriting. Monica winces at the heavy homesickness that flooded her with Beata's first letter at Mission House.

How much has changed as these nine months have flown by…and inched along. She feels she belongs to Moorty Mission now. Not that she's comfortable as a Westerner in India or a feminist at King Kevin's court, but she's found navigable waters. Her patients keep returning. She enjoys the health maintenance work. Even Kevin acknowledges her small success. Raul's gradually opening up and Brigid is less frosty. Her friendship with Sudha has grown beyond expectation. And Father Freitas has proved the best of spiritual advisors, helping her accept the Walshes and to be less self-critical. His wry wisdom and affection for everyone is contagious.

From the dining room, she hears animated voices: Brigid and Raul. They're worrying about the young girl with malaria. Malaria in winter. People in Minnesota couldn't fathom this, but the disease takes months to breed in the body before presenting. A cruel fever to spike in this bitter cold. Still, Anu will recover. She's got pluck.

Cook's preparing something spicy. Perhaps he's right that such heat sustains you in winter. Monica now looks forward to chai after lunch. Granted, Cook's chai isn't as rich as the precious cup Emmanuel's mother served her on the way to Moorty, but she's surprised by her new taste for sweet milky tea. The espresso craving is almost gone.

She runs her hands over the address label as if she might bring Beata closer. Well, she, herself, is arriving next month. What has she sent? No, wait until after lunch.

Brigid Walsh smiles. "Hi there. It's just us. Dr. Walsh and Father Freitas went down to the Lower Bazaar. Mrs. Mitra. It may finally be her time."

"I'm sorry," Monica remembers the old woman's reluctant acceptance of painkillers. "She's outlived the prognosis. And she's had those months with her family."

"Thanks to you," Raul says. "The hospice training has been transformational here. By now, everyone says so."

Brigid bites her lip.

"Why did Father go? I didn't think Mrs. Mitra was Catholic."

"She's not," Raul says. "You know *Padre*. They struck up a friendship in the ward. As an outpatient, she always visited him before returning down the hill."

"What do you suppose is in the package?" asks Brigid.

Taken aback by the warm familiarity, Monica shrugs. "I didn't want to keep you waiting. It's something from my friend Beata."

"Oh, the lady who brought you back to the Church."

Monica flushes. Why is she so cautious? She's glad Brigid is warming up. The woman has been more open since she followed Father's advice and invited her to lunch at the Kerala Coffee House. Brigid confided about losing her prematurely born twins. In turn, Monica offered confidences—about Beata, about the first retreat with Father Daniel.

"Yes, a very old friend."

"Isn't she coming soon? Beata, I had an aunt named Beata."

"Women! Talking. Talking. How about some action?" Raul teases. He's often good-humored in Kevin's absence. "Let's see what's in the parcel."

"You don't mind?"

"It's not every day we receive personal gifts from the outside world," Brigid says.

Ceremoniously, Raul carries the box into the dining room and sets it before Monica. He pulls a Swiss Army Knife from his pocket.

"You're prepared," she laughs.

"It's like an early Christmas," Brigid cries.

Monica won't spoil the good cheer. She prays the box doesn't contain something embarrassing like a walleye Jell-O mold. Beata has a certain kitschy Minnesota humor.

"Boots! Lovely!" exclaims Brigid. "May I?"

"Of course," she offers the box, delighted by Brigid's playful side.

"Luscious, fleece-lined, fine tread on the heels. Rich brown leather."

"Perfect gift," Raul nods. "There's a close friend: someone who knows your shoe size."

Monica colors at the attention. "We wear the same size. It's easy to remember." How clumsy. "Yes, Beata is the kindest person I know."

"But you said she does have a sense of humor?" Raul asks.

"Yes, a wicked wit. Sometimes a little corny, though."

"Then I look forward to the visit. You have good taste in friends."

"Sudha mentioned she saw you last week," Monica moves on nimbly.

"Yes, we noticed you in the Tibetan restaurant," Brigid perks up.

Monica stares into the middle distance to curb her astonishment at this new social curiosity from Mrs. Dr. Walsh.

Clearly amused by the female curiosity, Raul intercedes, "We were eating dinner as the Walshes walked into the restaurant." He turns to Brigid. "Sudha Badami is a teacher at the local school."

"We've met. I know Dr. Walsh is taken aback that he hasn't been invited to lecture at her classes as you two have done."

She still calls him "Dr. Walsh," like "Mr. Lincoln," even though Raul and Monica always use people's first names—with the exception of Father.

"I suppose she can't ask everyone," Raul tries.

Monica had been surprised when Sudha offhandedly mentioned the dinner. She said Raul wanted to discuss reading and math workshops in Manda, using her advanced students as tutors. But given how Sudha fretted over which sari to wear, Monica knew more was going on. Raul, himself, was particularly cheery last week.

Cook, the tactful choreographer, appears with steaming vegetable *biryani*.

Brigid bows her head. "Bless us, O Lord…and bless Mrs. Mitra. May she join the Communion of Saints before surrendering her mortal life. Amen."

Raul and Monica exchange glances.

Monica has heard gossip about Brigid secretly baptizing newborns, but keeps telling herself this is preposterous. Surely she'd lose her visa. And jeopardize the whole hospital.

Raul adds, "Please help little Gita. Amen."

To this Monica adds, "Amen." She's not confident for Gita.

Brigid passes the steaming fragrant *biryani*. "How is the child?"

"Holding her own," Monica shakes her head. "We've ruled out malaria, cholera, typhoid and encephalitis. The fever persists and the diarrhea."

Raul is tired and edgy, "We tested for salmonella, schistosomiasis, as well as shigellosis."

They sit in silence, half-heartedly eating the delicious rice.

"Monica stayed up all night with Gita," Raul shakes his head.

"I did not."

"I heard you return to the residence at 4:30 a.m."

Monica rubs her hands. "I sat with her a while, then fell asleep in the chair. Sister Catherine shooed me to bed. So you, my friend, are the night sentry?"

"No, I had a troubled sleep. The avalanche victim. Hopeless, given his state on arrival. I can still see his terrified eyes. His brother's anguished face."

"Very strange," Brigid whispers. "Rock slides in this season. So much more likely in late May, after the melting. But you did all you could. I noticed the night before you didn't come home yourself, until early morning."

"What's this?" Monica asks. "Doesn't anybody sleep around here?"

"Usually I sleep like a log. Perhaps I awoke when Raul crunched on the snow outside. Winter nights are so quiet. I love the snow reflecting the brilliant moonlight."

"Minneapolis is like this. Not mountainous, of course. But the snow illuminated by sun and moon. I love it too." How odd that Beata is coming in the cold season. Maybe she reasons she's just trading one winter for another.

They slip into separate reveries until Cook presents the tray of chai. Monica watches Raul add extra sugar.

"Looks like an overflow clinic this afternoon," she frets.

"Yes," Brigid says with satisfaction. "When we opened, we sometimes waited days for a patient to walk in."

"I hope we see them all. I hate asking them to walk all the way back tomorrow."

"We could use a few more docs," Raul murmurs.

She adds, "And a new surgical lamp, a stronger generator..."

"Dr. Walsh expects some large donations. He was very effective in Chicago."

Raul and Monica rise in unison.

"Thank you very much, Cook," Monica calls into the kitchen.

"*Muchas gracias*, chef!"

Traveling with Spirits

*****

Gita rallies a bit after dinner. Sitting with the child, Monica thinks about Father Daniel's quick response to that anxious email. Her loyal mentor and friend said she was pursuing the right tests and urged her to pray. Watching Gita's breathing, she wonders why she ever thought she had special gifts as a doctor. Because she cares? They all care. Raul also prescribes prayer for Gita. Still, isn't there some test they haven't tried?

"*Pani*," a little voice.

"Right here, Gita dear," Monica answers in Hindi and holds a straw to the girl's pale lips.

Such a pretty child, darker than many local people, with high cheek-bones and a nose that will one day be long and noble. There's already something valiant about her. She sees the pain in Gita's eyes and the loneliness. Also a kind of acceptance.

Her poor mother has five other children. Eyes filled with fear, she comes at least once a day to sit with Gita.

Gita manages, "Thank you."

The first English she's heard from the child. Who knows? "Thank you" is as much an Indian phrase as an English one.

"*Koi bat nahi*," she concentrates on Sudha's pronunciation of "You're welcome." She tries to remember the first verse of that simple Hindi lullaby she and Sudha practiced last week, "*Omana Thankal Kidavo*." Very softly, almost in a whisper, she sings:

> "Is this sweet babe the bright crescent moon,
> or the charming flower of the lotus?
> The honey in a flower
> or the luster of the full moon?
> A pure coral gem
> or the pleasant chatter of parrots?
> A dancing peacock, or a sweet singing bird…"

Gita extends her tiny lips to a half smile and closes her eyes.

Monica sings the verse again and again until Gita's breath evens out in sleep.

Sitting back, she surveys their clinic in the dim evening light. Here at the end of the ward, among the sleeping patients, she settles into a new contentment. Yes, she's worried about Gita. But the day has gone well. It was helpful to talk to Father Freitas about Kevin. As Father noted, the man works hard for his patients.

Monica breathes in the almost comforting scents of disinfectant and pesticide. Despite night-muted lights, she can see Sister's orderly desk. The sparkling instrument cart next to the door. The crucifix over the entry. Moonlight pours in the window, past the curtain, down by Mr. Singh's bed. He'll be recovered this week. She plans to take him up on the promise of a small bag of the sweetest winter apples from his stand.

Gita stirs. Steady breathing returns. A dream? A nightmare? How terrifying for a child to be in hospital. Especially a hospital with white doctors.

Gita mustn't feel abandoned. She'll sit up with her each night. It's unthinkable that this child might "leave us for Heaven," as Brigid would say. Unthinkable.

*****

"First you boil water," she says again. "*Then* you slip in the pasta."

"I never cook rice this way," objects Sudha.

"Rice is a different food." She laughs.

"Why should I trust you?" Sudha bends over the water, hands on her hips. "Murphy's not an Italian name."

"Someone who's lived in Britain should know an Irish name when she hears one."

" 'Britain' is an English word. Scotland is a country to itself. So is Ireland. The English claim everyone by using 'British' for Welsh, Scots and Northern Irish people."

"I see. You're not a Hindu nationalist. You're a Celtic nationalist."

"Less thuggish company."

"Depends on which Celts."

Monica tries not to worry about the R.S.S. They haven't come back for months, not since a long argument with Raul at the gate.

"Let's return to culinary issues. How are those diced onions?"

"All complete, see—onions, peppers, courgettes, everything sliced as per your rather peculiar instructions. Shouldn't we start them now?"

"Maybe the onions over a low fire. We want the vegetables *al dente*."

Sudha looks dubious.

"Now didn't I follow obediently when you taught me to prepare *porotta*?"

"No need to be from Kerala, *porotta* is an Indian food."

"At this point, *pasta* is an American food."

Sudha smirks, attentively browning the onions.

Monica concentrates on chopping tomatoes. Something about Sudha compels her toward perfection. It's not at all the kind of judgment she feels from Jeanne. Rather, it's a positive expectation. She often thinks that Sudha is rather perfect, herself: fiercely intelligent, funny, dedicated, beautiful, modest, generous.

They sit across the candlelit table. She runs her hand over Sudha's Ikat cloth from the *mela*, closing her eyes, savoring the almost Italian aromas. She'll ask Beata to bring proper spices. She says a silent prayer of gratitude for Sudha's friendship.

Is she in awe of Sudha the way she used to idealize Beata? No, she simply admires her. Each friend is so different from her beloved mother and troubled sister. Class: they both carry the poised self-assurance of people born into the upper-middle class. And she's enough of her own person that clear-sighted fondness for Beata has replaced idealization.

She opens her eyes to find Sudha studying her warily.

"Parmesan!" she declares to forestall her friend's mind-reading. "I'll ask Beata to bring a good chunk of Parmesan, too."

"This tastes good to me. You were right about the crunchy vegetables."

"So it's international cuisine week. Italian tonight. Tibetan last Sunday."

"Yes," she tries to sound off-hand. "Raul's proposal for tutoring in the remote areas is quite interesting."

She recalls that Raul credited Sudha with the idea. "You spent the evening discussing medicine and education?"

Sudha stammers, "W-we talked a little about our families." She pauses apprehensively. "Don't go presuming things, Dr. Busybody. As a feminist, I'd reckon you're used to ordinary friendships between women and men."

"Of course." Sudha can be very private. She'll learn the details in time. In time.

"And he started to tell me about St. Thomas. Fascinating. When the Walshes walked in, he got edgy. We left shortly afterward."

"Too bad."

"Still, I was curious, from a historical point of view. He said that Thomas came in the first century to Parthia, Kerala and then traveled to Tamil Nadu."

"So we're taught."

"I always wondered about those Syrian churches. Not only in Kochi, but dotted all through the back waters of Kerala."

"They say Christians have traveled here for centuries. Alfred the Great sent Anglo Saxon envoys to the Thomas shrine at Madras in the 9th century. St. Francis Xavier visited Goa in the 1500s. Robert di Nobili preached in Madurai in the early 17th century."

Sudha looks a little abashed by her suddenly instructive friend.

Monica explains. "I studied for months before I came."

"No wonder, then, there are so many of you people in my country."

"India had Christians centuries before Ireland, over a millennium before the Americas."

She mutters, "Just as well Dr. Sanchez didn't get into this. With you, I can argue. But I'm not so familiar with him."

"Sounds as if you're getting better acquainted."

"Speaking of growing acquaintances, isn't your Ashok due next week?"

"He's not my Ashok," Monica says, while noting the pleasure of hearing his name. "Yes, he's coming up. Then we'll take the train down together and I'll meet Beata at the airport."

"Ah, that train. You have a treat in store."

*****

Gita's mother weeps loudly into clenched hands.

Walking into the busy ward, Monica imagines the worst. This is her first break from the outpatient clinic today. Sister reported at lunch that Gita's fever was down and she allowed herself to relax. Damn. Didn't she learn anything from Mom's abrupt turn?

"Mrs. Roy," she bows. Immediately she turns to the child.

Gita's eyes are wide and bright, "*Namaste, ji.*"

Relieved, Monica smiles. "*Namaste*, Gita."

For Mrs. Roy, she summons her budding Hindi. "What is wrong? Gita's fever is going. That's a wonderful sign."

Sister Catherine intercedes. "She wants to take her home. But she's still short of breath, can hardly sit up."

Monica holds Mrs. Roy's hands. Calmer now, the woman weeps more quietly.

"Of course you long to have her home. We can help her more here. She's still quite sick."

"Gita doesn't want to go," Sister Catherine impatiently rubs her small hands together. "I told Mrs. Roy you would refuse to release her."

She blanches. "We can't refuse anything to a parent, Sister, as you know."

The usually sensitive nun turns on her heel.

"Sister is worried about Gita," Monica apologizes. "We all are. We are still doing tests. She does need to rest here a while longer."

Gita nods.

Still crying, Mrs. Roy kisses her child and whispers something.

"A few more days, then," she struggles. "We love our daughter."

Monica wants to say, *We love her too*. Instead, she replies, "We know that. More importantly, Gita knows." She guesses the girl will need to be here quite a while.

Gita smiles weakly.

Abruptly, Mrs. Roy turns to the door and departs.

Monica stands to go after the distraught woman, then turns as Gita reaches for her hand.

"Yes," Monica smiles. "I'll sit with you a bit. That's a better idea."

EIGHTEEN

November, 2001, Moorty

His train is late. Monica paces the windy platform, pulling up the hood of her down coat.

"The train is a far more sensible vehicle for reaching Moorty," Ashok instructed. *"Why did you allow Sister Margaret to book the plane and that ridiculous van?"*

A notably charming Indian trait is people's certitude in one of the most unpredictable places on earth. She worries about how exhausted he must be. They'll never do half the things she's planned for the weekend. Whew, this platform is bitter cold.

Ordinary friendship between men and women. Sudha's phrase is reassuring. Still the relationship between Raul and Sudha has become something more during recent dinners. More than her own connection to Ashok, who's coming here to relax from hectic Delhi. Despite his early gruffness, he does like Americans. He loves talking about grad school in New York. Clearly he's eager to discuss the Madison conference. They're drawn to each other's cultures. A sound basis for ordinary friendship.

"So sorry to keep you!" His bright brown eyes brim with distress. "You might have frozen to death. No need to wait hours here. I would have found the clinic."

She laughs, shaking her head.

He smiles cautiously, "What are you laughing at?"

"You. Your certainty." Now, to sidestep argument, she extends her hand. "It's good to see you. You must be very tired."

"Indians know how to travel on trains." He tilts his head from side to side. "I brought lots of work, plenty of food and water. I had my Walkman. I was perfectly..."

She's laughing again. Feeling ridiculously giddy.

"OK. OK, I see what you mean. Yes, maybe I am a little knackered," he admits. "That tie-up with the rails in..."

"They announced the obstruction. I was delayed in the same metropolis, myself, as I left in the airport van."

"The van, a bad idea. A very bad idea."

"Come." She pays him no notice. "Here's a porter to carry your bags. It's a forty-minute walk to the mission."

"Walking, yes." He looks crestfallen. "I had forgotten the environmental regulations against cars."

"We could stop at the Kerala Coffee House on the way, for some refreshment."

"A capital idea," he grins at her. "Capital."

"*Namaste, Doctor ji,*" The old waiter murmurs while scrutinizing her companion.

"*Namaste, Rabi.*" Then, in her best Hindi, "Are there seats at the back?"

"The usual ones, yes," he tilts his grey head.

They settle into the window table.

Ashok widens his eyes for effect. "A regular, I see. The usual seat. Name recognition. Property rights."

"Sudha and I have been here a few times."

"More than that, I reckon. Old Rabi inspected me as if I were a *dacoit* out to kidnap his only daughter."

She flushes, pleased.

"This isn't your India International Center window overlooking the gardens," she demurs. "But I enjoy lurking back here, gazing at Lower Bazaar. You can even see the *sabzi mandi*. That apple stand of Mr. Singh's has the sweetest fruit."

Ashok peers over his rimless glasses. "You sound like a girl in love."

"I don't know about the girl part, but Moorty does have its allure."

He watches inquisitively.

Rabi brings mineral water for her, plain water for him and coffee-spotted menus.

She introduces them, "Ashok is a professor from Delhi University."

"Delhi," Rabi repeats noncommittally.

"His family belongs to Kerala."

"Welcome," he says finally.

Ashok studies the menu. "Monica?"

He's caught her glancing down at the winter vegetables in the snowy market. "Monica, where have you gone?"

Surfacing, she realizes he's been musing about Mrs. Mitra's courage,

Gita's longing, Brigid's curiosity about Sudha and Raul. Her own curiosity. She's entered an entirely new world since leaving Ashok in Delhi.

"Aren't you ordering anything?" he asks in that recognizable, clipped voice.

He'll have to slow down to adapt to Moorty. "Perhaps *idli sambar* and *uthapam* for lunch."

He regards her querulously.

"I'd rate the food a cross between Nathu's and The Malabar Coast Café."

"That's a long chasm to traverse," he raises his eyebrows.

"Well, you could ask Rabi for recommendations."

"I'll stick with a more affable advisor, thanks."

Ashok happily munches his *idli sambar*. Between bites, he chats about Madison, says how much he likes the department there. He moves on to Delhi University politics.

She flashes back to that night at Lucia's Café. How different Ashok is from Eric, although they're both professors, both in their early forties and filled with intensities. Ashok has more fire, she thinks.

"Have I put you to sleep entirely?"

"On the contrary."

"I haven't asked about your patients. Your colleagues. What's the boss's name, Dr. Blowhead?" He studies her mischievously.

She slaps a hand over her mouth. "Did I put that in an email?"

He raises dark, thick eyebrows. "Your occasional irreverence is quite agreeable."

"Please call him Dr. Walsh."

"Blowhard. Blowhead. The name trips off a person's tongue."

"Time we started up the hill. They've forecast a storm. The porter will already have delivered your bags."

She slows to maintain pace with Ashok, aware that she's developed what Sudha calls "mountain legs."

"Wow." He stops by a bench at the ridge. "The peaks are high over there."

She grins, proudly, as if the Himalayas were hers to share.

"I see your backwater does have its compensations."

They resume the journey at a slower pace. She points out the stationers, the internet shop, the fancy comestible store. Imagining Moorty through his eyes, she sees again how picturesque it is, under snowy roofs in this November light. They stop at the newsstand. The vendor grins, handing her *The Herald Tribune* and *The Hindu*.

Ashok observes, "Rather decent range of media."

She rolls her eyes. In some ways he and condescending Kevin might hit it off.

"That's Moorty Playhouse, built in the 1890s. We have tickets to a performance there tomorrow night."

"Impressive building," Ashok notes, "even if the façade is a little rococo. Hope it holds up for another twenty-four hours."

"You'll have to lose that Delhi snobbery before we reach the hospital."

"You're not fun. Oh, I'm staying with a priest, right?"

"No. For an academic," she teases, "you're a little foggy with facts."

"Philosophers are more partial to ideas than facts." He laughs.

"Father Freitas is on holiday in Goa and has offered his room in the downstairs flat he shares with Raul Sanchez, my medical colleague."

"Very kind," Ashok says. "I promise to be a good guest."

He's winded. So she pauses, pointing to langurs huddling high in a tree.

*****

They trek down to the ridge wielding walking sticks on the icy road. An overnight storm has left a snowy blanket over the hillsides. She's grateful for Beata's boots and relieved Raul loaned Ashok some winter shoes. The man lives in his head. Doesn't he remember winter from New York? Well, his amazement at all things natural is as entertaining as it is trying.

"Too bad we don't have a sleigh."

"Next time, I'll order one," she says. *Next time*—she's making assumptions.

"Next time," he smiles, "I'll surprise you with my fancy polar anorak."

She slips.

He catches her arm for balance. "Are you OK?"

"That's what I get for my winterly superiority. I'm fine, thanks."

He continues to support her arm lightly.

She likes the steadiness and warmth of his hand.

They fall silent until they reach St. Michael's Church which the Anglicans are beginning to decorate for Christmas.

"Festive," he observes.

"Yes. Their choir sings lovely Bach Masses."

"Perhaps we can go hear them on Sunday?"

She's dumbstruck.

"Don't be like that. You know I like music. All good music."

"Sure. On the way to the train." Such a short visit. She takes a step, and breaking contact with his hand, notices a patch of cold above her elbow.

"It will be great fun to travel together to Delhi. A shame you and Beata can't stay longer in the city. I'd be happy to play tour guide next weekend."

"The hospital is already being generous with leave. Next time."

"Tell me about these people we're meeting at the Playhouse."

"Raul, of course, you know. And our friend Sudha."

"Are they partners or companions or…"

"Ordinary friends." She pictures Sudha's expression. "Ordinary friends, like us."

"Like us." He's suddenly tired from the walk. "Oh, right, precisely."

Women in glittering kameezes and luscious heavy silk saris swish around the ornate lobby. The gentlemen wear suits, fancy kortas and fine Kashmiri shawls.

"The State Governor is attending," Ashok whispers conspiratorially. "I heard two excited men chatting in the loo. You've brought me to the season's cultural event."

"We'll see." She peers around for Raul and Sudha.

"Why don't I find us seats? You wait for Raul and Sudha here."

Two young women appear in slacks and sports coats. Are they lesbians or trying to look cool or both? She doesn't think she's met any queer Indians. She's read Indian novels with gay characters. And she saw Fire before leaving Minneapolis.

"Hi Doctor."

"Hello, Radha, how are you?"

"Quite keyed up! My sister is dancing tonight."

"How lovely."

"Hello Doctor!"

"*Namaste*, Doctor Murphy."

Several other people nod or tent their hands in greeting. She wishes Ashok were here, to witness how she's become a small part of the community.

Rumor spreads about the Governor being delayed in traffic on the Cart Road. People secure their shawls and wander outside to the starlit mall.

Finally. Sudha and Raul. She wears a stunning rose sari; Raul looks spiffy in his golden kurta.

Ordinary friends. Monica recalls Ashok's reaction to the term.

"I hear we're waiting for the el gobernador," Raul snickers.

"Yes," she beams at the two of them. "Ashok is holding seats for us."

"Ah, the elusive Ashok." Sudha winks. "What are we doing out here? Who cares about the Governor? Professor Mystery awaits within."

"He seems a rather average bloke," Raul balks.

"Yes," Monica says meaningfully. Average. Ordinary. "Raul, I love it when you use British words like 'bloke.' "

"It means 'man,' yes? What would you say?"

" 'Guy,' I guess."

"Oh, I think you'd be more descriptive," kids Sudha.

Monica recalls the warmth of his hand above her elbow.

"Yes?" Raul encourages.

"No, it's Sudha who would be more descriptive, who specializes in embroidery. Come on; let's not keep our bloke-guy-man waiting."

Ashok has expertly nabbed seats by the aisle near an exit.

Monica recalls their discreet escape at the India Habitat Center. She hopes they'll see Radha's sister. Raj's sister.

Sudha sits beside Ashok and launches into spirited questions. Ashok seems to be answering with amusement and elaboration.

Raul, on the aisle, regards the tête-à-tête, then shrugs.

Monica, surrounded by friends, realizes she hasn't felt this light-hearted since she came to India.

Patrons in vivid saris and fancy kurtas and natty sports coats drift into the theatre.

Suddenly he's here, the Governor, standing on stage.

Polite clapping.

He lights candles before a small bronze statue.

"That's Saraswati, Goddess of Arts," Ashok leans over.

The first set is harmonium, sitar and tabla.

Ashok listens intently and she's pleased by his avid enjoyment.

Monica returns to the music, but her eyes glide up the rich brown, gold and white edging of the Governor's box. The ceiling is bordered with the same colors. The showy late Victorian skylight is cut in ornate stencil-like openings.

Sometimes she feels she hasn't just traveled to India, but to a different century.

Radha's sister is next, part of the *Bharatha Natyam* dance troupe. Such grace and discipline. She thinks about Raj. About how discipline runs in the family.

The audience loves this performance, interrupting frequently with applause.

During the next group, people walk in and out, handing cranky babies down rows to nearby relatives.

Sudha nods to Raul and whispers to Ashok. Her three friends stand to leave although the performance will continue for hours. Monica doesn't want to go. She wants to stay wrapped in the ornate décor, beautiful music and pleasant buzz of sociability. She's not ready for the next step, for Sudha's innuendo over dinner. Still, she is hungry. And Monica knows she can't stop the world from spinning on Sudha Badami's axis.

*****

Ashok falls into a deep, if not sound, sleep as their train rattles toward Delhi. Of course he was wrong about the train's superior comfort. The hot, noisy car clings precariously to the rails as they descend the mountains. No smoother than the van and a lot more chaotic.

They've found two seats next to a filthy, but translucent window. The atmosphere is earsplitting: ebullient men's voices, cawing children, mobile phones, rustling newspapers. Overhead racks are crammed with antique brown valises, purple backpacks and a few American-style roll-ons. The thick blue—grey—and formally white curtains bear an unfamiliar flower as the railway monogram. At each stop, the heating system shuts down.

Hours pass. Months, perhaps. Volume increases—phone chats; male camaraderie; babies crying; snoring.

How can Ashok nap trough this? The mountain weekend must have exhausted him.

She buys several curious-looking samosas. And one cup of tea. One suffices. One visit to the stand-up toilet on this ricocheting train.

Half-an-hour before Delhi, Ashok opens his eyes and stretches expansively.

He smells riper now and she likes this taste of intimacy. Wishes there had been more intimacy in Moorty. But how? At Mission Hospital?

"I must have dozed a few minutes," he mumbles.

"Try hours."

"We're almost home." He recovers his authoritative vigor. "You and Beata truly should spend more time in Delhi. The next two days are packed, but after that I'd love to—"

"Thanks, but as I said, I have to get back to the hospital. Gita—"

"Surely others are looking after her in your absence."

"Sister Catherine says the girl waits for me. Besides, I promised Beata the hill country. Mountain views. If she wanted a city, she could have stayed in the States."

"No cities like Delhi in the States."

"Indeed. Perhaps on her next visit."

Next time. Next visit.

"Then you are planning to stay in India a while."

Although he's trying to be ironic, she's touched by the intensity in his voice.

Reddening, she answers. "Who knows with the dicey visa situation."

He falls silent.

"Thanks for coming up this weekend and for escorting me down on the train."

"A sleeping escort. Very gallant." He shakes his head. "I slept an hour?"

"Perhaps three."

He looks incredulous. "Thank you for the hospitality. For showing me Moorty. For introducing me to your colleagues."

"*Koi bat nahi.*"

"For raising the concept of *ordinary friendship*," he adds archly.

Befuddled, Monica hopes he's trying to tell her something. The repartee is maddening. Still, he probably considers her an excessively literal American.

"Seriously, though."

He's clearly returned full force to advice mode.

"Yes, Professor?" She looks bright and attentive.

"At the station, I will escort you to a taxi and arrange the fare to the airport."

He's forgotten she lived in Delhi almost a month.

"Don't protest. And once you collect Beata take a pre-paid taxi to town."

"Thanks. I believe I've heard that advice before."

He continues earnestly, "Then ring me, please, on my mobile, once you're safely at the IIC."

How can she be irritated with someone whose face is so creased in apprehension?

"Will do, sir!" She grins, touched by his concern. She's elated at the prospect of seeing Beata, imagines the two of them gliding through New Delhi in a pre-paid taxi.

NINETEEN

November, 2001, Delhi and Moorty

Monica peers over the shoulders of huge welcome parties. She didn't expect to find six family members awaiting each passenger. The excited crowds transform the cold airport into a festival. So many people. What if she misses Beata?

A chauffeur waves his sign in front of her face: "Patel's Incredible India Tours." She inches to the left, clutching a receipt for the pre-paid taxi. Tonight is chillier than usual. She hopes Beata is warmly dressed.

There she is! Dearest Beata looking tidy and fresh in her cobalt blue dress, a black coat over her shoulders. Yes, the ubiquitous knock-off Coach handbag and sensible black roller-luggage. Clearly she knows how to fly. She's nothing like the bedraggled Monica of eleven months ago. Well, it does help that James bumped her up to business class with miles. Incredible that Beata is here and…

"Beata!" she calls. "Beata, over here!"

Her friend swivels. Their eyes lock. They each burst out laughing.

The Incredible India chauffeur glances at her, then at Beata and approves. "Friends. Very nice."

Finally at the end of the barricade, they embrace.

Her hands gripping Beata's strong shoulders, she declares, "Welcome to India!"

"Girl, it's sooo good to see you. You have no idea."

"I think I do." She's infused with nostalgia for Minnesota and their friendship deeper than anything she's allowed herself to feel this year.

"You look great!" Beata exclaims.

"You too." Monica notices a crease of fatigue. "You must be beat. Let's get a taxi and we'll be at the India International Center in no time."

"I thought we were staying at Mission House."

"We were. Then Ashok insisted that I shouldn't subject you to their damp guest rooms. And at the IIC we'll have more freedom during our two days in Delhi. Ashok is a member and made the booking."

"A man in the know."

"Quite," she says, stepping in to take control of the baggage cart. "You shouldn't be pushing that." She studies Beata's face, searching for changes.

"Ha, you should see how much I've improved at Body Pump since you left."

"I don't want to think about it."

The next morning, Monica settles in for breakfast at a window table. No telling when Beata will wake. She'll never forget her own long slumber the first night. Sister Margaret was far too understanding.

A small green parrot flies over a tree in the Lodi Gardens. Extraordinary all the things she's seen since that first parrot during her lunch with Ashok. She finds herself daydreaming about his laughter, even about their arguments. She's not ready to get involved. It's too soon after Mom's death. She still thinks about Eric. Not romantically, no, but she recalls the limitless kindness of the most innately sweet man she's ever known and feels a certain loyalty. She worries her interest in Ashok is confused with his connection to India, which she wants to embrace.

The waiter serves her a juicy slice of coral pink papaya, perfectly cooked poached eggs with toast and a spoonful of potatoes. A Western breakfast; she didn't know she was craving this.

"Another pot of coffee, please." Coffee. Real, filtered coffee.

Dad's letter is such surprise. She rummages around her Sportsac (far less orderly than Beata's handbag) and withdraws a white envelope to re-read his letter.

Dear Mickey,

How are you, way off in India? India! Did you get the traveling bug from your dear old dad?

She wonders. She likes to think she came to India rather than that she left home. Do people feel abandoned? Yes. Eric for one. Beata. Patients. Even some of her colleagues. Although she didn't leave a wife and kids, her journey isn't without cost.

I'm sorry I haven't written back since your mother's death. Are you and Jeannie doing OK? Her death hit me harder than I expected. Made me realize all the things I left unsaid, to Marie. To my girls.

He hasn't seen them since they were girls. Would they recognize each other?

I don't have a lot to write about our lives out here, but I wanted to touch base with you. Dorothea tells me I shouldn't lose you again by being lazy even though I'm not much of a letter writer. We are both in pretty good health. Sometimes we talk about selling the ranch and moving to Laramie.

Her heart catches. She sometimes fantasizes visiting him there.

But we're settled here. We'll probably die with our boots on. Write again. Don't give up on your old man. Remember riding together on the Hennepin route?

Let me know how you're doing in that far away country. Love, Dad.

That far away country. Wyoming.

"Here you are! I woke up and your bed was empty. Then I saw the note."

Monica beams at her friend. "Did you sleep enough?"

"Sleep, I only have ten days in India, do you think I want to sleep through it? Two days to see fabulous Delhi, five days with you in Moorty, three at Father Daniel's mission. I'm not going to sleep away my visit."

"Oh, Beata, I missed you."

"Vice versa! Now when do they bring the coffee?"

Monica signals the waiter.

"Oh, yes." Beata says. "An Indian breakfast. *Idili* and *sambhar,* please," she asks the waiter. "My friend has been raving about that musical sounding dish for months."

As Beata chats, Monica is suffused with joy. Also with wistfulness about home and the ease of life there. She wouldn't trade her days of discovery in India. Occasionally she does dream of a day's rest back in Uptown.

"So what would you like to do with your first day in New Delhi, Dr. Johnson?"

"Dr. Murphy will want to start somewhere earnest, the National Museum?"

Earnest, yup, she was about to make that very suggestion.

"I hear Delhi has terrific shopping and I was hoping to look for a shawl, cushion covers for the study, a few table cloths."

She laughs, remembering old debates about materialism.

"Oh, I know that look," Beata laughs. "You think your old friend is acquisitive. I am. It's a vice. A small one. I enjoy it. Some people don't enjoy their vices."

"I surrender!" She grins. "In fact, I've arranged for Tina to take you to Santoushti Village. First, let's go to the Crafts Museum. Artisans from all over India sell shawls and jewelry and leather work. It's close, a ten minute ride to Pragati Maiden."

"Oh, yes, and can we take one of those auto rickshaws?"

*****

"Funny we didn't meet in Minneapolis," Tina opens her white napkin at Basil and Thyme. "Monica tells me you met her when we were in med school."

"Actually, I was doing my residency. You were off to Kansas City by then."

"The 90s were a good time in the Cities; they were really coming alive," Tina says.

Beata is eating Tandoori Chicken. The others have opted for the "continental" option: fish stew. Monica wonders about this frequent term on Indian menus, "continental," as opposed to "subcontinental?"

"Yes, I often cursed my parents' move from New Orleans. I mean talk about alive! But the Cities have a lot to offer now. Good jazz everywhere."

"I wish we were in Delhi long enough to hear Indian jazz. Ashok took me to this fabulous concert."

"That's already on the list. Father Daniel has tickets to a club in Chennai."

"Father Daniel?" Tina asks. "In Chennai?"

"The person responsible for luring Monica to India," Beata says slyly.

"Oh, right, the retreat guy?" Tina says.

Beata takes the last bite. "Delicious. Good fuel for afternoon shopping. You know, I saw a midnight blue silk top—a tunic-like blouse—what are they called?"

"A short kurta," Monica explains.

Tina nods enthusiastically. "I saw that, too. In the second shop, Tulsi, right?"

"That's the one. Shall we?"

"Why don't you two go ahead? I'm going to indulge in coffee."

Collecting her purse, Beata mutters to Tina *sotto voce*, "I do wonder if she's a natural woman, sometimes. She is missing the shopping gene."

Tina smirks. "I bored her stiff one day getting my sapphire set and..."

"Girl, did you say *sapphire*?"

"Maybe we can stop at Capitol Jewelers on the way back to the IIC?"

Monica is content alone with her coffee. She loves her friends, but the shopping zeal is baffling. Sudha has a little of it, too. Monica recalls her booty from the *mela*. She'll be meeting Beata soon. What if they don't get along? Will they be jealous of each other? Can you introduce one part of your life to another? Could she bring Ashok to Minneapolis? Unthinkable. *Besides, it's not going to happen.*

*****

Their second day in Delhi starts with a visit to Mission House and ends with a saunter through Lodi Gardens.

"It's gorgeous," Beata exclaims. "A museum and botanical garden all in one."

Monica takes in the graceful trees, the rolling lawns, the lake, the striking Mughal mausoleums where children play and lovers rendezvous.

"Look at the strollers. Women in tennis shoes, wearing those beautiful long blouses and pants, what are they called?"

"*Salwar kameezes.*"

"Pretty as well as practical. But the tennis shoes?"

"Exercise. They wear sandals to work, tennis for walking." She thought Beata would like Lodi Gardens, this serene respite in the middle of one of the most vibrant, chaotic cities in the world.

*****

Brigid invites Beata to say grace. "As a welcome to our little communion."
Kevin watches.

"Yes, yes," Father agrees enthusiastically.

Raul looks down at his plate, something he often does when Kevin is present.

"Bless us, O Lord, for these thy gifts, which we are about to receive. Thank you for bringing me to see my old friend and to make new ones in these beautiful mountains. Amen."

After the collective "Amen," Father Freitas raises his glass. "We've looked forward to your visit for some time now."

"Thank you, Father."

"We know a fair amount about you," Raul teases.

He's lightening up. Monica can see the effect of hanging around Sudha.

"Even your shoe size," he says.

Brigid and Monica giggle. The others, including Beata, look perplexed.

Brigid explains, "Dr. Sanchez and I were here when your lovely boots arrived."

Beata smiles. "I feel I know all of you. For instance," she turns to Raul, "Monica has told me about your wonderful rural project."

Monica's heart sinks.

Kevin clears his throat.

Never a good omen.

"I received a letter from Mission House today," he intones as if reading an epistle from St. Paul, "about your special project, Dr. Sanchez."

"I sent them a report about the first six months."

"So it said."

Suddenly winter gusts into the room.

"Glad it arrived," Raul nods. "You never know with the Indian postal service."

Walsh ignores the comment. "In future, please do me the courtesy of running your missives by me before submitting them."

"You're the head doctor, but not the administrator," Raul says stiffly. Then more guardedly, "If you're interested I'd be happy to do that. Providing you don't censor them."

"Why on earth would Dr. Walsh do that?" Brigid sits straighter.

"We do have some disagreements about the rudiments of medical care."

"What might those be?" Kevin demands. "I believe in discussion, even debate. You've never raised this disagreement about 'the rudiments' before."

Raul hovers between exasperation and rage. "I've made some complaints. You refuse to protect women from unwanted pregnancies. And given the huge families…"

Father Freitas raises his eyes toward the ceiling. Monica knows he agrees with Raul on this, but can't contravene Vatican policy.

Walsh reddens. "Catholic hospitals do not dispense contraceptives. Why would I give birth control to a young girl in good health? It could ruin her body."

"Excessive pregnancies kill women at a far greater rate."

"Besides," Walsh clearly relishes certain arguments. "God has made his plans. Not every sex act leads to contraception. Why should we engineer systems to interfere with a power wiser than ourselves?" He looks to Father, who does not meet his glance. Walsh then continues, "We are not on this earth to tinker with nature."

Sister Eleanor excuses herself from the table.

"Therefore we shouldn't set Aruna's leg when she falls?" Raul retorts. "We should let little Gita die from her fever?"

"My friend," Walsh pauses theatrically, "you know the difference."

My friend, Monica notes, bad move. Raul gets more aggravated as Walsh grows bellicose.

"We're here to preserve life, not to destroy it!" Walsh waves his arms. "Providing contraceptives would kill my patient's child."

Beata squeezes Monica's hand under the table.

Raul's left hand is shaking uncontrollably. "You might be killing her starving children while cultivating an embryo."

"Baby," snaps Brigid. "Baby. The moment of conception brings us babies."

Monica hears so much in this voice: grief over lost infants; frantic defense of her husband's morality.

Everyone is bending forward, listening, arguing silently. Everyone except Father Freitas who has folded his hands and slid his chair back from the table.

How astonishing, Monica thinks, this is the first time they've all spoken about these issues as a group. Issues that have troubled her long before Raj's question, which grows more urgent for her each day.

Raul rests his left hand on his right palm. "St. Thomas Aquinas declared that male embryos don't have souls for forty days; for females it takes ninety days."

"You well know, Dr. Sanchez, as someone who studied for the priesthood…" Walsh pauses for a sip of water.

Monica blinks at this new revelation about her ever unpredictable friend.

Brigid intercedes. "We are forgetting our manners. Arguing in front of a guest. These important issues are best left to a staff meeting. Let's shift the subject and tone, shall we? Beata, will you tell us about your work in Minneapolis?"

*****

"Oh, Monica, I really blew it," Beata whispers as they hurry through the snow to the residence. "I'm so sorry I mentioned Raul's project."

She ushers Beata into the warm flat. She should have turned off the space heater during dinner, but so what, she's trying to be less of a good girl. The heat is welcoming.

"Let's make tea in the kitchen and chat."

"You've built up this collegiality for ten months now and I come in like a vampy home wrecker."

"Vampy. The perfect word. You're definitely high vamp." She holds Beata's hands. "Sweetie, don't beat yourself up. The conversation has simmered beneath a very thin surface for months. I'm grateful we've begun to talk. 'Begun' because the discussion will continue for some time."

"Aunt Honey always said I had a mouth on me."

"Aunt Honey, oh, right, from New Orleans. Wish I had met her."

"Auntie would say, 'We'll all meet up in heaven.'"

"One more thing to look forward to. I'm afraid St. Peter won't appreciate my silence about condoms. We'll never change the policy unless we talk about it."

"I was planning to ask how you deal with that retrograde dogma. It's one thing to be a liberal Catholic at home; quite another to work at a Catholic hospital here."

Monica drops into the chair and takes a long breath of steam from the fragrant tea. "I work in limbo, between good and bad. The hospital does do a lot of good here."

"Clearly."

"But we're falling short in all kinds of ways."

TWENTY

December, 2001, Moorty

Sudha and Beata stride ahead of her down the mall, laughing. Why did she worry about them getting along? They haven't stopped talking since they met.

Life would be perfect if Beata moved here. More realistically, Beata's visit reminds her of life in Minnesota, a life to which she might return any month. When she made the commitment to Moorty Mission, she was under the illusion the hard decisions were over. Nothing lasts forever, as the visa office continually reminds her.

Monica loves this route where the village rooftops are framed against distant white mountain peaks. She hears commotion as merchants make the last sales of the day. At the Tibetan residence, faded prayer flags flutter in the mild wind. Some houses in this part of town have been here since the middle Raj period, more English than Indian. A scratchy loudspeaker wails a Muslim call to prayer, followed by competing chants from Hindu and Buddhist temples. At least Catholics don't use these loudspeakers.

The Mayflower Hotel's grand lobby is decked with elaborate chandeliers, red brocade upholstery, stunning Persian and Afghan rugs. Sudha was right to pick this plush Victorian hotel for Beata's splurge night.

"My father would love this place," Sudha grins, ushering them into the lounge.

Monica nurses a Kingfisher as Sudha and Beata giggle over Mango Mama daiquiris. This place is beyond special in its over the top opulence.

"I've tried to get her to at least try on a sari," Sudha says. "She'd look stunning in a green Bengali silk one."

"Naw, Monica isn't interested in fashion. Believe me, I've tried. A shame with that great figure and gorgeous red hair. Yes, green would be perfect."

"Monica is right here," she reminds them. "Monica wears green blouses and dresses." And a green jade necklace from Eric. "But Monica doesn't want to wear a sari. I already told Sudha, I'd feel like I were at a masquerade."

"You could at least try…" Beata begins.

"Yes," Sudha agrees. "Do you find that our friend is a wee bit serious?"

"A wee bit."

"Now, I didn't invite Beata here to join you in a teasing match."

"But it's so much fun," Sudha says.

Mercilessly, they continue the wardrobe inventory. Then they move on to Ashok.

"It's an ordinary friendship," says Monica with a note of finality. There's no way that she's prepared to discuss her growing feelings. Not here; not yet.

"What does that mean?" asks Beata.

"A term people here use for platonic relationships," she replies.

Beata raises her eyebrows and Sudha shakes her head in amusement.

"I believe it's time for our dinner reservations." Monica stands.

*****

How can this be Beata's last day? Of course Monica would have a late afternoon emergency. The visit has raced by. Will she remember it next week?

Quickly, she changes clothes, determined to look stylish tonight when she meets her two friends at Sudha's. The blue dress should do it. And the purple shawl. It's true, she doesn't have much flair. Maybe it's a class thing. Mom always looked like an Irish housewife, even when she worked in the insurance office. Clean and neat was her motto. All those years of Catholic school uniforms left Monica clueless about dress. At the U, most girls wore jeans and t-shirts or sweatshirts. So she's not a Vogue model; she's still not as dowdy as Laurel and Hardy are making out.

Sudha ushers her in from the cold, takes her coat, offers her a drink.

"Beata's in the kitchen. Chicken gumbo tonight, well, a Moorty version, with Indian spices." She sets out a wooden bowl of salted lentils.

"Beata's chicken gumbo! We're in for a treat."

"I know." She grins, offering a glass of beer.

"Thanks, I can use this."

"Tell me about the emergency. Workers at a building site?"

"Two slipped off the bamboo scaffolding. One fractured an arm. The other, poor man, broke both legs."

"Ow."

"They'll be fine. The leg guy is in for a long rest, but the breaks were clean."

"Lucky for him you were there. It's thirty miles to the nearest government clinic. Rough with two broken legs."

Monica nods, gratified by the acknowledgment.

"Do I hear someone I know out there?" Beata calls from the kitchen.

Monica notices that Beata's voice takes on a Louisiana softness, as it always does when she cooks "home style."

"Yes," Sudha calls. "Come see her, all kitted out for our fashionista evening."

Beata appears, resplendent in a crimson sari.

Monica gasps.

Sudha and Beata are beaming.

"Gorgeous! It doesn't look like a masquerade costume on you."

Beata glows. "Getting dressed was a trip. Now, it feels perfectly natural. Something I don't want to take off."

"I knew you guys would get along famously, such refined, determined women. How does poor little mousey Monica fit in?" she teases.

"Mousey Monica," Sudha rises to the occasion. "The brilliant doctor who launches preventive health care systems, sets broken bones, conducts emergency surgeries. Mousey—isn't that the perfect word? By the way, you look super in blue."

"You may not be mousey," Beata says with mock impatience, "but you are a little tardy and my chicken is going to fall off the bone if we don't sit down."

Monica recognizes Sudha's block print table cloth from the *mela*. How many of these did she buy? The table looks lovely with candles and Sudha's best dishes.

Beata emerges from the kitchen gingerly carrying the pot well in front of her. "I'm terrified of spilling on Sudha's splendid silk."

"As I said, the sari is yours. It was meant for you. Suits you so much better!"

"No, I couldn't."

"This smells delicious." Monica realizes how famished she is.

"New Orleans comes to the Himalayas!" Beata is radiant.

Monica says a short, silent grace, then digs in.

For several minutes, they eat ravenously.

Sudha takes a sip of water. "Why don't you stay, Beata?"

"Pardon?"

Monica feels an odd mix of alarm, jealousy, excitement.

"Why don't you stay a while? You're so fascinated by the intersections of Buddhism and Catholicism. Moorty would be the perfect place to study, to meditate. And your work would be useful here. People deny the alcoholism, but I see it affect our families every day. Perhaps you could join the hospital in some capacity?"

Sudha's come a long way, Monica marvels, now enlisting for the Mission.

"How I'd adore your company. To be reunited with my old friend and to get to know my new friend. But I miss James. And I'm more timid than you two. You're searching, courageous women."

Monica's heart sinks. It was ridiculous to hope.

"Oh, come now," Sudha scolds.

"As much as I've fallen in love with Moorty and as much as I complain that the Twin Cities aren't New Orleans, I'm settled there. You both are strong and brave enough to leave home, to start new lives. No wonder you've become fast, close friends."

"We're all friends now," Monica declares. "All of us."

TWENTY-ONE

December, 2001, Moorty

Suddenly, she's gone. Monica resists sadness. Beata is not lost to her the way Mom is, in the way Jeanne might be. Beata will always be her friend. She'll see her in Minnesota. And Beata will return here. Missing is different from grieving; this longing is threaded with a spine of faith.

Days return to normal. Not quite. She, herself, feels more confident of her place here. And the dinner quarrel between Raul and Kevin echoes in her mind. At night, she's taken to pacing her flat, playing the arguments over and over.

The phone rings tonight during her restless walking.

"Oh, hello, Ashok." He's already called this week so she's surprised. "Is everything OK?"

"I just imagined you could feel, well with your friend leaving, a little lonely."

"How thoughtful." Her stomach somersaults at the intimacy. "I'm doing fine, thanks."

"You don't sound fine."

He finds his way to the topic of Kevin and Raul.

"No, I've vowed to myself not to talk with outsiders about this."

"I'm an outsider?"

"Of course not, I just mean…"

"Maybe if you told me what's bothering you, you could let it go."

"You've morphed into my confessor?"

"Try friend."

She releases a long sigh, repeating the argument over condoms and contraception.

"This is important. Why didn't you mention it?" He's clearly hurt.

"I've been praying about my own conflicts."

"And those are?"

"We could do so much good with condoms and birth control. But a Catholic hospital can't offer them. Otherwise we do help many people: accident victims; patients suffering from a huge variety of gastro-intestinal diseases," she goes on hectically.

He listens.

She can almost see his serious eyes when she says, "I thought I knew what I was getting into, but there's a difference between anticipating contradictions and living with them every day, facing women who don't want a sixth pregnancy, people of all ages contracting HIV and knowing we could have prevented…"

"Have you talked to your actual confessor about this? The Father you rave about?"

"I don't know."

"From what you say, he's a man of the world. From Goa, for heaven's sake. He must have experienced the same contradictions as you."

She shrugs. He's right of course. "I'll think about it."

"Good."

"Enough about me." She's calmer just for airing the worries. "How was the rest of the week at school?"

"Fine," he allows. "Every student passed the quiz."

"You're a good teacher, Ashok."

His voice turns abrupt, almost curt. "Listen, I want to suggest something."

"Yes?" She's pacing again, puzzled by her sudden nervousness.

"I was just invited to the Institute next month. I'm speaking on a Thursday."

"Yes," she says, reluctant to admit—or betray—enthusiasm.

"Since I'll be in your neighborhood, I could drop by Moorty for the weekend. That is, if you can cope with visits two months in a row."

"Yes, of course." She's thrilled, but should play it cool. "Everyone will be glad to see you, Sudha and Raul. And you'll get to meet Father Freitas."

"Everyone, oh good," he's more subdued. "I'll book the ticket. Perhaps we can attend another edifying cultural event at the Playhouse."

"Tell me truthfully," she's feeling giddy. "Didn't you find the theatre charming?"

"Charming might be going a bit far. But quaint, yes, quaint."

*****

"Welcome, to my cave," Father Freitas ushers her into his sparsely furnished office.

Three chairs and a small wooden desk. A crucifix hangs over the doorway. The concrete floor is warmed by a small Kashmiri rug. His bookcase is the only spot of indulgence, overflowing with novels, poetry, history and books on theology in English, Portuguese, Konkani and Hindi.

She takes a long breath and tries to discharge her anxiety, then relates the conversation with Ashok.

He listens intently, as if she were the only thing in the world that matters.

She longs to develop this kind of deep concentration. Yes, she does focus on her patients, but part of her is always worried about the next injury or illness.

After she finishes unburdening herself, he waits a few beats.

"I could say so many familiar things," he starts. "I, too, have differences of conscience with Vatican teaching on these issues."

She sees the pain in his eyes.

He exhales audibly. "You must listen to your heart. Many good Catholics oppose the Church's ban on condoms."

"But they don't work at Mission hospitals."

"Most of them, no."

She sits straighter, realizing Raul is probably dispensing prophylactics in Manda. How has she been so naïve? Ah, she's not here to talk about Raul.

"Monica, you've come with a theological and ethical quandary, yet, well, I wonder if your sleeplessness and distraction might have additional roots?"

"Such as?" She's taken aback.

"I've had the gift of knowing you for almost a year. I've come to admire Monica's ability to place herself where she is 'not Monica,' or to reinvent herself to the situation. Admirable. And tiring."

She's not sure she wants him to proceed.

"From what I know of your childhood, you leapt across social classes to become a physician and succeeded marvelously at that."

"To a degree."

"To a great degree," he corrects. "You've adapted beautifully here, learning Hindi, making Indian friends who trust you and, dare I say, love you."

This is not what she came to talk about.

"Perhaps you could be more accepting and come to like Monica, yourself."

He's knocked the wind out of her.

"You haven't had a holiday since you arrived."

"I just had several days with Beata in Delhi."

"Hardly a holiday."

Is he suggesting a leave? Is this his way of sending her home?

"Father Daniel and I spoke recently."

"Beata says he seems well," she stalls. "How did you find him?"

"Ebullient as ever, despite the heart trouble. He sends warm regards. In fact, he's planning a seminar on new gastro-intestinal protocols and thinks you'd be a perfect speaker."

"You're sending me to Pondicherry?"

"I'm not sending you anywhere. I believe it would be a blessing to Father Daniel and his colleagues if you traveled down there for ten days or so."

"Ten days." She's nonplussed and enticed.

"In March, before the heavy heat. Have you seen the Indian Ocean yet?"

"The ocean!" She's grinning. "Father, would you allow me to go?"

"How can we resist Father Daniel? Never underestimate the power of Catholics from Tamil Nadu."

She recalls Father Daniel racing after her in Minnesota with his email address. "He's a force, all right, this man who drew me back to the Church."

He smiles. "Your heart brought you back. Father Daniel would be the perfect person to discuss what's troubling your heart now. Frankly, I, like you, feel such conflict over these questions. He is a far better sounding board."

"I see." She's both reassured and shaken by this particular confidence.

"Shall I suggest he email you an invitation? That would be the next step."

"Yes, Father, the next step." She stands. "Let's take the next step."

TWENTY-TWO

Late January, 2002, Moorty and Rasik

In the thin morning light, the Pande Bazaar is a commotion of people greeting friends, shoppers dickering with merchants. Ashok shouts at the reckless bicyclists. Is the hubbub caused by unseasonable warmth? Is it always like this on the far side of town? She's only been here once before, at a dark 6 a.m. on an emergency call, fluttering in and out of the shadows.

One stall sells a cornucopia of adhesive bindis in many shapes. The next displays shawls. Another glows with a bucket of saffron.

She glances at the old snake charmer making a high-pitched whistle, summoning his cobra to ripple and swell upward from a round, tattered basket. She wants to watch, but Ashok gets even more cross. "No buses in sight. Not even an auto rickshaw."

"Relax," she says. "Moorty is a small place. It can't be far."

"It can be far enough for us to miss our bus," he glowers.

Ashok is a man of order, annoyed when things aren't clear, she notes once again. A rather non-adaptive trait for an Indian.

She asks several people before an old woman points to the "station" at the end of the street.

"Eureka!" The buses come into view. Six or seven. Without destination signs.

"Bloody bedlam," he protests.

Ten minutes to departure.

Nine minutes later, they're boarding the bus to Rasik.

"Whose idea was this?" he asks as they struggle past passengers storing cases, chatting in the aisle, to the only empty places at the back of the ancient vehicle.

"Ahhh," he emits a comic sigh and collapses into the seat.

"Actually, Sudha suggested Rasik. Relax, Mr. Curmudgeon, the worst part is over. We located the bus. We have our seats. Adjacent seats."

"Well spotted. I didn't see them. You're more nimble on coaches than I."

"My father was a bus driver. It's a perfectly safe, reliable form of transportation."

"How long have you been in this country? Nothing in India is a perfectly safe, reliable form of transportation." He shuts his eyes, rests his curly head on the window. "I should have hired a car. Who knows how many stops this tank makes."

A two-year-old in the forward seat has turned around and stares wide-eyed, fascinated by the gloomy Ashok.

She plays peek-a-boo and the child giggles.

Ashok opens one eye. Reluctantly charmed, he laughs. "You're good with children of all ages. Sorry for the petulance. My sister calls me a cantankerous traveler."

"Rasik is ninety minutes away. We'll be there by 11 a.m."

"They'll let us claim our rooms that early?"

"I checked. They're used to guests arriving on this notoriously trustworthy bus."

He releases a long sigh. "How do you know it's trustworthy? Did Sudha say?"

"No," she smirks. "I just wanted you to relax."

He laughs. Briefly.

She tries again. "Sudha says a maharajah from Rajasthan built Rasik Palace. He wanted a respite from the desert summer. Her friend Lakshmi says the palace is a huge yellow building set among manicured grounds with gorgeous views."

"Who's Lakshmi? Wait a minute, you mean Sudha hasn't even been to this place?"

She ignores the anxious question. "A hundred years ago they had fancy dress balls there. He was a Westernized maharajah even then. He hosted fabulous dinners, with wine from France. Quite a scene: the British vied with each other for invitations. He modeled his golden palace on a country estate he visited in Suffolk. Complete with a large stable for horses."

"Where are the maharajahs now?"

"After he died, his adult children used it less and less. His great grandson sold it to the Oberoi Hotel Chain."

"I can't wait." He closes his eyes. End of conversation.

*****

Two hours later the bus deposits them at an ornate wrought iron gate. They're the only ones alighting. She wonders if the skeptical professor might be right.

Ashok holds the heavy gate for her. They wheel suitcases up the cobbled path.

Here it is. The pale yellow 19th century dream haloed by shining, snowy mountains. She is twelve years old again and happier than if she'd gone to Disneyland.

"Interesting," he allows.

"Splendid!" she declares.

The huge front doors are weathered oak. Through their beveled glass centers: a blurry scene of green uniformed bellmen, stylish women and well-appointed men. She imagines them dining at candlelit table, soft music played by young Rajasthanis.

"Shall we?" Ashok opens the door and regards her curiously.

"I was daydreaming."

"Daydreams, not nightmares. Already, the curative powers of Rasik."

The young desk clerk hands brass keys for room 25 and 26 to the bellman, who whisks their bags up the opulently carpeted staircase.

Her room is the "Blue Boudoir." She walks over a threadbare teal and grey Persian rug to the Victorian vanity table, complete with oval mirror and azure flounced skirt. She lies on the robin's egg blue chenille bedspread, surprised by the firm mattress.

Clack. Clack. Horses? No: knock, knock.

Startled, she looks up, disoriented in the cerulean world.

"Monica?" His voice is concerned.

Oh, lord, it's one o'clock. She rushes to the door.

"Are you OK? Weren't we planning to walk before lunch?"

"Sorry, I tried out the bed and you woke me. I shouldn't have fallen…"

"Don't worry. You needed the rest."

Her breath catches at Mom's words. "*You must have needed the rest.*"

"We can walk after lunch. It's quite warm. Thirteen or fourteen degrees."

"January thaw, like Minneapolis," she sounds like an idiot. "I'll brush my hair and meet you downstairs, OK?"

"Take your time, Monica. This is a holiday."

What happened to the crank on the bus? The palace is working transformative powers on each of them.

She sits before the spotted oval mirror, inspecting the tangle of scarlet yarn on her head. How many lovely *maharanis* combed their rich black locks here? How many dithered between white and yellow sapphires? How many secret trysts occurred in that seductive bed? Her brush catches most tangles. She regards the green sweater: blah. Digging through the suitcase, she finds the purple turtleneck Beata brought from Minnesota. And the earrings Sudha bought in Moorty to match. Much more vivid. She feels a dreamy excitement. She's not used to dressing for a date.

Sun warms her face as they hike along the quiet road to the crest of the hill. Ashok wants to see the legendary cricket pitch. She's heard there's a *gurdvara* at the top. Monica inhales the benign, almost springlike air.

"Heaven," she whispers.

"Delightful. They're serving tea in the garden later. Imagine. In January."

"Oh, fun."

"Still, we don't want to get fooled," he warns. "Winter will return."

"OK, Dr. Nair, I won't put away woolies." Shedding her parka, she feels a slight breeze prickling through her sweater: delicious.

"That purple is very becoming on you."

"Beata's doing. She has great taste."

"Yes. In clothing. And in friends."

Two men drive by in a black pickup truck. They wave.

Flustered by Ashok's compliments, she's grateful for the distraction. The cricket pitch is nondescript. Aren't they all?

Ashok is entranced. They walk the length of the pitch. "What views! Imagine competing here, shouldered by these mountains. In this clean, clean air."

She doesn't know anything about cricket except that there's a wicket involved, so she murmurs, "Stunning."

"This India of *ours*, yes, I complain, really though, it's extraordinary."

India of *ours*. "Yes," she agrees.

They ramble along the road at a comfortable pace. Drivers wave, toot horns.

The *gurdvara* is a domed building flying a triangular orange flag, with the Sikh symbol.

A greeter welcomes the visitors warmly, advising her to cover her head and remove footwear.

They slip off their shoes at the door. After a year in India, she no longer worries about losing her shoes.

As they enter through the arch, she feels a tap on her shoulder.

The Sikh offers each a slice of coconut to make an offering.

Two devotees sit cross-legged on the carpeted floor.

Ashok and Monica tentatively approach the Guru Granth Sahib, eyes closed, before the holy book. They bow their heads. Is Ashok praying? she wonders. As if on cue, each leaves the offering and they exit silently.

"Lovely," she tells their host as she pulls on her shoes.

Ashok drops several coins in a dish and tents his hands. "*Namaste.*"

*****

Carefully, they pick their way downhill, avoiding patches of last week's ice storm.

"My first romance was with a Sikh girl," he muses.

"Oh?"

"Sanjana Singh. I think I fell in love with her name first."

"When was this?"

"I was what, twelve or thirteen," he pauses. "Romance is an exaggeration. Powerful emotions—or hormones—on my part. We went to one film."

"And?"

"There's no 'and.' Maybe she hated the movie. She avoided me after that."

"Sad," she says, amused as her twinge of jealousy dissipates.

"And you? Your first love?"

She rolls her eyes. "Not sure I'd call it love, but it was a deep crush. I asked a boy to the junior prom."

"Bold of you."

"We were studying feminism in Civics class. Besides, boys were put off by me."

"Too smart?"

"Something like that. So I asked this cute guy and we had a fabulous time."

"And?"

"Turned out he was gay. But it was the beginning of a long friendship."

"An ordinary friendship?" he teases.

She blushes, "We're still in touch. He's a neurosurgeon in Detroit."

*****

The garden is hardly blooming, but most of the snow has melted and the little tables are covered with white cloths and flowered plates.

Ashok ushers her to a table in the corner. "Better for watching the parade."

A young Tibetan man takes their order. Darjeeling for her. Assam golden tip for Ashok. Both without milk.

Other tables are filling with families. A pair of old women. Several couples. Monica notices she's the only non-Indian. She's glad Sudha suggested a place that wasn't packed with foreign tourists. What else would she expect from Sudha?

Inhaling the flowery steam of Darjeeling sweetness, she sighs contentedly.

"I had an interesting email correspondence last week."

The intensity of his voice makes her uneasy. "Yes?" she asks.

"From the department at Madison."

"Really?" she tries to sound neutral.

"They're inviting me to apply for a senior position there." The words spill quickly; his voice is high. "An invitation only. Maybe they're asking dozens of people."

She pushes through the weighty disappointment. "Don't erase the honor before enjoying it. You've talked about taking a break from Delhi."

"This would be more than a break," he says intently.

The small scar beneath is lower lip is reddening. She wonders if he fell on a bottle as a baby. No, certainly his mother breastfed him.

"It's a permanent post. Full professor."

"How do you feel about that?" she watches the afternoon's gaiety fading away.

"They have a great department. They 'get' my work. It's almost ideal."

"Almost?" Her chest tightens.

"I have, um, certain attachments in India." His gaze is fixed on his cup.

She sips tea, waiting, then selects a biscuit, nibbles the edge.

"Besides," he explains," I may not get the job."

"But if you did?" She shouldn't pressure him.

"That would be a hard decision." He's studying her again.

She nods.

"I could take a leave of absence from my post in Delhi just in case."

"That sounds wise. Alonso advised a leave from the clinic. I wasn't so wise."

"Monica, I wanted to say," he hesitates.

"Yes?"

Screeching. A monkey leaps up on their table. Higher pitched shrieking. Her voice. Ashok's. The culprit scatters biscuits and snatches two digestives, then leaps away.

Laughter from the other tables.

"Rascal," clucks a man to their left.

Hands on her chest, Monica's eyes are still popping out.

"Are you OK?" Ashok firmly grasps her arm.

"*Walk with a stick,*" advised Father Freitas. Tina warned, "*You'll need these shots because of the monkeys and…*"

She's shivering. Damn, she's let down her guard. About the monkeys. About so many things. She needs to be more realistic about this place and the people here.

"Monica?"

"I'm fine, thanks. I might have a short rest before dinner."

"Of course." He takes her elbow. "This is a holiday."

Holiday, yes, she ignores the fears about Madison, reminds herself to live in the moment.

*****

By seven, her good mood has returned. Maybe it's the collective vibes haunting this opulent bedroom. Vivacious spirits of maharanis past beguile her into dressing fastidiously for dinner. A leave of absence, he said, just in case.

She fingers a few pieces of jewelry. Nothing seems right. She hadn't counted on a real palace. Silver choker, jade beads, gold earrings, Sudha's purple baubles.

Sudha is such an advocate for Ashok. Annoying, yet pleasing, too. She wishes Beata had met him. At least her two girlfriends know each other. She thinks about the distinctions as well as the parallels. Beata is less cosmopolitan than Sudha. Also more droll. No one has ever made her laugh like Beata. Perhaps the jade. Eric wouldn't mind.

The necklace is perfect against the steel grey dress, the subtle colors accenting each other, Beata would say. Pulling her hair into a French twist, she thinks how her friend often complimented her long neck. Well, she's no maharani, but this will have to do.

Ashok stands at the front of the stairway, dashing in a navy kurta and matching slacks. He guides her to their table, set with candles, gold-rimmed china and crystal glasses.

"I feel like Deborah Kerr."

He holds the chair for her. "You don't mean *An Affair to Remember*?"

"Yes, actually. You know the movie?"

"My sister Manju's favorite. You share with her a certain…"

"Schmaltziness?" she laughs.

"No," he rubs the side of his chin. "No, a melancholy."

She's ridiculously touched to be compared to his adored sister.

"The film is much too sad."

But Kerr and Grant do get together, she thinks, after an absence.

The waiter delivers menus, then asks solicitously, "The monkey scared you?"

"A little," she admits. "I'm fine now."

"Really!" Ashok clears his throat. "Management should erect barriers."

"Yes sir," the waiter regards her with wry sympathy. "I shall return for your order."

"First, would you bring us a bottle of champagne?" Ashok recovers his equanimity. "This one," he points to something in the leather-covered wine menu.

Once the waiter leaves, she asks hesitantly. "Isn't this extravagant?"

"My treat," he smiles widely. "To celebrate our first holiday together in the land of maharajahs and monkeys."

Other tables begin to fill. She watches the dazzle of shimmering saris. In the corner, parents lead two well-behaved boys dressed in white shirts and ties.

"To the weekend," he raises a glass of bubbly.

"The weekend," she repeats. The weekend which is just beginning.

Their local lake fish is light and flakey. The chef has mashed his potatoes with garlic and butter. The fresh green beans are perfectly crunchy.

She savors every bite despite a sliver of disloyalty to Cook.

"Tasty," he murmurs.

"Very."

They chat for a while about Ashok's classes and Monica's patients. She reports on her talk with Father Freitas and the recent email invitation from Father Daniel.

"A break is a good idea," he agrees.

She is so at ease, happy, here in their private nook, feels intimate with this man, yet aware that there's so much she doesn't know about him. Hesitantly, she treads into deeper waters. "You never mentioned how your parents died." She watches him closely. "Are you comfortable telling me about that?"

"Very sad." He lowers his voice and fiddles with the highly polished silver pepper shaker. "Twenty years ago this month, actually."

"I didn't know."

"The sadness remains. Tempered by happy memories." His brown eyes soften into a rueful smile.

She aches for the time when her own grief lifts a little.

"They were in an auto accident. On holiday."

She recalls his warning, "*That road to Moorty is fairly labyrinthine. A three hour ride at least.*"

"How horrible."

"They say it was instantaneous. Still, yes, tragic."

"You and your brothers and Manju were all grown by that time?"

"Manju was in college at Miranda House, but my brothers and I were all working."

"You're the oldest by how much?"

"A year older than Ashish. No matter. The first child is always the boss."

"You know that about yourself?" she grins.

"I'm not wholly without personal insight," he feigns offense. "Our parents' deaths brought us closer," he takes a long breath. "Has that happened for you and Jeanne?"

"No, quite the opposite." She's dreading discussing Jeanne with him, should have at least begun to tell him months ago.

"I'm sorry," he says. Perhaps sensing her reluctance to discuss Jeanne, he goes on. "I think it made us feel more tied to Kerala, too, despite our Delhi lives."

"Kerala," she repeats. "Tell me something. When we first met, you must have known the long history of Christianity in Kerala."

"I'm an educated person," He refills their sinewy champagne glasses. "I was provoking you, slightly. My way of getting to know a beautiful foreigner."

"You make me sound exotic, like, oh, Sophia Loren."

"I didn't know you were such a film buff."

"I'm not, really. There's something cinematic, make-believe, about this castle in the sky."

He smiles. "A good recommendation from Sudha. I'm surprised she permits you to see me."

She bites her lower lip, but has no doubt her eyes reveal pleasure.

"You don't talk about your father. He moved to the Wild West?"

"He and his second wife Dorothea live in Wyoming. I got a letter from him last week." She pauses, finishing the potatoes, not certain she wants to discuss her father.

"A letter. That's nice."

"I'm kind of paralyzed about answering it. He wants to know how I'm doing. But part of me is still angry. How much does he care? I don't know where to start."

"Why don't you start there?"

"Pardon?"

"He must be a bright man if he's your father. He knows you're angry and sad about his departure. Maybe you need to get that out in the open."

How much more affection can she feel for this discerning man who poses as a gloomy crank?

Dessert is served.

As they reach the stairs, she feels light-headed from the two glasses of champagne. Ashok, who drank far more, seems perfectly sober. Obviously, she's over-reacting. At home she often splits a bottle with Beata.

From the dining room, she hears a piano. " 'Moon River.' I'm glad we escaped the entertainment," she laughs. "I hate Andy Williams."

"Another movie star?" He's amused.

"No, a schmaltzy singer."

"I see you don't like schmaltzy, whatever it is."

They giggle, ascending the regal staircase.

Her foot catches. A crease in the carpet? Her own clumsiness?

He breaks her fall with his arm.

This tripping and slipping with Ashok is getting to be a habit, she thinks. "Thanks. It seems to be my day for accidents."

His hand moves down her arm until their hands clasp.

She's breathless.

Too soon they're standing between their rooms.

"A lovely evening," she says, looking down at her shoes.

"Would you like a night…"

"I feel…"

Words, hopes, intentions, collide.

"Night cap?" he persists. "I have some excellent cognac in my room."

"I've drunk quite enough, thanks," she hears herself saying. Then the voice of Sudha, "I'd love to continue talking for a while, though." He smiles and holds open his door.

The room is as red as hers is blue. Crimson draperies, scarlet rug, ruby bed spread. Her head spins from the intensity, from the champagne.

"You look pale." He's uneasy. "Are you sure that monkey didn't nip you?"

"No, I'm fine. Fine." She drops on the plush burgundy velvet couch. "Your room is larger, grander than mine, a first class cabin," she burbles.

He's pouring two glasses of the aromatic cognac. Maybe he didn't hear her daft comment. How confident he looks. Confident and composed.

"Maharajahs need larger rooms. Wives had to cope with business class."

She laughs. "Wives. Oh, right."

"Cheers," he clinks his glass to hers.

The tawny drink is surprisingly smooth.

"Duty free," he smiles. "I've saved it for a special occasion."

"Delicious." This strange new contentment is edged with anticipation. "Mom loved a glass of brandy on special occasions. On Christmas Eve or her birthday, she'd bring out the brandy and the Waterford crystal glasses."

He sets down his glass and takes her cold hand in his warm palms.

"Christian Brothers," she natters nervously. "She'd say, brandy must be OK with the Lord if Men of God made it. Of course Mom was joking." She can't stop blathering.

"She was a remarkable woman who raised an extraordinary daughter."

Extraordinary. Ordinary.

He places her glass on the mahogany table and takes her other hand. She looks down, then up, into his fine, dark eyes.

"Monica," he whispers. "I have such feelings for you."

All she can do is nod. Then someone says, "And I, for you."

His moist lips brush her cheek as he draws her in. They embrace tightly.

He kisses her hairline, left ear, chin, proceeds up the other side of her face.

She turns his head and touches her lips to his.

"Enough," he says as if suddenly awake.

Shaking with disappointment, she's knows he's sensible to stop here, for now.

He catches her hand again and they are walking to the ruby bed. Perched on the side, they kiss, open their mouths to the warm wetness of each other.

The tip of his tongue is electrifying. A long sigh slithers through her chest.

He's slowly unclasping the beads, unzipping the dress.

She opens his kurta.

As he pulls the soft navy tunic over his head, she's engulfed in his sagey musk, back on the train from Moorty to Delhi and the pleasurable ripeness of his sleeping body.

He cups her breasts, runs his thumb over the satin of her slip, watching each nipple rise.

They turn from each other, remove the rest of their clothes and slip under the cool white sheets.

Propped up on an elbow, he gazes down, drinking her in. "Monica, dear Monica."

She draws him closer, feels his resistance.

"Let me look a moment longer. I want to savor this."

She runs her fingers gently over his amber chest. Light and shadow, their bodies together. At least. This feels so right, so normal and thoroughly unexpected. If she lets herself experience all the longing she's harbored, she'll burst with raw need.

"Monica, during the last year, I've come to treasure you. Your seriousness and your wit; your sweetness and determination, your never-ending curiosity."

She puts a finger to his lips. As much as she's ached to hear such words, she can't absorb them.

He kisses her finger, continuing. "What I need to say, dear Monica, is that I love you."

I love you, too, she thinks. Her chest fills with desire and apprehension. She has to answer. "I love you, Ashok."

He slides down in the now warm bed, whispering something she can't make out, then, "So happy. So happy."

She closes her eyes. "Yes."

Tongue on her thigh, he works his way down, licking her knee, her ankle. Then he moves back to the moist softness of her vagina.

It's been so long. She stops herself from counting the months. It's not hard because he turns her into a white hot pulsing sphere. She cries out in pleasure.

"Love," Ashok whispers. He rolls on a condom, raises himself above her, then slowly lowers his body.

She's stroking his bottom.

He enters her easily. Deeply.

She is so ready.

He pauses and looks for a long time. "We're together," he calls in wonderment.

"Yes," she smiles. "Finally."

Holding her breast with one hand, he wraps his other arm around her back and begins to rock.

She feels herself swelling with him.

"Oh, oh," she cries.

His own climax follows with a long, gratified moan.

She closes her eyes and sees glistening snowy peaks.

Monica wakes abruptly, enveloped by their mingled scents, by the tenderness of her formerly armored body. It's so dark, she can see stars through the window. Not many, but a few. She wants to linger in his sleeping warmth; she wants to wake him and make love again. Instead, she slides gently out of bed.

Her own sheets are chilly. Still, her body holds the heat of the night. She hears his words, "treasure, love." Impossible, yes, she feels impossible happiness.

Drifting back to consciousness at dawn, she tugs the covers closer although her bed is warm enough from the second rate heat of a single sleeping body. Happy in her own skin. She doesn't know if this is what Father had in mind. For the moment, she does feel happy.

For the moment.

Leave of absence.

Is that what Dad took, a leave of absence?

Let go, Monica. In this astonishing moment, your glass is full. Love. Now. The stars have disappeared from a pinking sky. She hears rustling in the trees. A dove coos. Groggily, she recalls how she used to confuse the calls of doves and owls.

TWENTY-THREE

May, June, 1999, Minnesota

The cell rings while she's parking. Eric. He's taken to checking in spontaneously. Sweet, she guesses. She doesn't know how she feels.

"Good morning, Eric." Not his fault she worried about Mom all night.

"Hi. Hey, I had a great idea. My friend's sister was visiting campus, you know, Pam, the one who runs the B and B in Pepin?"

She has to get to work. "No, I mean, yes, you mentioned her."

"It sounds divine and I thought we could go in June for a weekend."

"I don't know, Eric. Thank you, but I might be visiting Mom in Duluth."

"You can't go every weekend."

"I'm running late. I've got patients. Can we discuss this Friday?"

"Sure," he sounds hurt. "Let's do that."

She closes the cell and knows he's right. She can't go every weekend even if she does want to kidnap Mom back to her good life in St. Paul. So many reasons, she can't. And she's taking it out on Eric. On Friday, she'll apologize and treat him to dinner. Actually, a mini-vacation would be wonderful.

*****

"You're animated, today, Robert." She strides into the exam room. "Not surprising given the blood work."

"Oh, yes?" His gray eyes are expectant.

"Excellent count. Clearly you've been keeping up with the meds."

"Once I got them." His face shifts from exasperation to gratitude. "You were heroic badgering the insurance company."

She flaps her hands dismissively, recalling Louise's reprimand about exceeding professional roles. "I'm afraid I wound up shouting at the rep over the phone."

"Thanks to you, I've returned to work. My sixth graders thought they'd escaped the dreaded Mr. Welburn for the rest of the term."

"I can't imagine you as the 'dreaded' anything," she laughs.

He brightens. "They did throw a welcome back party, but that was clearly to curry favor and I sternly informed them it wouldn't work."

"I can picture your terrifying countenance."

He describes the kids' huge illustrated card, the singing. A lovely man.

Reluctantly, she checks the wall clock behind him. "So really, that's it for today. Unless you have any questions."

"Uh, yeah," he reddens. "Not about me. My friend Artie, he's been seeing Dr. Jill. I know she has a last name. All I can remember is that high-pitched radio squeak." He stops, alarmed. "Oh, dear, she's your colleague; I'm really screwing this up."

"Don't worry, Robert, go on."

"He doesn't seem to be getting the same treatment as I am and…"

"His case is probably different."

"Could be. Still, he can't get in to see her. She doesn't schedule regular blood work. He's so shy, kind of in awe of her. I tell him to consult with someone else, but he thinks that once you're someone's patient, you're enlisted for life. Or in his case, death. Sorry, I'm so mad. I was wondering, well, could you see him?"

She sits back. Her job is helping patients, not monitoring office politics. "Ask him to schedule another visit with her. If he can't get in, give him my direct line and we'll work out something—at least as a temporary arrangement."

"Thanks."

"Jill has a lot of pressure. It's hard to balance everything."

Robert cocks his head doubtfully. "Thanks, again, Doc."

"You're welcome, Mr. Dread."

She carries a cup of mint tea to the back office. Beata has nixed coffee at work. Beata, her medical advisor. Mid-morning is best for catching Mom. Jeanne is at the bank and Mom is most lucid, even perky, early in the day.

"Hello, there, Mickey, nice to hear your voice."

"How are things, Mom? Is it warm up there yet?"

"You know Duluth is slower to thaw than St. Paul in more ways than one."

"Have you made a few more friends—at church, maybe?"

"Father Olsen is so kind. He's invited me to Bible Study Group and the Share our Harvest Committee. I'll be meeting people soon."

"And the arthritis? Have you found a good doctor yet? Did you follow any of my referrals?" Monica can't tell if she's helping or nagging.

"Jeanne made an appointment with, oh, I don't know, probably someone from that useful list, dear, and I'm sure the date is coming up."

"OK, Mom. Is it bothering you much? Are you getting around?"

"We all have crosses to bear. This is a small one."

"You need exercise, friends. You can't stay holed up in Jeanne's little house."

"It's a lovely house, dear, with a kitchen overlooking the garden. I read my bible there. My magazines. The morning sun is lovely."

"Remember what Dr. Kim said about thrombosis. You have to keep moving. You don't want a blood clot or a—"

"I do quite a lot of moving around—cooking and cleaning. Jeanne says when the ice has fully melted, we'll stroll along the wharf, poke in those little shops. I know you girls have your differences, but truly, I'm just fine up here with Jeannie."

"All right, Mom, I don't want to bug you." She sips the tea, summons Beata's detachment. "Still, next time, I want a report about your doctor's visit."

"And you, Mickey, how is your nice man, Ernest?"

Eric, Ernest, does it matter. Easy to forget a name, given her parade of boyfriends in the last ten years.

"Fine. Eric and I might take a long weekend near Lake Pepin next month."

"Lovely, dear. It should be pretty in August."

"June, you mean. Next month is June."

"Of course. I mustn't keep you from patients. Say hi to Beata and Eric for me."

"Will do, Mom. I love you."

"I love you, too, Mickey. More than you'll ever know."

A rap on the door. Gao waits, looking sheepish.

"Message from Louise?"

Gao nods. "Your staff meeting started five minutes ago."

"Oh, god." How one's own memory crashes all the time.

*****

Chilly atmosphere. She wants to throw open the window to the May sunshine. Concentrate, she tells herself, choosing a seat between Gabe and Terence, avoiding Alonso's ironic glance. Best not to sit with him all the time.

"As I was saying," Louise looks at her pointedly, "Jill's media work is valuable to all of us in raising the clinic profile."

"It gives us a negative profile," Alonso persists. "She doesn't keep up with patient care."

Jill sits impassively, skimming titles on the bookcase.

Folding his hands and clearing his throat twice, Gabe intervenes. "Perhaps this is a personal matter best handled privately between Alonso and Jill."

Louise ignores the peacemaker. "Because of Jill, people know we do cutting edge work. The number of new patients has doubled in the last six months."

"What good is that if we don't treat them properly?" Alonso demands.

"Properly," Louise sits straighter and opines, Monica surmises, with the authority of a fourth generation doctor, "is a relative term. All top notch clinics are streamlining patient care. Focused attention is more beneficial than folksy visiting habits."

Alonso throws up his hands.

Louise glances at her notes.

Robert Welburn could take lessons in dreadly behavior from her.

"Well, Alonso, here's an item to warm your liberal heart," Louise moves on.

Monica shoots him a warning glance.

"After last week's tight, but decisive vote by the physician team, I have notified pharmaceutical reps that we'll end their free holiday buffets for the staff."

"Go Monica!" Alonso says under his breath.

Louise adds coolly, "Apparently we're one of the few clinics to be so, as the reps put it, 'super sensitive' to possible conflicts of interest."

Monica studies her cuticles.

Louise adds dryly, "The staff was disappointed, but professional in response."

"Did you tell them that Alonso, Terrence and I plan to provide Friday buffets?" Monica speaks louder than she intends. "We're rotating each week."

"We'd have to vote on that," Jill says. "We don't want the appearance of a rift in the physician team."

Inane, high-pitched little voice. Robert's words. Not hers.

Terrence shrugs.

Another battle lost, Monica thinks. What a ridiculous battleground.

Knocking on the door.

Louise consults her watch. "Time's up for today."

May is a surprising, abundant month. As Eric feared, they have one more snowfall, but it lasts half a day. The next week daffodils appear. Then lilacs and hydrangea. Monica watches the maple in her back garden grow greener each morning. Hundreds of people walk and cycle and skate around Lake Calhoun.

Saturday afternoon with Mom in Duluth is blessedly warm, too. They stroll along the lake side.

She's grown so stiff.

"I'm fine. Don't fret."

"You know, seventy-four is young these days," Monica says uneasily. "You need to get out more. Have you tried the exercise classes or the bridge games at the Senior Center?"

"Mickey, I'm ready for a quieter life."

Maybe she is pushing too hard. Still, there's something in her mother's voice, her face. A broken spirit.

The next day, she phones Jeanne while Mom is at church. Too early in the morning, she hopes, for her sister to be drinking.

"Yes, yes, an appointment in two weeks." She sounds more than usually annoyed.

Since the pastoral committee picks Mom up for church, maybe she woke Jeanne. "Sorry, if you're still in bed, just call me back."

"Bed, I've been up for hours, cleaning after Mom."

Her heart races. "After what?"

"She has these accidents."

"She's incontinent?"

"She pisses in bed if that's what you're asking. I change sheets two or three times a week."

"Jeannie, the doctor needs to know about this. Things can be done to—"

"Obviously. I'm not an imbecile."

"I don't want to be pushy, but why has it taken so long to get an appointment?"

"Some deal about the Medicaid forms. Red tape."

"But I'm paying for Mom's supplemental insurance."

"I decided to let that go. She agreed. It's an unnecessary expense."

"My expense," she raises her voice, quickly backs off. "I want to do that for her."

"What you could do, Big Sister, is visit her more often."

Monica counts to twenty, glancing out at the luxuriant back garden. She never wanted her mother living two hours away. Jeanne knows how often she visits.

"I'll be back in mid-June. A couple of weeks. Eric and I have a long-standing plan to go out of town."

"You have lots of distractions. I knew it would be better for Mom in Duluth."

"Jeannie, I appreciate all you're doing for Mom. She appreciates it too. When I ask about medical care, I'm trying to contribute."

"I know."

A softening? Regardless, she feels braver. "Will you call me after the doctor's appointment? Let me know how things went?"

"Right, I'll call Saturday afternoon."

"Actually, I'm at the Free Clinic then. What if I ring you Saturday night?"

"Darts at the Tav on Saturdays, my one escape during the week now."

"Next Sunday, then?"

"It'll be a nice break from the laundry."

*****

Crab apples. Shoots of hosta. Oak branches hidden by a canopy of fragile green leaves. Bicycling to work, she considers how she loves the impetuousness of spring/summer in Minnesota. It makes her feel great leaps are possible.

Good spirits are infectious.

Louise appears, a minute after she walks in, with a huge bouquet of irises for the reception desk. She's humming (humming!) under her breath.

Traveling with Spirits

*****

Monica calls Duluth more frequently now. Each time, Mom sounds slightly vaguer. Is she imagining this?

She's less successful reaching Jeanne on Sunday morning. Always the answering machine. Jeanne doesn't return the calls.

She's really worried, not sure what she'll find when she rings on Wednesday.

"Hello."

Such a little voice, as if she's disappearing. Anti-depressants might help. That and more company.

"Mom, I might cancel the trip with Eric. I could come up and see you."

"No, no, dear," she regains full voice. "You need to relax. Truly, I'm fine. Jeannine made an appointment with that doctor you keep talking about."

"I miss you."

"I miss you, too, dear. I want my lass to be happy. You shouldn't keep that young man wondering if you're interested."

She loves sweet, quirky, flinty Eric. Does she love him enough?

"You have my cell phone, Mom. And here's the number of the B and B."

"You left them last week. They're right here by the phone. Don't worry so. Go off and have a fine time like young people should do in the spring!"

Young. Spring. She hangs on to these words and the echoing lilt of Mom's voice.

*****

Eric looks fresh and energetic, positively handsome in a green cotton shirt under a v-necked yellow sweatshirt. She can tell by the loose-fitting jeans that he's succeeded in jogging off the winter paunch.

"Is my lady ready for *le weekend du printemps*?"

"*Mais oui, Monsieur. Un moment.*"

He insists on carrying her roller suitcase on his head.

At the last moment she dashes back into the apartment for a blue and green quilt jacket.

: time to put away dull winter clothes.

They cross the gurgling Mississippi, leaving Minnesota behind. Ripe green shimmers. Wildflowers ribbon the Wisconsin bluffs. Near Maiden Rock, they stop for a picnic lunch. Eric indulges her shopping in Stockholm; she finds pretty Amish hats for Mom and Jeanne.

The bed and breakfast is a charming old prairie style house. They're greeted warmly by the hosts, Gerd, from Norway, a big-boned woman with close cropped blonde hair and green-rimmed glasses, and her partner Pam, a short, black woman wearing cornrows and a contagious smile. Gerd and Pam escort them to the largest room, with a window overlooking this huge bulge in the Mississippi which everyone calls Lake Pepin.

"Summer! Finally!" Eric declares over dinner at the Harbor View Restaurant.

She takes his hand. Friday night at the Harbor View is always crowded and noisy and they're lucky to get a table in the side room. "Yes, it's been a long year for you with college politics and everything."

"I'm trying not to think about it. Two entire months before I contemplate another syllabus or attend a meeting."

"You deserve a break."

"You could also use some time off, Monie. Have you thought about my invitation to the cabin for a week or two next month?"

"I think about it a lot. But the clinic is hectic these days and there's Mom. How can I swing it all?"

"You've said you've seen too many burned out docs screwing up from exhaustion."

"I'm not that far gone," she says too defensively. He is being solicitous.

"I'm taking preventive medicine. Plus the cabin is closer to Duluth."

"You have a point."

"How's your mom this week?"

"Fading away."

"But seventy-four is too young for that."

"She's lonely, needs more stimulus, better medical care."

Eric watches her. "What can you do? Sounds like Jeanne—despite her drinking and such—is doing her best."

"She is devoted to Mom. Still, she's at the bank all day. Mom's alone and—"

"Monica there's no perfect solution. You've made the decision, hon.

You need to stop obsessing."

"I never made any decision," she sighs heavily. "I don't think Mom did either!"

The waiter arrives with their walleye and wild rice.

She tries to regain composure. In a subdued tone, "Jeanne, well—it feels as if she's hijacked Mom."

Eric studies his hands, salts the dinner, begins to eat.

"OK, Mom said she wanted to go, that she always loved Lake Superior, but…"

"Tell me, did you get them on the phone when I was jogging this afternoon?"

"No, only Jeanne's answering machine. They planned to take a shoreline drive. They both have phone numbers. Pam and Gerd seem conscientious. They'd give me a phone message right away?"

"Absolutely."

She can't abide his worried eyes. "Alright. I'll let it go for tonight. I have a right to one weekend respite. And so do you."

"And a couple of weeks at the cabin?" he raises a thatch of eyebrow.

"One week," she smiles faintly.

He raises his glass. "We've sprung the doctor from the asylum for a week."

She laughs, clinks her glass. Maybe Beata is right about Eric being the one. When he disconnects from college fixations, he's a dear.

*****

Lovely holiday, she reflects on the drive back to Minneapolis. Luscious sex, great meals, long walks, intense conversations. Ambling past pretty houses and well-groomed yards, licking ice cream cones. She hasn't felt this relaxed in six months.

All the way home they laugh.

She shouldn't invite him in because she has early clinic appointments tomorrow.

His face is both wry and woeful.

She can't bear to end the weekend.

They set her bags down in the bedroom.

Before she knows it, Eric has pulled her onto the goose down comforter.

She laughs. "Wait, we have to eat dinner. I need a shower."

He persists, kissing her forehead, nose, neck. Praising each body part in French, German and Italian. He hasn't been this playful since those first nights two years ago.

"Ummmm."

"Yes," he's unclasping her bra. "Ummm."

Reflexively, she glances at the answering machine, spots the blinking red light.

"Eric, dear…" Gently, she disentangles herself. "Just let me check the messages. I'll feel easier. I'll be more present for you."

He rolls his brown eyes. "OK, Dr. Murphy, zap the distractions."

The first message: incomprehensible mumbling and weeping.

She stiffens.

Jeanne's weeping.

"3:30 p.m. today."

The next message: a Nordic accent, "Monica, your sister is trying to reach you."

"4:00 p.m. today."

She presses the speed dial to Jeanne's.

The phone rings and rings. No answer. She dials Mom's new doctor.

An answering service, "I understand this is urgent. Dr. Truman will call you as soon as he can."

Eric reaches for her hand and she draws back.

"I don't understand. Two calls here this afternoon. Jeanne had my cell." She rummages in her purse. "Damn! Damn!" she shouts, "Damn! Damn! Damn!" She shows him the cold grey phone.

He waits uneasily.

"No bars. It was working yesterday morning. But I forgot to charge it in Pepin. I plug it in each night, here in this socket, each night." She can't stop rambling. "Each night except the most important one."

"Monica, we don't know what's happened. Everyone forgets to plug—"

"Something terrible has happened. Didn't you hear Jeanne wailing? The message from Gerd?" She shakes her fists. Not his fault. Her fault. Her fault.

Eric watches cautiously.

"Jeanne doesn't phone unless she has to. God, maybe I should jump in the car and drive to Duluth now."

"You're exhausted. At least wait until the doctor phones." He takes her hand. "Monica, let's make a pot of tea…have a glass of wine."

The syrah unleashes a litany of worries.

Eric listens.

Nothing he says calms her. She switches on the TV news.

Another glass of wine. A Red Lion Pizza.

The phone rings.

"Dr. Murphy?"

"Yes. Dr. Truman?"

"No, Dr. Tremblay. I was on duty at the hospital. Do you have a friend there now?"

She reaches for Eric's hand and he squeezes hard. She feels as if she's clutching air. As if she's about to fall a very long distance.

"What's wrong?" The sound of her own vacant words unsettles her. "How is she? I can drive up now."

"I am so sorry, Dr. Murphy, but I have very bad news."

"Tell me." Her steadiest voice.

"I regret to say that your mother has died. Your sister Jeanne followed your mother's living will directive and cancelled life support."

"How? Why? When?"

"This is awkward. I don't meddle in family affairs, yet if I knew that Mrs. Murphy had another daughter so close by, we would have waited."

"She tried to call," she mumbles. "But when? What happened to Mom?"

"Your mother suffered a severe stroke yesterday afternoon."

"Afternoon. Yesterday. Why didn't someone call yesterday?"

Dr. Tremblay stays on track. "We worked with her for hours. Your mother was unconscious. All her systems were down. We could have continued the life support, but your sister decided…"

"I could have got there in a couple of hours. Well, three. I could have said good-bye." Tears course down her cheeks.

"I understand this, now, Dr. Murphy. But your sister had medical power of attorney. She didn't mention…and of course I didn't know about the drinking problem until later, when one of the nurses mentioned it."

She can't hear him any longer. Because she's screaming so loudly. Flooded with rage and shame and grief. Screaming as if she could bring back her mother, could heal her sister, could redirect the course of all their lives.

TWENTY-FOUR

June, 1999, Minnesota

Jeanne pours a second cup of coffee in her small, neat kitchen.

Monica tries to compose her thoughts two mornings after Mom's death.

"Father Dolan will say Mass," she reports. Again.

Jeanne nods. Again.

Monica observes how soberly they talk, discussing the cremation and mass, planning where to scatter her ashes. They're being practical. Civilized. Cold.

She will not reproach Jeanne about Mom's medical care. It's too late.

"The Altar Society ladies are notifying Mom's friends at church," she adds.

Jeanne fixes herself another Alka Seltzer.

Monica believes this is all her fault. If she'd been more adamant, maybe, or less adamant. No, this is a useless train of thought.

Then she simply cannot hold back any longer. "Jeanne, there's one thing I don't understand."

"What doesn't the doctor understand?"

She concentrates. "After the stroke, well, that was Saturday afternoon. I was at the bed and breakfast. Why didn't you try to reach me in Pepin?"

"You said your cell phone was dead."

"At some point, yes. But why didn't you call the B and B? Eric was jogging and I was sitting on the veranda reading."

"Thanks for the thorough report. I was busy with other matters. Under a lot of pressure. So I didn't think of it, OK?"

"You could have reached me. You didn't cut off life support until Sunday morning. I could have made it to Duluth before—"

"It was too late. Too late!" Jeanne screams. "She was already gone." Tears stream down her swollen red cheeks. "What was the point? I called the B and B when it was all over. Once the hard work was done."

"But surely," she slows down here to be reasonable, desperately wanting to comprehend. "I, I had a right to say good-bye. To see Mom at the end." She wonders for the first time now if Jeanne really did try the cell phone.

"You made it clear you were busy in Pepin, that you needed a complete break."

Oh, damn, damn, why, why didn't she follow her instinct and visit Mom on the Friday? It's possible that even at that stage, she would have noticed, could have done something. Yet, she wanted to believe Mom when she said she'd be fine, that Monica deserved a weekend with her "young man." Imagine a holiday in Pepin in exchange for Mom's life. Of course she shouldn't think like this. But she's so ashamed. She should have been there. To attend to Mom. To say farewell.

"That's not fair."

"Whatever. You weren't there, OK? I can't make important decisions based on what I imagine your wishes to—"

"Imagine my wishes! What else would a person wish? You didn't let me say good-bye." She enunciates slowly as if precision will pierce her sister's shell.

"It's over now," she asserts resolutely.

Over. Monica understands that for Jeanne this is a profound relief as well as a grievous loss. But she, herself, will always wonder if Mom knew she wasn't there at the end.

"We've lost our Mother, Jeanne," she reaches for her sister's hand. "It's important to talk about that."

"There's nothing left to say," she glares. "Nothing left to do."

Monica is astounded by the blend of anger and satisfaction in her little sister's face. The little sister who somehow has become a kind of enemy. No, she wants to scream, don't vanish on me like Dad and Mom, We're the only ones left. I need my sister back. But she remains silent because she knows that for now, Jeanne is at a precipice and she doesn't want to be the one to push her over the edge, where she'd be gone forever.

TWENTY-FIVE

June, 1999, Minnesota

She walks along Beata's leafy, quiet street toward St. Luke's, having parked near her friend's apartment for a quick exit from the reception. So gracious of her to host the gathering after Mom's requiem Mass. The church parlor is too institutional. And her own apartment is too far away for Mom's older friends.

Jeanne bristled at the idea. "She's not even a member of the family."

Monica didn't reply, "She's the closest thing I have to a sister."

One of the many things she didn't say. For the moment, Monica has given up on family communication. Given up trying to understand why she didn't let her say good-bye. They only discuss practical details of the cremation, mass and reception.

"It's the one sensible plan," she answered matter-of-factly.

Jeanne surrendered. The right word. Accepted, agreed, understood: none of these concepts seemed to be in Jeanne's vocabulary.

She takes a long breath of sweet early summer air and continues toward church, where Jeanne and Beata and Eric will be waiting in the front pew.

He wanted to escort her to church. Jeanne said it would look weird if family appeared separately. Beata understood this walk was her one occasion for solitude today.

Her opportunity to be alone with Mom.

Monica pictures her now: the trim woman cooking corned beef in the kitchen, supervising the potato scrubbing and Jeanne's table setting. Always Dad's favorite dish on his birthday.

Mom smiling proudly at the U, taking a photo of Monica in cap and gown.

Mom walking warily along the wharf several weeks ago: a blurry vision of herself, but still there. Marie Murphy. Mom.

Now this gentle, loving presence, has evaporated. "Oh, Momma," she whispers, "I love you. I love you so."

She reaches St. Luke's five minutes before Mass. She'll chat with Mom's friends afterward. That will be enough.

The parking lot is full. Mourners stream into the church.

Stricken with panic, she's sure she missed it as she watches all these strangers, young and old.

This is someone else's funeral.

Her watch says 3:55. Father Dolan is waving from the steps. Smiling. He's happy to see her as if she is on time, in the right place.

Although Mom wasn't much on fashion, she would like her black linen suit, would approve of the green scarf. "A little bit of color," she'd say, "always makes the outfit."

Father squeezes her hand. "Bless you dear."

"Thank you, Father." He wasn't the kind of priest to say, "We haven't seen you in quite a while." Still, she's feared the encounter.

"All these people knew Mom?"

"Your mother was a blessing to parish and community. People have been phoning all week to check the time of Mass." He pats her hand.

She whispers, "I better get in there, then."

She nods to Mom's long-time St. Paul neighbors, then to the Somali family who moved in more recently. To Angela and Dorothy of the famous bridge club. Then, an even bigger surprise—Dr. Jill, herself, sitting with Alonso and Terrence. Don't think about motive, not here, not now.

Beata has carefully arranged seating in the front pew. Jeanne is at the center aisle. Eric beside her, Beata next to him, saving a place by the far aisle for her.

She takes her seat and holds Beata's warm hand. "Thank you."

"Bless you, Monica."

The first notes of "Amazing Grace" strain as Father processes to the altar.

Everyone stands.

Monica thinks how Mom loved this hymn, even when it was considered "Protestant." A natural ecumenical, Mom embraced Vatican II and the vernacular mass. But she once confessed, "I can't get used to guitars in church. Maybe, dear, it's because the Larsen boys are always off key."

She gazes around reassured there are no guitars or tambourines, just an organist. The Larsens moved to Eden Prairie years ago.

Mass proceeds, as if in a childhood memory. The old words and music are comforting. After so many masses, confessions, rosaries, the Church has marked her indelibly.

Father Dolan stands before them. "Eternal Rest grant onto them, O Lord…" She remembers how much Mom loved his lush, baritone voice,

"And let perpetual light shine upon them."

Monica is glad Jeanne also nixed inviting speakers from the floor. They both want a simple Mass. Mom hated being center stage. Dad was the one who enjoyed spotlight: when he fled West, they were all a little confused about where to focus their attention.

Now Monica recalls the shock and sadness in his voice when she phoned him on Monday. She pictures the yellow roses—her parents' favorite flower—he sent to the funeral home. Sees Jeanne tossing them in the waste basket.

"Marie Murphy was a true Christian," Father Dolan begins. "Deeply involved in worship and service. She reared two fine daughters, Monica and Jeanne, who now grace the world with their different talents in medicine and business."

"Believe in God?" Her fifteen-year-old sister demanded one night after Mom had gone to bed. "Would a loving god give Mom this cruddy life? Tear her away from Ireland? Take her husband off to Nevada?"

"Wyoming," she whispered.

"Wyoming, who cares," she sped on. "Would a god give her arthritis? Leave her with a mortgage and a paltry salary?"

She still has no answer. She wonders if Jeanne was drinking then, in high school.

"Many here don't know each other. Marie Murphy's generous spirit extended so widely—the food shelter, the library literacy program, St. Luke's Good Neighbor Committee. Some of you had the joy of working with her for thirty or forty years."

"Momma, I love you. I miss you. Please know I would have come." She's kneeling now, praying directly to Mom. Praying for herself and Jeanne. It's been a long time since she felt the kneeler. Odd how she and Carol Fitzpatrick planned to become nuns when they were in seventh grade. Carol writes, occasionally, from her climate field station in Tanzania. They had been so sure in those days. She doesn't know about Carol, but her own certainty turned upside down at college where she learned to ask questions.

She glances at Jeanne, the once open-hearted child, now harder and wider from years of drink and lousy diet. Through all her disappointments, she remained fiercely dedicated to Mom. Jeanne's barely holding herself together. Her face is set just so; the wrong word from Father will spring her into a rage or a loud wail.

"Therefore, let us pray for those who have lost a great friend and neighbor. Let us pray that Marie's example of Christian charity will shine forth in all of us."

She pictures Dad driving the bus along Hennepin. Where is he at this moment? Drinking coffee and surveying the range? Riding a horse through the hills? She had to phone him about her death, of course, but was unprepared for his long, ragged moan, which said everything about regret and resignation.

The communion line is short. Neither Monica nor Jeanne receive. Not even today, she thinks, not even for this woman who lit all those candles.

Now it's over. Father instructs them to stand, to go in peace. She's supposed to walk outside. Pretend Mom is truly gone. Spend the rest of her life without her.

The organist plays "Jesu, Joy of Man's Desiring."

Beata takes her arm, whispering. "Come, they expect us to be the first to leave."

Already Jeanne and Eric are in the aisle behind Father, who leads them to the door.

Dazed, she walks along, holding Beata's hand.

Jeanne stands next to Father Dolan, numbly accepting condolences. Monica takes her position on the other side of the priest.

Sometime in the late afternoon, she notices Beata's spacious flat is packed with people enjoying plates of ham, chicken and potato salad. The Altar Society ladies have brought cookies and pies. Eric has supplied cold drinks and is supervising the coffee and tea. She's so lucky to have attentive, abiding Eric in her life.

Jeanne looks calmer. Monica maintains her distance, still afraid of what she might say, also leery of smelling her sister's breath.

During a lull in the sincere, effusive, overwhelming condolences, she drifts over to the window and glances at the back yard.

Mom never did take down the swing set.

Every night of summer vacation, she and Jeanne played on the swings after dinner. Monica loved to soar high, high above and dream about the chain looping over the top as she made a beautiful circle. Maybe one day she'd fly hot air balloons or airplanes. Jeanne preferred a shorter, boring rhythm closer to the ground.

"Come on, try, Jeanne, you can get this high too."

"I don't want to. I'm fine."

"Come on, it's fun..."

"Not my kind of fun," she grumbled.

Monica watched the pretty, apple-faced girl sway monotonously back and forth.

"You're just scared," she prodded.

"You're nuts!" Jeanne shouted. "Nuts. Nuts. Swings are dangerous. Kevin O'Reilly spent two weeks in the hospital. Do you know people can die? Mom and Dad could die, you and I could..."

Baffled by this cautiousness, Monica cajoled. "Come on, nobody's going to die. Not for a while. You're six years old. You're smart enough not to go too high."

Jeanne jumped down and ran to the back porch. She picked up Felix and stroked the cat ardently.

Monica shakes her head, startled to see that the swing set is painted blue, that it resides in Beata's back garden. That's right, they sold the house when Mom moved to Duluth. The swings are gone; the homestead is gone. Mom is dead.

A tap on her elbow.

Mrs. Wilson looks healthy, alert, a little tired, with sweat along her hairline from the June humidity. "I'll be going now, dear."

"Thank you for joining us, Mrs. Wilson."

"Of course. Marie was the model neighbor. She was lucky how successful, yet dutiful, her daughters were in different ways. What a saint Jeanne was at the end."

"Yes," she nods numbly. "We both loved Mom a great deal."

"Yes, both of you. She was so proud of her daughter, the doctor. There weren't many children from our neighborhood who went as far as you did."

She smiles faintly, wants to disappear.

Now that it's evening, her attention clicks on and off. One minute, she's thanking Eric and the next she's silently arguing with Jeanne. One minute she's talking to Father and the next she's wondering when Mom will show up at this lovely party.

Time to go. Does she imagine this? Is she being released? All the guests have gone. Jeanne, too. Washing up is finished.

"Thank you, thank you. She throws her arms around Beata and Eric. "You're the best of friends."

They all hang on tight, swaying affectionately.

Monica sighs, detaches, reaches for her purse. "I have early morning patients."

"No, Monica," Eric demurs. "Beata has made a dinner reservation at Frosts. To unwind. You don't want to go back to an empty apartment."

Empty apartment. There's nothing she craves as much.

"Yes, Monica, it will be good for all of us to debrief," Beata tries, "or even to sit quietly over a glass of wine in a room without funeral echoes."

"Sorry. You've both been very, very kind. I need to be alone. So much to absorb."

"Monica," Eric takes her hand, "stay."

"No," Beata touches his shoulder. "If solitude is what she needs, we must let her go."

"Okay," he says reluctantly. "Remember we love you. Call if you want company."

She nods, afraid that if she says another word, she'll burst into tears.

Hours later, she's still driving the streets of St. Paul. Very dark now, it's time to head home. On the freeway, she feels queasy but she makes it safely to the Hennepin exit. She pulls over and starts walking, starved for fresh air.

The sky is that majestic blue-black before the night shade is completely drawn. She hopes Beata and Eric aren't trying to reach her at home. Finally, the temperature has dropped and there's a slight wind. Or is that the breath of cars zipping along Hennepin?

Dad will be by soon. She looks for him on each bus. He has to pass here. She buttons her sweater. Mom will be mad she's left home without a jacket.

"Spare change, Lady?" The skinny man reminds her of Armand Millar from fourth grade.

"Spare change, Lady?" he says more loudly, as if she's really a lady.

"Sure," she digs in her pocket for a dime. She won't need bus fare. Dad always let her ride for free and she's not allowed to tell Mom, who is strict about the seventh commandment and doesn't believe in cheating the bus company.

"Thanks, Ma'am." He shuffles off.

"Ma'am," imagine that.

Her watch says 11:30. Mom will be frantic at this hour. She must wonder where Dad is, too.

A police car pulls over, idles nearby.

Two concerned cops hop out and approach her. One officer, the woman, sits beside Monica at the bench. "Waiting for a bus, Miss?"

"I'm not a miss," she says for some reason. "I'm a doctor. Dr. Murphy. Well, I plan to be a doctor when I grow up."

"Dr. Murphy," the officer repeats solemnly. "May I see your ID?"

She hands over a big wallet. Where did she get that?

Something cracks. The breeze stops. Monica is freezing on a dark bench talking to a police woman. Crazy. They think she's crazy.

"Yes, officer," she pulls herself together. "I had a problem with my car. My mother died and…" She's weeping uncontrollably. Sobbing as she couldn't sob at home, at church, keening at midnight at a bus stop on Hennepin Avenue.

"There, there, Doctor," the officer places a light hand on her shoulder. "I see you live about a mile from here in Uptown. Why don't we drive you home? Is your car safely parked?"

"Yes, yes."

"Is there someone we can call? A relative?"

"No, no relative," she panics.

"Perhaps a friend?"

"Beata," she says numbly and recites her best friend's phone number.

TWENTY-SIX

September, October, 1999, Minnesota

Beata lounges across from her in the blue easy chair, reading a novel. Monica stares out at the yellowing gingko and the fiery maple. Soon the early dark will be upon them. And perhaps sleep will come easier than it has this summer.

Beata looks up. "You OK?"

"Fine, just thinking about autumn."

"Great colors this year, they predict."

"You're really the best."

Beata frowns doubtfully.

"Spending all this time with me. Being good company, reading or watching silly videos. I'm so grateful."

"This is what friends do, hang out together."

The telephone rips through the evening's hard-won tranquility. Monica's nerve endings are completely exposed.

Deliberately, she returns to her book.

The ringing persists. Does it grow louder?

Beata watches her.

"Machine will get it," Monica says, eyes fixed on her book.

Two clicks, then: "Monica, it's Eric. Again. Please pick up. Why are you avoiding me? Did I do something? Not do something? Please call. I've put off going to the cabin for weeks and I should leave soon. Call me, Monica. Please." Click.

She gazes out the back window.

"So what's going on?" Beata asks.

"How do you mean?"

"Why aren't you answering his calls? OK, you needed space the first few weeks, but he's been ringing a very long time." Her brown eyes round with worry.

"I can't take care of anyone right now."

"What if he wants to take care of you?"

Jeanne sat on the swing, her face wrenched with anguish. "Do you know people can die?"

She shrugs.

"Are you angry with him?"

"Why would I be angry?" she flares. Startled by her intensity, she adds quietly, "What makes you say that?"

"You feel this groundless guilt about Marie's death. Maybe you think he was some kind of accomplice?"

"Thank you, Dr. Johnson, for your shattering insight."

Beata sits back. "Sorry, that was intrusive."

Monica can't hold back the tears. "No, you've been wonderful, Beata. Eric, yes, in some twisted way, I may hold him complicit in that awful weekend. I feel so ashamed."

"There was nothing shameful about it."

"Then why do I feel so god-damned guilty?"

"Because it's easier than feeling other things?"

"Like torment about not saying good-bye to Mom." She pounds the arm of the couch. "Like rage at Jeanne."

Beata joins Monica on the couch, slips an arm around her shoulder. "Maybe, yes."

"And betrayal. I failed utterly in the last, most important time. I abandoned her, like Dad. I feel so alone. I'm grateful for your friendship. And for Eric. I truly wish I knew how to take him back into my life."

"You could start by answering one of his calls, just talking."

"I don't think I can risk it, the disappointment. Deep down, I feel all alone now. So alone."

"Monica, there's something I've been wanting to mention."

She looks up, wiping the tears with the back of her hand.

"Now don't get upset."

"A shopping expedition?" Monica aims for a change in tone. "Another big shoe sale?"

"Metaphorically speaking," Beata studies her. "Shopping for equanimity."

Monica adroitly extricates herself from Beata's embrace. Yet she knows she'll acquiesce. There's no choice.

"A retreat but not what you think. This is ecumenical: Buddhist and Catholic, considering the Paramitas from different spiritual traditions— at St. Ursula's in a few weeks. Fall is stunning out there. We could take walks. You could attend as few sessions as you liked."

Most days are slow, ponderous. One early Friday morning, before anyone arrives, she reviews patient notes. It takes a while to settle in, the grief counselor says. Monica has given the same advice to her own patients. Even after years in Medicine, watching people die, helping people die, it's completely unbelievable that her mother is gone.

A rap on the door. "Monica, are you there?" A woman's voice.

"Yes."

"It's me, Jill." A pause. "May I speak with you?"

Cautiously, Monica opens to the door.

Jill holds out a book. "This was really helpful when my dad died. I hope I'm not intruding."

"No," she says, suddenly aware of her defensive posture. "Would you like to come in?"

"For a moment," Jill says. "I have to be at the station by eight. But I didn't get to speak with you after your mother's Mass."

"Thank you for coming." She is chastened.

"I hope you are taking care of yourself. I'm doing a series on family leave this month. Paternity, caretaker, grief. Have you caught any of the spots?"

"I'm afraid not."

"Compassionate leave is an important preventive measure. And if you need more time, I'll talk with Louise."

"Thank you. Really, thanks." She can't think of anything she'd like less than Jill appealing to Louise or being the poster child for her radio show. She should be grateful. The woman is trying to help. Like so many people. Eric urges her to come up to the Boundary Waters. The grief counselor invites her to join a group. Mrs. Wilson calls every week, offering a home-cooked meal.

"It's the least I can do." Jill takes her hand.

"Actually, Jill, work is the best therapy for me. Thanks so much for coming by. And for the book."

Jill touches Monica's arm. "Just let me know." She closes the door softly behind her.

Head on her desk, Monica sobs in dry heaves.

*****

The room is almost monastic, well, cheery monastic. A single bed and a small sink. A bathroom shared with the neighboring cell. Straight back chair with a small desk facing French doors which open out to a woods of oak and maple. She thinks about Carol Fitzpatrick and the certainty of their youth.

Monica unpacks and pulls out a map of local hiking trails.

The opening evening, Beata has promised, will be light on ritual.

*****

She sits beside Beata and watches the speakers appear. The round, sixtyish woman named Mary Arneson, is a Buddhist teacher. The priest from Pondicherry, Father Sanjay Daniel, is as thin as his colleague is round and as dark as she is fair. Perfect Minnesota nod to diversity, she thinks sardonically, checking out the audience, mostly white, save for Beata and a Southeast Asian man near the back.

Beata pats her hand encouragingly.

Pay attention, Monica. Don't waste the entire weekend stewing in suspicion.

Mary Arneson introduces each of the Paramitas: Generosity. Morality. Renunciation. Wisdom. Energy. Patience. Truthfulness. Determination. Lovingkindness. Equanimity. Her long dark hair falls to the shoulders of a shapeless blue dress, a tent capacious enough to contain all these virtues and more.

Father Daniel explains that they'll review five Paramitas on Saturday and five on Sunday. Each afternoon there will be a general discussion. Monica likes his informal authority and openness.

"A room at the south end of the building is always open for silent meditation." He tugs absently at his clerical collar. "Curiosity. Dispute. Enthusiasm. Skepticism. All attitudes are embraced here."

*****

She follows Beata in the cafeteria line and they snag places at a corner table. She prefers a personal chat to a "getting to know you" chat with five unknown seekers.

Dusk huddles in. Autumn days are growing shorter. Orange and red leaves glow in the last light.

"May I join you?" A high-pitched, familiar voice.

Monica's heart sinks at the thought of being trapped in "community."

"Certainly, Father," Beata answers for them. "Please sit down."

She recovers. "Yes, welcome, Father."

"I'm eager to meet Americans on their home turf, as it were," he speaks with British-inflected English. The crisp lyrical accent Monica enjoyed this afternoon.

"You've never met Americans before?" Beata inquires.

That's it. Let Beata handle him: she loves priests. Monica can zone out. Maybe excuse herself early and read in the room.

"Oh, I know Americans in India," he smiles. "Several work in our medical mission."

"Medical mission?" Monica asks.

Suddenly, they're the only ones left in the cafeteria. Beata sips her tea and watches happily as they chat.

"You know a fair amount about India," Father Daniel is pleased.

"Not really. A grade school project. Close Indian friends from med school. And I devour novels from South Asia."

Beata stretches, "If you'll both excuse me, I should prepare for bed. I understand tomorrow is a big retreat day."

Father Daniel throws up his hands. "Apologies for monopolizing your evening. I didn't expect to find another doctor here and someone like you, Beata, so well-versed in public health questions. Thank you for a most enlightening conversation." He bows and departs.

Monica studies his light tread, head bobbing from side to side. She checks her watch. "Oh, shit, I had no idea."

Beata is grinning. "Retreats are like this. Time flows. Flies. Floats."

"Come on. We were talking about ideas, not—"

"Not what? You didn't expect to think on a retreat?"

Monica yawns. She doesn't know what to expect. She does know she's not going to win this round with Beata.

At sunrise, Monica rambles in the woods. She loves early October when the colors are most vibrant and cool mornings lead to warm afternoons. Light is sharp and bright. If only this lasted longer, if only…

She finds a seat at the back of the hall, on the aisle: her customary location, a position for slipping in and out unnoticed.

Mary Arneson speaks simply and clearly, about the Buddhist concept of generosity, the habit of sharing, of letting go of need. Her dark hair is pulled back in a silver barrette. She's persuasive because of her indifference to persuasion.

Father Daniel exhibits the same disregard for conversion. He provides colorful examples from the New Testament of Christ's generous nature, about the satisfaction of being a good neighbor, about the manifestation of joy through giving.

All sensible, straightforward concepts. None of it seems religious at all. Fervent young Carol Fitzpatrick would be very disappointed as would her pious friend Monica. She's not sure how the current Monica feels about...anything.

She ducks out before the session on "Renunciation." A useful topic, but she's too fragile with guilt and shame. She showers and lies down for a few minutes.

Wakening an hour later, she gapes at the clock. She hasn't napped since childhood. She holds her forehead, but finds no fever. Actually, she feels invigorated.

The second day passes swiftly. Mary's talk about Lovingkindness feels like a testament to Mom. There are degrees of virtue Monica knows she'll never achieve. She does agree with much of what Mary and Father say about patience, truthfulness, determination, but she's irritated by their enthusiasm. Their spiritual gusto.

The afternoon is intense with eager people testifying about their successes and failures with equanimity.

Monica likes the other participants, although some are rather earnest. She glances out the window at an orange maple.

Then she finds her hand in the air.

"Yes, Monica," Mary calls on her.

"Equanimity is the one I have the most trouble with."

Father Daniel regards her playfully. "Why do you think we left it for last?"

She persists, "This accepting—surely some things aren't acceptable. Many of the most vocal anti-war activists are Buddhists and Catholics."

Mary mulls this over. "We work for social justice and to assuage pain when we can, but sometimes—"

"That's it," she interrupts. "How can God or 'the Spirit' allow war? How can you believe in a power so unfair, cruel?" She hears Jeanne's voice. Finally, an accord.

"A fascinating challenge, Monica," Father Daniel acknowledges. "Tell us what you mean by fair and unfair."

A bell rings.

End of session. They often end like this, on a question. Monica doesn't know if she's more relieved or aggravated.

The final ritual is inclusive and brief. She doesn't pay much attention, still chewing on the question. She does feel respect for the retreat leaders and gratitude the weekend didn't turn to be sanctimonious or woo-woo.

Beata hums as they pack for the car. Monica is still brooding about unfairness.

"Monica!" someone calls.

Father Daniel rushes toward them, breathless, holding a small white card.

"Oh, Father, we were coming back to say good-bye."

"I trust you found the weekend…" he regards her mischievously and pauses as if wishing her to finish the sentence.

What does he want to hear? Instructive, inspirational, useful? Honesty, she tells herself and out spills, "Provocative."

"Precisely," he declares. "I, too. Please take my email address."

She smiles in surprise.

"We do have email in India. In fact, we are a nation known for our techies."

"Yes, of course."

"Minnesota isn't far from Tamil Nadu when you connect electronically."

She hands him a business card. "It would be fun to hear from you."

They drive back to the Cities in silence.

As Beata takes the exit for 35 W, Monica says, "Your powers are unpredictable."

"Yes?"

"Of all the outcomes I might have anticipated, I never thought I'd wind up with a priest as a pen pal."

"Don't forget, he's invited you for haute cuisine in Pondicherry."

"Right," Monica says as they pull up to her apartment. "I'll book a flight next week. And be sure to send you post cards."

TWENTY-SEVEN

October, 1999-August, 2000, Minnesota

It's a symphonic autumn morning, Monica thinks, the crisp edge of cold. On the lawns of grand lakefront houses, Japanese maples pulse fiery red. The lofty gingko in Adam's yard is sheer gold now, on the cusp of dropping leaves. She loves the Sunday morning walk around Lake Calhoun, watching joggers, bicyclists and skaters. And people strolling in jeans or Sunday dresses. Since Holy Spirit parish is directly across the lake from her, she has a chance to think over the sermon. This brisk late October day feels ripe with unfamiliar contentment.

The phone is ringing when she opens the door. Monica runs up the stairs and is breathless as she lifts the receiver. "Hello."

"In the middle of calisthenics or something?" Her dear, deadpan sister.

"No," she pants, surprised that she didn't screen the call. "I ran upstairs."

"Oh, hanging out with your friend Beata at the Coffee Shack?"

"I'm coming back from Mass," she says without thinking.

"Church?" she exclaims. "You've gone over to the dark side looking for Mom?"

Settling by the window, she drinks in the late autumn colors. "This isn't about Mom," she murmurs. Charity, she reminds herself, lovingkindness.

"You have to face facts, Mickey, she's gone. You can't go into some airy fairy hereafter looking for her."

Monica holds her tongue. If she's learned any spiritual practice it's silence.

"I guess you called about the financial papers?" Lately this is their only topic.

"Yeah," Jeanne says. "I've made some kind of order. Her affairs were really a shambles."

"Jeanne, I don't mind doing that work. You've done so much." She hates bookkeeping, but hates it less than her sister's carping. Besides, this is her responsibility, too.

"If there's one thing I know how to do, it's accounting," Her voice rises. "No, no, I'm only trying to locate the final sale papers on the house."

Monica wants to ask, *You mean the house you made her sell?* Instead, she says, "I'll check my folders. I don't think I have anything, but I'll look."

"Fine," Jeanne answers, hanging up before either says good-bye.

Monica recalls Mom in the little kitchen, burns on her arms where she wasn't black and blue. She smells chocolate and oatmeal rising from the cookies. Why did it take her so long to notice the bruises and blisters?

Three Canadian geese fly by the window, heading south for winter. Time is short. With patients. With Mom.

Jeanne is wrong about why she's been going to Mass. She wants a different perspective on Mom's death, on her own life. Maybe she won't continue attending. Who knows?

The garden comes into focus. And the brilliant oaks across the alley.

*****

Lucia's Café is louder in the cold, dark months. Snow on the ground since the first week in November. She waits for Eric at "their" table by the window, trying to concentrate on the book about lovingkindness for her study group. She hopes this is the right choice for their first dinner since the funeral in June. And their first meeting since they broke up over the phone in September.

"Hello there!" Eric looks sharp in the maroon cardigan she got for his last birthday. His smile is provisional.

The earth has revolved a thousand times since that interminable day five months ago. She's been to Hades and back, with no sighting of Persephone.

He bends over, kisses her cheek.

Feeling the familiar heat, she is touched by nostalgia rather than desire.

"You look great," he declares.

"You, too."

Glancing up from the menu, she confesses, "I'm sorry I ignored your calls for so long—"

"Monica, don't worry, I understand."

"I'm sorry," she persists. "I was too full of grief. The suddenness of her death was unbearable." She pulls out a tissue, but she's resolved not to cry. "That and the shame. When I wasn't numb, I was scared, guilty.

My whole body was a huge ache, as if someone had ripped out major organs."

"Monica you have no reason for guilt. When my dad died his best friend said, 'You'll always think you could have done, or said, one more thing.'"

She nods, remember his loss.

"I guess you implicate me, unconsciously. She died during our get-away."

"No," she takes his warm, comfortable hand.

The waiter recites specials. They both order arugula salad and trout. Nothing has changed. Everything has changed.

"I should have been less persistent, more patient," he says.

"Monica, please pick up the phone and let me know you are okay."

"I don't blame you. And breaking up has nothing to do with—"

"Don't worry, Monie, I'm not going to ask you to come back."

Something in his voice, or her heart, makes her wonder.

"I just don't want to lose my best friend. I miss our talks and your wicked wit."

She clutches the tissue, surprised, a little sad that he's not trying harder. No, what she needs, and seems to have is a loyal friend.

The arugula is accented with sun-dried tomatoes and a dust of feta. Yuletide colors. Advent. Season of waiting.

"Tell me about the church stuff. Is the bible class interesting?"

"It's a study group. We read books about Islam, Judaism, Christianity, Daoism, Buddhism." She doesn't mention attending Mass. She hasn't told Beata.

"Is it those people from the retreat?"

"One of them, Mary Arneson, gave a stunning talk last night about the engaged spiritual life."

"The what?"

"About finding a deeper way to practice your convictions by contributing…"

"You already do that. At Lake Clinic. At the Free Clinic. With your tutoring. Your whole life is working for others."

"It's about being mindful, too."

"Beata tells me you have a pen pal in India."

"Father Daniel wrote the day he returned home. I think we're developing a kind of friendship."

"What do you write about?"

"Medical stuff, like preventive health programs." She doesn't mention her spiritual questions and his judicious suggestions.

Eric looks relieved.

"So tell me about Macalester? That drama with the dean?"

"They hired a firecracker in the development office. So I don't have to hit people up for money or their kidneys."

She manages a couple of bites of the fish. Even the wild rice tastes too rich. She moves the food around her plate, hoping he won't notice how much is left.

"I've missed our talks."

"Me, too." Sipping the wine that appeared on their table at some point, she worries about her tendency of jerking in and out of focus like an old TV.

Eric describes his freshman seminar. She loves his enthusiasm and marvels at her own impatience with this lovely guy.

"And Doctor Jill?" He surfaces from school. "Are you booked for a guest spot?"

"Now, there's someone I could practice lovingkindness on."

"Loving whatness?"

"I'll explain as I walk you to your car." She's suddenly wiped out. This exhaustion comes at odd moments and she can't shake it.

"I had to park way off, near your apartment. Uptown is hopping tonight."

She buttons her quilted parka. A little premature, but she's feeling the cold lately.

"I have a feeling we're going to get hit with a blizzard."

"Eric," she pokes him in the side as they walk outside. "You start fretting about icy roads in July!"

*****

Monica slips into her favorite place, the aisle by the wall in the last pew. She kneels, rests her head between her hands. This is the right place for now. She glances at the altar—at the purple and green banners proclaiming, "Agape." "Peace." "Faith."

Beata walks up the aisle with Marion Bradley. Of course! Her old school friend is delivering the homily today. Monica evades Beata's curious glance. How embarrassing. She's been waiting for certainty before telling Beata. When will she be certain? She's tried Quaker and Unitarian services, the Zen Center and none of them feels right. Is she comfortable here because the smells and colors and words are familiar?

It's childish to hide like this. She kneels straighter.

Beata turns again, catches her eye, winks.

She may not be ready to tell Beata. But Beata is ready to find out.

On the way to the vestibule, Beata links arms with her. "Morning, sister."

"Hi there, old pal."

"Shall we go out for Sunday coffee?"

"Aren't you going to the breakfast for Marion? It was a fine homily."

"He'll be swamped by people. I've already said congrats and good-bye." Her voice is no-nonsense. "Explained I saw someone I really need to catch up with."

"I know we need to talk, but I can't do coffee. I have an appointment with Father Tom in forty-five minutes. Maybe we could sit in the parish library?"

She rounds those intense brown eyes and purses her lips. "Parish library. Father Tom. You know your way around. Is there something you haven't told me?"

She ushers Beata into a long room filled with books. On the far wall is a projector and CD player. Beata sits on the green leather couch. Monica takes an easy chair.

"Nice to see you," Monica tries.

"Come on, hon, what's going on? You're going to Church?"

"To this one," she whispers tentatively, "sometimes."

"Why not St. Olaf's? My parish?"

"Because it's your parish. Your priest. Your community. I also didn't go to Mom's parish. I needed my own place."

Beata is beaming.

"Don't get carried away. I simply wanted to explore different spiritualities, as Father Daniel would say."

"Father Daniel? So you're having a good dialogue with him?"

She nods.

The scents of coffee and hot sweet rolls and re-heated quiche rise up through the vents from the parish hall. Monica wishes they were mingling with Marion Bradley's fans and not having this private, strangely raw conversation.

"Will you tell me more?"

Monica looks at her watch; it's almost time to meet Father Tom.

"Right, your appointment. OK, I'll stop badgering now. But this is topic number one for Saturday night. Deal?"

"Deal."

*****

She kneels in the confessional. The old church is redolent with scents of furniture polish and stale flowers and holy water. Cold in here this December afternoon.

"Bless me Father, for I have sinned."

"You don't have to be this formal, Monica."

"It has been sixteen years since my last confession."

"You're so tense. We could simply sit and talk."

"Thanks, I prefer kneeling. I need…" She sniffs into a tissue.

"There's nothing to be frightened of. Relax if you can."

Nothing to be frightened of? Her whole life has crashed. Mom has died. Jeanne is drinking herself into oblivion. She hardly hears from Dad, despite his promise to be in touch. She hates her colleagues and for months she's been prickly at work.

"Tell me, what's on your mind," Father Tom suggests.

"I feel so guilty, ashamed about Mom's death. I should have been more alert for at least a year before. The burns, the bruises, the forgetfulness." She can't face the vastness of her neglect.

"You visited her often. And you had patients, volunteer work, a life."

What does well-meaning Father Tom know? She's wasting their time and is glad he can't read her face through the grill. "I should have noticed more."

"But you didn't."

Silence between them. Footsteps in the aisle. A squeaky kneeler being lowered.

"Can you accept, admit, that you didn't notice?"

"Admit," she's disgusted with herself, "admit that I caused—or at least contributed to—Mom's early death."

"Monica, God took your mother. You weren't ready for her to go. But God was. And maybe your mother was, too?"

"Admit," she repeats to keep afloat in the wreckage of blame and remorse.

"Admit," he advises, "in the sense of acknowledge. Yet also in the sense of 'let in, give access, allow to pass.' "

"Forgive myself?" she flares.

"Admit, first, that you are human."

"Of course I know I'm human. A failed human. If I had understood Dad's longing, I could have talked to him. And Jeanne, I'm a doctor and I can't stop her drinking. Then Mom, the person I loved most, I failed to save her, too."

"Monica, doctors do help people. But do you ever save them?"

"Certainly not," she snaps.

"And those people you failed, you didn't put yourself on the list."

"What do you mean?"

"I suspect the place you've truly failed is in loving yourself."

"Oh, come on."

He waits.

She starts to cry. "I'm so flawed. There's so much I've done wrong."

"How are you responsible for your father's departure, Jeanne's drinking or your mother's death? Does it hurt more to think that perhaps that you couldn't prevent the losses?"

She's had enough. What's the exit line? Buttoning her sweater, she runs her hands over her cold arms. Time to go.

"Monica, you have many fine qualities. But your humility could use some work."

"What is my penance, Father? Will you absolve me and give me penance?" Although she doesn't believe in sacraments, she's superstitious about simply leaving.

"What do you think your penance should be?"

Her knees hurt from the kneeler. She can't think of an answer.

He leans his head toward the grill, as if to hear if she's still breathing.

"Are you cold in there?" she asks.

"Not particularly. What kind of atonement would you like to make?"

"A rosary?"

He's quiet.

"Two rosaries?" she tries. Maybe they've upped the ante since she was a kid.

"Monica, do say the rosary if you're inclined, but I'd like to ask you something."

Nervously, she tuches her head to the grill to catch his words.

"This week, only for one week, I want you to do a kindness for yourself each day. Can you do that?"

She refuses to cry. Quickly, she says, "Yes, thank you, Father."

*****

The lake is another world during the short January day. Frozen to the center. Still. Skeletal branches of black trees chatter. A few birds peck through the snow over the dead grass. How do they survive? Strollers are bundled in parkas and face masks.

Beata's solution is to stride vigorously and Monica works to keep up with her friend's long legs.

"Lucky with this sun," Beata says. "Sun on the snow. All this brightness."

"So you're converting to winter?"

"I'm accepting winter. I'm admitting winter."

Admit. Monica smiles tightly.

"Friend, I owe you an apology," Beata says. "When I tried to drag you over to my parish, it was so wrong."

"I should have told you earlier."

"You weren't ready." She waits for Monica to respond and when she doesn't, softens her voice. "I'm here when you want to talk."

"I have questions. But at Holy Spirit people talk about morality and ethics. I sort of traded those concepts for politics at the U. I wanted to be a good political person. Righteous. Progressive."

"You are."

"I want more. I want to work in a place with people who share my values."

"Don't we all?"

"Lake Clinic has some fine people, but it isn't the practice where I can contribute how I need to."

"Now you have Father Tom, the study group, others at Holy Spirit."

They're passing the docking area where all the row boats are tied for the season.

"I've found comfort in the past few months, but I can't buy the whole program. The Church's stand on contraception, on condoms in the midst of an HIV/AIDS crisis."

"Many of us disagree with that. Catholics for Choice: I recently joined this group to lobby for women priests."

"How do you accept the contradictions?"

She's staring at the small hills: Dakota burial mounds they were taught in school. A young man jogs by, followed by a golden lab.

"Things will change," Beata says. "The Church is a social institution and people are contradictory. Rome has to adapt. You need faith."

"That's what Father Daniel says."

"How often do you guys write?" Beata quickens her pace.

Monica catches up. "You seem bothered."

"Bothered," Beata repeats stiffly. Wind gusts around the lake. She pulls her hat down. "Why do you say that?"

"Your voice, whenever I mention him."

"You mention him a lot."

She's hurt by the tone. "We're not having a romance or anything."

"It's a little odd. A doctor and a priest. He must be a busy man yet he regularly emails a stranger on the other side of the earth."

"Small world," she repeats his farewell at the retreat. "He's become a kind of spiritual mentor. I thought you'd be pleased."

"I'd be pleased if you found someone closer to home. Pretty soon, you'll be headed off to India!"

"Oh, sure!" She laughs. "He challenges my dogged questions. And after all, maybe I'm incapable of faith. Doctors look for symptoms, evidence. Faith is the opposite."

"Sometimes you have to be OK with not knowing."

"Perhaps that works for you, Beata, but it's not in my nature."

"Humility," she bursts out, "that's what's not in your nature."

She steps back, stung.

Beata takes her hand. Her red leather glove over Monica's blue polar tech mittens. "Monica, I love you. But you're so demanding—of the universe, of yourself."

"What's wrong with that?"

*****

Monica waits at an outside table, preparing herself for Beata's objections. On this sweltering August night, they'd be better off inside the air-conditioned bistro. But she needs to contain the imminent explosion. Beata's last phone call was angry and distraught.

She wants a glass of chilled white wine. She might have several glasses tonight. For the moment, she needs to stick with ice water and slow breaths.

Cars zip by. Several lumbering trucks groan and wheeze. The exhaust is irritating. All this will aggravate Beata's mood. Should they move inside?

"Hi there!" Beata bends down, hugging Monica. "Nice to return to the old hang out."

She kisses Beata's moist cheek.

Monica recalls that frigid January night when they talked about work and family here, when Beata tried to lure her to the Lutsen retreat. She remembers the bad art. And how Beata was turning heads then in her splendid coat, as she is now, in her close-fitting yellow cotton dress. "Good to see you."

Beata orders a Sangiovese. "Red wine is good for the heart, right?"

"A certain amount, yes."

She can't hold back any longer. "A medical mission in the foothills of Northern India?!"

"Sorry I couldn't find a warmer place for you to visit." She gulps the water, glances at the traffic. "But Pondicherry Mission is full and Moorty badly needs staff."

"Why did I ever bring you to that retreat? Why didn't you become a nice domestic Buddhist? That Mary woman was pretty impressive."

Actually, Beata did bring her back to church. First the retreat. Then those books, Thomas Merton and John Henry Newman being the most important. Beata sharing her doubts about papal doctrine. Beata's example of tranquility.

"Who says I'm not a Buddhist?"

Beata shakes her head. "I support any decision you make."

She's not persuaded.

"But I have to ask the hard, obvious, almost patronizing question."

"No, I'm not running away." Monica faces her directly. "You implied that on the phone. I do need to leave for a while, but I'm not running away."

As the waiter takes their drink orders, she resolves to lighten up, maintain her convictions and embrace Beata's concerns.

"But India! How will you deal with the restrictions of a Catholic hospital there? We're not talking progressive Catholic like our parishes. As you know, you'll be facing women who need to limit their pregnancies.

And..."

"Yes." She has practiced the answer. "Still there are many contributions to make. People suffer enormously from eye and gastrointestinal diseases. Besides, didn't we have this conversation before? Didn't you vote for contradictions?"

They order dinner. A brief détente.

"After years of reconciling triage with good health care at Lake Clinic, I do know something about ambiguity."

Beata's eyes are red. "But there are Catholic Worker Projects all over the US—hospices and so forth."

"And far more people in India without medical care."

"What about the dangers? Bombings? Kidnappings?"

"Dear, dear friend, I know you're worried. But I've thought it all out. I'll take whatever faith I have with me. That and, I hope, your prayers."

"Certainly," her voice is hoarse.

"You do think I'm crazy."

"In the most admirable way," she digs into her purse for a tissue.

That knock-off Prada bag is always neat—comb, make-up kit, velvet pouch for her rosary, slim red wallet. Monica knows there's also a picture of her family. And a photo of Beata and herself at Eric's cabin.

They hold hands until the puzzled waiter appears with two seafood salads.

Monica takes a deep breath. "Will you write to me?"

"Every week," Beata smiles faintly, "until I come check on you in person."

TWENTY-EIGHT

March-April, 2002, Moorty

Stepping off the train at Moorty, Monica is astonished by the cool sunshine. A world away from Father Daniel's mission in Pondicherry, where temperatures have already hit forty degrees Celsius. What an inspiring visit, but she's grateful to return to the bracing air of the foothills.

The thin porters are soon out of sight, carrying luggage and small gifts from Pondicherry to Moorty Mission. What a crystal spring day. Right, this week is Holi. Ten days ago, when Monica left for the seminar in Tamil Nadu, she trudged through icy slush to the Moorty Station. Now that's all melted. Distant mountains are still snow-covered, but here in town flowers are budding, trees filling out.

"Ah, Moorty," Father Daniel's colleagues swooned. "You're lucky to be going home to Moorty."

Home, she muses, before beginning her hike to the hospital. Has Gita recovered from the relapse? Someone would have contacted her if she had a downturn. Surely.

The walk feels both familiar and different. She waves to Rabi, who stands, arms akimbo, outside the coffee shop.

He squints, waves back.

The Playhouse is advertising a sitar concert on huge blue and yellow posters. Moorty Heaven. It's so temperate these next few months when much of the country bakes or boils or in the case of Tamil Nadu, sizzles.

*****

"Monica dear, please take more tea," Father Daniel smiled curiously that last evening. The others had returned to the hospital or their quarters.

"Thank you," she obeyed and poured half a cup.

"I'd like to discuss something."

"Yes, Father?" Had she done something wrong? Was Mission House disappointed? Did Kevin file a negative report? Was this whole assignment to Tamil Nadu a gentle thank you and farewell? She searched Father's kind, dark eyes.

"About the nature of vocation," he began.

"*Vocation*," she repeated, alarmed, as if to stay on track.

"*I've watched a number of doctors and nurses from Europe and the Americas over the years*."

She drained her cup, noticing he hadn't touched his, and as Father loved tea, she grew worried.

"*You have a strong vocation and you're an excellent doctor. We all learned from your seminars this week. Everyone admired your generous, modest spirit*."

Relieved, she now teased, "*But not my equanimity*."

"*I do remember your question from the retreat*." He grinned. "*And I suspect you need to keep searching for that answer*."

"*Yes, Father?*" She waited.

"*I don't mean to interfere, but sometimes I worry that, well...*"

"*Please continue, as my spiritual advisor*."

"*Advisor is too strong. Perhaps a spiritual friend to a wise woman. But yes, I shall continue. I do worry that you don't realize you have a right to be happy*."

She waited.

"*That's it. See, you don't even perceive this as a matter of consequence. You are so busy thinking of others—about your patients, colleagues, Ashok's academic dreams, your sister, your dear, departed mother, your friend Beata—a lovely woman. I wonder where Monica is in all that? Do you understand?*"

"*I guess so. I don't think about my happiness much. Sorry*."

"*No, no, no!*" His voice pitched higher. "*This is not about apologizing*."

"*Of course, sorry*," she looked at him, catching his laughter.

"*Now, Monica, just be aware. Be open to happiness as it comes*."

*****

Mr. Sood fusses with his papers at the news stand. He's wearing the same clean, ironed lunghi and kurta he wore all winter. "*Namaste, ji,* you were out of station?"

"*Namaste,* Mr. Sood. I was in Chennai and Pondicherry for ten days."

"Ah, very hot. Very hot. One day I would like to see the beaches."

"Lovely white sands," she nods, paying for her usual papers.

"You've returned in time for Holi!" he declares. "Good fun."

"Yes, spring seems to be blooming all over."

"Wait until you see the daffodils on the road between Billington's Hotel and the hospital. Oh, my, such yellows. Like the sun. Welcome home, Dr. Murphy."

"Thank you, Mr. Sood; it's good to be back."

Home, the idea pleases her. Unnerves her. She's not Indian, as the immigration authorities in Delhi remind her with regular visa appraisals. She doesn't want to presume an intimacy she hasn't earned. Did Annie Besant feel at home? Foster? Orwell? Kipling? Does she want to be Indian? In some besotted way, she does. How much of that is wanting not to be American?

The carnations are bursting in red and white by the Anglican church where she and Ashok enjoyed the Bach concert that snowy day.

Home. She is returning to a useful job. Perhaps that's the best one can expect. She thought she belonged in her family. Now they've drifted off or died or dismissed her. She thought she belonged at Lake Clinic before the personalities became unbearable. She belongs to Moorty, at least for now.

Passing Billington's, she spots Mr. Sood's miraculous daffodils. Do news vendors in Minneapolis talk about daffodils? The question is—does she talk to news vendors in Minneapolis? She pays for *The New York Times* online. The difference is that she, herself, is more open in this new place.

Is this the happiness Father Daniel proposed? She is happy learning so much—about Mughal architecture; Tagore's poetry and music; Ray's films; the exquisitely varied landscapes. OK, people can be abrupt in crowds. She's not partial to the large Delhi and Chennai middle classes with their imposing houses and BMWs. But each day here brings a new surprise, which she cherishes, as she does the breakfast mango or papaya. Papaya for breakfast, no better definition of heaven.

A momentary feeling—that's not what Father Daniel is talking about—rather he urged a practice of happiness. First comes the openness, he advised. Then, maybe a habit. No small challenge from her spiritual friend.

It's tea time as she reaches Moorty Mission and she's ready for chai. The grounds have transformed. She sees patches of muddy earth where snow mounted ten days ago. She's never noticed the peeling paint on the south side near the refectory.

Angry voices.

Reluctantly proceeding, she hears Raul shouting at Kevin about evangelizing.

Kevin is outraged about Raul's latest Manda trip.

"Welcome home!" calls Sister Catherine, seated alone at the table.

"Thank you, Sister. I see attendance at tea is sparse today."

"Yes, Dr. Sanchez is packing for Manda. Mrs. Walsh has a touch of flu."

"Sorry to hear she's ill." Monica sits, winded after the long walk. Has she grown out of shape in ten days of Tamil Nadu cars and rickshaws?

"*Namaste, ji,*" Cook appears with a tray of tea and biscuits.

"*Dhanyavad,* Cook."

He bows. "The porter left your luggage at the residence."

Sister grins, "Someone in the ward will be glad to know you arrived safely."

"Gita," she draws a sharp breath. She's prayed every night for the child.

"She's stronger by the day. This relapse is her mother's fault. She pulled her home too early last year."

"Now, Sister, we all do our best."

Sister Catherine ignores this. "She's been cranky in your absence, I'll say."

"I'll finish this lovely chai, have a quick wash and drop in on the miniature curmudgeon. It's good to be back." Yes. Savor. Practice.

*****

Holi dawns on a sparkling morning, a day so clear she can touch the mountains.

She and Sudha stroll into town, laughing as children sprinkle each other with pink and purple and green powders.

"If they're this colorful in the morning," Monica grimaces, "how do they look at bed time?"

"By then you couldn't describe the hue. Everyone is a sunset. You really missed the whole thing last year?"

"Emergency. A road accident, I recall." She's wearing old clothes as Sudha advised, almost looking forward to being pelted with the vibrant powders.

"Be prepared. Getting pelted is an expression of camaraderie. You have to be in the mood."

She recalls Mr. Sood's daffodils. Holi, Spring Festival of Colors.

"And what news of *Monsieur* Ashok?"

"Oh, we talked several times when I was in the South. He's doing well." She's too shy to go on, shy and little superstitious of revealing her feelings. "Look over there, the snow on the peaks!"

"Come," Sudha clutches her hand. "Let's sit here and watch the mountains. This is the clearest time of year. Once when I was on a course in Darjeeling, we all got up and journeyed to Tiger Hill to see the sun throw its colors on Kanchendzongha."

"How wonderful." She's fascinated by recent revelations of Sudha's romantic nature. How much does this have to do with Dr. Raul?

"And look here," Sudha continues rapturously. "Oh, they are gorgeous this morning. My heart aches to get closer. I'm not a spiritual sort, as you complain, yet one feels, I don't know, called to go higher into the mountains when they're this close."

"So why don't we?"

Sudha turns, blinking in hesitant anticipation. "What do you mean?"

"I've seen signs in several shops about jeep trips to the Western Himalayas. We could go to Shimla. It's only a day from there to Sarahan, I understand."

Sudha stares, dumbfounded.

"We could stop at Narkanda and Rampur on the way." She's warming up.

"The old Hindustan-Tibet Road."

"They say it follows the Sutlej River most of the way."

"I had no idea you were interested, well, quite so interested, in the mountains."

Monica watches Sudha curiously. "How can I live here and not want to climb higher?"

"But we are two women."

"Is my feminist ally demurring?"

"Still, the expense. A car and driver!"

"I have a holiday coming in May," she says impulsively. "I have money in my account at home. I'd be happy to pay for both of us."

"No, I couldn't possibly."

"Consider it a token resetting of international economic scales."

"Don't be silly." Sudha stands, stretches, glances once again at the mountains and pivots toward town. "Are you ready for coffee? We haven't seen Rabi in weeks. He must be wondering what's happened."

"I'm completely serious." Monica's chest expands in anticipation. "I'll check with the shops this week and bring itineraries to dinner on Saturday."

Sudha gasps, "Uh, oh, here we go!"

Monica looks up. Too late to move or duck.

Vivid powders rain down on both of them. They're caught in a fit of giggles, their laughter louder than the children's.

"This old dress is much improved," she laughs. "And your *salwar kameez*, my dear, is absolutely dazzling."

Sudha grins. "They should let us into the coffee house now."

*****

Monica sits in bed, leafing through brochures, trying to determine her favorite routes before presenting them to Sudha. This is a chance to reciprocate for Sudha's kindness and hospitality. It's the journey of a lifetime.

Sangla has a campground—a posh site with fancy tents and pre-pared foods—an adventure. The next stop might be Kalpa, at 10,000 feet, where Shiva went to smoke pot and where marijuana still grows wild.

With each new day in India, Monica is a little more confident. More accepting of unpredictability and fate and faith.

Heavy footsteps. A tired tread tramping downstairs. Raul is always exhausted returning from Manda. While he's away she worries he'll run into animals, *dacoits*, the RSS. Sometimes she thinks he'll decide not to return. Sudha worries about this, too.

Shutting the light, she imagines Sudha and herself watching the winding Sutlej River as the jeep climbs higher and higher into those inscrutable mountains.

*****

Gita's mother has brought a new coat for her daughter and small gifts for the staff.

Monica watches wistfully as the little girl stands, nimbly slipping her arms into the coat.

Sister Catherine beams. "Wonderful, isn't it? God's miracle. When she arrived the second time, I was sure she'd only last a few days."

"Yes." Monica murmurs.

"She's returning to her family, to school. Oh, Doctor, you must be gratified."

She steps forward, lowering her voice. "Sister, do you think, rather do you sense, she isn't quite ready? Does her family have the capacity to care for her?"

"Love," Sister Catherine grins. "That's what she needs now. You've done a fine job. Look how well she is."

Monica stands straighter. "You've double-checked the blood tests?"

"Yes, Doctor. You and Our Lord have brought back little Lazurus," she whispers. "Now it's time to see her off to the happy family."

Suddenly the girl turns to her.

"Doctor Murphy, I shall miss you!" She wraps her arms around Monica's waist while her mother looks on with a mixture of embarrassment, gratitude and surrender.

"We will miss you, too, Gita. But we'll schedule a follow-up visit next week. To make sure you are keeping well."

"May I come back? May I?"

How the child's English has developed. Monica notes Mrs. Roy's faint smile of pride.

"Your mother can make an appointment. I look forward to seeing you."

"Thank you, Doctor Murphy! Thank you, Sister Catherine! See you next week." She waves shyly and accepts her mother's hand.

Monica excuses herself to the loo. Grateful to be alone, she clicks the cubicle door shut. Tears stream down her face. What's happening? She's thrilled to see Gita thriving. This is what doctors do, if they're lucky, help people recover. She's witnessed miracles, as Sister Catherine would call them, dozens of times. Each newly healed patient leaves her energized for the next case. What's wrong with her today?

"Doctor Murphy?" Sister Catherine's worried voice.

She flushes the unused toilet, hoping her sniffing wasn't audible. "Yes?"

"There's well, a rather critical situation in the waiting room."

Another auto accident? Mrs. Sing's heart finally giving out?

"I'll be right there, Sister."

"I'll tell them, Doctor."

She washes her hands, splashes her face. Better. Not a complete transformation from the clinging sentimentalist, but the best she can manage.

Sister leads nervous patients out the door.

R.S.S. She says a quick prayer.

"Yes, how can I help you?" she addresses the three men perhaps too abruptly.

"You are English."

She remembers from the first terrifying visit that this one's name is Arjun. She tries for Raul's cool method of response.

"*Nahi, meh* Minnesota *say hoon.*"

He brightens, breaking into English. "The Metrodome. Famous Dave's in Calhoun Square. I did engineering at Iowa State. We went to the Cities on weekends."

The older man shifts from one sandaled foot to another.

"What branch of engineering?"

"Chemic..." he regards his dour comrade and stutters, "I, we, don't have time for personal questions." Resuming in Hindi, "We've come on business."

"So you said." Inadvertently, she checks to make sure her white lab coat is buttoned professionally over her green blouse.

"What visa do you carry?"

"I don't have time for personal questions." She hopes to sound nonchalant.

"This is not a personal question, madame."

"Sir, you are not a government official." She's startled by her self-confidence.

"We have many colleagues in government. My cousin, Ramesh, works in the Delhi visa office. Perhaps he will give us a more courteous, complete answer."

She ignores the chill around her neck.

They turn to one another, whispering.

Arjun addresses her. "You may tell your colleagues we will return in one month. Before that if Ramesh has interesting news."

"Our clinic is open to all with health concerns." She holds the door open.

They file out silently.

She stands stunned, relieved, incredulous.

"Dr. Murphy!" exclaims Sister Eleanor.

"They left faster than when Dr. Sanchez talked to them," Sister Catherine adds, her face moist with perspiration.

Monica stares blankly into the bright afternoon. "For now they're gone, Sisters." She feels the adrenaline coursing through her veins. "Let's return to work. They want to stop us, but we will carry on." Does she sound like General MacArthur?

*****

The April morning is brilliant with colorful birds and flowers as Monica strides to chapel. This would have been Mom's 77th birthday. She always dreamed of a big party for her 80th. And now she's in the Himalayan foothills walking to a memorial Mass for a life cut short. Still, she replays that weekend in her mind. If only she'd stayed home or called Duluth, herself. Father Freitas's offer to say a memorial Mass is a surprising balm. How her mother would have liked the genial, generous priest. Mom, who spent years praying to save "pagan babies," would be astonished that people in India were praying for her.

Most of the staff regularly attend morning Mass. Today Raul is here. And Sudha in a back pew by herself.

She slides in next to her friend.

Sudha registers her surprise. "When Raul told me," she whispers," I knew this was important to you. As your friend, I wanted to be here."

"You are so kind." She hugs Sudha.

"Hardly." Sudha puts a finger to Monica's lips. "Do nudge me along. I don't know the drill."

Monica lowers her head in prayer. When she looks up, Father is approaching the altar. Sister Eleanor has gathered a luxuriant bouquet of daffodils.

She's counting losses: Mom, Dad, Jeanne, Eric. In a world devastated by war and famine, she's gotten off lightly. She misses Mom the most. At odd times, Jeanne's disappearance is the most poignant. How did she lose her sister? When and how did Jeanne lose so much of herself?

Of course she hasn't completely lost Dad. She owes him a letter. Odd how they've been in somewhat closer contact lately. Maybe the distance makes him feel safer.

Sudha seems fascinated by the prayers and hymns.

Kevin has chosen a passage from the Gospel of Luke.

She receives communion now, as she wishes she could have done at Mom's funeral mass.

And Eric is quite a presence in her life again. Dear Eric, whom she ignored so long during her shadowy paralysis. Each week he emails news and jokes. Despite her initial jealousy, she's glad he's found Loretta. It's good to be friends. You can count on friends.

Ordinary friends. This month she's tried not to dwell too much on Ashok. What if he takes the job in Wisconsin? What if she loses her visa here?

During the final prayers, she thinks of Gita. Thank God this beautiful child has been restored. If only she'd been able to tend her own mother…then she begins to take it in—why has this taken so long? Caring for Gita allowed her to make some small amends for that other absence, she thinks sadly.

✶✶✶✶✶

After Mass, she and Sudha return to her flat for a cup of tea.

"I do love your place." She surveys the long, tiled living room-dining room-study. "The kitchen is a little pokey. It was probably built for the servants."

Monica pours steaming water into the pot.

Sudha parts the flowery curtains. "Ah, yes, your view! On clear days like this you can see the temple. Beyond that the peaks. Extraordinary!"

"I wish I had more time to enjoy it," she calls from the kitchen, "but I don't get back from work until after dark."

"You have a full day off now. Don't you take time for contemplation?"

"You sound like Beata." She sits on the couch and pours the tea.

"Beata! I enjoyed her. We emailed for a while, but both got distracted. How is she doing?"

"She has news." Monica hands Sudha a cup. "James has proposed."

"Didn't like it that she went traipsing around the world without him, eh? So what did she say?"

"That she'd have to think about it."

"Savvy woman!"

"Beata enjoys her life. Her stimulating, if sometimes overwhelming job, her cozy condo, her meditation, church, friends, scouting the sales. It's nice to have a man in her life, but she's not lonely."

"Good." Sudha readjusts the lime green dupattas over her shoulders. "Loneliness is a rotten reason to pick a man."

Reason and romance: do they have anything to do with one another? Uneasily, she changes the topic, "So Raul says the tutoring project is a success."

"Yes," Sudha's eyes shine. "And an excellent experience for Raj and Vikram."

"Very different students." She harbors a certain loyalty to her first eye patient.

"Both idealistic in their own ways. Vikram has the softer nature, but they're each good-hearted. In fact, they learned from one another as well as from the Manda children. And emerged with such admiration for Raul."

"The program will continue, then?"

"Absolutely. We have students clamoring to sign up."

"How about your own program with Raul?"

She frowns incomprehension.

"You're still going out to supper, I notice."

"A discerning woman."

"And you're a suspenseful one. Do I detect a touch of romance?"

"I suppose." Sudha paces back to the window. "I'm happy with my days—students, community work, our friendship, good books." She turns to her friend.

"But?"

"Not but, rather and."

Monica sips tea, observing.

Sudha stands straighter. "Raul is a smart, kind, cosmopolitan man who does important work. And," she pulls an impish face, "for a Christian, he's rather broad-minded."

Monica shakes her head. "And?"

"I don't think I'd ever meet anyone else so compatible, so exciting."

"Wow! I didn't expect this much. So you're talking happily ever after?"

"It's been broached." She turns back to the mountain view. "We'll see what the universe offers."

"Would your parents accept him? Would you marry in Bombay?"

"Hang on. You're much further along than we are. As for my parents, they would be disappointed that he's not a nice Hindu man. They might be relieved I found anyone. A doctor is respectable. I should avoid mentioning the mission at first."

Monica bites her lip. A few years ago, she, herself, would never have considered marrying a Catholic missionary doctor.

"They would like Raul." Sudha walks over and takes Monica's hand. "They would embrace you as their own daughter. Mother would help you select the perfect sari for the wedding since you would be in any ceremony of mine."

Tears again. What a day. Monica hopes she can stay in India long enough to attend. Her turn to glance out the window. She hopes Arjun's threat about the visa office was an idle one. She doubts it.

TWENTY-NINE

April, May, 2002, Delhi and Moorty

The Bengali Market buzzes with late afternoon shoppers. Monica feels at home and not—wistful about those first innocent days in Delhi. When Ashok pops into the stationer's for paper, she waits outside, enjoying the parade and looking for recognizable faces. This is her Delhi, the chaotic, vivacious neighborhood near Mission House. Each of those first weeks now seems as long as a month in Moorty. She wishes she were as porous as when she first arrived. She's begun to take her place for granted, foolish given her imminent supplication at the visa office. She'll be returning to Mission House too soon for an exit visa.

"You were right," Ashok breaks through her reverie. "They had the ideal paper. In the Bengali Market, who would have thought?"

"Snob. You're like New Yorkers who never leave the Upper East Side."

"You can hardly compare my shoddy campus in North Delhi to the Upper East Side." He puts an arm firmly around her shoulders.

She inches closer. This feels right.

Last year, when they lunched at the IIC, she never would have imagined them as a couple. A couple of what? For how long? For now.

She pecks his cheek. "The Bengali Market is a cornucopia: stationers, green grocers, post office, Krishna convenience store."

"A regular Walmart, I bet."

Ignoring his sarcasm, she peers at an ornately garbed elephant lumbering up a residential side street. "Don't Hindu weddings happen in January and February?"

"Most. But April is the season for hotel workers."

"Pardon?"

"Weddings are big business. *Lakhs* of rupees. *Lakhs*. Waiters and bellmen and clerks work double time in the winter. So they marry now that the larger nuptial extravaganzas over over."

Nuptial extravaganzas. She reminds herself that love is different from commitment. Besides, how could she possibly marry this peevish character?

"Down there," she points past the elephant, "and around the corner, is where I bought my skim yogurt from the Mother Milk stand."

"You bought Mother Milk? Foreigners don't have the enzymes to drink that stuff. Indians shouldn't drink it either. Remember that scandal about selling correction fluid as milk? Scores of babies died."

"That wasn't Mother Milk." Then to distract him from further disquisition, "Look at the magnolias and dahlias. India grows the most beautiful flowers."

"Yes, yes. That gives me an idea."

As Ashok picks through the floral display, the one-eyed vendor smiles at Monica. She'd like to think he recalls their encounters from last year.

"For the lady," Ashok hands her a bouquet of red roses.

"Stunning," she says. "Thank you."

At Nathu's, she can't help but pause and stare at the array of buttery, nutty, creamy sweets in the window. Ashok shifts from foot to foot. His face, reflected in the glass, grows long. "Just why can't you stay at my flat? We're adults, after all?"

This grouch, who rails against anything that defies his own logic and values, is used to getting what he wants. Turning from the window to face him directly, she takes his hand. The roses are so fragrant, she's momentarily speechless.

He gazes at her.

"It's a question of propriety," she explains again. "For the first night, I'll stay with Tina—in case the hospital calls. Kevin was reluctant to let me come to Delhi and I don't want him to think I'm here on a tryst."

He takes her hand. "A two day trip to renew your visa? That's hospital business. Besides, I thought Father Freitas was the Director."

"Kevin is the senior doc. It's hard to explain where he gets his authority."

"Maybe you just give it to him."

"Come on, now—"

"Monica, you're on a bureaucratic errand," he raises his voice.

"If he found me staying with you, he'd think I had ulterior motives."

He pulls a face, "I should hope you do."

"Let's just say my primary motive is that visa. For lots of reasons."

Ashok takes her hand; the hairs on her arm lift and she flushes.

"My cousin's working hard on your case. Janardhanan has all the papers."

"Let's hope we can celebrate tomorrow night," she tries.

"I'm counting on it," he squeezes her hand. "Just the two of us."

"That will be perfect," she tries to convince herself of this, to ignore tides of fear.

The driver cautiously navigates the roundabouts on the way to Tina's. She marvels at the greening city: blossoms everywhere. Soon they are on the Ring Road, driving past Haus Khas, Greater Kailash, toward Tina's flat in Vasant Vihar, too far from the action, as she complains, but convenient to work.

They pass through three check points before they pull up to the Embassy compound. A guard orders the driver to open his trunk. Two men inspect the underside of the cab with mirrors attached to long poles.

Finally, the guard approaches her window.

"I'm Doctor Murphy," she speaks slowly and clearly. "Here to visit Dr. Nelson."

He lights up. "Dr. Nelson is a very nice lady."

Tina's always charmed the men. "Yes," she agrees. "An old friend of mine."

"Welcome. Please proceeed. Dr. *ji's* house is fourth one on the left."

"Good to see you," Tina rocks her in an embrace.

"Perfect timing." Monica is winded from the bear hug. "Your door opens as we arrive."

She's laughing. "No secrets in the fortress. Amit rang as you passed through."

Slipping off her shoes, Monica is astonished by the spacious, light-filled house. "Gorgeous," she declares. "But the entry is like a citadel."

"Since 9/11, embassy security has been a bear. In Calcutta, the American Center is protected by sand bags and rifle-bearing guards."

"Remind me not to lose my passport in Calcutta."

"Let me give you a tour."

Tina's lavish living room is furnished with a white sofa and matching chairs. Potted palms flourish against one wall. A stunning painting of an Indian mandir hangs over the fireplace. Monica is disoriented, a little jealous, in the five star flat.

"This mahogany table," Tina says, "you're wondering how I meet expenses."

"No, I wasn't actually." Of course she was.

"Beautiful furniture is so cheap here, if you know where to look. These mission style chairs match perfectly. I couldn't afford them at home."

"Home?" She's startled. "Are you leaving? You never mentioned anything." She realizes now how comforting it's been to have Tina in Delhi, a phone call away.

"It's crossed my mind," she says dismissively. "More anon, as your sweet mom used to say. Let me show you to the bedrooms."

They pass a study, bright with bay windows and a skylight. The bedrooms are at the back, overlooking a landscaped garden. Tina's room is fitted with stripped sheets and a duvet cover she bought from Anokhi when they shopped with Beata last December.

"This is your room, old friend. Any time. The key is yours."

"Thank you." She sets her bag next to an elaborately carved teak bureau.

"May I offer you some liquid refreshment on the back veranda?"

Tina makes a strong martini. Monica sips slowly, nibbling on the olive. "Tell me, what's up? Where would you go if you left the embassy hospital?"

She pours herself a second drink, glances at Monica's half-glass and shakes her head. "I don't know. Government medicine is so much paperwork. Rules change monthly: who you can treat, what you can prescribe. I like my Indian colleagues—the office staff are great fun—but some of the American docs are, well *American*, if you know what I mean. Fans of the administration."

"Of Bush?"

"Yup."

She takes another sip. "I guess every job has trials. Lake Clinic had Captain Louise. And you know my reservations about Kevin Walsh."

"Reservations? More like despair and rage, I'd say."

Monica shrugs.

"At least you're *doing something*, Monica. You're helping people who have no resources, who would die without your hospital. And here, well, I don't know. I'm treating visiting senators with diarrhea and obese children of embassy hot shots."

"You're attached to India, to your Delhi friends. How could you leave?"

She half smiles, clinks Monica's glass. "We all have to return, hon, eventually."

*****

Tina's driver makes sure they're both belted up before heading to the visa office.

Monica closes her eyes and prays silently. If it is Thy will. Help me carry out Thy will. She tries to mean this. She wants the visa, isn't ready to leave. Thy will. It's hard to concentrate after a restless night thinking about Arjun's cousin. Yes, the R.S.S. are known for their empty threats as much as their terror tactics. She woke at 3 a.m. in Tina's lush bed hearing, "We all have to return eventually." Yes. One day. She's not ready yet. Not my will, she prays, but thy will.

Tina pats her knee. "I'll play it low key," she says brightly. "I'm just your friend. I won't mention the embassy unless they get nasty."

She's not prepared for nasty. Then again, she hasn't been prepared for much of what she's experienced since arriving in this country.

Monica spots Janardhanan immediately: a younger, plumper version of Ashok.

"Yes, welcome, Dr. Murphy and Dr. Nelson. Ashok has spoken about each of you." He studies Monica carefully, with no pretense of discretion.

At his invitation, they sit on plastic folding chairs.

"I believe I've located all your papers." He taps two large files.

She asks, as casually as she can, "Do you have a colleague named Ramesh?"

"Ramesh, no. This is a large office, but I've been here a while, why do you ask?" Suddenly he looks ten years older, seated behind folders holding her past and future in India.

She explains about the last visit from the R.S.S., about Arjiun's warning.

He whistles through his teeth. "Truthfully, I mean no offense, I don't know which is more detrimental to your status, Dr. Murphy, your Church affiliation or your government's behavior."

"Hey, no offense taken," rejoins Tina. "We didn't vote for Bush."

Janardhanan looks curious.

So much for low key. Monica can't tell if Tina's comment is helping, but she doesn't want to leave him in doubt. "Like many Americans, I actively oppose U.S. aggression in the Middle East."

Jananardhanan tilts his head. Impassively, he runs down a list of questions.

An hour later, he says, "I think I see some windows here."

"Oh, thank you." Monica sits back, rubbing the knots in her neck.

"I can't guarantee anything. But we can build a case to extend the visa. After all, this is a special situation."

"Special?" she asks nervously.

"Of course I have to be discreet. But my elder cousin Ashok has never before asked a favor. He raised me when my parents took ill. Indeed, I owe him a life of favors, but I am surprised at this one."

"What's so surprising?" Tina demands.

"I've known Ashok since we were lads and he's never held truck with any religion. He's no Marxist, but he does agree with that 'opiate of the people' line."

"I know." Monica smiles diffidently.

He rises. "Now that I've had the pleasure of making your personal acquaintance, Dr. Murphy, I think I'm beginning to understand."

As she gets up, her legs creak to life.

"How long?" Tina asks. "Until we hear?"

*****

Ashok sets the dish on his prettily laid table.

The room is fragrant with coriander, hot peppers, mint and a dozen aromas she can't place. His table is draped with an embroidered white cloth and matching napkins.

"Please be seated, Madame, and welcome to the Café Nair." He suppresses a smile, lights two beeswax candles. The rich scent of honey mingles with the other fragrances.

"A hidden talent, Ashok. I couldn't have imagined. This all looks lovely."

"Ah, one of those sexist women who thinks men can't cook."

"Hardly." She's not in the mood for his adversarial jousting. She's faced real opponents lately. "But you never talk about liking to cook."

"There's a lot we haven't talked about."

"Yes." Unnerved by the rapid intimacy, she takes a bite. "Delicious."

"So, Janardhanan called."

She's breathless. "Already?"

"Nothing official to report. But he was quite impressed with you. Impressed with me knowing you."

"Are all the men in your family flirts?"

"Did he flirt with you?" His jaw tightens slightly.

"No, no. He was entirely professional. Cordial. And he has a great regard for his cousin. He told us how you took him in."

He balks, "Nothing to it. He was a teenager, almost grown. Please," he says, "please eat before the meal gets cold."

She does eat, with gusto and to his pleasure, asks for second helpings of each. A splendid meal, a light wine from Nasik, serious talk about jobs and families.

"A *petit digestif* in the living room?" He gestures to the couch.

"A very *petit* one." She's excited, wary.

His futon couch is smaller than Tina's with thinner, firmer cushions. She notes details to calm herself, not sure she's prepared for what follows the brandy. A small television is stored in the corner, covered by a black and white Ikat print. He's decorated the wall with masks.

Ashok follows her gaze. "This mask is from our home near Kochi. This one comes from Shillong. And that one, that's an Ojibwa mask from Wisconsin."

She's trying to ignore his fondness for Madison. Naturally, if she gets sent back to Minnesota, she'd be delighted to know he was so close. Might be so close. They have no commitments. They are simply savoring moments; they've both agreed.

As he pulls out two crystal snifters, she recalls sipping cognac from plastic cups at the Razik Palace. That evening unfolded so easily. Tonight, she feels tongue-tied.

He hands her a generous globe of the aromatic liquid.

"Too much!" she protests.

"Enjoy what you like," he says, settling in close, resting an arm on her shoulder.

As they sit together sipping the brandy and listening to the cacophony of Delhi horns, sirens and shouts, she knows she's a world away from Tina's flat. A universe away from Moorty.

"The clamor, does it bother you? I can close a window, but I'm afraid the air conditioner isn't working," he speaks faster. "I could adjust the ceiling fan." He rises.

She pulls him back down. "This is lovely as it is. Relax."

He moves closer, brushes her lips with his.

She sets down her brandy snifter. He sets his next to it.

"Monica, Monica," he whispers, the softness of his breath arousing her.

She draws her face closer.

*****

Mrs. Habib is frightened but brave as she heads into her tenth hour of labor. Monica does what she can, then leaves Brigid in charge.

An hour later, glancing into the birthing room, she watches Brigid take the patient's hand, wipe her face with a damp cloth. She's a good person, totally devoted. Monica has been so judgmental.

As she strolls into the darkened ward, she feels grateful for this eventful, if tiring, day. The appendectomy patient from Koti is doing well. The young man with pneumonia is now OK. In midday she enjoyed a chat with Gita who is more vibrant with each visit. Her bouquet graces the ward desk. And the visa—the visa!—arrived. She is safe. Once again. For now.

Ritu is sleeping soundly. How Monica wishes she had come to the hospital earlier. There's so much they can do for diabetes. But at this stage? The first job is to save her toes. She stands by the bed, thinking of her friend Ritu in medical school, a world and a life away.

A whisper from the far end of the ward, past the partition, in the men's section.

She turns, catches Kevin's eye. He slips something in Mr. Patel's bedside drawer.

Two hours later, after Aymen Habib arrives in the world, Monica passes the birthing room. They need more than one delivery station. She hears a sound and looks through the glass slit in the window.

Brigid is still there, although she's had plenty of time to wash the infant and return him to his mother. What is she doing, exactly? Her back is turned and her voice is low. Some kind of prayer? Monica makes out a cruet of water. No, she can't be baptizing Aymen. Mrs. Habib is a devout Muslim. She must be imagining this. She stands, paralyzed, thinking about Brigid's lost twins. Please God, let me be imagining this.

Casually, Brigid sets down the cruet and turns, smiling. She's rocking the baby. Protecting his dark little body with her strong, freckled arms.

Monica turns on her heels, furious. At Brigid, at herself. She wants to wake Father Freitas. Instead she ventures back into the ward and checks on Ritu, who is still sleeping soundly. She walks past the partition into the men's section.

Mr. Patel's slumber is also deep. He lies on his side, breath moving like huge waves through his exhausted body.

Quietly, she reaches for the nightstand drawer.

"Oh, Doctor *ji*," Mr. Patel looks up, "Good Evening."

"Checking in on you. Good night for now, Mr. Patel." She walks quickly to the exit.

*****

She's halfway out her apartment door, late to meet Sudha for their Saturday shop at the *sabzi mandi* when the phone rings.

"Moorty Motor Tours, here, may I speak with Doctor Murphy."

Her heart bounds. "This is Dr. Murphy."

"We've had one cancellation."

The Hindustan Road. Sudha will be thrilled. She's too numb to speak.

"Beginning May twenty-seventh or twenty-eighth."

"So soon? Couldn't we move that into June a bit?"

"Timing, Madame, timing. We want to go after the snow melts, before the rains."

"But I didn't think the monsoons started for a while."

"Madame, we have a waiting list. If you've changed your mind, we shall move on."

"No," she says and thinks, yes, maybe, who knows. When she first mentioned the trip she ran into all kinds of flak from Ashok and Kevin. Now it's real. She and Sudha are headed for the mountains. "Yes." She laughs. "I'll be by with the payment this afternoon."

"Very fine, Madame. And may I be the first to welcome you to Moorty Motor Tours, a First Class travel service."

*****

During their usual Tuesday call, Ashok's voice is tense. He's trying to be reasonable. "You know this is dangerous, Monica."

"They've run these trips for twenty years."

"But what kind of driver will you get?"

First class, the man said, but she holds her tongue. "Really, Ashok, I think it will be perfectly safe."

"Nothing is perfectly safe."

"You're just a worrier."

"Can't you hear I don't want to lose you? You've become a huge part of my life."

In spite of herself, it slips out. "Oh, you'll forget me once you get to Madison."

"Monica," he grows more serious, as serious as she's ever heard this serious man, "Monica, I could never leave without you."

Heart in her throat, she manages, "When will you hear?"

"Funding is up in the air." He's disappointed, impatient, eager to resume admonishing her. "Typical academic hold-up."

Now that she has her visa, Ashok can't leave, he just can't. But it's not her choice. Thy will be done.

"Back to the point," he insists. "Do check this outfit out thoroughly, Monica. I'm not happy about this at all."

"Sudha isn't getting this kind of discouragement from Raul any more."

"Raul is a cowboy."

"You're certainly no cowboy." She laughs. Thank God, she hasn't fallen in love with her father. Still, is she, perhaps, a cowgirl?

"I have an idea. I'll contact my cousin in tourism."

"How many cousins do you have?"

"Enough." He is no nonsense, "Ashish can look into things for me. For us."

It's late. She has an early surgery. Still, she'll finish the letter to Beata. She's relieved to unload the anger and frustration about her evangelical colleagues. This is good practice for the talk she must have with Father Freitas. She ends the letter on a grateful note, because, despite the difficult week, she feels blessed.

So you see, it's all settled. The visa. Our dream trip. I can't believe how lucky I am. Kevin balked at first, but he admitted I haven't had more than a few days of real holiday since I arrived in India. Sudha is giddy as a school girl. I wish you could join us. Then it would be perfect.

THIRTY

May, 2002, Himalayan Journey

Spicy deodars scent the early evening air. Setting a suitcase on the step, Monica notices wild pink roses and purple irises. Radiant red rhododendrons shine from high branches.

Before coming to Moorty, she never imagined rhododendrons as trees. Nearer the ground, here, grow foxglove and periwinkle. Late May is the prettiest season she's known in the Indian hills; this is a mad time to leave. Yet they have a narrow weather window for the trip. From the tenuous season to the rugged route, the whole journey does seem precarious. She tries to ignore Ashok's worried echo.

"Hi there, traveler," booms Father Freitas. "Ready for adventure?"

Of course Father would give her a cheerier send off than the fussy professor.

"As ready as I'll ever be." She grins. "Thank you for your blessing this morning."

"I shall keep you in my daily prayers."

"Hola!" Raul swoops up her bag. "The Jeep is here. Padre, shall we escort the dama to her chariot?"

Monica follows, clutching her purse and pillow. She recalls Jeanne and Mom helping her move to the medical school dorm. She feels that familiar jumble of excitement, confidence, fear and perhaps a touch of hubris. What is she doing setting off to the Himalayan Mountains? Well, Father says she's taking a classic Indian trek. Although Kevin maintains grave doubts, he did advise a pillow for her spine. Raul nodded in agreement. Sudha considers the pillow silly, for she believes in karma. Monica has sent too many SI victims to physical therapy to believe in spine karma.

Sudha steps down from the jeep and waves as they all approach.

Shankar, tall in his seat, hand gripping the wheel, leaps out for her luggage.

She watches Raul and Sudha beam at each other. Subtle deportment and palpable attachment. Father Freitas's eyes shine knowingly. No one else at the hospital has been told of their betrothal. Surely Brigid and Kevin suspect.

She raises her hands in *Namascar* to Father and Raul.

Sudha does the same, then holds the door open for her.

"Bon Voyage."

"Hasta luego."

"Welcome, ladies," Shankar says in careful English. "Please inform me if you require anything."

"Dhanyvad, Shankar," Monica replies, explaining in Hindi that they speak both languages.

"No, no, English only. I am a first class driver, offering a first class service."

He's facing forward, sitting erect in a freshly ironed beige shirt. Monica catches his face in the rear view mirror—young, confident, handsome.

As they wind down the Cart Road, Monica fumbles around, digging her hand beneath the seat and back rest.

"What's the matter?" Sudha asks. "Have you lost something? Already!"

"The seat belt." She gropes. "The mission jeep is just like this. The seat belts are usually attached at the door frame."

Sudha is laughing.

Shankar shakes his head.

"Welcome to India, where young men cut the seat belts from their cars," Sudha explains. "A matter of pride."

"And stupidity: do you know how many car accidents we get at the hospital?"

He interrupts. "Don't worry, you are in the back seat. No problem."

"Don't be silly," Monica says.

"No accidents," he says confidently. "First class service. I have never had an accident."

She sighs and fusses with the pillow feeling irritated and embarrassed. Well, they all have Father Freitas' blessing and continuing prayers. All of them.

*****

"Breakfast at Narkhanda," Shankar announces the next morning as they leave the Shimla hotel. "You will like. Ladies always like pretty views."

She and Sudha fall silent, enjoying the orchards of cherries and apples.

Monica is startled by the intense green of the nimbly terraced farms as they climb from 2,205 meters to 2,608 meters. She's imagined journeying into Himalayan whiteness, pictures Minnesota in January with more contours. Near the equator, she's slowly learning, people cultivate at high elevations.

"This truly is the Hindustan-Tibet Road." Sudha leans over. "Can you imagine the centuries of trekkers and traders who've preceded us? I'm beyond excited. This trip is too generous of you."

Suddenly their jeep jolts to the right.

"Durga Temple," Shankar explains. "I shall make a small offering for safety."

Monica assents. Durga, Shiva, Krishna, he can stop at any shrine he likes. They're going to need all the help they can get on this steep, twisting road. "God speed," Father Freitas said. They're not alone. *Hasta luego* means, "See you later."

Shankar resumes his cautious, almost balletic steering, weaving them seamlessly from paved to unpaved road. He maneuvers around crowded coaches and brightly painted lorries. An hour into the trip, Monica sees a truck tipped over in a muddy ditch.

Shankar slows, chats with the driver. He resumes guardedly.

"Bengalis on pilgrimage," he turns half-way to address them.

Monica wishes he wouldn't swivel around so often. They can hear perfectly well.

"Help is on the way. Crazy driver though. He took the turn fast. No worries with Shankar at the wheel."

"Good to know," she says encouragingly to him, to Sudha. To herself.

Narkanda is all he promised: a lush respite steeped in sunlight. Outside in the crisp air, they devour a breakfast of chapattis, fruit and yogurt.

Monica stretches back, drinking in the fresh air. "Ah, lovely. This *is* a holiday."

"Such an intense time for you. New country. New hospital and colleagues."

"New friends!" she toasts Sudha with her tea cup.

Sudha raises her cup. "I haven't felt this free in years. The sense of possibility, adventure. It reminds me of when I set off for Saint Andrews."

"That must have been a huge shift—much bigger than my coming to India. You were so young—seventeen or eighteen." Monica finishes the last *chapatti* and wants another. No, her stomach is quite full. Her appetite for everything swells now as they set out. She needs to slow down, to concentrate, to be more mindful.

"Who knows! The other choice was J.N.U. in Delhi. That, too, is a world away from Bombay. Besides I had Scottish teachers in school. I understood that soupy accept when I got to St. Andrews. And, perhaps this is perverse—I sometimes consider Oxbridge and St. Andrews as a cultural outpost of India. So many of us go there."

"Nice post-colonial twist."

"Ladies, Ladies." An aggrieved voice. Shankar approaches politely, determinedly. "We were scheduled to meet at the jeep a quarter hour ago. At this rate, we'll be late to Rampur."

"Indeed," grins Sudha. "Rampur has been on the Silk Route for thousands of years. I suspect it will be there, Shankar, whenever we arrive. Still, I thank you for the courteous reminder about time."

They travel East and North, deeper into the ancient Himalayan Kingdome of which Rampur was once the capital. Impossible to continue chatting now. Just as well, for Shankar has been listening avidly, eager to join their conversation and opine on matters from politics to film. Besides, Monica is absorbed by dramatic scenery and shards of remembered history: Some caravans took twelve months to complete the 4,000 mile Silk Route. They traded for wool, glass and ox hide as well as silk. Religion, too, was spread along this trail: Buddhism, Islam, Nestorian Christianity.

After Rampur, they proceed up, up, up. She gazes at the Sutlej River coursing brown foam from its Tibetan font toward Govind Sagar in Western Himachel Pradesh. They pass waterfalls, cedars, lofty pines.

The Sarahan hotel is modest. Their turquoise and yellow room has two decent beds and a deck overlooking the mountains. After unpacking, Monica suggests tea on the balcony.

"Veranda," Sudha teases. 'We call it a veranda."

Draped with shawls in the crisp mountain air, they settle down to tea and biscuits. "Imagine, being surrounded by the Himalayas with my good friend."

Clouds float over distant peaks, one lifting enough to reveal a snowy ridge.

Monica grins. Sarahan is one of the most beautiful places on earth. Why not spend the rest of their holiday here. "Tell me more about St. Andrews."

Sudha sips her tea slowly. "When I went to Scotland, I felt I was an international citizen. Bombay is a huge port and very cosmopolitan. We have large populations of Muslims, Christians, Jews, Parsees, people from Africa, China, Europe. And of course the Britishers. Or the half-British. And from the Commonwealth."

Monica waits.

"St. Andrews felt provincial compared to Bombay. I became more aware of my difference. Oh, I had Scottish friends, dear friends. Yet I came to know in some deep way that I would always be Indian. Maybe part of it was the Scottish Nationalist Movement. If they were separating from the English, why did I hold on to my Anglophilia? By the second year, I knew I'd return to India. I became more certain of my identity."

"And less certain?"

"Less certain that being Indian was an identifiable identity. I belonged to Bombay, but it was the differences in India that appealed most to me."

"That's why you left Bombay?"

"Bingo! If I returned from university to Bandra, I would always be a Bombayite. Also, there are some aspects Indian families—even liberal ones like mine—that shape and narrow your destiny. If I wanted to understand India as a whole country—as a nation of distinct ethnicities and traditions, I needed to leave home."

"You were so much farther thinking," Monica shrugs. "I went from the Minnesota biological sciences to the U's med school to Lake Clinic." She studies the now cloud-shrouded mountains, realizing Minnesota is so much smaller than she has ever imagined.

Sudha shakes her head fondly. "My parents are well-traveled intellectuals. Your mother was a secretary and your father a bus driver. You ventured further—across classes."

She half smiles. "And you forget, Dad is now a cowboy."

"How could I forget?"

In the early evening, they amble over to the Bhimakali Temple with its six silver-coated gates and red carved, slanting roofs.

"Both Hindus and Buddhists pray here," Sudha explains.

Monica knew they would encounter more Buddhists in the north and east. The pagoda-like roofs remind her that they're getting close to Tibet and China.

They slip off sandals and enter the temple.

Abruptly, a bayonet. The young army guard asks them for their watches.

Monica complies, quickly, noting how she's grown accustomed to following incomprehensible directions these last seventeen months. She hopes he returns the watch. Despite the bayonet, the guy doesn't seem menacing. "Why the watches?" she whispers.

"I'll explain later," Sudha says.

They stand outside a locked door. Soon they're joined by six young Himachali men in green, red and yellow woolen caps as well as by three women in green head scarves.

"Wait," says one of the visitors in English.

A small man appears. He leads them up the winding stairs to a small sanctuary where people are praying.

Monica feels one of the women handing her something. Slices of coconut. Once again, she's forgotten an offering. She bows her head in thanks. Praying silently, she calls on Jesus, Durga and Buddha to stay with them on their journey. The jeep is big enough for all of them.

*****

Day three. Hairpin turns, loose gravel. Sheer drops. Shankar points out two golden eagles—huge, magnificent animals overlooking their precarious path from high perches. The crows, who own these skies, exude a different dignity as they sail sleekly across the horizon.

In midmorning, Shankar stops at a roadside temple dedicated to Ganesh.

Sudha wanders around the jeep, peers down over the edge of the highway.

Monica stays seated, praying. She adds an invocation to the elephant god.

Late in the afternoon, they reach Bajara Camp, near Sangla. 8,500 feel in the air. No, she thinks, 8,500 feet on earth. Their earth is rising.

She and Sudha drop their bags in a luxurious tent and head out for a stroll in the afternoon sun. Shankar has recommended nearby Basteri Village.

Within ten minutes of climbing, goats and sheep stream toward them. Hundreds of animals.

Shepherds look astonished at the two travelers—one in a sweatshirt and black pants; the other wearing a purple salwar kameez.

Finally, a young man shouts, "Where is your home?"

"Moorty," Sudha calls back.

Monica's impulse is to say "Moorty" as well. But it doesn't feel earned. They probably couldn't place "Minnesota." "The U.S.A." sounds alien to her. Finally, she responds, "North America."

He grins, "Welcome to our India!"

They linger a while in the model village, admiring mountain peaks to which they're getting closer every day. On the way back down to the camp, they watch a herd of cows headed to Basteri, apparently without the prodding of dog or human.

"The cows are coming home!" Monica laughs. "If I were a cow, I'd come home to this lovely village."

A downpour commences about 4:30 and rain continues into evening. They arrive in the dinner tent as soggy as the other campers. Good cheer prevails. Many guests simply relish the novelty of camping in the wilderness. Monica notices that she and a Dutch couple are the only "Euros" here. Other guests come from Calcutta, Jaipur, Chennai. Sudha gets into an animated conversation with Saroj and Ashwin from Bombay. An hour after dinner, Monica is exhausted, as if she's walked up the mountain rather than being chauffeured by First Class Shankar.

The bedding is plentiful and cozy.

Darkness. Camp noises. Voices. Rain. Monica feels full with so many extraordinary moments from the day.

"Are you asleep?" whispers Sudha.

"Not yet," she answers reluctantly.

"When do you think Ashok will hear from his American university?"

"Who knows?"

"That's hard."

"Yes," she answers with a finality she hopes will end the conversation.

"And?"

"Sorry?"

"You've taught me persistence. What is happening between you two?"

Monica feels a huge breath escape her chest.

"I've answered all your questions about Raul. Turnabout is fair play."

"Love your Anglicisms!" She rolls over and faces the tent wall. Really, she doesn't want to discuss this. The mountains are meant to be a retreat—from work, family ghosts, decisions.

"Don't disgress."

She moans. "He's hinted…"

Sudha sits up.

Monica turns to the dim outline of her friend's face.

"How could you keep such a thing from me?" she shrieks hoarsely.

"I don't know how I feel." She sits up. "I haven't responded. You could say I'm keeping something from him, too."

"What's the problem? You're clearly in love."

She sighs. "Really?"

"Go on! Think about how you talk about him. Your eagerness for his emails and calls. The look on your face during his last visit."

"Yes, I'm drawn to Ashok. He's a fine man, but…"

"But what?"

"His work is in Delhi. If he stays in India, he wants me to move to Delhi."

"Delhi isn't Bombay, still, it's not the end of the earth."

Monica laughs, "I love Delhi. But my work is in Moorty."

"There must be other doctors who could come to Moorty."

"I've been trained. Developed programs. There are patients who rely on me."

"Surely that would all happen in Delhi. They need more doctors there, too."

"So what about this?" Monica can almost see Sudha's eyes in the darkness now. "I would miss you. What would I do without you?"

Sudha sniffs. "You'd be fine. I'd miss you, too, of course, but we would visit."

"Listen, Sudha, I don't want to visit. I want to be in Moorty, at the Mission with my patients, with Raul, Father Freitas, Sister Catherine, Sister Eleanor. And you."

"Let's talk about this another time. You're tired."

"Do you truly believe I need to move to Delhi and get married to be happy?"

"I believe we each flourish near someone who loves us the way

Ashok clearly loves you. I think you've needed to be loved for a very long time."

"What I need now is rest. Good-night, my persistent friend." She's too stirred up for sleep. But quiet will be good. Monica doesn't tell her Ashok also wants her to move back to the States if the Madison job is funded. She tries not to think about it. Yes, quiet. For a few hours.

"Good night Monica."

"Sleep well, Sudha."

Brilliant sunshine fills the morning as they eagerly head out to explore Chitkul. The jeep climbs to 10,000 feet; the sun growing brighter and the wind fiercer.

Carefully, the friends tread to the edge of newly cultivated fields bordered by a glacier. What rewards: wild strawberries, giant butterflies and scores of dazzlingly colored birds.

The nearby village, larger than Basteri, is distinguished by delicately carved wooden houses with pagoda slate roofs. Strolling through the streets, they are greeted by women sewing and weaving, children playing and men intent over card games.

"*Namaste*."

"Hello!" An old woman looks up.

"Good morning," says a neighbor.

Monica fantasizes that someone will invite them for tea. Sure. Just how many strangers did she invite for tea in Uptown? They continue meandering around the village and hours slip by.

Monica stares out the jeep window trying to imprint the image of these mountains on her mind. They remind her of the Rockies, her favorite American range, but the Himalayas are so much larger and even at 10,000 feet, there's substantial vegetation. She finds herself resisting the Himalayan beauty because she doesn't want it to be more stunning than the Rockies.

"It's extraordinary," Sudha declares. "How changed the landscape and architecture are from Moorty. Do you see what I mean about different Indias?"

"Absolutely."

"No, Ma'am, I beg to differ." An assured voice from the front seat. "This is all one India. Very large. This is why our India is great."

Sudha winks at her. "You have a point, Shankar."

After dinner, in the strong sunlight, they trek the banks of the Baspa River. Discovering a meadow, the women stretch out, savoring the late warmth, the fresh scent of grass and pleasant sensations of well-used muscles.

Sudha holds her head back, watching the clouds.

Monica has never seen her friend so relaxed.

"Today reminded me, in odd way," Sudha sits up, her blue salwar kameez as unwrinkled as it was this morning, "of Saturday family walks on Malabar Hill."

"I've heard it's a lovely spot."

"We would always picnic at a special spot overlooking the Arabian Sea, which my Admiral father insisted on calling 'the Indian Ocean.' "

"Perhaps Shankar is a distant cousin of your father?"

"No doubt," Sudha shakes her head. "The Our India Is Great campaign is grating. I fear it's not far from that sentiment to the ideology of those thugs who made 'reconnaissance visits' to your hospital."

"Your father is sympathetic to the R.S.S.?"

"No! He's very sensible for a military man. My mother has seen to that! Right now, I'd rather think about the color of Malabar Hill and the smell of the sea. Oh, look at the time!" Reluctantly, she rises, brushes off her clothes and offers a hand to Monica.

As they head back toward camp, Monica asks "Were you close to your brother and sister?"

"When we were children, especially to my Sister. Meena is a year younger, only."

"Odd they both left India. You did, for university, but you came back."

"Not odd. They're part of the Indian Diaspora."

"Do you miss them?"

"Yes and no. I miss some idyllic childhood years before Naren went to boarding school. Then I was sent off. And Meena attended a different school. These children's prisons are a British hangover. I got a reasonable education in certain subjects. However, you're taught to see yourselves as individuals rather than in relation to others. The impresario of your future success."

"That's fairly American, too." She studies the tension along Sudha's jaw line.

The descending sun plays pink and red on distant mountains. They stop to watch.

"You've recovered from that, though. You returned from Scotland."

"I'm more distant from our parents than Meena and Naren in some ways. They live in cosmopolitan cities. Father doesn't know what to make of his country recluse."

"Recluse!" Monica laughs. "You're one of the busiest people in Moorty—on this committee and that, doing more projects than I can count."

Sudha shrugs, "Tell me more about Jeanne."

She gazes at the mountains, continues walking. "We were closer as children before Dad left."

"That must have been so hard."

She's lost in the lingering sunset. She wants to be in the Himalayas. With Sudha. Not in Minnesota. Certainly not in her childhood. "Mom and Jeanne were distraught."

"I mean," Sudha takes her hand, "hard on you."

Her eyes fill. She's not going to be one of those Americans who crack up in India. No, she takes a breath. Everything happened so long ago. She studies the soft sunset colors. "Must be the altitude," Monica forces a laugh.

Sudha frowns.

"Come on, comrade," Monica squeezes her hand, "the sun is going and I'm worried about these flashlight batteries."

THIRTY-ONE

May, 2002, Himalayan Journey

She sits outside their tent in the high desert, soaking in the golden mountains. Atop the tallest ones, glaciers shimmer. On this sunny, windy afternoon—too windy for Sudha, who lies in the tent reading—the campground is decked with white and purple irises, pink rock roses and a violet sweet pea ground cover. They've landed in Paradise. Birds call from the bushes as the Spiti River surges and spurts into the gorge below. Really, you could step into Heaven from here.

Dear Beata,

The route from Kalpa got steeper and steeper and yet we remained in the middle of nowhere. We passed dozens of road workers. The men never acknowledged our car. Invariably, women workers stopped and waved. Most drivers and travelers are male, so perhaps the women were happy to see us? What hot, dusty, treacherous work. More admonitory signs up here. "One Blunder and You Go Under."

Back to Kalpa. The sunny Kinnauri village is distinguished by sloping slate roofs on beautifully made buildings. We visited a Buddhist temple and several Hindu temples, passed tailors and shoemakers and grocers. At the edge of the village, we took a long road leading to the highway. Evening light was exquisite and we felt so tranquil that we walked over an hour. At one point, we saw a shepherd in a Kinnauri hat herding her small flock of sheep and one yak. On her back, she carried a large load of firewood. Suddenly, she turned and all the sheep as well as the huge yak followed her down a set of steep stone steps.

Monica tugs on her shawl. Despite the wind, it is splendid out here.

One groundless fear: they're the only two guests. Girish, the camp manager, says the tents are usually full. Not to worry they'll get extra attention from the cook, the housekeeper and himself. All men. Extra attention? Monica remembers Sudha's early reservation, "But we are two women." Well, hasn't God taken them this far?

"Hey there!" Girish appears with a telephoto Nikon protruding from his chest.

"Good afternoon." She stands, anxiety dissolved by his friendly directness. She tries not to think of Beata's crack about his "phallic neck piece."

"I'm going to Tabo Monastery this afternoon and I wondered if you ladies would like to join me. I could show you around."

This tall, handsome guy in his late twenties ties his long black hair in a ponytail and wears second-hand R.E.I. pants, a grey sweatshirt and a Tibetan shawl. His shoes are Munros, circa 1970. He looks like someone working at Ragstock on Lake Street. She remembers Girish explained that he gave up his teaching job in Lucknow to meditate here in Spiti. That he spent last winter in an isolated cave and plans to pass next winter in a remote monastery. The camp job covers his yearly costs. He's a spiritual seeker. What is she worried about?

"Let me ask Sudha."

Sudha pops out of the tent wearing two shawls. "Sudha says yes. We were looking forward to the monastery. What could be better than a personal tour?"

Several minutes out of camp in Girish's rickety sedan, they pass a thin man, walking purposefully, red robes fluttering in the wind. He stops and waves.

Girish pulls over and opens the door. They exchange a few words in Bhoti. Then the monk bows and smiles warmly to Monica and Sudha.

"Great luck!" Girish turns, as confident as Shankar, driving with one eye on the road. "My friend has keys. He'll show us the ancient part that most visitors never see."

She and Sudha grin at one another.

Tabo Monstery is a series of one-and-two-storey yellowish buildings. Not the crumbling 10th century edifice she expected. More like a scene from 19th century New Mexico, something out of Death Comes For The Archbishop.

The oldest section is guarded by statues of gruesome figures who ward off evil interlopers. They pass through a gallery of sculptures— gods and goddesses. Resting on a throne at the center of the room is a color photograph of the Dalai Lama. Behind that revolves a sculpture with heads of four distinct Buddhas.

Girish and the monk lead them from the altar to view the one-thousand-year-old murals on the walls and ceiling. Finally, they enter a room devoted to a massive sculpture of a new Buddha, a gargantuan child.

"He would have been eight years old when discovered," Girish explains. "People during this period are reputed to have grown into giants."

Girish shows them the elaborate library. Sudha leafs through a book. After a while, Monica shuts her eyes, trying to absorb the fact that she's really here at this remote and venerable monastery. She imagines centuries of prayer and meditation. Who would have imagined her long, long, journey from Father Daniel's retreat to Tabo?

Dinner is served in a tent like the one at Sangla. Girish joins them at a small, candlelit table. Electricity, he's explained, went down last week.

"You're both from Moorty?"

"More or less," Sudha says. "We live there now, but I belong to Bombay."

He turns to Monica who is savoring the *sag paneer*.

Odd he hasn't asked before, she thinks. "I'm from Minneapolis."

"The University of Minnesota. It has a famous South Asian library."

"The U, yes," she's pleased. "You've heard of the Ames Library?

"I almost went there for a Ph.D." Girish shrugs.

The guy is full of surprises. "But you decided against it?"

"Why travel to Minnesota when you can come to Tabo? Why study when you can absorb and practice spiritual discipline in this venerable place?"

Absorb and practice spiritual discipline, she muses, how close has she come to that? "Will you become a monk?"

He laughs, then stares at the shadows playing on the tent ceiling. "Once I thought that was my path, but," he pats the Nikon, safely placed on a side table. "I'm too curious about connections between spirit and earth. Perhaps one day I'll write a book with photographs. When I have enough pictures. When I'm wise enough."

"How will you gauge that?" Sudha asks in a teacherly voice.

He opens his palms. "What do you do in Moorty?"

"I teach secondary school. And Monica is a doctor at a local hospital."

Not Mission hospital, Monica notices. Not Catholic hospital. Not subversive neo-colonial institution.

"You know," he says with practiced casualness. "I had an idea about tomorrow."

"I'm not surprised." There's an edge to Sudha's voice.

Monica wonders if her friend is also a little fearful. Because they're surrounded by men? Because Spiti feels too perfect?

"How would you like to see Lalung?"

"Lalung!" Sudha exclaims. "It's so isolated. Really quite Tibetan."

"Ya." Girish's tongue dislodges a kernel of rice from between two front teeth. "Tibetan, but officially Indian as these things go. The people speak Bhoti. It's about an hour away. Depending on the rock slides, et cetera. If your driver has the petrol, we can go."

They look at each other, flabbergasted.

"My young friend, Norbu, hasn't seen his grandmother for months. I don't suppose you'd mind giving him a lift? He could translate for us."

"The jeep has room," Monica rushes on. "Four passenger seats."

"We will ask Shankar," Sudha hesitates.

"I asked this afternoon. 'First Class Service,' he said. 'Whatever the ladies request.'"

"That was foresightful," Sudha says coolly, "to inquire about logistics."

"I trust that you don't find it impertinent—"

Monica follows their volley warily.

"Let's stick with foresightful," Sudha frowns. "The trip sounds like an adventure. I vote yes."

It takes a beat before Monica sees they're waiting for her. "The vote is unanimous."

Two lanterns cast a yellow glow inside their little tent. Comforted by the mellow light, Monica is glad the electricity is down. Sliding under heavy covers, she's eager for sleep after a startling day.

"Monica, I've been wanting to ask you something."

Her shoulders tighten. Is Sudha suspicious of Girish?

"Yes," she answers reluctantly. Bedtime is not her favorite hour to chat.

"Raul and I have been making plans."

She waits.

"Tentative plans."

"About?"

"Manda."

The word strikes like a rock. She expected "wedding" or "children." Plans for Manda means she'll be losing Raul and Sudha. "He's going to open a clinic there? A full-time clinic?"

"Yes," Sudha declares. "Monica, do sit up a moment. I need to talk with you."

Sleepily, she rests a pillow under her elbow and faces her friend.

"The tutoring project has gone magnificently. And there's a huge medical need. We both feel we've done what we can in Moorty."

She sighs, shrugs away her selfishness. "That would be brave of both of you."

"One does what's next."

"The hospital will sorely miss Raul."

"Delhi will send a replacement."

"That's not the point."

"No."

"And I shall miss you, dear friend. Yes, I know this is right. Hard and daring and right. Be prepared for frequent visits from a certain Moorty doctor."

"Monica, thank you." She closes her eyes and takes a long breath. "I knew you'd understand. Nothing will happen for a while. There's so much planning. He's just begun fundraising. It could be months. A year."

Monica fights her feelings of abandonment. People move on. Sudha and Raul love each other and they'll flourish in Manda. Besides, who knows how long her visa will last. "I hope the visa comes through and I'll be there to say *Hasta luego*! And, as threatened, to visit often."

"The best kind of threat." Sudha slips beneath the covers. "We'll talk more tomorrow. You're exhausted. I just wanted to start the conversation."

Start the conversation? Monica wonders.

After a hearty breakfast, they climb into Shankar's chariot.

Norbu is a quiet, polite kid of eighteen or nineteen. Shy with the women; at first he speaks only in answer to questions.

Their route winds past mountain after mountain as they follow the blue grey Spiti River.

"Those giant rock formations," Sudha points out the right window, "remind me of the Olgas in Australia. Meena took me to visit the Northern Territory."

"The Red Center," muses Norbu.

"An educated young man," says Sudha.

He blushes, falls silent.

Up, up they travel. Monica's spine twists with the sudden turns. No room for her pillow with two extra passengers.

Road workers cover their heads, mouths and noses with scarves and shawls against the biting dust. Coated in pale dirt, they look like ghosts. Monica imagines a Greek chorus warning them. Of something.

"Oh, look, there," Sudha declares, "at those weird formations."

Glad for the distraction, Monica says, "Like the Badlands of South Dakota."

"The Badlands," Norbu brightens. "Sitting Bull and General Custer."

"That's right!" she waves to him.

"Norbu reads a lot," Girish says. "We have good conversations."

Suddenly the jeep skids to a halt. It takes a moment for Monica to leave the Badlands, to notice the huge boulders blocking the highway. Dozens of them.

Girish leaps out. Then Norbu. They haul rocks to the roadside.

Monica and Sudha join in, tossing smaller rocks.

Reluctantly, Shankar emerges from the car. Clearly moving rocks is beyond the call of "First Class" duties.

Monica supposes he's finally realized the jeep isn't going anywhere blocked by these boulders. Eventually, they manage to clear a path for the car. Catching her breath, Monica feels refreshed by the exercise. It's good to do something on a holiday. Looking down, the River seems to take on a new life.

*****

Lalung, like most villages up here, perches on a sheer hillside. All dwellings are the same beige-tan-taupe color. Dust covers the people, too. Girish explains it protects their skin against ravaging winds.

They stride past basic abodes which remind Monica of Pueblos. Otherwise, this looks like an ethereal realm. She notices a satellite dish on a distant roof. So much for unearthly!

"Our monastery is ancient," murmurs Norbu. "We will meet the monk."

They climb and climb up steep village roads. Monica and Sudha pause several times to catch their breath.

Norbu halts at an unprepossessing door and rings the bell.

Minutes pass. A quarter hour.

An old monk in a red baseball cap appears, bows at his unexpected guests.

"Our monastery," Norbu translates the monk's words from Bhoti, "is exactly the same age as Tabo. In fact it was founded on the same night all those centuries ago."

Girish, turned away from the group, snaps photos of the austere buildings in the haunting landscape.

The monk escorts them to a room with a prayer wheel. Its old walls are lined with vibrant, almost gaudy images of the Buddha in erotic poses.

What would it be like to live in a village where, for centuries, everyone shared the same faith? Tabo and Lalung in one week. Monica has fantasized about peaks, not monasteries. She's not prepared for the sacred nature of this mountain journey. She feels a pang of regret about her continuing search for spiritual community.

The next chamber is tiny. Very dark. No electricity in Lalung either. He props the door to admit sunlight on the elaborate rainbow-colored carvings. The centerpiece is a four-bodied Buddha on a wheel.

"The wheel hasn't turned in five hundred years," Norbu translates.

"Well, let's not try it today," Sudha whispers.

Norbu concurs solemnly.

Now they enter a library where each sacred text is bound in an ancient saffron cloth.

"It's all too extraordinary to absorb," she whispers to Sudha.

Norbu waits outside in the sunny, windy morning.

Girish waves from a high rock, hundreds of yards away, then points and clicks his Nikon.

*****

Tonight Norbu joins them in the tent for dinner.

Monica watches the two young men filling their plates and wonders: mentor and student? Friends? Lovers? She still has trouble reading body language between men here. The tent is cozy with battery-powered lanterns and a kerosene heater. Their adventure has given her a large appetite for the delicious curry.

"Did you enjoy your visit?" Norbu asks bashfully.

"Your village is stunning," declares Sudha.

Norbu beams.

Monica thinks of Basteri, Chitkul, Lalung, all places she couldn't have imagined.

"I've been wondering," Girish pauses from his meal, "what kind of doctoring you do in Moorty. I don't remember a hospital there."

"Oh, yes," Sudha interjects, "it's been there ten years. Small. Excellent staff."

Monica studies her friend. Has she changed her mind about the clinic because of Raul? Herself? Or is she forestalling a young man's rant about Western busybodies?

"Forgive me for being personal," Girish persists, "but why would an Indian hospital hire an American doctor?"

She draws a long breath. "I work at Moorty Mission Hospital. A Catholic-sponsored facility. Normally, it is staffed by Indians, you are right. This is rather an anomalous moment."

"Why did you come to India?"

"To contribute what I could."

"Ah, an evangelist." He's clearly teasing.

"No, my goal is to help people get well."

"Do you tend their bodies or their souls?"

Monica sees genuine curiosity in the eyes of this contemplative photographer.

"Can one separate the two? I focus on the body, of course. I'm a physician."

Sudha pays close attention.

Norbu's voice is faint. "I went to a Mission Hospital once. My appendix burst. The care was first-rate."

Sudha stands and passes the dessert try. "Sweets anyone? A game of Scrabble?"

As they prepare for bed, Monica says, "Interesting intervention."

Slipping into a flannel nightgown, Sudha asks, "What do you mean?"

"Serving dessert like the camp chatelaine and then changing the topic to Scrabble."

"OK. OK." Sudha perches on the bed. "I didn't think Girish would understand the kind of work you and Raul do."

"I see." She's annoyed but also touched. "Well—" she shouldn't continue, "do you?"

"Do I what?"

Monica slides between the cold sheets, then reaches over for her shawl. Why didn't she bring that silk underwear she uses in the Rockies? Sudha taps her foot.

"Do you understand our work?" Monica lifts her head from the pillow.

"Some of it."

Monica closes her eyes, lies back down. She should let this go.

"Do you understand its implications?" Sudha asks a little sharply.

"Some," she answers honestly. "I've given good care. The pre-natal and preventive health programs are useful, but—"

Sudha waits.

"As time passes I feel desperate about the condoms which would do so much good. That question Raj asked a lifetime ago is still fresh in my conscience."

"Ah, Raj."

"I don't convert my patients, but some of my colleagues aren't so judicious."

"Brigid," Sudha sighs. "Raul has told me. About the 'spiritual check-ups' she does with patients."

Monica shakes her head angrily.

"And the baptisms."

"How often has he seen it?" She should have told Raul about the Habib baby.

"I couldn't say."

"Is this one of the reasons he's so eager to leave for Manda?"

"One of them."

Monica groans, heavy with shame.

"I shouldn't have said anything," Sudha apologizes. "Not at bedtime. Brigid does provoke me. But we need rest. General Shankar said 'bright and early' for our journey to Losar."

Losar. Monica hopes to dream about this village 13,500 feet high. Imagine. Rest. Sleep. Dream. If only she could.

Girish and Norbu stand outside the breakfast tent, waving farewell.

Sudha calls out the window. "Hope you have more guests this week."

"Yes, a family from Gujarat is arriving today," Girish assures her. "And some people from Delhi the next day."

"Good luck with the electricity," Monica adds. "Thanks for everything."

She wonders if Girish's visitors are imaginary. Maybe their own stay was a fantasy.

Thousand-year-old monasteries.

Villages pulsing under blankets of dust.

Rotating Buddhas.

Mystery, not menace.

"*Jule*," Norbu shouts in Bhoti.

"*Jule*," Monica and Sudha call back.

Shankar guns the engine and they set off at a gallop.

THIRTY-TWO

May, 2002, The Himalayan Journey

Sudha sits in front, absorbed by the mountains.

Monica adjusts the pillow behind her back and prays. She begins each day asking that their travels go well, that she will know God's will and have the strength to carry it out. This morning she also prays for guidance about Moorty Mission. Surely Father Freitas will direct them well. Surely she can put the Walshes' evangelism out of her mind until the end of this trip. Can try to put it out of her mind.

"Oh, look," Sudha points.

Monica takes in a spectacular waterfall streaming from the rock face.

"Many waterfalls now," Shankar declares. "Extra beautiful route for you."

"Indeed," Monica nods in gratitude.

"Did you enjoy Spiti camp?" he asks.

"Very much, Sudha answers.

"Only women," he mutters.

"Pardon?" Monica finds it hard to hear him from the back seat.

"You were the only women there."

"Yes." Sudha's exasperation is returning.

"Were you not afraid?"

"No, should we have been?" Sudha regards him curiously.

Flustered, he concentrates on the road, then speaks up. "My company usually escorts businessmen through the mountains. Sometimes married people. This is the first time to drive two ladies traveling alone."

Monica refrains from repeating that they are traveling with each other, not alone.

"Well, aren't you lucky then?" declares Sudha. "How interesting for you."

His face grows serious. "Interesting. It is interesting."

"I'm glad to hear that," Sudha says flatly.

Monica manages a half smile, as reluctant as Sudha to learn more about Shankar's opinions about women travelers.

They arrive in Losar just after 4 p.m. Almost 13,500 feet. She's never climbed this high in the Rockies. Do Dad and his cowgirl do much hiking? He didn't answer the last letter. She hopes he's OK.

The small crossroads town is hectic with people purchasing supplies for even farther flung areas. For millennia traders have visited from Tibet and India. The crowds reflect this history—faces from Central Asia, Lhasa, Delhi. Afternoon streets bustle with lorries and coaches and a few jeeps like theirs. In nearby fields, some still dusted with snow, she sees crops of potatoes and carrots. The junction town is bordered by silvery mountains, some as high as 20,000 feet.

"Don't you want to keep going up, up toward those beautiful peaks?"

Sudha laughs. "Yes, I always like to go farther, to see what's next."

Shankar's voice darkens. "Kunzum Pass after this. Then we go down. To the Kullu Valley, to Manali, to Rohanda and then we return to Moorty. This is our package. According to the signed contract."

"Yes, Shankar," Monica says impatiently. "Don't worry. We're being fanciful."

"Fanciful," he weighs the word. "I think it is a woman's trait, yes?"

"Among many assets," Sudha says.

Apparently not knowing what to make of this, he says, "I drive now to the Government Guest House. Special place. These other jeep travelers stay in the two town hotels. Not so nice. Not so clean. Yet even they are all booked now."

"We appreciate your careful planning." Monica sighs, dying for a shower.

On the edge of Losar, they stop at a small, blockish structure. Shankar knocks. He knocks again, more loudly. Then he calls through a crack in the door.

Finally, a monk in red robes appears.

"The manager is temporarily absent," he speaks impeccable English. "Perhaps I can be of assistance?"

Shankar is opening the trunk, carrying out their bags.

"We have a booking here for tonight," Sudha explains.

The monk tilts his head skeptically. "Perhaps there has been a mistake. This is a government Guest House."

"Yes," Monica concurs. "We have a booking through Moorty Motor Tours."

"I see," he reflects. "Please come in. This is the common room. I am next door. There is one more guest chamber at the end of the house."

They enter a murky parlor sparsely furnished with two small tables and six chairs.

"I'm afraid we've had no electricity for days. And the water is limited."

Monica's heart sinks. So much for a shower.

A small, round man bursts in. "Hello. Hello?"

"Ah, this is Mr. Sharma, the manager. And these are your guests from the Jeep Company."

Mr. Sharma looks puzzled.

"These ladies have a booking for tonight."

"Impossible. Impossible," he grumbles. "No booking."

Monica feels the weight of the day, of the whole week, on her tired, dirty body.

"Is the room reserved for someone else then?" Sudha steps forward.

Monica thinks of her authoritative friend on that first visit to the clinic.

"We must hold for possible arrival of a government official."

"We have nowhere to go," Monica says plaintively. Where is Shankar? Why isn't he straightening this out?

"I have an empty storeroom," Mr. Sharma hesitates. "No bed, but I can give you a comforter," he says kindly, doubtfully.

Shankar overhears this as he appears with the rest of the bags. His voice is uncharacteristically belligerent. "Our guests always stay here. Moorty Motor Tours. My manager rang you three days ago to confirm."

"No phone service," Mr. Sharma shakes his unhappy head. "No electricity. No booking!"

The monk steps in. "Certainly a local family would put you up."

Sudha shakes her head. "So clearly there's been a double booking here."

"No booking." Mr. Sharma displays the reservation log which lists only the monk. "Maybe government official will not come. They have a right to arrive until 4 a.m."

"How about this?" Sudha tries carefully. "We sleep in the room. If your official arrives—which looks doubtful given the hour and the difficulty of traversing these mountains in the dark—we will surrender the bed. You keep your rules. If the official doesn't appear, you'll receive a night's payment you would otherwise not have had."

Monica is astonished at her friend's quick, agile wit. After all, it will either be this wager or a night on the concrete floor.

Mr. Sharma frowns.

"A resourceful solution," the monk says gently.

Mr. Sharma wraps his arms around a barrel chest. "As long as you agree to surrender the bed. I don't see why not. If you have eighty rupees."

Monica notices a flicker in the monk's eyes.

Sudha maintains, "We have sixty rupees. More than the room is worth."

Mr. Sharma wags his head from side to side.

The monk smiles.

They have a deal of sorts.

"You understand," Mr. Sharma continues. "No electricity. No coal for heating."

Sudha shrugs.

He turns to Monica and lowers his voice. "Indian-style toilet."

She keeps a straight face. "This will be most adequate, Sir. Thank you."

"You are welcome." A relieved smile. "Both ladies are welcome. Welcome."

They set out for a stroll in the darkening afternoon, taking a long, empty road toward the highest mountains. Here at the edge of town, Losar is quiet. The last light is thin, tranquil. They're near the summit of their trip. Only Kunzum Pass will be higher. Then they begin the descent. Moorty will appear before them. How much longer will she have the company of Raul and Sudha? She wants the trip to end here, wants it never to end, wants to rewind and set a different course. Hubris. Selfishness. They all have their own paths. She should be grateful she's shared Sudha's for a while.

Back at the guest house, they wait for supper, huddled in three layers of clothes, reading by flashlight.

At dinner, Monica is charmed to find the dining room lit with the dim bulb of a flashlight, the top screwed off, providing a candle-like glow. "Where do you think the monk is?" she whispers.

"Perhaps we imagined him."

She feels a chill.

"He probably eats alone," Sudha says more seriously.

The vegetables and rice are simple fare. Miraculously prepared, given the cooks have only flashlights with which to navigate the pitch blackness.

They eat eagerly, in silence. Again, Monica feels the load of their long day. At another time, with a roaring coal fire and flickering candles, the guest house room might be comfortable, even charming. Tonight, it's a rough way station and Monica prays that they'll be sheltered until dawn.

They fumble around the room, washing their hands with cold water from a plastic pail and crawling beneath the covers fully clothed. The comforters are so redolent with lanolin, it feels they've bedded down with a yak.

Sudha giggles.

Monica follows suit.

"It's so hilarious," Sudha gulps a breath. "Two sophisticated women bundled in bed, wearing all their clothes in case they need to make a midnight getaway."

"Oh, don't even think about it." She falls into a fit of giggles.

"This reminds me of sleeping with Meena, on that childhood holiday to Moorty."

"Yes," Monica reflects. "Jeanne and I loved Nicko's attic bedroom overlooking Lake Superior. We'd stay up hours talking and laughing."

"So what should we talk about?"

"Don't you think we should get some sleep?" she yawns. "In case Mr. School Superintendent or Mrs. Treasury claims our bed?"

"You're too practical," Sudha complains. "Actually, there is something I need to ask you."

Exhausted as she is, she can't say no to Sudha, who clearly savors bedtime chats.

"What's that?"

"Would you consider joining us in the Backcountry Project?"

"That's a good name for it," she stalls.

"No, really. The three of us would make a superb team."

"Two days ago you were sending me to Delhi to marry Ashok."

"You said no."

"You knew I would."

"I want you to be happy. Moorty isn't the place for that."

"I made a commitment to the Mission." She feels torn.

"We could enlist Ashok, too. He's interested in this kind of project."

"He's interested in his academic career."

"He's interested in you. And he has a conscience."

"Of course," she says heatedly. "What use would he be in Manda?"

"He's a great supporter of rural autonomy. Philosophers write about everything, no? He could investigate values in indigenous healing arts. Philosophy of medicine. He could teach at Delhi during alternate terms. Or get a job at one of the universities in this state. I bet his articles would be invaluable for fundraising."

"Dear friend, you're getting carried away," Monica sighs. "My dad calls this blue-skying." Surely Sudha knows that erudite philosophy articles are more likely to drive donors away.

"I'm serious," she whispers. "Raul and I have discussed this for weeks. You could do so much…"

"Sudha, I'm flattered. Honored…"

"Stop there." She puts her index finger over Monica's lips. "Just say you'll think about it, that's all. That you'll think about it."

"OK," she surprises herself. "I'll think about it."

"Good." Sudha sinks beneath the covers.

"Now you owe me some serenity. Let's discuss something calming. Tell me more about your childhood trip to Moorty."

They are up at 6:30, pacing in the sunny courtyard to keep warm.

"Oh, delicious!" Sudha exclaims.

Monica turns to see the cook carrying out a tray of tea and steaming chapattis.

"Bliss!" Sudha declares. "The mountains. The sun. Fresh, hot chapattis. My dearest friend. I don't think I've ever been happier."

THIRTY-THREE

June, 2002, The Himalayan Journey

After breakfast, Monica and Sudha pack quickly, eager to go. On this crisp, clear morning, at the edge of the world, Monica imagines they might be able to see into eternity.

The first class vehicle takes longer to awaken than the passengers. Finally, Shankar admits his battery is dead.

"In Minnesota, we plug cars into electric block heaters each night."

"Not very practical in a land without electricity."

"Right," she feels foolish. Her reflexes are still so American, so presumptuous. "Moorty is beginning to feel like the French Riviera."

Sudha rolls her eyes. "I'm grateful we had a bed last night. If we'd slept on concrete floor, we'd be in the same condition as Shankar's chariot."

Monica doesn't want to be stuck here. One night with the yak is enough. She aches to wash her hair, her whole body, in warm water. Where is her patience? That elusive equanimity?

After an hour of tinkering, Shankar finds someone to push the jeep downhill. To everyone's relief, it sputters to a start.

"Onward to Kunzum Pass!" he declares merrily.

They both sit in the back this morning. Monica takes the place behind Shankar so Sudha has the unobstructed view.

"Onward," they say in unison.

The good humor is short-lived. The steep roads are the most difficult they've encountered so far. They'll have to ascend 1,500 meters on winding, rock-strewn surfaces before Kunzum Pass.

Monica gazes out the window, praying for safe passage.

They creep up the sheer grade.

Do they really need to get this close to the top of the world? Monica begins to sense a grave, if irrational, dread.

At the next turn, she watches their ascent steepen.

"Damn!"

They've never heard Shankar swear before.

"What is it?" Sudha forces calm into her voice.

"Flat tire." He draws a sharp breath. "Can't you hear it?"

"Oh, no!"

"Bad roads," Shankar explains needlessly. "Frequent problem. I will fix it."

They step out and wait on the side of the rugged highway, clutching their shawls close to their bodies, against the wind.

Sudha suddenly flies to a high rock. "Come here. Might as well enjoy the scenery. This is as close as I, at least, will get to Heaven."

"Sudha, be careful. That's not safe."

"Each day here is a wager," she laughs. "Thank about last night. We got to sleep till dawn with that stinky yak."

Cautiously, Monica picks her way toward Sudha. "Thanks to you."

Shankar examines the tire. He studies it from another angle. Then another before slipping his jack beneath the car.

Minutes pass. Half-an-hour.

He fiddles with a bolt, which is locked in ice.

A tractor driver pulls over and Monica sees he's hauling an open cart crowded with six dusty women road workers wearing protective scarves over their heads, noses and mouths. She is suddenly nostalgic for Lalung's dirt roads and neat dwellings. Were they deeper in the Himalayas in that village or here on this isolated rocky road?

The tractor driver stands with hands on his hips giving Shankar advice.

Shankar ignores him, his face a study of staunch determination.

A woman calls to Sudha and Monica.

The tourists from Moorty pick their way down the hill, approaching the cart tentatively.

Mixing Hindi, English and sign language, they all manage to communicate, amusing themselves. The giggling women belong to Chatru.

Behind them, Shankar and the tractor driver lift and bang and grunt.

The sound of clapping turns the women's attention. The tractor driver is grinning jubilantly. Shankar stands, wiping his hands, looking annoyed.

"Ready, Ladies?" Shankar is edgy.

Monica looks at the bald tire and their exhausted tense driver, then at Sudha. She says, "As ready as we'll ever be."

When the jeep pulls away, the road workers are waving and whooping. For one dislocated moment, Monica sees klieg lights on an eerie green football field, maroon-and-gold clad cheerleaders waving pom-pons toward Kunzum Pass. Whoop. Whoop.

Sudha and Monica grin at the women, waving back.

Silence descends. Clearly all of them are lost in thought or relief or foreboding.

For an hour, they ride in silence.

Monica peers out anxiously for a roadside shrine. Something to cheer Shankar. To buoy all of them.

Sun cuts through the cold. She breathes in the welcome warmth.

At the same moment, Shankar points to a dhaba, making a swift left turn. The sign reads, "Omlettes, Lemmon Tea, Beans and *Chapattis*."

"Perfect!" Sudha pronounces. "Sun. Air. Food. A chance to stretch."

The café owner, a slim man in jeans, parka and green woolen cap, nods to them, then continues retouching his shingle, Vijay's *Dhaba.* "Fresh, new paint," he explains to the hungry visitors, "to draw people in."

Vijay's other customer camps at the end of the long outside table, nursing a Coke and listening intently to a short wave radio.

Monica has noticed dozens of people listening to short wave here in the Himalayas. Of course. How else would they get the news?

The three pilgrims sit, waiting silently for Vijay to reassure them with warm food.

Quickly, Vijay serves generous plates of rice, beans and chapattis. Vijay tells them he lives farther south in Manali with his wife and children seven months of the year. "I come up here May to October—to escape the mosquitoes and tourists in Manali."

"Doesn't it get a little lonely?" Monica asks.

He stretches his arms wide and studies the mountains. "Not with such company."

"I see what you mean."

"Where do you ladies travel now?"

"The Kunzum Pass. Then down to Rohtang Pass," mutters Shankar, probably still stewing about the dead battery and the flat tire.

Vijay draws a sharp breath. "Bad weather this afternoon. Snow and rain. Rock slides. Safe drive."

"Certainly," Shankar answers curtly. "Safety is our motto."

They continue traveling toward the summit. Soon they will be at Kunzum. Now all the surrounding mountains glisten in brilliant whiteness.

It's sunny enough, Monica notices, relieved Vijay was wrong about the weather.

Every ten miles or so, they pass a "Free Tibet" sign on the roadside. Or another car.

Most of the day, it's just the little jeep limping along the jagged mountain edge.

Then, finally, suddenly, too soon they arrive.

Kunzum Pass is packed with snow. 15,085 feet.

"Yay!" shouts Sudha, then grabs the hands of her fellow travelers. "We did it! We made it."

Shankar nods, nervously, perhaps unused to ebullient reactions from his businessmen passengers.

Monica laughs, then kisses Sudha on both cheeks. "Yes, yes. We're here at last."

Sudha leaps from the car, tugging her shawl after her.

"Here, at last," Monica muses. Pensively, slowly, she puts on her wool hat and gloves. Outside in the crisp air, she says a prayer of thanks, realizing she's reassured as well as sad that they've reached the goal. It's down, down from here.

They stop at the Kunzum Buddhist Temple. Monica photographs a radiant flank of Tibetan Liberation posters. She wants to concentrate on this place, the pinnacle of their trip, but her mind drifts backward to the Raj trappings of Shimla, the sunny morning tea at Narkanda, the temple at Sarahan, the lovely village near Sangla, the astonishing dust of Lalung.

"Do we have to go down?" Sudha asks, shifting from one foot to the other to keep warm.

"It is heavenly," Monica laughs, "but just a little chilly to be heaven itself, I think."

"Yes, we must continue to Rohtang Pass," Shankar says, "as we agreed in the—"

"In the contract," Monica and Sudha finish his sentence.

Relieved, Shankar consents to have his picture taken with each of them. Monica sees his impatience, perhaps nervousness, about reaching tonight's hotel before dark.

As they leave, he drives clockwise around the temple for an auspicious journey.

*****

Light is fading fast. Grey clouds sail swiftly across the filmy sky. They're riding into shadow land.

A fine mist has coated their windshield.

Shankar switches on the noisy wipers.

"In Ireland," Monica hears her own inanely cheery voice, "They call this 'soft weather.' "

"Hard to drive," Shankar stretches his neck. "Hard to see."

Silence again. Monica broods over Sudha's startling invitation to work in Manda. She's touched that they want her. Flattered. Yet how can she possibly leave Moorty Hospital? A long sigh runs through her tired body (she didn't sleep so well with that yak and the imminence of midnight eviction). Equally, how long can she survive the reign of Kevin Walsh?

Sudha reaches along the back seat for her friend's hand.

Monica looks up, questioning.

"We're going back down now. Back to earth. You know Rohtang Pass is 'only' about 13,000 feet. Very terrestrial."

Monica shuts her eyes, ready for a shower and electricity, regretful their trip is ending.

"I want to thank you. For the adventure. The beauty. For your friendship."

Monica squeezes Sudha's hand. She'll miss her when she leaves for Manda. It will be hard to phone. Even hard to get mail in and out. She's certain, however, that her own work is in Moorty, that she must keep her commitment to the Mission. Of course, that's the right decision.

The rain increases. The windshield is a blur. Afternoon dims. Darkens.

Suddenly a deluge. Torrential water courses heavier and heavier. Sheets of it. A river. They are surrounded by wetness and noise.

How did Noah steer the ark? Monica wonders. Can you survive a barrel ride over Niagara Falls?

Shankar accelerates. Then slows down. Clearly he doesn't know what to do.

The jeep jerks sharply to the right and rests on a narrow shoulder, huddled against the silver-white mountain.

Monica looks over Shankar's shoulder at the steep highway ahead.

Sudha stares out her window at rain coursing down the road. "It's like a river."

"Not good to drive in this," he declares.

"Of course," Monica agrees. "Best to wait. We have these downpours in Minnesota during thunderstorm season. I always pull over to the side of the highway." The side of a well-paved, graded freeway, with broad safety shoulders. Near an emergency call box.

Sudha sighs, wraps her shawl close and closes her eyes.

The rain slows. Just as the storm abates and Shankar puts the car in gear, they hear the noise.

A deep rumble.

A roar.

"What the—" Monica begins.

"Rockslide!" Shankar shouts. "Out. Out! Against the mountainside. Now!"

Monica opens the door, reaches back for her suitcase.

"No, no time. No time!" he screams. "Out!"

"Slide toward me," Monica calls to Sudha. "Safer over here."

"Faster this way," Sudha says, opening the door on the far side.

Another earsplitting crack.

Shankar carefully edges out, flattens himself against the wet mountain.

Monica follows, all the while, keeping an eye on Sudha.

Giant rocks and sheets of dirt pummel the jeep as the ground shakes fiercely.

"Sudha? Where are you? Sudha?" Monica screams.

Immense boulders and oh, no, a wall of rocks and snow and earth itself.

Monica bolts toward the car, shrieking, "Sudha! Where are you, Sudha?!"

Shankar yanks her arm. He's too strong.

"Nothing," he says breathlessly. "Nothing you can do—force of the landslide."

They stare at this broken world. "Ma'am and the car are gone. Swept away."

"No, no, no!" she pleads. "Sudha, where are you, Sudha?"

Shankar hangs on to her with one hand and dials his satellite phone with the other. He's saying something in a calm, clear voice. Speaking in English. But Monica cannot hear anything except the growling earth.

Monica watches the landslide go on and on. It is probably over within minutes. But Monica is frozen, caught in the eternal flow of rock and dirt and trees and—

When she stops shaking, Shankar releases his grip.

Numbly she walks across the road.

"No, Ma'am," he calls.

She's moving too fast for him. If she doesn't look down, if she doesn't say good-bye, she'll never forgive herself. Still, she can't believe this is all happening.

Oh, what a horrendous sight: the wash of broken boulders and splintered trees and no, it's too deep, she can't see the car. She imagines Sudha's terror, oh, God, why did this happen? Why Sudha, who was, is, treasured by Raul, her family, her students, all of them. Why beloved Sudha?

Monica feels Shankar's firm hand.

"Ma'am," he speaks softly, firmly. "We must wait over there. I have contacted headquarters. Help will come in a few hours. Do not worry."

"An ambulance!" she shouts frantically. "Call an ambulance for Sudha. A helicopter would get here faster. She's alive down there, just trapped, trapped—"

"Come," he says kindly. "We'll wait on the other side, out of the wind. We must try to keep warm."

"But the medical helicopter," she demands loudly. "They've sent some kind of ambulance?"

He looks away sorrowfully.

She rocks back and forth between searing pain and numbness. "Sudha. Sudha," she prays. She can't go on without her. They all need her. "Sudha!" she shouts at the top of her lungs.

Another rumble from the earth. A loud, deeply vibrating hum exploding into a groan.

The globe, itself, is shifting.

THIRTY-FOUR

June, 2002, Moorty
They stand at attention in the damp auditorium of Walkerton School as a monsoon rages against the high windows. The students all look crisp in their green and white uniforms.

"Please be seated," announces Sri Dal, the headmaster.

Monica sits awkwardly on a wooden folding chair between Ashok and Sudha's mother. When she tried to sit at the back of the auditorium, Sri Dal ushered her to the front row.

Ashok has been so kind and attentive.

"Of course I came," he whispered. "I was terribly worried for you."

Mrs. Badami's green silk sari rustles as she shifts in her chair.

On the train platform, she said to them, "Call me Rajul."

Indeed the handsome, sturdy woman with the jet black hair and ageless skin seems a contemporary, but something in Monica maintains a distance.

"Dear esteemed guests and students," Sri Dal speaks with gentle authority, "We gather today to honor a devoted teacher and admired colleague, Sudha Badami, who served Walkerton School for five memorable years. As you know, today we are privileged by the presence of her beloved parents, Sri and Srimati Badami. Doctors Murphy and Sanchez and Professor Niar, who were friends of our cosmopolitan teacher, also privilege us with their attendance."

At the station, Rajul tried to put them at ease. "Sudha spoke so often about both of you doctors. I know how much she admired your work and how greatly she cherished your friendship."

Santosh Badami was more formal. The tall, trim man seemed to wish he could evaporate in this thin, hill station air. He was cordial, unsurprising for a well-traveled naval officer, but remote.

"Our first speaker today is Vikram. Vikram has worked with Sudha Badami for two years now and has grown proficient in English."

Soberly, Vikram climbs to the stage.

He surveys the audience. Catching Monica's eye, he offers a half-smile.

No trace of the gawky boy who came with his prickly teacher to the clinic. Her breath catches at the memory of Sudha in her sari with the blue trim. She sees her as clearly as if she's standing next to Vikram now.

"I think you are the perfect person to present a lecture on hygiene for our students. Do you ever get away from the hospital?"

How intimidated she felt by the refined, confident teacher.

Sudha persisted, "So when you come, you will not speak about religion?"

"She taught us all the literatures. She explained that only when we know about the world can we understand our own country." Vikram speaks confidently. "I shall miss Madam Badami." He chokes, then regains composure, as his teacher would have expected. "And I will never forget her."

Ashok squeezes Monica's elbow.

Murmurs of agreement and approval echo in the room. Vikram gives a slight bow and exits.

Rajul's eyes are full. Small hands—so like Sudha's—are folded in her lap. Next to his wife, Santosh sits erect and attentive. Yes, these are the people who gave Sudha her grace and certainty.

She watched the landslide go on and on.

She couldn't hear the car. She imagined, felt, Sudha's terror. Oh, God.

"Ma'am," his voice trembled as he tried for an authoritative tone.

"An ambulance!" she demanded. "A medical helicopter!"

Raj climbs the steps solemnly. He's grown taller and more handsome in the last sixteen months. His voice is deeper than Vikram's, but no less mournful.

"Madam Badami helped us develop pride in our country and tolerance of others. And appreciation of others. She instilled in us the belief that we could make great contributions. It is because of her provocative, patient, authoritative instruction that whatever gifts I have will be better used."

Their journey to Manali in the rescue van was a blur in the lashing rain. The driver told Monica and Shankar about other deaths. A whole family from Patna. A school group from Jaipur. She couldn't absorb the details. She didn't care about the others. She ached for Sudha.

The hotel had electricity and excellent phone service. Hysterically, Monica kept thinking how happy Sudha would have been here, showering and washing her hair after all those grungy days on the road. Monica didn't care if she ever showered again. She didn't want to eat. She didn't want to sleep. She wanted to die.

Instead she phoned Raul.

With him, she wept as she could not do before.

Raul was the first to compose himself. "I will ring her family, the head-master at Walkerton," he said shakily.

"You have enough strength for this?"

"I will find it. But how about you? I'll come and drive you back to Moorty."

There was nothing more in the world she wanted. Another three days with Shankar seemed unimaginable.

"No, please. You have so much to do there. No, I'll be fine. I'm not hurt, just wet and dirty."

"You are also in shock, Monica. I'll ring you in an hour to check."

The third time the phone rang, she watched the black instrument from her bed, willing it to be silent. He was trying to draw her from the hole of despair, where among the splintered trees, the sundered boulders, some-where, she knew she would find Sudha.

The ringing subsided. She closed her eyes.

Ten minutes later: bloody phone again. She started to throw it against the wall.

Ashok's voice, full of concern. "Raul rang. I'm so very sorry. How are you? Why didn't you phone me?"

Before she had a chance to answer, he interrupted. "I've booked a coach for Manali. I arrive tomorrow about 10 o'clock."

The teachers are speaking now. About Sudha's diligence. Her loyalty. Her creativity. Her bright spirit.

Former students climb the steps to add words of appreciation and grief.

Monica listens gratefully. She hopes Raul will speak, but he's already told her he has no words yet. Nor does she, of course, because she can't get beyond, "Helicopter! Ambulance!"

Sri Dal ends the memorial by asking everyone to observe a moment of silence.

*****

Lunch at the Mayfair Arms is painfully stilted for the first half-hour. Monica wishes Ashok hadn't left for Delhi. He was so adept in social situations. Still he'd already spent more than a week away from the university.

"Please tell us about your hospital here," Rajul asks. "Sudha said you were doing good work, each of you."

Santosh is gradually disappearing into the William Morris wall paper.

Monica fixates on the ornate silver butter dish. The background music, a Handel sonata, is counterpointed by the occasional chime and clink of crystal and silverware.

A stocky waiter in a white suit too tight across his belly serves her filet of sole and Dover potatoes. Where has he come from? Is he wearing slippers?

"And Monica," she hears Raul talking, "has done wonders with preventive health care."

Santosh tucks into his roast lamb and mint sauce.

Sudha would laugh about her memorial lunch being held at this classic colonial dining room. At first, Monica assumed the Badamis chose a posh Western restaurant to make their guests comfortable. Then she recalls Sudha's long ago comment about how her father would love this place. She sees that urbane Santosh feels at home here and that Rajul is striving for an atmosphere of composure.

"Yes, tell us more about the program, won't you, Dr. Murphy?"

"Please call me Monica."

"To be sure," Rajul dips her head, "And you do a lot of prenatal care as well?"

Monica is touched that Sudha reported so much to her parents.

"You do what is asked." It does seem as simple as that.

Rajul nods.

"Sudha made real contributions," Monica feels blood rush to her face at the palpable memory of Sudha's endless vitality. "You heard about her teaching today. She also worked in the Manda project with Raul, encouraging her students to learn by teaching others."

Santosh speaks for the first time. "That's our Sudha. Always busy, always taking one step beyond. She was that way, even as a child."

"Tell us what she was like as a girl?" Raul asks.

Plates of ham and chicken salad. The Altar Society women brought a full bakery of cookies, cakes and pies. Mom would have loved the food, would have fluttered around checking that everyone had enough to eat.

The cat-footed waiter pads up behind her. "May I show you our pastry tray?"

She wants to say, you can show me a stiff glass of single malt. But Sudha's parents don't drink. And, as always, she's aware she could turn into Jeanne.

"By all means," answers Santosh, who has relaxed. Eyes bruised with grief, he is nevertheless becoming the classic, generous Indian host.

Each of the others orders a pastry; Monica isn't hungry.

Bracelets chiming, Rajul points to the tray. "Come dear. How about the berries? Healthy, beautiful berries? They're so tasty this time of year. Sudha told me you had 'an appetite for life.' She talked about those cooking classes. You know she was very proud to make us *pasta primavera* on her last visit to Bandra."

"The vegetables were perfectly *al dente*," Santosh smiles for the first time. "Delicious, indeed. *Pasta primavera* from our little mountain eccentric. A wonder."

Overwhelmed by longing for Sudha, undone by Rajul's reference to the "last visit," she feels tears stinging her eyes. Monica tells herself that crying is self-indulgent in the presence of Sudha's parents and lover. Their pain is so large and deep. Yet she does carry something they do not bear. She is responsible for her friend's death. She planned the trip, paid for it secretly without telling Sudha. With privileged American presumptuousness and reckless spontaneity, she risked her dear friend's life. And lost it.

"I'm so sorry," she suddenly confesses to Rajul and Santosh. "It's my fault. The trip was my idea. If only--." She is sobbing. "I'm sorry. So unutterably sorry."

Raul bows his head.

Santosh studies his plate.

Rajul gazes at her, then takes her hand. "No, please listen. Sudha was not a follower. She cherished you as a spirited companion. She rang us the night before your journey, of course. She was thrilled beyond excitement."

Santosh intercedes, a catch in his voice. "I tried to tell her. I know those mountains from my brother who did war duty there. I said, 'Go later in the season. The rains are treacherous.' Sudha never listened. My fault. If only I had been a stricter father."

Monica hardly hears his words.

"No. No. No!" Rajul declares. "No one's fault. Sudha was Sudha. Our Sudha always traveled the furthest. Yes, Meena is in Australia and Naren flies back and forth from Toronto and Leeds. But our Sudha always had her eyes in the stars. She ventured farthest in her imagination. And now she is at rest in her beloved mountains."

"But you 'recovered;' you came back to India," Monica said.

"Not to Bombay. In some senses I am as distant from my parents as Meena and Naren. At least they live in large, cosmopolitan cities. My father, especially, doesn't know what to make of this daughter, the country recluse."

That night in Sangla, Monica knew their friendship would go on and on.

"Our Sudha treasured you both. Monica and you, Dr. Sanchez..."

"Raul, please."

"We look forward to welcoming you to Bombay. A beautiful city. Especially in January and February."

Politely, they nod.

Monica knows her assent is more than courtesy. She is bound to Sudha's parents, Sudha's spirit.

THIRTY-FIVE

June, 2002, Moorty

Birds chatter outside the window. It's safe to open her eyes now. One more sleepless dark has passed. Rising, she finds the room surprisingly chilly for summer.

Another night reliving the accident. Revising it.

Ignoring Shankar.

Reaching into the jeep and yanking Sudha to safety.

Yelling, hurry, hurry, forget your stupid purse, hurry, hurry.

Always the same image. Sudha can't hear her. Can't see her. The curtain drops.

Shankar pinning Monica against the mountainside shouting, No you cannot move. The jeep disappeared. The earth shifted.

As she boils water for tea, Monica thinks how she has talked it through time and again with Ashok. Why? She asks him: why couldn't I help her? And he says it was too late. It happened too fast.

Is Sudha in Heaven? Sister Mary Thomas said only good Christians went to Heaven. Monica remembers coming home from the first grade crying because the Cohen family next door weren't going to Heaven. "Whatever makes you say that?" Mom consoled. "God has room for every good person."

It takes all her effort to dress.

"So if you don't believe in Heaven, do you think you'll be reincarnated?"

"No, I'll just vanish," Sudha smiled. "Disappear into the universe. Recycled."

Monica stared at her, for this is exactly what she used to believe.

"So will your body. We'll mingle together for eternity. Your lovely blue eyes are made of the 10^{80} particles that have been roving the universe for zillions of years. You just return those particles."

Monica shrugged.

"I don't mean to make light," Sudha softened. "Your religion, I know how much it means to you. Does it bother you that I'm not going to Heaven?"

"Yes," she rejoined. "It's your choice. But it will be lonelier without you."

What made Monica confident she was going to Heaven?

It's already a lot lonelier here without her. She moans, yearning for Sudha's radiant smile, her quick repartee.

Combing her knotted hair, she stares at the mirror, "How can God be so unfair?"

"I will pray for you," Father Freitas said. "And when you find the strength to offer your own prayers, God will hear them. Give yourself time. Give God time."

He's a good man, but right now, it's hard for her to believe in his prayers. Harder still to believe in her own.

Forcing her steps toward the refectory, she knows she has to face them. She has to return to work. Eating is also a good idea. Not eating is more appealing. A quicker route to her dance with the 10^{80} particles.

Sister Catherine greets her at the door, sniffing into a white handkerchief.

Monica squeezes the nun's free hand.

"May God rest your friend's soul."

Monica nods to console the good woman.

As she enters the dining room, Sister Eleanor reaches forward.

The nun embraces her. She, too, is crying. Restrained Sister Eleanor.

And now frigid Brigid. The spiteful epithet leaps to her mind in the midst of a consoling hug. Monica recoils at the touch, even as she hungers for warmth.

The first day back at work passes in a fog. Grief hits at odd moments. While checking Ritu's blood work. While walking to dinner. How can she cope with these sad, sympathetic people? How can she face Raul? When it's her fault. She had boldly divined the trip, persuaded Sudha to come. Yes, her fault. Her most grievous fault. No matter what they say.

Monica retires early. Everyone understands; they are so damn understanding without understanding a thing.

Dusk when she enters the flat. She sits in dimness, gazing at Sudha's favorite view of those treacherous mountains. She is literally surrounded by danger and threat. She always was. Birds sing evening songs, calling her to another sleepless night.

The phone's ringing crackles through the flat.

"Monica?"

"Beata!"

The dam breaks. Sorrow and pain and anguish and guilt race through her exhausted body.

Silence on the other end. Maybe she's hung up. Maybe she's abandoned her too.

"I'm sorry," Monica manages. "This is an expensive call just to hear someone weep futilely."

"Not futilely," she says with familiar tenderness. "And this is what money is for."

Suddenly she's angry, flailing at her friend. "Tell me, Beata. How can God do this? Why is it that everyone I love leaves? Why?"

Beata is quiet, or rather engaging, Monica imagines, in "active listening." She can feel her bloody Christian concern all the way from St. Paul.

Monica moans. The flat is dark. Birds are silent. The mountains invisible.

"Not everyone," Beata says finally.

Monica sighs.

"You have me," Beata says softly.

Friendship, Monica corrects herself, not Christian concern.

"You have Ashok."

"I know. I know. I should get on with life." She regrets the brusqueness, can't help it. "Get prepared to slam into another brick wall."

"Have you talked with Father Freitas about this?" Beata tries. "Or Father Daniel?"

"They've both been so kind. Father Daniel invited me down to Pondicherry. And Father Freitas is full of good counsel." She's not being ironic, although she can't accept his support. "He offered to say a memorial Mass."

"That might be healing."

"Oh, Beata," she erupts, regretting it immediately and unable to stop herself. "What's the point? Sudha wouldn't even be there in spirit. She's too busy communing with the other 10^{80} particles in the universe."

"Pardon?"

"Sorry, I'm so sorry, dear friend. I should go. I'm exhausted. Making no sense. I didn't get much sleep last night."

"I'll call in a couple of days, OK? Saturday or Sunday?"

"I'm so tired, Beata. So tired."

Monica forces herself to brush her teeth. (Did she say good-bye to Beata? Did she hang up the phone?) Her body feels so extraneous now.

What is she doing with it?

The sheets are cool and as soon as she turns out the light, heartache engulfs her. Dear Sudha, I miss you. Dear Sudha, I am so sorry.

Giant rocks and dirt pummeled the jeep.

Where was Sudha?

Immense boulders and no, an avalanche of rocks and now the earth itself.

She bolted from the car for her.

Shankar's grip was too strong.

"Nothing," he said. "Nothing you can do."

Mea Culpa. Mea maxima culpa.

The landslide went on and on. Oh, what a horrendous sight, the wash of rocks and splintered trees and it was too deep. She couldn't see the car. She could feel Sudha's terror. Oh, God—

Mean and merciful dawn comes once again. The irritating chirpers return. At least she's liberated from her bed. No more pretense of sleep until tonight.

Morning sky is streaked with pink clouds which remind her of the weeping cherries at home. Monica used to enjoy the lingering sunrise in Moorty. But not today, perhaps never again. Nevermore. Are there ravens in Moorty? Never-ever-ever more.

The room is full when she arrives for breakfast.

"Good morning," she manages.

They're all a bit wary. Is she imagining this? Why does she assume she's the center of attention?

"Did you sleep?" asks Raul, his own eyes circled in darkness.

"Did you?" She resists his concern. How can he show her such kindness, such forgiveness?

"A little better," he says, "I took a pill."

"Not a bad idea." Kevin says to her. "You have to sleep."

Of course, she thinks; otherwise we'll be useless to the hospital.

"Dr. Murphy, have you considered a short leave?" Father asks.

"I've just had a vaca--," she stops herself.

"Father Daniel emailed, suggesting you might want to do a brief retreat in—"

"Thank you, no. Thanks to everyone for your concern. But I'll be fine. I'm feeling better every morning," she lies.

THIRTY-SIX

June, 2002, Moorty

On Sunday afternoon, Raul suggests a walk. This is the last thing she wants. Yet how can she refuse him?

The last few days have passed in a stupor. A walk. Air. It will be good for both of them.

They wind up at a bench looking out toward the mountains, holding hands, crying.

Gently, she pulls away, relieved not to be touching, not to be touched.

He glances at her, seems to understand. "This was your bench. Yours and Sudha's." His voice is trancelike.

She's surprised.

"She showed me, the week before you set off. She was so excited, you know. She told me you two used to sit here dreaming of the peaks together."

Together.

His tone grows sober. "We must go on." He pauses, holding back tears. "She would want us to go on. We need faith. In our work. In God."

"Faith!" she rasps. "Where do you find faith? After losing her. And your father?" She wonders if she's losing her own faith permanently. If so, how genuine was her conversion? Her commitment? Will the real Monica please stand?

"Besides faith," he asks her faintly, "what else is there?"

"Sleep," she says desolately, "That would be a start."

*****

Monica notices the blue vellum envelope on the postal tray. Clearly Beata's letter would have been written before the avalanche. There are a couple of other pieces: a card from Eric, probably a sympathy note. Some Global Priority thingee from Chicago. She checks her watch. Four p.m. She can still do another hour's work. She should check on Aruna in the ward and gauge the tightness of her cast. But truly, she's overcome with exhaustion. Kevin has told her to take the whole day "for herself." A quaint expression, as if she might pop down to the spa for her regular pedicure. Instead, she walks down to her all too silent flat.

Monica settles into the creaky chair by the window with a cup of tea. Her eyes are caught by the embroidered throw pillow—bought at the *mela* with Sudha long ago. OK, get on with it, she can hear Sudha's voice. Read your friend's letter. Aren't you curious?

Dear Monica,

I guess you've been waiting for this. You often know things before they happen.

She smiles, for she does know what's coming although they haven't discussed anything except the accident on the phone this week.

James reserved a table at a charming French Canadian restaurant. White tablecloths, candlelight, fresh roses. We had a superb meal. He ordered in French naturellement. I know I sound like a school girl and not the 47-year-old been-around-the-block woman I am. But there's something about this man! By now you will have guessed. He brought a tiny package.

Inside the lovely satin box was a gorgeous, I do mean gorgeous, blue sapphire ring. I asked him if I had mentioned how the Indian jewelers pronounce sa-fire.

He laughed. "That's how I knew you loved blue sa-fires."

And so, dear friend, I finally said "Yes."

Yes. Yes, Beata. Good for you.

I'm hoping against hope that you'll be able to be my Maid of Honor. We're planning on October. I'll understand if you can't do it. Your work is so important. But I had to ask. Your presence would make everything perfect.

Monica closes her eyes, imagining the power to make everything perfect.

She should phone Beata to congratulate her. She should answer the other emails of concern that had come—one from Eric, two from Jill, none from Jeanne—during the last blurry fortnight. She'll do that soon. Right now she needs to sip tea and re-enter the world she inhabited before her life collapsed.

She needs to be alone; needs time to recover from the police investigations and physical examinations and tributes and commemorations. Opening her purse she finds the vial of pills she finally accepted from Raul.

He's made her promise to be careful.

Still, it's hard not to consider permanent departure.

Her eyes fall on the Global Priority letter from Chicago. Chicago? Who does she know in Chicago? Something about last year's taxes, maybe? Warily, she opens the envelope.

Dear Dr. Murphy,

Let us begin with condolences. We here at the Chicago Mission House have just heard about your accident and your great loss. We know you are surrounded by loving people of faith. We join your colleagues there in praying for your peace of mind.

The impetus for this letter began several months ago and its arrival unfortunately coincides with your recent tragedy. Please forgive us for intruding.

We would like to invite you to return to the U.S. to help train medical personnel for our missions. As you know, it's rare for an American doctor to work in an Indian mission as you do, but our doctors go all around the world. You have had such success that we wondered if you would share your expertise back home for a while. The contract would be for six months. It is renewable. However, if you prefer, you could return to your post at Moorty, where you are clearly valued.

But she just got her visa.

Is this Kevin's way of expelling her?

Father Daniel and Father Freitas have praised your ideal combination of faith and skill, your understanding of local people and of medical advances.

Skill? Kevin has had to step in for her at least three times this foggy week.

Faith—in what?

"Faith," she told Beata, *"is imaginary."*

"Sometimes you have to be OK with not knowing."

Oh, that infuriatingly patient voice.

Faith and skill? Monica is back at the beginning of her preposterously naïve spiritual journey. Back to the doubt and grief that engulfed her after Mom's death. And guilt. There's so much she didn't do. For Mom. For Sudha.

*****

"How are you?" Ashok's voice on the phone is kind, quiet.

"I slept last night," she reports grudgingly.

"I'm relieved."

"Raul's pills."

"But still."

She flares. "I can't take pills for the rest of my life."

"You'll get better."

"Time cures all?" she snaps. No, she's not angry at him. She can't quell or even predict this volcanic rage.

"Monica dear, you know what I mean. I wish you would let me love you."

"I do."

"I don't think you do. Your guard is up, far too high to let me in."

She will not weep. The effort silences her.

"I want to hold you."

The news about Chicago spills out.

"Wow!"

"You're the only one I've told, so—"

"This is wonderful, Monica. We can go to America together."

"You've heard from Madison?"

"No, but they're making more promising noises. The appointment is with the provost now."

Promising, she wonders, promising to whom?

"Monica?"

"Yes."

"Monica, I love you."

"I love you, too, but…"

"But what?"

The nagging worry: "What if we only love each other in this place at this time?"

Ashok is silent. Then, "Love isn't like that," he says fiercely. "Love transcends the temporal, the spatial."

"That's right, we're all part of the 10^{80} particles recycling in the universe."

"I don't mean that kind of transcendence."

THIRTY-SEVEN

July, 2002, Moorty

She opens the door to find Ashok standing outside her flat with a bouquet of roses. How amazing. Her heart pounds.

He was just here last month.

One horrendous month. Unbearable month. He's completely surprised her. Is she happy? Thrilled? Everything is hard to read through the numbness of grief. But she can feel her heart pounding.

Once inside the flat, he draws her to him tightly.

She holds on, sobbing.

"Yes," he says. "Yes. Cry as long as you need."

That evening they walk down the mountain to Lhasa Café, the Tibetan restaurant on the edge of town.

"It's lovely to see you," she beams. "I didn't know how much I needed to be held. You were very patient this afternoon. So kind."

"I only wish I could have returned sooner." He watches her uneasily.

The waiter looks so much like Norbu, their young friend from Spiti, she has trouble concentrating on the menu.

"I can only stay the night." His words are gentle, somehow weighty. "I, I wanted to see you for several reasons."

Her heart races. Another change. Whatever it is, she's not ready for it.

"I have news."

"Yes," she asks cautiously.

"The Madison job." He clasps and unclasps his hands. "They sent the formal offer."

"Terrific. What a wonderful opportunity." Someone is saying this; meanwhile, she feels as if a lead weight has dropped on her head.

If he loves you, he'll find a use. He could investigate indigenous healing arts. Philosophy of medicine…

"What's wrong?" He takes her hand.

"I'll miss you." Her eyes fill. No, she will not cry, will not mar his big opportunity.

He shakes his head. "Not necessarily." The smile is diffident, nervous.

She's gazing out the window. Dark already.

"Monica?"

"Sorry, I got distracted."

"I wanted to say something else, or rather to ask." He studies her face.

She looks deep into his brown eyes, finding edgy apprehension, hope.

"I wish we had a fancy table cloth, music in the background, but—." He takes her cold hand. "I would hope we might marry and return to your beloved Midwest together."

She's crying and laughing. Shocked. Elated. Scared. Of course she expected this some time. She stares at him with love and amazement.

But not now. Not yet.

How good it would be to live near Beata again. And maybe the proximity to and distance from Jeanne—a state away—would allow her to reconnect with her sister. What a relief it would be to return to a country so easy to navigate. To work in a clinic with a full inventory of medical supplies. Or she could take the Chicago job, commute to Madison on the weekends. Oh, to be liberated from the melodrama of Dr. and Mrs. Walsh and the pagan babies.

"Monica?" Ashok asks with that characteristic mix of irritation and concern. "Are you OK, Monica? I know this is an awful time in your life. I understand."

"I'm OK, Ashok. It's just that all this is somewhat…startling."

He drops his head. "I just got the letter and ran for the train. I, I'm so insensitive. You're still in shock from the landslide from losing dear Sudha. You look better, but still—"

She dries her eyes on a paper napkin.

"All I ask is that you think about it. Will you at least promise to do that?"

"I promise."

*****

Monica takes in the tense silence as she arrives for dinner.

Cook places food on the side table and heads bow in preparation for Father to offer the grace. Monica is distracted from her prayers by

Ashok's proposal, by the palpable hostility in the room.

Something has shifted in recent days, like a season changing. Perhaps the monsoons are making them all edgier. Tonight's conversation is louder now, more about work, unusually charged.

Before. Will she always live a life parsed by "before" and "after?"

"Thank you, too, for our dear colleagues," Father continues with the grace, clearly trying to lighten the mood.

Monica is not ready to let go of Sudha. She tries to concentrate on the present—caring for her patients, praying for serenity, even writing to Jeanne. She ardently wants her sister back. Yesterday, reading Rajul's note inviting her once again to Bombay, Monica sobbed for twenty minutes. Sudha was going to take her home next year; she'd promised a stroll along Marine Drive and a hike up Malabar Hill.

"Amen," says Father Freitas. He smiles at Monica.

She thinks about his advice to go to Chicago, to take a leave of absence here. She'll always be welcome back. Leave of absence. She thinks of her father. Of Ashok.

Raul is saying something about condoms. His voice has become jittery since Sudha's death. He's lost the little elasticity he ever had.

Reluctantly, she tunes in, mid-conversation. How did they get to this subject so early in the meal?

"As you know," Kevin says, "Since the doctrine of the Immaculate Conception was declared in the 19th century, the Church has held human life begins at conception."

"That doctrine was conveniently divined to propagate the faith when the Church was losing millions to the potato famine." Raul's left hand tightens into a fist.

"Thank you for your historical interpretation. Our charge here is not to theorize about dogma, but to humbly follow it." Kevin pushes his half-eaten meal aside.

"Who says you have a right to let your conscience dictate someone else's health, someone's life, someone's survival?" Raul is quavering.

"Conscience is part of my medical expertise," Kevin shakes his head sorrowfully. "Doctors have applied ethics to medicine since Hippocrates."

"How ethical is it to restrict condoms during a pandemic? Within eight years, India will have one the highest rates of HIV in the world."

"Please, please!" Kevin holds up his hand.

The debate is clearly over. Monica waits for pronouncements.

"We have an excellent HIV/AIDS education program organized by Dr. Murphy. We do outreach to the schools and with all our patients at the clinic."

"I agree with Raul." She can't help herself. "The prevention work goes only so far."

Sister Eleanor appears at the door. "There is an emergency arrival. Another motor accident. Three people. One is bleeding very badly."

The Walshes rush out first. Father Freitas follows at a measured pace.

Raul turns to her and places a hand on her arm. His voice is urgent. "I know Sudha must have talked to you about joining us."

She nods, incapable of anything else. The emergency returns her own accident back to the wide screen.

"I don't want to pressure you," he hesitates. "Then again, we feel I must."

She waits. *We. Sudha and Raul.*

"Now more than ever," he urges, "we need you. I can't continue otherwise. There is too much, too much. Please." He studies her face. "Promise to think about it."

He's heartbroken, Monica sees, desperate.

"I promise to think about it," she whispers.

THIRTY-EIGHT

Fall, 2006, Koti

Sudha chats contentedly with her imaginary friend on the faded pink couch in one of India's shabbiest hotel lounges. A bilingual friend, apparently, as Sudha switches merrily between Hindi and English.

Monica marvels at how her beautiful daughter's eyes flash when she plays. Do all children have such wild imaginations? Will Sudha grow up to become an actor? A painter? Those rich, dark eyes mirror her father's intensity.

From a desk at the back of the lounge, Raul glances at a news report on the fuzzy television and listlessly fills out a report. Raul turns to Monica, laughing ironically, "Government funding. I'm grateful we have it, but damn this paperwork! I thought bureaucracy was elaborate in Argentina. Indians make a science out of it."

Monica looks up from her letter. "I can take over if you like."

"No, you don't have the patience for it, really."

"And you do?"

"More than you."

"Hmm."

She changes the topic. "I don't want to sound like Pollyanna," she begins.

"Heaven forbid," Tina sets down her book.

Monica ignores her. "But think of it. Four years ago, who could have imagined this: Biju taking over the Manda project, bringing in Anuradha and Rabindra, getting everyone government funding, having secure visas—"

"Slightly secure visas, Ms. Optimist," Tina says dryly. "When I worked at the embassy, I had a secure visa."

Monica shrugs, diverted by Sudha's dancing. Sometimes when the girl dreams like this, Monica thinks her dear mom is in the room. Mom before Tim headed West, when she used to say, "Life is as it should be."

"Imagine," Tina teases. "I gave up a visa and a decent flat in Vasant Vihar for tenuous security in the Backcountry Project and or current residence is this—what is it—half-star hotel—while we get the lodgings finished in Koti."

Biju clears his throat. The wiry young man peers through the dim lounge at a blueprint. "You're the one who lobbied for this satellite center. It's not as if we don't have enough to do in Manda."

"Yes, but don't you think we'd be more comfortable at the Westminster Ridgetop?" she jokes, "where the American Consul is staying?"

"Sure," Monica laughs. "When we start wasting funds on a place like that, it's time to go home."

"Monica is right about the visa security," Raul says. "We're much safer now than at Moorty. Remember the trips to the visa office. And those cordial RSS visits?"

Monica winces. Sometimes she does wait for the thugs to appear in Koti or Manda. Even though the RSS has quieted down since Congress came to power in 2004.

"Yes," he continues, stretching his strong arms wide. "Compared to Moorty Mission days, we're more secure and doing better work."

"Different work," Monica corrects quickly.

Tina shakes her head affectionately. "You two sound like an old married couple."

Monica laughs. Raul too.

"Better not let Ashok hear you say that," he feigns alarm.

Monica sips her tea and returns to the letter.

Tonight, especially, I am missing you my dear, and our sweet little Sudha. I am just home from a dreary dinner party hosted by Robby Robinson in Geography. His wife, an intense person, is principal of a public school outside Madison.

"Robby tells me you're in a commuting relationship," she said. "Tell me, where is your wife?"

Of course she's never heard of Koti, but she looked worried at the sound of it. When I explained further, she fairly exploded in bewilderment.

"Oh, dear, couldn't your wife get a visa here? I hope the INS is not making difficulties."

Naturally, I burst out laughing, then clarified that my cousin was helping you get a more secure Indian visa. Covered in confusion, she moved on to chat with the others. Thank god.

Monica grins. This is the sort of encounter that appeals to Ashok's absurdist taste. She hopes he told the poor woman that he spends summers here, that he'll have a whole sabbatical year with his wife and daughter in Koti beginning in January. Maybe not, since he likes to make out that things are dire. She marvels, as always, at his elegant cursive. She types her letters for he nags her so about her illegible hand writing.

I was reflecting on that first year here in Madison. Our Saturday campus walks. Dinners at Lombardinos, films at the Orpheum. And when Sudha arrived, the amazement of witnessing her inch by inch growth. When you returned to help Raul "shore up" the project, I had no idea you'd be gone so long.

He reminds her of this in each letter. Truthfully, she hadn't expected to be here for two-and-a-half years. She misses Ashok dreadfully. Yet he feels the separation more. After all she lives with the grace of Sudha. She loves her work, feels it's far more useful than anything she's ever done.

I know, I know we've discussed this. And I'll be there in January. But the cold days until final exams feel endless. When I get there, will Sudha recognize her father?

Monica will reassure him when they Skype on Saturday. Tina wonders why they write such long letters when they manage to Skype or email once a week. You say different things in a letter. Monica learned this from Beata years ago.

Last weekend with Beata and James—no doubt we'll talk about all this before you get this miserably slow letter—was excellent. They taught me to cross country ski at Lake of the Isles. Beata was oddly preoccupied by her decision to move back to Minneapolis. Their new house is closer to their jobs. She thought you'd be pleased, though, that she'd left St. Paul. I didn't catch the point, actually.

*****

Half-star hotel, Monica considers brushing her teeth. Tina loves to impersonate the spoiled American, but she's become an invaluable member of the team. Oh, no *that* word. Yet, here they are a *team* with common goals rather than running on parallel high-powered career tracks. Tina is tireless, inventive, always challenging them to do more. She and Anuradha have developed a model inoculation program and their proposal to UNICEF is sailing through committees.

"Mama, Mom!"

Monica rushes into the candle-lit bedroom. "I'm right here, sweetie, right here."

The sprite looks at her with one eye open.

Monica grins, in spite of herself. "I thought my beautiful daughter was asleep."

"I want a doll like Meenakshi's," she says in a most wide-awake voice.

"Meenakshi?" The full weight of her exhaustion descends. Monica perches on Sudha's bed. "Remind me, who is Meenakshi?"

"You know."

She draws a blank. It's especially humbling to confess ignorance in the face of a three-year-old's certitude.

"You've met my secret friend."

"Yes, of course," she whispers, "I'm so sorry."

"May I have one, please?"

"One what?" Monica yawns. It's been a long day, examining people in their makeshift tent clinic. More exhausting without the proper supplies, without a building that was supposed to be finished weeks ago.

"Maaama!" Sudha claps her hands.

"Sorry dear, I don't remember." All day she's been obsessed with tomorrow's fundraising meeting with the ridiculous American Consul. Concentrate on your daughter, she tells herself. Otherwise she'll be calling her *ayah* "Mama."

"You know. You know."

Monica shivers. Meenakshi, the niece. The Haryana doll for the traditional child that Sudha bought at the *mela*. This isn't the first time Sudha Badami has appeared in her daughter's imagination.

"May I, may I have the doll?"

"Maybe when Daddy comes. Maybe we can go with Daddy to a *mela*."

Sudha nods and slips down into the covers. "Nightie night."

"Sweet dreams," Monica smoothes the child's black hair away from her tightly shut eyes and kisses her forehead, right on the two freckles which seem to be the only part of her appearance she's inherited from Monica.

Sudha smiles serenely.

Monica finishes brushing her teeth in the damp bathroom. A semi-functioning shower has drenched the floor and made subsequent access to the toilet or sink a soggy adventure. Newly constructed plywood cabinets reek of camphor ball disinfectant. She hangs her skirt on the door latch. At least they have clean towels. After days of asking. She shouldn't complain. They've lived in sparser conditions in camp. She's never fully described the hotel to Ashok, by far, the most fastidious member of their family. By the time he comes, she'll be back in comparatively developed Manda.

*****

Amit drives a little too swiftly for Monica's comfort, but the speed and traffic don't bother her as much as they once did. What can she do? These hill roads are being expanded by good government schemes which will take years to realize. Meanwhile, the route is teeming with ox-drawn carts, hundreds of bicyclists, honking, multi-colored wooden lorries, pedestrians, meandering cows, spanking new Ambassadors and trucks groaning under building materials for the future of this ambitious nation.

"What's a two-word synonym for India?" Ashok asked her one morning in their new Madison house. He relished the sleek lines of their kitchen cabinets, the lush pile in the bedroom carpet, the intense quiet in this cul de sac on the edge of town.

"I give up."

"Well, that could be a three-word synonym," he grinned. "No, the answer is Under Construction."

Monica understands his ironic distance and his fierce attachment to India. Being a foreigner—still, despite her years here, despite her Indian daughter and husband—she can't afford, doesn't actually experience—ironic distance. "Sense of possibility" would be her three-word answer. There's something invigorating about this place where everyone is on the move, where people are so literally engaged with the growth of their country.

The van swerves around a dawdling white cow.

"So sorry, Ma'am," Amit grins into the rearview mirror. "Close call, yes?"

"Indeed! Not your fault, don't worry."

On the roadside, teenagers in salwar kameez school uniforms carry backpacks adorned with logos of U.S. companies. Every tenth shop advertizes phone service: STD/ITD. One shack bears the sign, "Friends' Books and Electricals."

Despite the bumpy road, she studies her notes for the meeting. Assistant Consul Geoffrey Marshall is Tina's bright idea. From her Delhi days, she knows the embassy has deep pockets and an intense interest in making friends in remote areas. Assistant Consul (that's his title, isn't it?) Marshall will be in the state capital for four days to open an American Corner reading room and preside at local functions. He's agreed to meet with Monica for lunch. A three hour journey for lunch.

"*Why don't you go?*" *Monica nudged her friend, who was altogether more suited for diplomatic hobnobbing.*

"*Oh, no, I'm not on the favorites list of Mr. America.*"

"*Mr. Who?*"

"*He's this young guy—maybe twenty-five—who has a master's in international studies from Brown and thinks he profoundly comprehends the world.*"

Monica regarded Tina skeptically. Hard to believe her old med school pal had so much grey hair now. Of course the silver didn't show so much in blonde hair. She was ripening into a beautiful middle-aged woman, just as she'd been a gorgeous student. "*Now tell me, we're sure to hit it off as two blue bloods from The Main Line?*"

"*No, really, he'll like you. You're not sarcastic. You're a nicer person.*"

Monica shook her head in exasperation with Tina, who had intentionally left out the background story on Mr. America when she made the appointment.

Tina shrugged.

"*OK, but you owe me one.*"

"*I owe you a thousand.*"

Monica is astonished at how different parts of her life have come together. Imagine, Raul and Tina are both her colleagues now. It's all coincidence. OK, Sudha would call it Karma and Father Freitas would say Providence. When she returned to help Raul, Tina came for a visit. And she decided she was ready to leave the embassy, but not India.

The work here is so different from Moorty. She could never return to the Mission. Not just because of the Walshes. No, her work there left her with too many moral and spiritual questions.   ❧

She misses going to Mass, but feels like an imposter in church now. She sometimes thinks of seeking out a really liberal parish, but that's getting harder with this new German pope. Oh, she still believes in some kind of spirit. An encompassing power and presence. Jesus now has become a loving model, a bodhisattva, a brother, not a deity. When she talks with Father Freitas and Father Daniel, they each advise her to have faith in faith.

Yes, maybe someday things will become clearer, as clear as they were to Mom, as they are to Beata. Right now, she's fine. When pressed, for Indians are preoccupied with spiritual questions, she says she believes in the practice of compassion. In Manda and Koti, there's plenty of opportunity to be useful and loving without the restraints of a diocese or dogma.

Ahead of them, Monica sees rolling hills, rice paddies, palm trees. She should be strategizing about fundraising, but her thoughts keep jumping around.

Somehow here, she's found a spiritual community. They all share a similar sense of service. Her colleagues come from such different backgrounds. Rabindra from a Calcutta Marxist family; Anuradha from a secular Punjabi community. Raul still believes in his own Argentinean-Indian-American Catholicism, but can't stand the current pope.

Monica wonders if she herself is agnostic. She prefers the word "seeker," but that sounds too sentimental, too Hermann Hesse-ish.

As they approach the hotel, she returns to her notes, reminding herself that this trip has an urgent material goal. Focus, Monica.

THIRTY-NINE

December, 2006, Moorty

A day by herself in Moorty: what luxury. Monica misses Sudha, but someone has to collect supplies from Moorty station and she knows the inventory best. All morning she's been washed with nostalgia. Moorty in December. Cold, crisp air. Snow shoveled to the roadsides. Blue skies opening to views of distant, white peaks.

"*Namaste, Doctorji!*"

Monica turns, "Mr. Sood, excellent to see you."

He hands her a *Herald Tribune* and a *Hindu*.

She reaches for her wallet, but says, "No, no, we are gladdened to have you back!"

Monica grins, "Very kind. Thank you. I do miss Moorty, but alas, I'm only here for a day to collect supplies."

"Oh, shame, shame. You are much missed. Much missed."

She continues down the hill, started by the expanded Moorty Internet Shop, which has taken over the storefront next door. Now what was there before? Oh, yes, the old telephone stalls. These days so many people have mobile phones. How much has changed in a few years.

At Moorty internet, a banner reads, "Rent your DVDs here." Peeking inside, she sees shelves of supplies for home computers. She's wistful about her Tuesday afternoons eagerly waiting at the screen for messages from Beata and Tina. And Ashok.

Dear Esteemed Dr. Murphy, he wrote to tell her about that Chicago trip, full of exuberance and adventure. *But I am dashed at the thought of missing you.* Dashed. Maybe she fell in love with him right then. After four years of marriage, she finds his combination of diffidence, chivalry and zeal just as beguiling.

Radha Agarwal is busy at the cash register. Monica notices her brother Raj, now quite manly and handsome, helping a customer in a sleek new computer station.

Radha glances up and waves happily, urging Monica to enter.

"Later," Monica mouths and she does hope to find time after having lunch with Brigid Walsh and collecting supplies.

Lunch with Brigid Walsh at the Lhasa Café. Monica shakes her head. This year she's enjoyed several lunches with Father Freitas—as well as his visit to Manda. Otherwise she's been completely disconnected from Moorty Hospital. Her departure wasn't as abrupt as Raul's. She finished out her contract. The Walshes couldn't object to the state of holy matrimony and Monica "following" her husband to Wisconsin. Still, there was an edge to their farewells. Monica knows that recently Kevin has scuppered at least two grants to the Back Country Project by registering protests about expertise and equipment.

So when Monica received the pale jade linen envelope addressed to her in Brigid's inimitable hand, she felt mildly panicked. The cryptic note did nothing to assuage her dread.

Dear Dr. Murphy,

When you next come to Moorty, I would be grateful if you would be my guest for lunch at the Lhasa Café. As Christian women, I believe we need to have a conversation. I hope all is well with you and your family.

Regards,

Brigid Walsh

Conversation? To what end? Retribution? Forgiveness? Instruction?

Monica thought about it for a week and wrote back that she would be pleased to join her on 7 December, if that suited.

The All Purpose Stationers is still flourishing. Monica notices the same display of "holiday" cards in the window since July. *"Why not?" Mr. Patna explained. Everyone is always happy to receive 'Season's Greetings,' January, June, whenever. So many holidays."*

Monica feels buoyant about being home in Moorty. Maybe next month when she and Sudha come here to meet Ashok's train, the three of them can take a weekend holiday, eat at the old cafés, attend a performance at The Playhouse.

Rabi stands in front of the South India Coffee House in a thin kurta and lunghi. The man must carry Kerala heat in his blood.

"*Namaste*, Rabi."

He peers at her.

Monica's breath catches at the memory of her visits here with Sudha and their special table overlooking Lower Bazaar.

"*Namaste ji,*" he says, perhaps recognizing her.

Monica checks her watch and hurries along.

Now, on a quieter street, at the far side of town, Monica breathes in the scent of Deodar cedars. She calls up the day she came across that group of boys pointing and laughing at the bright orange monkey swinging from an electrical wire to a high branch.

Suddenly, Monica is gazing down a sharp slope at the small brick school.

Her heart sank at the first sight of Walkerton's broken windows and shabby grounds. Numbly she followed Vikram through the dilapidated corridors past a courtyard of sad trees and shrubs into a windowless anteroom.

And then, the apparition of Sudha, lustrous in her deep purple silk sari.

"Namaste, Dr. Murphy. Welcome to our school."

Now their little jeep was being pummeled by rocks, dirt and oh, no an avalanche of snow and boulders and the entire weight of earth itself.

Still, she wakes at night panicking for Sudha, pulling her quickly from the car. Just another minute—half-minute—and she will be fine. Another 15 seconds.

"Sudha!" She must be calling out loud because Ashok takes her in his arms and rocks her. Lately the nightmares are less frequent. And in daylight, she usually can focus her thoughts. Saying farewell to Walkerton now, she recalls that crisp dawn in Losar.

"Bliss!" Sudha had declared. "The mountains. The sun. Fresh, hot chapattis. My dearest friend, I don't think I've ever been happier!"

She will bring Sudha Badami to this curious lunch.

The Lhasa Café is unchanged: the same rudimentary furnishings and Tibetan weavings on the walls as on the night of Ashok's astonishing proposal. Sudha was with her that night, too.

Brigid is seated by a sunny window. In this light, Monica can distinguish lines under her eyes, creases in that lovely porcelain skin.

She stands in greeting.

Monica is once again amazed by the woman's height. There's always been something about her demeanor, especially her deference toward Kevin, which makes Brigid appear shorter than she is. This afternoon her green eyes are as piercing as ever.

"Monica, welcome back." She extends both palms.

"Brigid." She squeezes her hands. Of course they are on a first name basis, released from hospital hierarchy. "Great to see you." Monica is abashed that she means this.

Brigid lights up. "Yes, I feel the same. Let's sit. You're looking well. How are your husband and daughter?"

"Fine, thanks." Does she know Ashok is still teaching in Wisconsin? "Sudha is three now. And full of beans."

Brigid folds her hands

"She cherishes the Christening cup you sent."

"I'm pleased," Brigid blushes. "I still have mine from Aunt Maeve."

Monica omits the detail that Sudha has never been baptized. She hopes Brigid won't ask about the ceremony.

They drift into silent contemplation of the menu until the waiter appears.

"May I have the house special?" Monica wonders what the woman wants from her.

"I'll order from the Indian part of the menu," Brigid says. "May I have the *biryani* and a side order of *brinjal*?"

"*Baingan*," Sudha had instructed. "Not *brinjal*. You want to learn Hindi not Rajtalk."

Monica sighs. This wasn't the kind of company she needed from Sudha. Still, why does she expect her friend to be any less contentious in death. She smiles to herself.

"Did I mispronounce something?" Brigid asks. "I do that, sometimes. After all these years."

"Sorry I was … (Well, why not tell the truth?) … having a memory of Sudha Badami teaching me to cook eggplant." She would not say *baingan* and embarrass Brigid.

"Eggplant? Yes, that's the odd word Americans use. We say *aubergine*."

Monica tilts her head. "How are the good Sisters Catherine, Melba and Eleanor?"

"Very well. Each went home at a separate time to Kerala for a fortnight last spring and returned most fortified. They did ask me to give you their warmest regards."

Monica's eyes fill. How kind—and discreetly helpful—each nun was. "So how is…your husband keeping?"

"Fine, thank you. Dr. Walsh is in good health. We like all the new staff, Dr. Raina and Dr. Rai and Dr. Sen. It's now the largely Indian crew it should be."

The waiter serves a bottle of mineral water.

Pouring Monica a glass, Brigid says, "You must be wondering why I invited you to lunch after, well, after such a long interlude."

"Yes," Monica sips the water nervously. Ridiculous to feel anxious.

"As you know, Father Freitas is my confessor."

Monica's eyes widen. She should have prepared for deep water.

"Which has complications—your confessor being your colleague— and blessings. One of the latter is that he knows so much about my daily life—and the lives of those around me, and those formerly around."

Monica feels a brief reprieve when the fragrant *biryani* is served.

After a few bites, Brigid resumes, "And I felt contrite about, well, about the way I treated you at the clinic. I'm afraid I was overly critical. Frankly, somewhat jealous."

Monica listens carefully as she eats.

"While I still maintain my views about the importance of missionary work, offering baptism to babies and instruction to adults ..."

Oh, no, please, please, Monica thinks.

"... I have come to respect what you're doing at the Backcountry Project. You reach people we can't."

"Thank you, Brigid," Monica says, nervously searching for a change of subject.

"I think Dr. Walsh understands the importance of remote outreach better now. A little better."

Monica doesn't ask why he's sabotaged their grants.

"However, between us, I don't think he'll ever forgive Dr. Sanchez for stealing Cook from the Mission." She smiles mischievously.

Monica knows she's supposed to laugh, but she's overwhelmed by sudden intimacies and confidences. She smiles faintly. She does look forward to reporting to Raul tonight that the lunch with Brigid Walsh was quite worthwhile.

"And so," she reaches into her purse for a jade linen envelope. "I would like to make a contribution."

Monica takes a long drink of water. "Why thank you."

"A monthly donation will follow. I wanted to present this first envelope in person, so you would understand the context."

"How generous," Monica responds. "Everyone will be most grateful."

"I would be grateful if you kept the source of the donation anonymous. The money is my own, naturally. From a small trust fund. Dr. Walsh doesn't need to know."

How Monica has longed to hear such words from Brigid.

"You may make up an imaginary donor, if that's easier for you." Brigid looks into her eyes. "This is between us."

"Of course."

"Between us and Our Lord."

FORTY

February, 2007, Manda

Ashok laughs, chasing Sudha around a chair in the sitting room of their modest, comfortable flat which still smells of fresh paint and sawdust.

Monica sips tea, watching contentedly.

"Oooooomph," Ashok exhales, sinking into the couch beside her.

Sudha tugs at her father's stockinged feet. "More, Daddy, more."

"Not just now, my sweet. Daddy needs to rest." Ashok grins. "Perhaps you could play with dolly for a while."

"OK, if you promise to be Monkey again. Promise?"

"On Jakhu's temple. I vow Monkey will return."

He wraps his arms around Sudha and Monica snuggles in close.

Sudha skips away with her doll.

"Life is as it should be," he sighs, "Home. Monkey. Children. Dolly."

"Oh," Monica sits up. "You want a dolly for yourself?"

"Cheeky girl!" he kisses her nose.

"Or more monkeys?" she grins to forestall the inevitable conversation. *Children*, he had said, *children*. One is enough for her. She can't imagine loving another child the way she cherishes Sudha. Besides, she's forty-two.

"Sudha, Sudha," Rabindra calls from the garden. The child darts out the door.

She takes a deep breath. "Children, I know we talked about two children, darling, but Sudha has a big personality. And I'm not sure..."

"No, hold on!" Ashok assumes that maddeningly professional bearing and cadence. "I suggest that we first settle the small matter of the seven thousand mile distance between us."

Odd, how they've exchanged lives.

Odd and wonderful how he's devoted to Beata and James and she's been welcomed into Ashok's family. Manju visits often. Ashok's brothers are always inviting Sudha and herself down to Delhi for a long weekend. At first she anticipated their objections about marrying a white American from a Christian family. Ashok had assured her that they were all brought up in a secular, cosmopolitan home. In fact, Monica feels that she belongs with the Nairs in a way she never fitted with the Murphys. Here she doesn't stick out as an intellectual and professional. With Manju and the brothers and their wives, she can converse unselfconsciously about books and theatre and film and politics.

"Let's not think about the miles," she says. "We have you here for a whole year. Our family is together. You're finishing the book. I have useful work at the new clinic."

"OK, we will postpone, but not abandon, this discussion. I agree that a little enjoyment is in order. But then we must get serious about our future."

"Yes, of course." She grins. "I'm so jazzed you invited Beata and James to visit this fall. Beata has only come once and James has never been to India."

"They're great people."

"On another important matter—what's this about you being Sudha's monkey?"

"Really, don't ask," he says.

She laughs, realizing she's giddy.

"This seems to be your month for family," he changes the topic. "Sudha's birthday card from Jeanne."

"Let's just hope she stays in AA more than a month this time." Monica is caught between fear and self-righteousness. "Let's just hope she doesn't get in another car wreck."

"She's trying, Monica, you have to give her that."

"Yes," Monica agrees, wondering how her compassion and patience instantly evaporate when it comes to her sister.

Ashok muses, "I keep thinking about that last sudden note from your father, with the Wyoming T-shirt for Sudha."

"It might fit her in a year or two."

"What matters is the contact, the gesture."

"Yes," she admits, knowing that the estrangements in her family trouble Ashok. "But then Tim was always a bit of an apparition."

"Well, I don't want to be Tim."

"Pardon?"

"I don't want to be the father who disappeared from Sudha's life."

Monica feels the tears welling.

Cook has worked for days preparing the feast for Father Freitas' visit: *aloo gobi, sag paneer, baingan bharta*, chicken *tikka* and a special Goan curry. All morning the aromas waft through the clinic grounds.

Monica finds herself unexpectedly nostalgic for Moorty hospital.

"He's here! He's here! He's here!" Sudha runs into her mother's small office.

Monica grins at the girl's affection for the priest.

She shuts her notebook and slips on a shawl.

A small, graying man extricates himself from the van.

"*Namaste*, Father," Monica beams.

"*Namaste*, my friend," he hugs her.

"Cook has prepared tea and your favorite biscuits."

"No, no," he protests, in that familiar, high-pitched voice. "Just as I'm retrieving my youthful figure."

Monica laughs. "As a doctor, I always prescribe chocolate biscuits to aid travelers overcoming long, winding van journeys."

"It is rather a marathon ride as these things go," the priest concedes.

"I'm glad it's just the two of us for a moment," Father says as they sit at the dining room table.

"Raul is eager to see you. But he had an emergency surgery and Ashok will be back in ten minutes. They'll all be here by the time Cook serves."

"We need a private moment. I have sad news."

About Sister Catherine or Sister Melba or Brigid or someone else from Moorty?

"Our dear Father Daniel. He passed away yesterday."

"Oh," she feels wind and spirit leave her. "No, oh no."

Father Freitas takes her hand.

"I was making plans to visit," she shakes her head. "If I had only known he was so ill."

"Quite sudden. Quite sudden. Fortunately, I was in Chennai for a conference."

She shudders with sobs.

Father takes her other hand.

"I got to say good-bye to him."

"Wonderful." She tries to hold back the tears. "That's wonderful for both of you."

"He asked after you several times."

Monica nods, her mouth pursed.

"I tried to reach you but I couldn't get a phone connection."

"Yes," she says, "we've had problems with the new system." She takes a long breath. Despite all the losses, she doesn't seem to get any better at handling grief. Father Daniel has been a spiritual parent; she never imagined him leaving her. A selfish way to look at it—him leaving her.

"He was worried."

"Worried?"

"Worried that he had brought you to India and now your love for this country and your sense of duty are separating your dear family."

Monica sniffs.

"He had no advice. That was his Buddhist-Catholic way. He did ask me to remind you that God wants us to be happy in this life."

Monica smiles. "So like Father Daniel. Pain is inevitable. Suffering is elective."

"Precisely," Father returns the fond expression.

She's filled with memories. Dinner with Father Daniel in Minnesota. Their long email correspondence before she came to India. Her happy visits to Pondicherry. Their ongoing discussion about finding equanimity.

"Do you have any plans, you and Ashok?"

"Many options, Father. Ashok may teach in India again. I may return to Madison. We may continue the commute. We're open to many possibilities."

"Possibilities are good."

After they are all served, Cook takes his seat at the end of the bountiful table.

Father Freitas offers grace.

Raul, Monica and Sudha join in. Ashok, Biju and Rabindra bow their heads.

Monica hopes Tina and Anuradha will return from Koti in time to spend at least a day with their visitor.

"Oh, I almost forgot." Raul pops up and retrieves two bottles of Goan wine.

"Ho, ho!" Father slaps his chest. "You trekked some distance to find that."

"Friendship is worth all kind of journeys." Raul narrows his eyes enigmatically.

"To friendship!" Ashok raises a glass. "To the company of those we love."

She thinks about her dear friends here today and the traveling spirits who have passed on—Mom and Sudha and Father Daniel—and the ones who seem to inhabit a netherworld, Dad and Jeanne.

"Friendship!" They clink glasses.

For this moment, she knows, *I am happy in my lucky life*. Monica gazes at her family and friends. She remembers Father Daniel's wise retreat talks. And Sudha Badami's delicious cooking lessons.

END

Traveling with Spirits

Acknowledgments

I am grateful to the many people and institutions that helped support my work on Traveling With Spirits during the last ten years.

I was fortunate to have residency fellowships at the MacDowell Colony, Ucross Foundation, Hawthornden Castle, Hedgebrook and the Virginia Center for the Creative Arts. The staff at each of these places welcomed me "home" to comfortable work places, peaceful surroundings and stimulating company.

The McKnight Artist Fellowship and the McGinnis-Ritchie Fiction Prize gave me practical and artistic encouragement in pursuing the story of an American working in India, first through short fiction and then through this novel.

Many thanks to the University of Minnesota for a sabbatical supplement award, a Graduate School Faculty Summer Research Fellowship, and a Faculty Humanities Research Fellowship.

I am very thankful for the skill and advice of many librarians, archivists, and others who helped me with research. Although, Mission House, Moorty, Manda, Koti and other locations are imaginary places, the book is deeply informed by my own experiences visiting and working in India for decades. Authenticity is crucial to literary fiction. So, too, is respectful artistic liberty. Thus some details, like Monica's visit to Spiti, would not have occurred during the exact year of the story because of large rock slides that closed the roads.

Joe Taylor and his colleagues at Livingston Press have brought this book to you. I am grateful for their engagement with the novel and their hard work in all the complicated processes of publishing.

David Schorr's beautiful cover reflects his passion for India and its people. Thanks to David for sharing his art and many years of wonderful conversation about India.

I first started going to India in 1988, at the invitation of writer and activist Kalima Rose. In 2000, I received a Fulbright Senior Scholar Award which supported my teaching at the University of New Delhi (Miranda House), the University of Calcutta and the University of Himachal Pradesh.

I've returned to India to give lectures, readings at workshops in 2003, 2007 and 2010 in Jaipur, New Delhi, Calcutta, Berhampur, Bhubaneswar, Bombay, Nasik, Aurangabad, Trivandrum and other sites. These visits were made possible by K.S. Bijukumar, Smita Basu, Rajul Bhargava, Veena Chawla, Elizabeth Corwin, Aruna Dasgupta, Mariam Dossal, Anne Grimes, Muthukrishnan Janardhanan, Hameed Khan, Almitra Kika, Anuradha Marwah, Saroj Merani, Sunrit Mullick, Sudha Rai, Lea Terhune and others. I appreciate all they taught me about Indian cultures and histories and landscapes.

A number of stalwart friends and colleagues read entire drafts of the novel and offered detailed, helpful criticism. These people include Chitralekha Basu, Arundhati Das, Kath Davies, Janice Eidus, Zoe Fairbairns, Elizabeth Horan, Deborah Johnson, Helen Longino, Susan Mahle, MD, Rashmila Maiti, Kat Meads, Ranjini Obeysekere, Eve Pell, Rose Pipes, Pamela Satran, Mandira Sen and Sonja Swenson.

I relied on the innovative and diligent work of research assistants at Stanford University and the University of Minnesota. No question was too large or small for these sleuths and I appreciate the many kinds of work they did to make this novel possible: Jennine Capo Crucet, Ellie Freedman, Lori Hokyo Misaka, Scott Muskin, Elizabeth Noll, Anna Rafferty, Jocelyn Sears, Sonja Swenson and Andria Williams. Jovel Queirolo was crucial in the proofreading process.

Gary Garrison at the Institute for International Education offered incalculable support and advice over many years. Thanks to Annu Matthews for help with research questions. Friends are the main reason I keep returning to India. Amit, Amita, Anuradha, Ashok, Atiya, Bina, Dhruv, Irfan, Jan, Jasodhara, Madhvi, Mandira, Manju, Mimi, Naren, Rajashri, Raji, Rajul, Ritu, Shefali, Sudha, Urvashi, and Veena—Thanks to you all for your gracious hospitality, provocative company and many kindnesses.

There would be no pages here if it were not for my best critic, beloved partner and traveling companion across the astonishing Indian subcontinent, Helen Longino.

Valerie Miner is the award-winning author of fourteen books. Her novels include *After Eden, Range of Light, A Walking Fire, Winter's Edge, Blood Sisters, All Good Women, Movement: A Novel in Stories*, and *Murder in the English Department*. Her short fiction books include *Abundant Light, The Night Singers* and *Trespassing*. Her collection of essays is *Rumors from the Cauldron: Selected Essays, Reviews and Reportage*. In 2002, *The Low Road: A Scottish Family Memoir* was a Finalist for the PEN USA Creative Non-Fiction Award. *Abundant Light* was a 2005 Fiction Finalist for the Lambda Literary Awards.

Her work has been translated into German, Turkish, Danish, Italian, Spanish, French, Swedish and Dutch. In addition to single-authored projects, she has collaborated on books, museum exhibits as well as theatre.

Winner of a Distinguished Teaching Award, she has taught for over thirty years and is now a professor and artist in residence at Stanford University. She travels internationally giving readings, lectures, and workshops. She and her partner live in San Francisco and Mendocino County, California. Her website is www.valerieminer.com